THE CROWN BREAKER

CONQUERING IMORIA'S MAGIC DUOLOGY
BOOK 1

T. B. WIESE

For everyone who finds the villain more interesting

AUTHOR'S NOTE

The Crown Breaker is a DARK adult fantasy MM romance. It contains elements of language, explicit sex, murder, graphic violence, sadism, physical & mental torture, drug use, and physical & emotional child abuse.

OTHER BOOKS IN THIS WORLD

- (This book) - The Crown Breaker
- Book two - The Broken King

1

My dagger dances between my fingers as I watch the man on his knees before me. My lips pull up with a grin as he tries not to tremble and fails. Good. He should be afraid.

My blade glints in the light of the setting sun, spilling golden rays through the glass doors and windows along the west wall of my throne room.

"Ryd—"

Looking down at him, I lift a brow, silencing Sakara's words of familiarity. I may have taken him to my bed ... several times. I took what he offered, but we are past that now.

Sakara bows his head, and I fight back a chuckle as he whispers, "Sire, I don't understand."

Oh, but he does.

I circle him slowly, the room silent. My soldiers standing at the edges of the room hold back their amusement, keeping their faces blank. They are well aware of the game I'm playing with Sakara, even if he hasn't caught up yet. He is the fly in my web.

As I step behind Sakara, my gaze snags on the movement of someone stepping through the door behind my throne. My captain, Lucaryn, comes into the room, stopping next to my throne with feet planted slightly wider than his hips. Light from the windows to his right highlights his brown skin and black hair. I imagine the unlit chandeliers overhead are jealous of the sunlight touching his skin. Luc's broad palm rubs his chest before he crosses his arms. I raise an eyebrow, but he shakes his head, almost imperceptibly.

Damn. I was so sure we had found it this time.

My focus turns back to the man kneeling before me. I lean over, my breath fanning Sakara's dark cheek, my beard barely scraping his smooth skin. I place my right hand on his shoulder, and I almost laugh when he glances at my empty middle finger.

Sheathing my dagger, I hold my left hand before him, palm up. He stares at it for a second before tilting his head back at me. He presses his lips into a tight line, and though he's silent, that doesn't stop me from knowing what he wants to say.

My magic swells as I push the mental voices of everyone else in the room into a dull background noise, focusing on Sakara. His thoughts are spiraling in a panic, and to snap him out of it, I curl my forefinger and middle finger in a beckoning gesture.

I let a chuckle slide from my lips as his thoughts stall, eyes glued to my fingers. His thoughts flash through my mind as he recalls the memory of my hands skimming across his naked skin, teasing between his thighs, teeth skimming his neck, my hard length pressing into him from behind as he fisted the sheets of my bed ...

My cock grows hard at the images and the remembered passion we shared. I grip his long black locs, pressing my lips close to his ear, but my voice is loud enough to be heard throughout the throne room. "I enjoyed having you in my bed, but that's over now." Chuckles float from a few of the soldiers, and Sakara's cheeks redden. I flex my fingers again. "Hand it over."

His body trembles under my grip, but he doesn't move. I sigh, releasing him, and step back. I wave a hand at the nearest soldier, who steps forward. Starting at Sakara's head, the soldier runs his hands over his scalp, feeling down his locs before trailing his hands down his neck, patting his tunic over his shoulders, and running his palms down his arms. His hand slides down Sakara's shirt and around the waist of his pants. Sakara grips the soldier's wrist, flinging his groping hand away.

I tsk, bringing his gaze back to mine. "I did ask nicely. Now you either submit to this search, or I make you."

His nostrils flare, fisting his hands at his sides, but he bows his head, and a tingle of pleasure shivers down my spine at his reluctant submission. I nod at the soldier, and he resumes his search. His large hands pat down Sakara's waist, his back, over his hips and ass before lifting his shirt, running his fingers inside the waist of Sakara's pants. He pauses near Sakara's left hip, digging his fingers into the fabric at his waist. The soldier stands, holding out a gold ring with an embedded raw green stone.

I step forward, holding out my hand. The soldier drops the ring made warm by sitting so close to Sakara's skin, onto my palm. I stare at it a second, the raw moldavite stone dull against the shine of the gold, before I slide it onto the middle finger of my right hand.

I lean down, malice coating my words. "Sakara, my pet, did your Queen really think sending me a spy wrapped in such a tempting package would be all it would take to get her hands on the Mind Stone?"

His breath hitches, but there's fire in his eyes as he tilts his head back to meet my gaze. "It almost worked. My Queen knows your weaknesses, *Rydel.*"

My right brow lifts, and the soldiers stiffen. No one addresses me so informally, no one except Lucaryn.

I round him again, smirking at his slightly trembling shoulders when I step out of his view. "You think you were close to succeeding?" I chuckle, and Sakara's shoulders tighten even more. "Just because I fucked your Queen once, does not mean she knows me." Sakara's fists are so tightly clenched, his knuckles are white. I wave my hand at him. "I fucked you ... more than once. Do you claim to know me and my supposed weaknesses, Sakara?"

I press my boot to the middle of his back and kick him forward. His hands hit the beige stone floor with a loud smack as he catches himself. I stalk back around him until I'm facing him once again. He slowly walks his hands back, lifting himself to kneeling, and I can't help but grin at his scowling face.

My dagger is once again rolling through my fingers, eager to be

3

fed the blood of my enemy as my eyes travel down his body. What a shame. Queen Ravaxina Lurona is a fool to waste such talent on trying to steal the Mind Stone from me.

I have accepted many defectors over the years, which is how Sakara first came to me, a spy of Queen Ravaxina's court, claiming to have defected. And the fact is, I would have welcomed Sakara into my court. He would have been perfect to send back to Ravaxina's kingdom to join the other spies I currently have planted in her kingdom—two of which are defectors from her court.

But like Sakara, many so-called defectors come with hidden intentions. I always see through the lies. I pluck the truth from their minds and do with them as I please. A lie has never passed my detection, not since I took the Mind Stone ten years ago from the former king of Leiren. One well-timed swing of my sword sent King Ammeryn's head thudding to the floor, and the gaudy necklace holding the Mind Stone slid with a wet thunk from his bloody neck. He never saw it coming, despite the Stone's power.

But the stone in my ring, the stone Sakara tried to steal for his Queen, is a fake.

The real Stone—embedded in my back over my left shoulder blade and covered with thick scar tissue—warms as the magic flares. I cross my arms, tapping my dagger against my bicep. "Did you really think you could get past the Mind Stone?" I wave a hand dismissively. "No, don't answer. You had such ... faith in your lies. And *truth* be told, the idea of adding another spymaster to my court pleased me. But alas, your loyalty is not to me, and I can't let that stand."

Sakara's mind is a whirlwind of thoughts, trying to find a way out of his predicament. Thoughts fall like arrows, never lasting more than a moment before they're eclipsed by another. *Convince Rydel I've actually defected. Should I defect? Yes. No. No. It might save me from Rydel, but my Queen ... my Queen.* His eyes flick to mine, suspending his panicked thoughts. He knows I've heard everything.

I chuckle. "Quite the predicament."

Sakara frowns. "Does your cruelty know no end?"

I shrug, dagger dancing in my left hand. "You came to me. You tried to steal what is mine. Is my cruelty not justified?"

His eyes narrow. "Only someone with a soul as black as yours would ever consider cruelty justified."

Luc shifts, and I'm sure he's a heartbeat away from leaping the three shallow steps of the dais to run his sword through Sakara's chest, but a shake of my head holds him in place.

I grin, stilling my dagger, using the blade to flick dirt from under my nail. "My soul may be as black as the pits of hell, and if I believed in the gods, I'd surely pray to Pravum." Sakara's eyes go wide, and his face pales at the mention of the god of depravity. I shrug. "But I'm not beyond gratitude." My eyes meet his. "So, thank you."

His jaw flexes as he fights to keep his words contained, but I answer the question that's spooling through his mind. "At least you gave me something in return for trying to steal from me." I let my eyes suggestively travel down his body, and if his glare could kill, I would be dead at his knees.

Lucaryn laughs from where he still stands at the dais, and Sakara's brown eyes narrow even further. "I didn't enjoy being in your bed."

The Mind Stone warms again under my skin. "We both know that's not true. I never take what is not willingly offered ... to my bed, anyway."

Sakara crosses his arms, straining his tunic over his broad chest, trying to look tough even kneeling as he is. "I've been here for weeks. If you knew, why did you let me roam your kingdom and your castle so freely? Why let me steal it?"

My dagger stills, the leather wrapped hilt creaking under the force of my grip. I stare down at him. "It was amusing." I catch my reflection in one of the large mirrors along the side wall and gesture at myself with a cocky grin, turning back to Sakara. "Plus, I read you as soon as you arrived. My appearance surprised you. You came here thinking you were going to have to seduce a hellish creature as ugly on the outside as inside—the fearsome Crown Breaker. One look at me, and relief poured from your mind. You were glad your Queen picked you for this assignment. You looked forward to getting into my bed." I lean down again, our lips a whisper apart. "And well, I'm just a man, after all. I figured, why not enjoy the gift Queen Ravaxina sent me?"

I see his intentions a second before he acts, and I stand and step back a step before his head can strike mine. I grin down at him. "It's hard to surprise the owner of the Mind Stone."

He snarls at me. "I'm amusing? You enjoyed the gift, like I'm an object?"

"Your Queen treated you as such when she threw you at me, yet you condemn *me*?"

"I could have killed you many times over."

Sakara jerks as I laugh, the sharp sound bouncing around the room, and several soldiers chuckle along. "Killing me was the last thing on your mind, lovely Sakara. I was just surprised it took you so long to make your move." My dagger picks up its movement once again, flicking through my hand. I tilt my head, my grin widening. "You enjoyed yourself, and for a while, I thought you might actually defect."

"You think too highly of your cock."

I shrug, wiggling my fingers, showing off the green stone in the ring. "Regardless"—I tap the tip of my dagger to my temple—"This game was stacked against you."

He unfolds his arms, letting them hang at his sides. "A game."

"It didn't have to be, but here you are, holding tight to your loyalty to your Queen. I commend you, but you've lost."

"And now?"

The Stone warms, almost painfully, as I stare at him. "You die." I'll give him credit. He doesn't react other than a small, sharp intake of breath. "Or ..." I almost close my eyes with anticipated bliss as his thoughts erupt with hope. Here comes my favorite part.

When hope crashes to make way for ... the fear.

I tap his forehead with my finger. "Or, I could imprison you in your mind. I've plucked a few choice memories to punish you with." I tilt my head. "The fire." His eyes go wide, and I smile. "Your brother's screams. Your nails breaking off as you clawed your way out."

"No." His voice is a strangled whisper, and tears rim his eyes.

Yes. My head is pounding from focusing the magic, but the chaotic fear dancing through his mind like yellow lightning is delightful. I fight to keep from adjusting my half-erect cock as his terror washes over me.

I step into his space, kneeling before him. His dark eyes reflect my bright green ones, and I cup his cheek. "Death or imprisonment?"

His eyes flick between mine. His thoughts spool through my head, and I barely avoid rubbing my temples. The finality of death tilts his decision toward imprisonment until he begins considering the horror of being trapped in one of his worst memories. His mind skips between his options: death, or terror of going mad within his nightmares.

I sigh, bored. "Time's up."

My dagger severs the pulsing vein in his neck as it slices across his throat. Sakara's hot blood spills down his front and sprays across my chest. He falls to the side, choking gasps escaping him until he falls silent, eyes staring at nothing.

Wiping my blade on Sakara's pants, I stand, sheathing my dagger, letting my fingers linger on the hilt for a moment. This dagger, the blade I swiped from a drunk soldier when I was nine-years-old, soothes me like a warm blanket would soothe a baby. The dagger was meant to be sold to buy Luc and me some food. We hadn't eaten in days, but Luc had wrapped his hand around mine on the hilt, urging me to keep it. Sometimes I can still feel the warmth of his hand when I hold my dagger.

Striding toward the dais, Sakara's blood quickly cools, sticking my shirt to my skin. "You know what to do."

Soldiers peel away from the wall, gathering Sakara's body to send back to his Queen—as a message. Ravaxina is pushing my limits. She's always been a thorn in my side, but I found it amusing and challenging to thwart her desperate efforts to steal the Stone and take my kingdom. But after ten years, Queen Rava's actions are losing their amusement and are becoming annoying. One day she's going to push too far.

My thighs flex as I climb the three steps and clap Lucaryn on the shoulder, drawing a small wince from his face. We head through the heavy wood door he came through earlier, closing off the bloody throne room behind us without another thought.

Luc smirks, bumping me with his shoulder. "Fearsome Crown Breaker?"

A grin pulls at my lips. "Well ... "

We both chuckle as I angle my head toward him. "Welcome home. What's got your face pinched in pain?"

He shrugs, his black hair falling over his forehead from where he had tried to brush it back. "Kahar."

Luc is my family—my chosen family. I have absolute trust in him, which allows me to keep the magic out of his mind. I never hear or see Luc's thoughts unless he pushes them at me. Like now. The Stone in my back warms, and images flit through my mind. I see Luc bent over with his black steed's front leg bent and held between his thighs. One of the horse's shoes had come loose, twisted, and punctured the soft part of his hoof. Luc gripped the twisted shoe and pulled, but it didn't come loose. Kahar reared forward, knocking Luc on his back and slammed his bleeding hoof into Luc's chest, cutting through flesh and muscle.

I shake my head, our footsteps echoing down the windowless stone hallway, torches flickering golden-orange light around us. "I don't know why you insist on keeping that hell horse. He's a menace. We have a stable full of horses."

Luc rubs at the left side of his chest. "I like him. Plus, he's as fearsome as my reputation. I've got to stick with him at this point." He rolls his shoulder with a grimace. "Though the bruising's going to take forever to heal, and I'm going to have a pretty big scar."

"Re'ashe'ar iyai suhfs." *Serves you right.*

He just snorts a laugh as we pass a single guard with a nod and climb the wide staircase that leads to our private wing.

We are silent as we approach the large wood door to my suite. Two guards stand on either side: one who's been with me for ten years, the other a defector from King Erathan's coastal Kingdom of Adren to the southwest. They nod as Luc and I pass through, closing the door behind us.

My fingers work down the buttons on my once white shirt, now turned a dark red with Sakara's blood. "So, no luck on finding the Heart Stone?"

Luc walks to a cabinet built into a nook in the stone wall, opening a glass door and retrieving a bottle of whiskey. He uncorks the top with a pop and takes a swig straight from the bottle. "All the markings we read about were there, even the inlaid trap at the cave entrance. It looked promising."

A sigh slides from my lips. I, along with seemingly everyone else in Imoria, have been searching for the Heart Stone for generations. The two Stones of power are the only remnants of magic left in the country, maybe in all the world. I thought that having the Mind Stone in my possession would give me a leg-up in the search for the second Stone, but so far, every lead we've chased down has been fruitless. There's so very little lore left on magic. Finding anything I haven't already read and ruled out on the two Stones is becoming harder and harder. I'm afraid there might be no more information to be found. The centuries have swallowed the mysteries of magic.

But I won't give up.

I cross the room, entering my washroom. Wetting a towel, I wipe the blood from my face and chest. The blood has darkened, blending in with the swirling tattoo on my left shoulder and across the left side of my chest, so I scrub the towel over the intricate inked design. I come back into my sitting area, sliding a blue tunic over my head. As I tuck it into my pants, I turn, facing Luc. "We have to find it. Before anyone else."

We both know the importance of possessing the Heart Stone. We grew up together, the best of friends bound through violence and hardship. After *that* night, I vowed to do whatever it took to rise to the top. I would hold all the power. I would fear no one. They would fear me.

But having the Mind Stone will not be enough if someone else finds the Heart Stone. I need both. I will have both.

Luc takes another big swallow of the whiskey before holding it out to me. "Ry." His tone tells me I won't like what he has to say. I take the bottle, letting the amber liquid burn its way down my throat, warming my stomach, not unlike how the Mind Stone warms my back.

Luc takes the bottle back, running a hand through his dark hair, sending it sticking out on top of his head. "I ran into a search party from Adren."

My head snaps up. "And?"

"One got away." He stuffs a hand in his pocket, and he slouches like he's bracing himself. "I think they might have gotten to the Stone before me." Luc winces at the look on my face. "The man who ran off pulled something from his saddlebag and slipped it into his cloak before he galloped off. I didn't get a good look. I can't be sure. There's still a chance—"

"But?"

"But, whatever he had was small and a deep pink."

"Fuck!" My arms snap out, swiping the books and papers from my desk, sending them fluttering and thudding to the stone floor. Breathing hard, I brace my hands on the top of the desk, trying to bring my anger under control. My fingers dig into the leather-inlaid surface as I inhale, hold it, then slowly exhale. And again. And again.

Finally, I kneel, gathering up the mess I made, placing neat piles back on the desk.

Luc remains silent as I collect myself, and when I finally turn, there's a smile on my face. "Well, if King Erathan does have the Heart Stone, at least that means we'll know where it is."

I tap my lip with my finger, then spin, snatching up a slip of paper, scribbling a quick note. Turning, paper clutched in my fist, I stride to the door, opening it and handing the paper to one of the guards. "Send this to our spies in Adren."

He nods, taking the paper and walks off with purpose. I close the door, crossing back to Luc. I snag the whiskey bottle from him and drink deep.

"Ry—"

"It's okay, Luc. We'll wait to hear from our spies. I want to be sure before we make a move on Erathan." Luc takes a deep breath, and I cross my arms. "So, what happened?"

"I sent Carelle and Anare to an adjoining cave system to search there." A shadow passes over Luc's face as his lips turn down. "I left Merith at the entrance to keep watch. When I came out, he was on the ground, two arrows in his chest."

I pass him the bottle, and Luc takes another deep gulp before holding it back out to me.

"I'm sorry, Luc. I know you liked Merith."

I didn't know the man well, but he was Luc's second, the first man to earn a spot in our elite unit, the Sagas. Luc nods, keeping his eyes cast to the floor.

"How many of Erathan's search party did you take out?"

"Six. After I took out the first three, they focused their attacks to allow the one with what might have been the Stone to escape. By the time Carelle and Anare returned, it was over. I'm sorry, Ry."

I wave my hand; the whiskey sloshing with the movement. "Seriously, Luc, it's okay. One against seven is not great odds, even for you." We both snort a laugh, and my shoulders release some tension at Luc's small smile. "I'm just glad you're okay." I lift the bottle but pause before it reaches my lips. "Were you still on Adren land?"

"Yes."

I hum a small sound of thought as Luc takes back the nearly empty bottle. "Well, Erathan won't be happy about that. If he does have the Heart Stone, once he learns how to use and control the magic, he might demand retribution."

"Do you think he'll make an attempt for the Mind Stone?"

"I'm not sure. So far, he's basically left us alone. He's never been over-zealous in his endeavors of my Stone or my kingdom. He's seemed content with trying to find the Heart Stone and ruling his slice of Imoria. But we'll have to be vigilant. What do you think of moving a few of our spies out of Trislen and into Adren?"

Luc swirls the whiskey in thought. "Is it wise to take eyes off of Queen Ravaxina?"

I shake my head with a chuckle. "We can leave a few in place. Once she gets wind that King Erathan might have the Heart Stone, she's going to lose her shit. It'll be quite amusing to see what her desperation drives her to do."

Luc salutes me with the whiskey bottle. "Indeed. I'll arrange to have some of our players moved around in the morning."

I nod, and Luc stretches, his spine popping, and his muscles flexing. My eyes snap to the sliver of brown flesh revealed between his shirt and pants. I swallow, allowing myself a moment to appreciate him.

We've never talked about us beyond our friendship, and Lucaryn is the only person in this world that I trust. I'm not about to ruin our friendship by making advances he might not want. And, no, I'm not brave enough to use the magic to find out if …

His hand rubs over his chest. "Okay. I'm sore and tired. I'm going to wash and get some sleep, unless you need anything else?"

I shake my head, heading to my desk. I sit in the uncomfortable wood chair, staring at the neat piles of books and papers. The window at my back is now dark, the sun gone for the day. The smaller blue child-moon hangs close to the horizon. The larger white mother-moon won't make an appearance tonight. Torches have been lit in each wall around my rooms, and a fire crackles off to my left near my bed. "No. Go rest. While we're waiting to hear from our spies in Adren, I'm going to plot a few other locations I was researching." I sigh, rubbing a hand over my face, my trim beard scraping my palm. "Though I'm running out of places to look. We've practically exhausted the references we've found over the years. Beyond just searching blindly, I'm not sure where else to look."

Luc rubs his chest. "Well, maybe our search is over, and Erathan's just holding it for us until we can … liberate it?"

A chuckle bubbles from my lips. "Maybe. We'll continue to send out search parties, just in case. Plus, that'll keep Rava's and Erathan's spies guessing."

Luc nods, his eyes pinched in pain. "Do you ever worry … about the power?"

I shrug. What texts we've found on the lore of natural magic and magical items all come with ominous warnings of going mad, of being consumed. "I've had the Mind Stone for ten years." He raises an eyebrow, and I laugh. "Okay, yes. That first year was tough—"

"Tough?"

I roll my eyes. "It was hell. But I've adapted. I'm in control."

Luc tilts his head down, looking at me through his lashes.

"Mostly. I'm in control, mostly."

He chuckles. "See you tomorrow, Ry."

A hum of noise is my only response as I pick up an old book with a peeling leather binding and aged pages that look like they might crumble to dust at any moment. I've read this book cover to cover several times, but maybe I've missed something.

My eyes skim over the page without taking in the words. I *knew* the Stone was in that cave system at the edge of King Erathan's territory. I should have gone with Luc. But there's nothing to be done about that now.

With the Heart Stone in play, either in Erathan's hands or still lost, I can't rest knowing the magic to manipulate and influence feelings and intentions is out there, waiting for me. I'll cut down who I must. I'll burn my way through the country. There's nothing I won't do–as King Ammeryn found out when I, one of his 'trusted' soldiers, cleaved his head from his body.

I know I'm the villain of most people's stories, and I'm not bothered by that in the least. It's said that evil will inevitably fall to the good deeds of men, and I smile at that thought.

I guess we'll see, because I won't stop.

Not until I have all the power.

2

I jolt upright, slamming against the back of the hard wood chair. Peeling away the piece of paper that's stuck to the side of my face, I can't help but glance at my hands to make sure the blood from my dream is not coating my skin. I shake my head, trying to physically dislodge the image of my mother's empty, smiling face from my mind.

I smack my hand against the arm of the chair. "Useless." I picked this chair because it's so uncomfortable it keeps me from falling asleep while I'm working. Usually.

My beard scrapes against my palms as I rub my hands over my face. Pulling the tie out of my hair, I sigh, letting the shoulder-length blond strands fall around my face. The books piled before me are familiar, and my eyes land on the paper that was stuck to my face. One line of script stands out with mocking clarity, bringing old memories to the surface.

*'He who claims an item imbued with Magic, has the power
to wield its power, no matter the location of the item.'*

I learned the truth of those words within days of taking the Mind Stone from King Ammeryn. The pain, the excruciating agony of being bombarded with thoughts and images not my own made me constantly nauseated, my head pounded ceaselessly, a thin layer of sweat always coated my skin, and I couldn't see straight. For long stretches of time, I couldn't be around anyone other than Luc. Finally, on the third day after taking the Stone, I woke up to Luc shaking me awake from where I'd passed out in the main hall. I shoved the Stone into his hands, my own shaking uncontrollably, begging him to take it away.

Luc took it to the west wing, but the thoughts of everyone in the castle, the courtyard, the barracks, and even from the outer edges of the city kept screaming through my mind. I thought I might go mad from the noise of thoughts that weren't my own. So, Luc took the Stone out to the stables, then into the city, then deep into the eastern woods. He took it farther and farther, even going into the mountains until I realized the magic was stuck to me and would be stuck to me until someone took the Stone with the intention of keeping it for themselves. The magic works off intent.

Luc offered to claim the Stone for short periods of time, but I refused. As my captain, he had enough to burden him. He didn't need the pain and distraction of the Stone on top of everything else. I could endure.

If I couldn't escape the magic, I decided I'd keep it close where I could protect it. So, I had Luc cut into my back, digging the Stone into my flesh before sewing it up. I dealt with the pain, the torture of the magic, until I learned to control it. I bore the weight for Luc and me, and now the power only hums with a buzz of sound in my mind until I focus or get physically close to someone.

Once, when Luc asked what it was like, the best way I could describe it was like being in a crowded room where the rumble of many voices creates a low ambient noise until you start walking through the press of bodies and start picking up pieces of conversation. The closer I am to someone, the sharper their thoughts become, and if I concentrate, I can push the magic toward a certain person or persons and pick out their thoughts. It hurts, bordering on agony sometimes, but I'll bear any pain to have this advantage over ... everyone.

I crack my neck, the paper crinkles as I shove it to the side, grabbing my notes from last night from two books and one scroll that mention the Heart Stone's possible locations. The scripts are vague, and I'm more than likely drawing conclusions that aren't there, but it's something.

My obsession with magic is well known, and I'm watched by other magic hunters. Any hint that I'm on a trail gets around fast, and now, that rumor mill will work in my favor. I'll keep them guessing—does Erathan have it? Do I? Is it still lost?

Smirking, I stand, shrugging out of my shirt and dropping my pants in a pile at my feet. My eyes longingly glance at my bed, but the dark purple of the sky tells me morning is approaching, and if I lay down now, I probably won't get back up until lunch. And there's too much to do.

The always-present throbbing in my temples is moderate this morning, but still, my gaze snags on the drawer of the table next to my bed, and the shaking in my hands gets worse. I can practically smell the sweet dead-rose scent of the street drug I used to take to find some peace from the magic. It's been years since I've indulged in the drug, and I've long since cleared it from my rooms—from that drawer, but the urge still hits me, and I hate myself for the weakness.

Clenching my hands, I pull on new clothes—black pants and a deep forest-green linen shirt—strapping on my black leather chest harness, sheathing several knives and daggers. I run my fingers through my blond hair, pulling half back into a tie to keep it off my face.

Grabbing the glass on my bedside table, I down the contents. I smack my tongue against the roof of my mouth with a shudder at the bitter taste. The healer brings this contraceptive tonic to my rooms each night, and I take it each morning—I love sex, but I don't love the idea of an illegitimate heir being thrown in my face.

With a nod to the guards outside my door, I walk down the stone hallway, torchlight interrupting the shadows. Giant tapestries depict the landscapes of my kingdom, Leiren, and more detailed scenes of the capital city, Farden. They do their best to add some warmth to the perpetual cold of the castle, but the chill seems to hold on to the stone walls like a petulant child.

Shivering, I smile, thinking of the quickly approaching winter solstice, which means my kingdom is about to be flooded with citizens from all around the country, as it is every year for my big solstice celebration. Despite the crush of people, voices, and thoughts, I love solstice and I *love* a good party.

I come to Lucaryn's door, and the sound of my knuckles hitting against wood interrupts the silence.

"Enter."

I'm not surprised he's awake at this early hour. We've always been early risers, mainly because we both suffer from the same memories that fuel our dreams—though Luc would call them nightmares.

Stepping inside, leaving the door half open behind me, I take in his rooms. I've known Luc my entire life, but I'm still shocked by how chaotically he lives. I step over and between discarded clothing scattered across the floor. My nose wrinkles at the rotten smell as I move a plate of half-eaten food from who knows how many days ago, in order to sit in the plush chair in his sitting area.

"How do you live like this?"

He pauses in fastening his pants to look around the room. His lips lift in a little smile as he shrugs. "I know where everything is. There's a system."

His sheets are rumpled, there's the glint of a sword on the floor beneath his bed. Through the open door to his washroom, I spy wet towels piled next to his tub, and there's a fresh towel draped over a tattered privacy screen.

I shake my head. "If you say so."

As he leans down, picking up a black shirt that's more wrinkled than our 92-year-old gardener, I notice the wound over the left side of his chest. The angry red cut, as long as my finger, has been crudely stitched, and a bruise darkens his brown skin.

"That looks pretty bad. Maybe you should have the healer look at it."

"Ry, I'm fine."

He's the only one who calls me that. To anyone else, I am King Rydel Wescaryn.

I catch the wince he tries to hide as he tugs the shirt over his head.

"It looks worse than it is. Besides, the healer would just cut out the stitches, douse me in alcohol, and stitch me back up again."

"Okay, fine. Breakfast. Then we can go over the locations for the search parties and discuss Erathan and Ravaxina."

He nods, distracted as he looks for the partner to the boot he holds in his hand.

Leaning over, I drag the boot out from under the chair and hold it up with a grin. "Some system."

He takes a step toward me, but I toss the boot at him, and he catches it one handed.

We head out together, our strides keeping pace, until we arrive at the dining hall. It's fairly empty this time of morning, with just a couple of servants cleaning the long wooden tables, benches, and chairs, and a few soldiers eating their breakfast in silence, some coming off the night shift, others readying for morning rounds. These are the soldiers of my elite unit, The Sagas, who enjoy the privilege of eating here in the castle instead of the mess hall off the barracks.

Luc peels away from my side, aiming for a soldier who I'd guess is coming off the night shift. Their voices are low, accompanied by little nods and shakes of their heads.

When I appointed Luc as my captain, he took to the position like he was born for it. We may not have the largest army in Imoria, but I'm proud to say we have one of the fiercest fighting forces in the country—especially within our Sagas unit. These soldiers were hand-picked for their skill and ruthlessness. Luc has done his job justice, curating a top-level unit that every soldier in my ranks aspires to join.

I grab a plate, piling it high with baked cornmeal, sausage, roasted vegetables, and bread. My legs protest as I sit on the hard wood bench, still not recovered from sleeping in my damned desk chair last night.

Eating slowly, I watch Luc absently rub his chest as he talks with the soldier. She's been with us for a few years now—another defector from King Erathan Bryrel's army. She was stationed at one of Adren's port cities—a tough and demanding job.

I recall the day she arrived ...

Three of my soldiers flanked a woman as they walked into the throne room. *She held her head high, her dirty-blond hair pulled back with three braids crowning her head, and loose strands spilling down her back. Her leathers were stained, and I suspected that was blood on her sleeve. Stopping before me, she held my gaze.*

Brave or too stupid to know better? I hoped she was the former.

I could have slid right into her mind and let the Mind Stone reveal her to me, but I enjoyed trying to assess a person's character. I liked to test myself on how reliable my intuition could be, so I simply asked why she had come.

Her back was straight, and she held her hands relaxed at her sides as she requested to join my army.

I lifted an eyebrow, drawing my dagger and letting it play between my fingers—accusing her of being a spy.

She didn't so much as twitch at my accusation before calmly denying it.

When I asked why she'd leave Adren, the wealthiest kingdom with the largest army in Imoria, her answer dripped with mirth. "It was comfortable enough … until it wasn't."

I tilted my head at her. "And that means?"

Her feet shifted ever so slightly as her left hand clenched. "Until a soldier I was on duty with decided my body was his for the taking."

My eyes traveled down her body, picturing lean muscle under her clothes. "And did he? Take it?"

"No, your Majesty. I refused him, and when he … insisted, I killed him."

I glanced at the dark stain on her sleeve. "So, what's the problem?"

She sighed, holding up her left hand, showing me the two missing fingers—third and fourth. "This was my punishment for protecting myself."

"You mean your punishment for killing a soldier."

She stiffened at my statement but held my gaze. I let the silence draw out. The other soldiers in the room stood still, waiting for the real test.

Finally, I smiled, waving a hand. "Well, good for you. If I allow you to join my army, you are welcome to kill anyone who advances on you without consent."

Her eyes widened at that, and I laughed. "We are a band of fighters, misfits, deserters, criminals, and killers. We are not the most morally upstanding group, but we operate on loyalty—first to me, second to each other. Every one of my soldiers earned the right to be here."

I leaned forward from where I sat on my throne, bracing my forearms on my knees. "I have just one rule."

I stood, descending the three steps at a leisurely pace until I was toe-to-toe with her. I had to look down, and she tilted her face up, her eyes holding fear.

"Don't betray me."

The Mind Stone warmed in my back under my skin as I dove into her mind. I saw the attack from the soldier. I witnessed how close he had come to raping her. She gasped as I made her relive her trauma. She had fought him off with quite a decent amount of skill. That pleased me. She would be an excellent addition to my army ... if she proved to be true. Finding her opening, she had driven her sword into his belly, leaving him to slowly and painfully bleed out on the damp wood of the docks.

So that story was true.

She jerked but stood her ground as she relived the blade slamming down on her hand, leaving her bloody fingers behind on the scarred wood table.

I pressed deeper, searching for any order, any whisper that would indicate Erathan—or anyone—sent her to betray me or to take my Stone.

I heard my soldiers move in, knowing what to do as she started shaking under my assault on her mind. They grabbed her by the shoulders, holding her up as her knees buckled. I searched everything, making special note of any memory that brought her pain—like when her lover died of sickness two years ago. Her whimper echoed around me, mirroring her whimper in her memories as she clutched the frail hand of her lover, a small woman with red hair, her pale skin almost bruised by how thin she was. Her chest was still, no breath leaving her cracked lips, her green eyes glassy and staring sightlessly at the ceiling.

I smiled at the pain in her memory. Bad memories are my weapon of choice, besides my dagger.

When I'd seen enough, I stepped back, locking my knees to hide how shaky they were, having learned long ago how to hide how much the magic takes out of me. I met her gaze with a nod, my lips pressed in a hard line as I glanced at her left hand. "Can you still wield a weapon?"

She stiffened her spine, her soldier's pride showing through. "Aye. I can wield a bow as well as before ..." She held up her mutilated hand. "And I am just as capable with a sword in my right hand as I was with my left."

Her thoughts supported her confidence, and I nodded. "We'll see. Captain Lucaryn." *Luc stepped forward, standing at my side.* "Take her to the barracks. Let her rest, then have the grunt unit show her the ropes."

Luc turned with a nod, and the woman managed to get her feet back under her. "Thank you, your Majesty."

I grinned. "Don't thank me yet. We are a hard bunch. You'll learn. Or you'll die."

She nodded, a flash of fear making her thoughts slightly chaotic. I stilled my dagger, gripping the hilt. "And you know, now, that you can't deceive me, yes?"

She nodded again, bowing her head. "I will serve with loyalty."

"Good." *I sheathed my dagger.* "Welcome to the army of Lieren, ...?"

"Carelle, your Majesty."

I blink away the memory as Luc pushes away from the table, leaving Carelle—who is now in the coveted Sagas unit—to finish her breakfast.

After loading up a plate of his own, he joins me. "So, where am I sending the search parties?"

The flavors of fennel and fat coat my tongue as I take a bite of sausage. "One group will go to the other side of the mountains in the Varyen Desert." Luc's eyes un-focus as he thinks over who he will send to the 'cursed' high desert. "The second is deep in the forests bordering the village of Keenor."

His brows raise as he shoves huge helpings of baked cornmeal into his mouth. "The hunting village in Trislen? Wouldn't Queen Ravaxina have already searched there if there was any hint of the Stone being in her kingdom?" Bits of food fling onto the table at his words, and I laugh, shaking my head. He's always such a mess.

"I'm sure she has searched that location, but it will drive her mad when she learns we have people in Keenor. Hopefully, she'll think she missed something. I want her to doubt any information she receives about Erathan possibly having the Mind Stone."

Luc chuckles as I go on. "The last location is at the sea cliffs along our southern border. In two days, you and I will ride with that party."

Luc opens his mouth, holding up a finger, but I halt his words.

"Casin will take over as acting captain. He's done it before. Unless you have someone else in mind?"

He shakes his head, the tapping of his fork against his plate drumming a metallic rhythm.

I nod. "The location is not technically in Adren, but it's close enough to put us in striking distance as soon as we have confirmation on whether Erathan has the Heart Stone."

His fork pauses halfway to his mouth before he nods and continues eating. King Erathan and Queen Ravaxina have eyes on me —I allow them to have eyes on me—and any move on my part will quickly get back to the other two rulers of Imoria.

And of course, there are the independent hunters who watch the movements of us three royals—those who search for the Stone for themselves hoping to become, well ... me. A nobody who rose to become a King.

The three kingdoms of Imoria have tolerated each other for centuries, and neither Queen Rava nor King Erathan have been willing to go to war against the King of the Mind Stone. Not yet anyway.

But now ...

As if sensing my turbulent thoughts, Luc leans over, placing a hand on my shoulder. "We'll get it. Even if we have to burn Adren to the ground. Uss a uhnasuhu zuhss az sa iyai." *All of Imoria will bow to you.*

I grin. "Imoria will bow to *us*, my friend."

I push away from the table, leaving Luc to finish demolishing his breakfast.

Yes, I will rule all of Imoria. It's what I was made for, after all. How else would I have had the strength to cut down my first enemy at only seven years old? A boy that young should have felt horror at the scene before him, but I only felt joy, absolute glee at what I'd done.

It's been twenty-seven years since *that* night, and I haven't turned back since.

3

I grip my shirt and yank it over my head, tossing the sweat-drenched garment to the side. Holding up my fists, I circle my opponent, Casin. He's a beast of a man in my Sagas Unit. He has at least five inches on me, and I'm six foot two. And despite his size, he's fast.

I duck, feeling the breeze of his swing as his fist screams past my face. I throw a punch, missing, then follow it with a kick aimed at his knee. My boot connects, causing him to stumble back, but he doesn't go down.

I vaguely hear the grunts and thuds of others sparring around us, and I know Luc is out here somewhere sparring with his own partner, but I don't chance a look around. I keep my focus on the man before me.

He swings again, and this time, when I duck, I push into his space, wrapping my arms around his torso, locking my arms as the side of my face presses against his sweaty skin.

He grunts and slams his clenched fists into my back, knocking the air from my lungs, but I don't let go. I dig my heels into the dusty ground and push harder.

When he wraps his arms around my middle, my feet leave the

ground and as the world turns upside down, I know this is going to hurt like a bitch.

His arms squeeze me until I'm sure a rib is about to crack, but before he has the chance to drop me on my head, I lean into his hold, twisting just enough to slam my elbow into the soft flesh above his kidney.

I scramble to get my feet under me as he releases me and stumbles back. We circle each other like stalking mountain cats. My fists clench and unclench at my sides, itching for my dagger, but there are no weapons today.

We've been sparring for at least twenty minutes, but I feel more restless than when we started. I'm eager to get on the road–to do *something*. Plus, I can't figure out what my move should be if Erathan does indeed have the Heart Stone. Do I go in with a small covert group, or do I invade with a show of power and make a spectacle of stripping him of his newly found magic?

A moment of unfamiliar doubt shivers down my spine. *If* I can take the Stone from him. While I can see and even influence thoughts, he will have the ability to know and influence my feelings. Erathan could snuff out my anger and lull me into a state of calm serenity. He could make me doubt my own strength and crush my spirit under the weight of fear. He could make me believe I'm loyal to him and him alone and turn my feelings against those under my protection, against my kingdom, against Luc. *If* he has the Stone, I need to act fast while he's still struggling with the new power.

I huff a breath, shaking off my fears, tucking back a few strands of hair that have fallen from my tie. I have to get that Stone.

The big man before me grins, actually grins, and I return it as I charge. I could use the Mind Stone and end this fight in seconds, but where's the fun in that?

I land a crushing right hook followed by a brutal jab to his gut which folds him over at the waist. Before he can right himself, I land a kick to his left knee, this time dropping him to the ground. Pain blooms up my side as he slams his fist into my ribs, but I push closer, cracking my knee into his chest before I punch him in the nose.

Blood pours down his chin, dripping onto his bare torso, mixing with his sweat. I spin, wrapping my arm around his neck, locking my wrist in my other hand, and squeeze. His nails dig into my flesh, tearing grooves down my arm, but I don't register the pain. All I care about is the win.

His boot kicks at the dusty ground, trying to gain leverage, but I lean into him, adrenaline coursing through my blood like lightning.

His movements become slower, and his breaths gasp in short bursts.

Luc's voice rings out across the training area. "Tap out, Casin."

The training yard has gone silent, and a crowd has gathered. I lean so close into Casin, my lips almost brush his ear. "Do you yield?"

There's a smile behind my words, and he shakes his head with a grunt, picking up his struggles for a few seconds before he weakens again. Sweat drips down his face, pooling between my arm and his neck. His muscles strain against me, trying to find a way out of my hold, and I can't help but appreciate his sculpted body struggling under me. I'd offer to take this sparring match to my rooms, but the ink running down the back of his left hand tells me he's married. Shame.

I keep my elbow locked but release my other hand to deliver another sharp punch to his kidney. His back arches with a grunt as I regain my choke-hold.

He barely maintains his hold on my arm as his body begins to go slack.

"Rydel. That's enough." Luc is closer now, standing right outside our sparring circle.

I lean into Casin. "Is it enough?"

He doesn't respond, and I can feel his muscles trembling.

Luc crosses to us, dust kicking up behind him. "Ry."

My skin feels too tight, and my hands shake with the need to feel the sharp release of pain that comes with striking your opponent.

I release Casin and round him, landing three quick punches to his face. Blood flies both from my split knuckles and his cheek. His left eye is swollen shut, bruises already rim his eyes from my hit to his nose, and his bottom lip is split. He topples to his back, and I follow, landing another sharp punch to his face.

"Do you yield?"

In anser, Casein thrusts his hand up, catching me on the jaw. My teeth snap, and I taste blood. Spitting to the side, I smile down at him as he tries to hook his foot behind my knee to flip our positions. I pin him with my thighs and shins, punching him over and over with meaty thuds. My anger is a living thing as I recall being young and scared, falling helplessly time and again under angry fists. I was just a child! He should have loved me, protected me, not ...

Drawing my bloody fist back again, I'm halted as a hand grips my arm, yanking me away.

Panting, I stand to face Lucaryn, hands fisted at my sides. He tilts his head, holding out his arms. "You want to go?"

My breath heaves out of me as I force my anger to drain away. The white rage recedes from my vision, and I slowly uncurl my fingers, rolling my shoulders down my back. Luc watches me, holding my gaze. I take a slow breath. Luc nods, and I nod back, letting him know I'm in control.

There are a few thoughts of concern and even fear from the soldiers surrounding us, but most are amused or indifferent. Sparring usually gets rough. All sorts of issues and anger get worked out in the rings, and I've been training with the Sagas since I created the unit 10 years ago.

Casin coughs as he pushes himself up to sit. "Good match, your Majesty."

"Likewise."

I leave him where he is, turning before scooping up my shirt. I use it to mop some of the dust, blood, and sweat from my skin.

Luc matches my stride as we head toward the castle. "Feel better?"

I flex my fingers. "A little."

He shakes his head with a smile as we climb the stone steps to a pair of double doors standing open to the morning air. "Maybe you're trying to scratch the wrong itch."

"What does that mean?"

He huffs, turning his gaze skyward. "You need a good fuck, Ry. Have you had sex since Sakara?" He glances at my spread, flexed fingers. "Other than your hand?"

I recall how Sakara's skin pressed against mine, sweat-slicked with pleasure. I grin. "No. Are you offering?"

He throws his head back in a laugh as we pass through the doors, nodding to the two soldiers standing on either side. "You couldn't handle me."

Oh, you have no idea. I keep my grin in place. "Indeed. You're probably a very needy lover." He laughs again as I aim for the stairs that lead to our wing, tossing the words over my shoulder, "I'm going to get cleaned up, then finish packing for tomorrow."

Luc calls after me. "Are you sure it's wise for you to leave the capital right now?"

I pause. "Erathan won't make a move. Not yet. If he *does* have the Heart Stone, now's the time to strike. He's going to be struggling with the power for a while." I barely hold back a shudder as I once again recall the intense headaches and hallucinations brought on by the new, overwhelming power of the Mind Stone.

Luc doesn't move, and we end up in an awkward stare off. A sliver of doubt slides into my chest. If he's this concerned, maybe I should stay here. Why push my luck? I chew on my bottom lip, my left hand reaching for my thigh sheath where my dagger usually sits, but it's empty. My fingers fiddle with the leather straps instead.

Luc steps back, rubbing his chest and shaking his head. "Never mind. You're right, it's a good move. Dinner in your rooms tonight? We can go over the plan."

"The first search team is leaving tonight?"

He nods. "The other party will leave in the morning a few hours before us, and the bird master knows to send a bird as soon as confirmation one way or the other arrives from our spies in Adren."

"Good. Hopefully, our search parties will give Erathan a false sense of security. And it will drive Rava mad." I bark a laugh, and Luc grins, rubbing his chest again as he walks off, disappearing around a corner. My earlier unease at leaving the capital to go on the hunt vanishes. Luc will be at my side. We'll have a few of our soldiers with us, and I have the power of the Mind Stone. We'll be fine if our enemies decide to engage.

Halfway up the stairs, I pause again. Turning around, I head through the east wing of my castle. I could bathe in my rooms, but the spring in the grove outside the orchards is calling my name. I need the space. I need the open air.

A guard trails me under Luc's orders, and I shake my head, annoyed but appreciative of my friend's protectiveness. As I walk through the halls, snippets of thoughts flit through my mind, like ghostly voices of the people who live and work in my castle. *'I heard the King is leaving tomorrow'* ... *'Hunting the Heart Stone'* ... *'I'm hungry'* ... *'I can't keep up with these fires. There are so many hearths in this castle'* ... *'I wish I would have been picked to go this time to join the hunt'* ... *'I've heard that possessing too much magic destroys your soul'* ... *'I wonder if I can convince Laurel to take me to her bed again tonight'* ... *'Will the King invite the other royals to his winter solstice celebration this year'* ... *'Magic disappeared from our lands for a reason. The Crown Breaker courts disaster with that Stone'*

I force the Stone's magic to quiet, blocking out the voices as much as I can until they become a low rumble of noise.

Suspicion and fear call to the Stone, giving me the secrets of those around me. And I'm suspicious of everyone ... except Luc. So, I've learned to read people quickly and either feed or lessen my distrust. If their thoughts are disloyal, the magic rages, flaring with heat and pain. If they're harmless, the power recedes to a mere dull throb.

If Erathan does indeed have the Heart Stone, he's going to be plagued with the overwhelming feelings of everyone around him.

A smirk crawls over my face. I hope he does have it—that would make things so much simpler.

I squint as I step back outside; the sun climbing higher toward afternoon. Following a worn path that leads through the fruit orchards, I notice the trees are nearly bare, having shed most of their fruit of the season. The overly sweet scent of rotting apples fills my nose as I pass through the break in the stone fence and into the copse of trees making up the grove that shields a natural spring. The sound of the guard's steps fades as he moves to stand in the shadow of the trees, leaning his shoulder against the trunk of one.

Stripping quickly, I wade into the water, rolling my shoulders down my back with a sigh, recalling the many times as children Luc and I bathed in that freezing river outside our small village.

My arms pull me through the water, my feet kicking lazily. With a deep breath, I dip under the water, enjoying complete silence. Early on in my reign, I used to spend hours here, holding my breath under the water as long as I could just to have a moment of peace.

I grit my teeth as an image pops in my mind. Someone's here, and they're close enough for their thoughts to breach the water. The angle of the image is from the spring's edge, looking down at the rippling water.

I calmly let my head slip to the surface, letting the water drip down my face as I glance at the trees, seeing the slumped form of the guard on the ground. I turn, facing a cloaked figure standing over my clothes with their arms at their sides and a dagger glinting in their hand.

I can't see his face, but his voice is deep with a rumble of amusement. "Hello, keeper of the Mind Stone."

4

"Is my man alive?"

He remains still and silent, but I catch a faint thought, *I'm not a monster, you are.*

I smirk. "So, who are you?"

He lifts his arm, pointing his dagger at me. "No one."

He's trained for this moment. The only word I'm getting from his mind is *'Stone.'* And the only image I'm getting is the raw, green shimmer of moldavite—though it's obvious he's never seen the actual Mind Stone because he's picturing it much bigger and shinier than it is.

I stroke my arms over the water, lazily propelling myself backward, ready to test his mind.

"You're here for the Stone."

It's not a question, and a bit of fear skirts around the edges of his concentration before his focus dives back into the image of the Stone, and his hood bobs with a nod. "Yes."

Skimming my hands along the surface of the water, I keep my hands visible, showing off my naked fingers. I took the fake ring off this morning to spar. I float back, exposing my naked body, before rolling to swim slowly toward him. "As you can see, I don't have it on me."

He flicks his wrist, causing the blade to flash in the sunlight. "You will tell me where it is."

"And what, you're going to waltz into my castle and retrieve it?"

He tilts his head. "If I need to, but I think you're the kind of man who likes to keep what's important to him close by." His boot kicks my pile of clothes. "It's not tucked away here, so maybe you have it *in* you."

Panic stalls my breath for a moment before I get the flash of an image of my ass. I stop my lazy strokes, standing chest-deep in the water and throw back my head with a great laugh. "You think I've shoved it up my ass? That would be most inconvenient, don't you think?"

He shrugs, sending the black folds of his cloak swirling around his body. "Regardless, I'll search your body, and if I can't find it, I'm sure a knife to your throat will get your captain to reveal the Stone's location."

I take another step; water rippling and splashing at my waist. "What makes you think he knows?"

"A hunch."

"I'd hate to be tortured on a hunch."

The more he talks, the more his focus on controlling his thoughts crumbles. It's extremely hard to talk about one thing while trying to get your mind to focus on another. As I keep my steady pace toward him, I get brief flashes of thoughts and memories, like getting an impression of a landscape in the dead of night through lightning strikes.

I'm now only calf-deep in the water. He reaches out, pressing the tip of his dagger to my chest. "The Stone."

"That easy? Come on. There are only two magical items left in this land. One is lost, and I have the other. And you think you're going to take it with a dagger and a demand?"

He moves to press the blade deeper, but I lunge to the left, grabbing his wrist and twisting. His mind opens to me as his focus shifts to keeping a hold of his blade. My hand is wet, and I'm unable to get a good enough grip to force him to drop his dagger, but I have his mind, and that's enough.

I sift through his memories as he swipes at me. The water around my feet slows me down, and I clench my teeth, catching the edge of his blade along my side. Blood drips down over my hip and onto my thigh before mixing with the water.

He lunges again, stepping into the water with me. His pupils dilate and sweat beads on his forehead as he realizes I'm in his mind. Panic swirls through his thoughts as he tries to shut me out, but I already have him.

I grin at the delicious fear and panic. All he can focus on are the memories he doesn't want me to see.

It's heady. Even after ten years with this magic, I still get a rush when I hold a person's mind, their thoughts, their memories, the basis for who they are, within my power.

Neither King Erathan nor Queen Ravaxina sent this man. He's acting on his own. He's out for his own glory. I can respect that, and I'm impressed at how far he made it. But today is not going to be his day.

And then I find it. Everyone has at least one—one memory or fear that has the power to drop them to their knees.

A smirk pulls up my lips. His eyes go wide, and his body goes stiff as I grab onto and pull up the scene.

His eyes are locked on a young boy, maybe six. No, his thoughts say ten. But the boy is small for his age. Skinny and curled in on himself, his blond hair is dirty and sticking out in all directions.

A short man with a fat face and protruding belly pulls the boy back by his shirt, ripping the collar. Sweat plasters the man's wispy hair to his bald head and glistens on his pale skin.

The boy chokes on a sob, eyes begging for help. "Silas."

His brother.

"Let him go." Silas' voice is desperate as his eyes dart between his little brother and the sneering man.

"You have the money?" The man's voice is hard and filled with greed as he tugs the small boy tighter against his large stomach.

Bile rises in Silas' throat. "You know I don't. I need more time." His fear is frantic, and I smile. Such a perfect memory.

The fat man presses a dirty knife to the boy's throat. "You knew who ya were borrowing money from, boy."

Silas moans as his little brother's pants darken with his urine and his weak voice murmurs, "Please."

"This was ya third and final chance. Time's up."

Silas screams as the blade rips across the boy's throat. Blood immediately covers the front of his small body, and the fat man pushes him into the mud at his feet, stalking away with a grumble. "What a waste. I shoulda known better than ta offer my money and kindness ta street trash."

Silas skids to his knees, gathering his brother into his arms. The boy tries to say something, but it comes out in a gurgle of blood. He coughs, spitting blood into Silas' face before he goes limp.

Silas' pain is exquisite, sending tingles down my spine and a smile across my face. Tears stream down his cheeks as he chants, "I'm sorry. I'm sorry. I'm sorry."

I loop the memory.

Silas stares into the eyes of his ten-year-old brother, skinny and curled in on himself. His blond hair is dirty and sticking out in all directions.

A short man with a fat face, protruding belly, wisps of hair plastered to his bald head, and sweat glistening on his pale skin, pulls the boy back by his shirt. The collar rips, and the boy chokes on a sob, eyes begging for help ...

Sliding from his mind, I walk up to Silas, now on his knees, the bloody spring water lapping at his waist. His eyes are unfocused and rimmed with tears as he relives his little brother's death over and over.

Grinning, I pull back his hood, revealing short-blond hair, much like his dead brother's. His eyes are brown too, but with a ring of light-brown, almost gold, at the outer edge. His lips are slightly parted, and the first of what I know will be many tears falls down his cheek.

I lean down, close to his ear, knowing my words will whisper through his mind. "Nice try."

Gathering up my clothes, I pull on my pants, shove my feet in my boots, and ball up my shirt in my fist. I check on the guard, finding a bruise on his temple, but his breathing is even. Turning back, I pat Silas on his shoulder. "Wait here. A couple of my soldiers will be along in a moment to show you to your room."

I chuckle as I head back through the orchard, squishing a few soft apples under my boots on the way. It must have been nice for Silas to have a brother who cared, who loved him ... unlike my sister. But in the end, what good did it do him?

A pair of soldiers making their rounds through the eastern grounds come into view. I lift an arm to hail them, and they jog over.

The taller of the two, his skin startlingly pale, even though he spends a good deal of time outside, picks up his pace as he draws his sword. "You're injured, my King." His braided red hair bounces around his shoulders and over his chest.

Oh yeah. The cut from Silas' blade. I forgot about that.

I wave them off, the other soldier having drawn his blade as well. "It's nothing. I'm fine, but my guard was knocked out. He'll have a monster headache but should be fine. There's a man at the spring." I tilt my head back in the direction from which I came. "He came for the Stone. It was a good effort, but ..."

The second soldier, his short, curly brown hair catching the sunlight turning it copper, smirks with a bark of a laugh. "When will they learn? They keep coming, thinking they will be the one to get past the magic."

I grin, huffing a chuckle with the two men. "I mean, *I* did it, so I can only blame myself for giving them hope."

The red-head's grin widens. "How *did* you do it?"

"Ah, that's a secret I'll take to my grave."

Still grinning, they cross their right fist to their hearts, bowing slightly before heading to the grove. "We'll get your guard to the barracks and will escort your guest to his cell."

I continue toward the looming castle before me. Many people have claimed seeing this castle makes them feel cold, a sense of dread coming from the large grey stones stacked heavily atop each other. But I've always felt nothing but excitement every time I walk through the thick wood-carved doors to *my* castle. The giant slabs of stone feel solid, secure. And the large expanses of windows down the western face, balances the weight of the stone.

The thick tapestries, telling the stories of our country of Imoria and my kingdom of Lieren, dampen the sounds of boots traveling the halls. Plush, expensive carpets add color and warmth to almost every room, and the kitchens are always stocked, so I never have to worry about where my next meal will come from.

So many rooms, several I have absolutely no use for. And it's all mine.

I fought, scraped, lied, cheated, and killed my way from that disgusting shack of a house to ... this.

My guards open the door to my suite, and I'm just over the threshold when I see red—anger.

A hand shoves into the center of my back, and I stumble forward. The door slams behind me. "What the fuck, Ry!"

5

I let the momentum of Luc's push carry me farther into my rooms. I slow my steps and stop, turning to face my best friend.

He's thrown on a shirt since I last saw him and has rolled the sleeves up to his elbows, revealing the many scars criss-crossing the brown skin of his muscular forearms. His chest expands with every deep breath, and the muscles in his arms are strained with his clenched hands.

"Why didn't you call for backup? He knocked out Lero." My brows furrow, and Luc huffs. "Your guard." I shrug as Luc rubs his chest. "He could have ... " His words trail off with fear flooding his eyes.

I cross my arms, the tattoos along my left shoulder and chest flexing with the movement. My skin pebbles with the chill of the stone walls around me, the thick rugs, tapestries, and curtains doing what they can to warm my expansive rooms, but without a fire in the hearth, the space remains cool.

"I can handle myself."

He waves a frustrated hand at me. "E'a fas sa iyai, Ry." *He got to you, Ry*. "What if you hadn't been fast enough?"

Once again, I had forgotten about the cut along my side, and his attention to it sharpens the slight pain. There's concern under his anger, and I do my best to keep my voice calm.

"It's a scratch. And he's now drooling in the dungeons." I take a deep breath, releasing my arms and shoving my hands in my pockets. "How do you suppose he made it so close to the castle? I didn't think to search his mind for the answer at the time."

Luc's jaw flexes as he grinds his teeth. "I'm not sure. But I'll find out."

My fingers itch for my dagger, but I keep my hand firmly in my pocket. "I'll go down tonight and get the information from his mind."

He nods, but I can tell he's still unsettled by his stiff posture. "Luc, you know I can take care of myself."

He runs his hands through his short black hair as he paces.

"I know, Ry. But you have a target on your back—you have since the day you killed King Ammeryn and took the Stone. You made me your captain for a reason ... to watch your back."

"And I trust you explicitly, Luc. In all things. I always have, and I always will."

He pauses, hanging his head, his shoulders slumping.

"I can't help but worry, Ry. After everything, I can't lose you."

My steps are silent against the thick weave of the blue, gray, red, and cream rug under foot. I place my hand on his shoulder.

"Nor I, you. We've been together since the beginning, and I wouldn't be here if it wasn't for you." His bright blue eyes meet mine, the edges still creased in worry.

His head bobs in an almost imperceptible nod, and I pull him into my chest in a tight hug. I've got a few inches on him, but his build is bulkier than mine, making him feel solid and strong in my arms. We hold each other for a few minutes, taking comfort in the safety and trust of our friendship before he steps back.

The loss of his body heat sends a shiver across my skin, and I head to my washroom, calling over my shoulder, "I'm going to get cleaned up, *again*." He snorts a laugh behind me, and I smile. "Then I have a stack of letters to review from our spies, as well as some reports of bad weather and even worse crops from the eastern villages. I'll have to assess that situation and decide on this season's taxes and food stores." Pausing in the washroom's doorway, my fingers unfasten my pants as I toe off my boots. "I imagine that will take me up to dinner, so I'll meet you back here, let's say, an hour after sunset?"

He nods. "I'm working with the grunt unit today. They're going on the mountain trial tomorrow."

I laugh, shoving my pants to my ankles and kicking them to the side. "Oh, they're going to hate you."

He shrugs, chuckling, the sound deep and familiar.

I smile back before turning into the washroom, the stone cool under my bare feet. I hear the door to my rooms close behind Luc, and I turn the lever. Water rises through a pipe that opens in the ceiling in a corner of my washroom. It's like standing in a warm rain shower, and I'm the only one in the kingdom with such a luxury.

My mind snaps back to *that* night, twenty-seven years ago. The water in the languid river outside my village was freezing, as usual. Luc and I washed the blood from our clothes and bodies, and my teeth chattered loudly. The cold pebbled Luc's skin, and his lips were turning blue. Though we were both used to bathing there, it never got easier to deal with the cold.

I usually went there to bathe because I wasn't allowed to bathe at home until my father had washed. And once he was done, I'd make sure my sister had a dip in the semi-warm water in our tub before I quickly scrubbed my mother down. After, I'd stare at the cold, dirty water with hatred. I despised that tub, and I rarely used it.

Luc would come to the river with me because it was easier than hauling water to fill his tub. Plus, I think by bathing in the river with me he was showing solidarity—best friends suffering and struggling together.

When Luc's parents died, he moved in with his elderly aunt who needed help to do *everything,* and she never left the house. But her reclusive nature paid off when she died several months prior to *that* night. In the dead of night, I helped Luc bury her in the small patch of land behind their house. We were young, but we were no strangers to death, and we kept this one a secret. No one knew Luc was alone except me. If anyone found out, the king would have seized his house, and the soldiers would have sent Luc to live at the church in the next town. We were not willing to be separated, so we pretended his aunt was still alive, running the usual errands for her, and kept her garden weeded and thriving as she would have demanded.

Scrubbing ourselves clean *that* night, there were wide grins on our faces, knowing that would be the last time we'd have to endure that particular section of the freezing river. We were free. There were many more freezing baths after that, but not there.

As I turn my face up under the hot shower, it brings a sigh from my lips. All the pain and death I've dealt along the way was worth it for this alone. I smile into the water before grabbing a bar of oatmeal soap from a marble table to my right. Paying special attention to the cut on my side, I scrub myself clean. The wound really is a mere scratch. It's not even bleeding anymore and should scab over in a few hours.

I turn the lever off, toweling myself dry before leaving the washroom for my bedroom. I open my walk-in wardrobe, grabbing a pair of black pants and a forest green tunic—the same color as my eyes. Dressing and sliding into a pair of soft, fur-lined leather boots, I head back out of my rooms and down the long hall of my wing until I turn the corner into the common spaces, heading to the main library.

Sunlight paints squares of golden light onto the grey stones through the windows of the west wall. As I pass through the open doors of the library, my boots leave the stone flooring, sinking into plush carpet once again, this one with a deep green and gold weave.

My desk stands in the center, framed by a large window overlooking the gardens standing bare other than the few evergreens showing off their color amid the naked, cold branches. And much like my desk back in my room, neat stacks of books and papers cover the surface, but these have nothing to do with magic lore or the history of the Stones. These are all pertaining to my kingdom and my people. The burdens of being King.

A servant appears in the doorway as I sit in the padded chair, much more comfortable than the chair in my room. He clasps his hands before him, bowing his head slightly. His shaggy, brown hair falls over his forehead.

"The usual, your Majesty?"

"Yes."

44

I pick up a stack of papers as the servant slips silently from the room. A cursory glance tells me the situation in the eastern villages is indeed dire. The papers are coarse against my fingers as I spread them out on the desk, looking them over closely.

A glass is set on the desk by my left arm, and the sound of the servant's soft steps recedes. Without looking, my fingers wrap around the glass, and I bring it to my lips, taking a sip of the spiced whiskey. It burns down my throat and into my stomach, warming me like an inner fire.

I'm not known for my altruism, quite the opposite in fact, but I won't let my people starve. I do just enough to avoid an uprising. It's a fine line of keeping the masses 'satisfied.' Too much comfort, and they start to take for granted what they have and start demanding more. Too little, and they rise up, believing a new ruler will change their circumstances.

I snort out loud, grabbing another stack of papers. People can be smart, but put them in a group, and they act like any other pack animal ... panicky, reactive beasts.

It seems the port town of Joxsis on our western border has done quite well this season. I can send some stores of fish, blubber, salt, and kelp to the eastern villages.

Leafing through a few more pages, I nod. I can compensate Joxsis with two new ships. It's been on my to-do list for a while now, and I set aside the necessary funds last year, so I won't be giving anything up. But the people of Joxsis won't know that. This way I can keep the tax rates, and if all stays on track, I'll be able to raise the taxes for the coming spring season.

I stack the papers, tapping them on the desk before setting them to the side. I reach for the four letters, still sealed with wax, from my spies in the kingdoms of Adren and Trislen. Reading each carefully, I sigh, releasing tension from my shoulders. There are confirmed reports from my spies that Erathan does have a pink stone in his possession, but he hasn't used the magic and isn't exhibiting any signs of distress.

I frown, running my fingers over the words on the page, my gaze going distant. Erathan has a stone, but is it *the* Stone? He would definitely be in distress if it was.

I shake my head. I'll know soon enough.

Focusing on the other letters, I relax a little more. There's nothing else going on in Imoria that I wasn't already aware of. These are all basically check-ins.

Good.

I go through a few more papers and reports from around my kingdom. There have been more than the usual animal attacks in our northern villages. The cold weather is moving in early, driving the predators out of the mountains in search of an easy meal. A village to the south is requesting maintenance and widening of the road they use to get to and from the capital. That might be a worthwhile expenditure, but I'll speak with the soldiers I have stationed in that village to see just how dire the road condition is. A few of the other southern villages are concerned with the condition of the border walls. We don't have a huge problem with people sneaking into our kingdom, but those that do always provide me with delicious entertainment. I'm not worried about the border, not right now, anyway.

A knock on the open door brings my head up. Blinking, I look around. The room has dimmed with the setting sun, and I've been squinting without realizing it. I crack my neck, rubbing at my eyes.

Two servants glide into the room. The same one from before crosses the room with a covered tray in his hands. He sets it on a low table to my right before taking the empty glass from my desk and replacing it with a full one.

I stretch my arms overhead, enjoying the popping the movement sends down my back. "Captain Lucaryn is eating with me tonight. Bring a second tray."

He nods and silently slips from the room.

I palm my dagger, spinning and twirling the blade as I sip the whiskey deep in thought. The second servant, a small woman with delicate features, small hands, and long brown hair, stoops over the hearth, building a fire. Her thoughts whisper through my mind, the same voice I heard before. '*Endless fires. This place is so big. All day and night I light*

46

and tend fires. It's to the point I dream of smoke and flame.' Once the fire has caught, she stands and lights the four torches that line the room on the opposite side of where the bookcases stand. *'The scent has permanently stuck to my hair, no matter how often I wash it. Maybe I should shave it. Sometimes I wish stone could burn. I'd light one last fire and be done with it.'*

Luc strides in, quickly followed by the servant carrying a second tray of food.

As the woman turns to leave, my voice rings out, halting her steps. "You wish to burn my castle to the ground?"

Luc pauses, watching the woman who has frozen by the door. She spins, her eyes wide, and her mouth drops open before her small hand covers her lips as tears rim her eyes. "No!" She drops her hand, bowing low at the waist. "It was an unconscious thought. I would never, your Majesty. My mind conjures these thoughts when I'm tired. I'm grateful for this job, your Majesty. Please."

Luc crosses his arms as the other servant quietly leaves the room, his thoughts floating out with him. *'How many times have I warned her? Focus on the task. Don't let your mind wander, especially around the King.'*

I watch the woman as she clutches her soot-stained fingers in front of her, the coal blending with the marriage ink on the back of her hand.

My sharp tone makes her flinch. "This is going to hurt."

I don't give her time to brace herself before I dive into her mind, yanking at her memories, dreams, and thoughts. I could do it gently, but I don't. Her body tries to fight the intrusion of my magic. Sweat slicks her skin, and her shoulders begin to shake. I'm satisfied that she's harmless, just tired as she claimed, but I keep going, because I can.

I observe her time here.

She arrived at my gates, starving and desperate. Years before, her parents had died, leaving her alone and without a coin to her name. She begged for a job, opening herself to my magic to prove her innocence and despair. She has worked hard, usually with a lightness that reflected her gratitude for having a job, money, food, and shelter. But

47

winters are hard with the stone castle fighting against the fires she lights to try to hold back the cold.

A soft whimper slides from her lips as her knees give out, and she crumbles to the floor, clutching her head. My own head is aching, so I pull out of her mind, and she falls forward, pressing her hands to the floor, heaving deep gulps of air.

I relax back into my chair. "Finish your duties for the evening. You're dismissed."

She lifts her head, her hair framing her face, lips trembling. "I still have my job?"

I nod, waving my dismissal. "Yes." I consider her for a moment. I don't want her random thoughts of exhaustion to turn into actual desires. If I'm not around to catch her thoughts ... "I will have someone else assigned to the west wing fires during the winter. Once spring arrives, you will return to tending the entire castle."

She struggles to get a foot under her, kneeling a second before pushing herself up to standing. Keeping her head bowed, she whispers. "Thank you, your Majesty."

"Go."

She turns on shaky legs and quickly leaves the room.

Luc flops down on a large cushion on the floor at the low table as the door clicks shut. Lifting the lid off the tray, he sets it on the floor. "That was rather nice."

I roll my eyes. "She's a hard worker and wouldn't have acted on her thoughts ... yet."

"Worried about all your pretty things going up in smoke?"

"Well, yeah."

Luc laughs as he pours water from a pitcher into a glass.

I smile, blade still playing in my hand. "The grunts give you trouble?"

He takes a big gulp of water before tearing off a huge hunk of bread with his teeth. He mumbles around his mouth-full of food. "Nah. They just had to be reminded they are at the bottom of the rung, and that they haven't earned shit yet."

I laugh, pushing back from my desk, absently sheathing my blade before joining him on my own cushion across the table. "It's always the same."

"And it's always fun breaking them."

We clink glasses in salute as we say in tandem, "Se'aiy e'auhse'as se'auh, as se'aiy suhe'a." *They either break or they die.*

Luc grins as he stabs a slice of roast duck with his fork. "At least this group seemed to catch on faster than the last. Only one died today. Though I suspect we will lose more tomorrow on their first night in the mountains and even more throughout the week."

I nod, chewing a bite of roasted potato; fat, rosemary, and salt coating my tongue.

The mountain trial is a tradition of my reign. Luc and I picked this time of year for the volatile weather in the mountains. Here, at the base of the northern peaks, the weather is still warm during the day, the last of summer holding on. But in the mountains, the snow has already started to dust the ridges, and temperatures are known to plummet with no warning. The winds are brutal, and the animals that make their homes in the craggy mountainside are vicious hunters, looking for much needed food to help them through the coming winter. So, surviving the mountain is a task all in itself, but we also have a few of the Sagas soldiers stalk the grunts, driving up their anxiety. Sometimes the Sagas engage, sometimes they don't. It's all part of the game. Fights between the grunts, sometimes to the death, are not uncommon as they scramble to make it to Dagger's Peak. It's not the highest peak of the Imoria mountains, not by a long shot, but it's still treacherous. If they do reach the summit, a patch awaits them.

There are equal numbers of patches for three of the units; The Annarr, The Prioi, and The Sioastr. But there is only one patch for the Sagas unit, so getting to the peak early has its advantages.

Those that make it back will advance from the grunt unit into the unit whose patch they recovered. One will advance to the Sagas unit. Right now, there are only twenty-three soldiers who wear the Sagas symbol on their leather armor—a crown with a crack down the middle, symbolizing my nickname when I strung up King Ammeryn's headless body to the front gates of this castle and tossed the pieces of his crown at his feet.

49

The people called me the Crown Breaker. Some still do.

Luc sets down his fork and knife, crossing his legs as he picks up his glass of whiskey. "So, tomorrow."

I mirror his posture, smiling. "I was thinking we could head straight west and travel down the coastal trail."

"That's pretty open territory. Maybe we should go south through the forests. It'll add a half-day, maybe a full day depending on weather, but it'll be safer."

I consider his words but shake my head. "The coast might be more open, but this time of year, the trails will be fairly empty, and it'll get us to the border faster."

Luc nods. "The first group left for the desert an hour ago."

"Any trouble with"—I waggle my fingers in the air—"superstitions?"

He chuckles. "No. In fact, there was actually a small fight about who would get to go. There were challenges flying across the barracks and coin changing hands on who would be able to handle the high desert trip."

I grin, running my hands through my hair. Nobody lives in the high desert. Not anymore. And there's little to be found of water or game, so it's a true survivalist's journey.

My territory technically ends at the mountain range that spills from the north, down the center of the country. The three kingdoms of Lieren, Adren, and Trislen border the western half of Imoria. Beyond the mountains to the east lies the Varyen desert, once ruled by Queen Alea, the possessor of the Heart Stone, centuries ago. But both her kingdom and the Stone vanished over five hundred years ago. No one knows what happened. Whether it was invaders from across the sea, famine, a desert storm, or magic gone awry ... her kingdom was wiped out. There were rumors of where the Heart Stone ended up, but until recently, no one had found it or any trace of Alea's once fairly substantial kingdom.

And so, the Varyen desert is considered cursed and remains desolate.

I take another sip of whiskey. "And the group heading to Trislen?"

"Packed and ready, excited to see how Queen Ravaxina will react to their presence if or when she finds out."

I toss back the last of my whiskey. "How many are coming with us?"

"I've selected five. Two Sagas and three from The Annarr unit."

I bend my leg, resting my forearm on my knee. "Good. Large enough for decent protection, but small enough to pass detection if needed. Who are you leaving in charge?"

Luc nods before getting up and crossing the room to refill his glass at my liquor cabinet. "Casin or Carelle."

When I stare blankly at him, he smirks. "Really, Ry. Would it kill you to learn their names?" I just shrug with a small smile, so he continues, "Carelle is the Sagas with the two severed fingers."

He rejoins me at the table, flopping down on his cushion.

"Ah. Either is a fine choice, but I like Casin."

"That's because he nearly beat you today."

I raise an eyebrow. "He didn't."

Luc huffs a laugh, shaking his head. We continue to chat, talking about matters of the kingdom, then trading stories from our childhood.

Eventually, my eyelids grow heavy and Luc stands, saluting me with his glass. "Here's to finding what you want tomorrow."

I smile. "To finding what *we* want."

He returns my smile before leaving my room, closing the door quietly behind him.

My eyes unfocus on the flames in the fireplace, and I don't realize I've slipped into sleep until the dream begins, and I find myself seven years old and covered in blood.

6

Frost crunches under my boots as I make my way toward the stables, rolling my shoulders. Morning came too soon. I awoke from the dreams feeling like I had run with a pack full of rocks on my back all night. Every time I slip into the dream, I pray that some new memory will unlock, filling in the reality of what Luc told me I did, but clarity never comes.

The smell of horses and hay fills my nose, but running steps halt my progress. I tilt my head back with a sigh, my leather harness stretching across my chest.

"Your Majesty."

I turn, watching the male soldier jogging in my direction. He stops before me, and I see the patch of the Prioi unit on the right shoulder of his uniform. As he pants, catching his breath, I notice his leathers are too tight, and I cross my arms, impatience building. He continues to huff great breaths until I can't take it anymore.

"Why would a quick jog from the castle send you so out of breath, soldier?"

His eyes go wide, and the Stone warms with his fear-filled thoughts. He snaps his mouth closed, his breaths somehow coming out even louder through his nose.

"I ... Well ... your Majesty ... I ...The stairs from the dungeons, and ..."

I grit my teeth and simply reach into his mind. It takes a second to push past his terror to find the reason he came for me.

Sweat beads on his face as I sift through his thoughts, and when I release him, he slumps. With another sigh, I rub my hand over my face.

"Go to the stables and tell Captain Lucaryn that I'm going to be late."

"Yes, your Majesty." He tries to stand taller, but his chest is still heaving.

"Then tell the Captain that you are going on the mountain run today."

His eyes go wide. "But, your Majesty, I ran the trial four years ago."

I narrow my eyes, sliding my hand into my pocket. "You either run it today"—I flick my dagger into my other hand—"or I demote you to the grunt unit, and your new job will be to clean up after the soldiers you've let down. I have no use for a soldier who can't run a few stairs. I should kill you right here." He steps back, eyeing my dagger. "You have allowed yourself to become a weak link."

Finally straightening his spine, he snaps to attention. "It will be an honor to run the trial again, your Majesty."

I walk past him without another glance, listening to the sound of his heavy footfalls taking him to the stables. I give him a thirty percent chance of surviving the trial. But there's no reason he should be so unfit.

Retracing my steps, I hasten back to the castle, but instead of heading up to my wing, I turn left. My boots thud on the stone floor as I unlock and push through a thick iron door. It takes a moment for my eyes to adjust to the sudden darkness, and my hand skims over the cool, slick walls as I descend the curving staircase.

By the time I hit the last step, my breath is fogging in little clouds from the cold. As I walk down the narrow strip of walkway bordered by iron bars, the only sounds that reach my ears are the soft breaths of the prisoners and the scurrying of rats.

Weak light filters through high-set barred windows, giving me just enough light to see into the cells, some occupied, some not. I wave with a grin as I pass the cell holding Silas. His gaze passes through me as drool slides down his chin.

The soft orange flicker of a torch up ahead illuminates the dark, damp stones, and the guard stands, saluting with a fist over his heart.

"Your Majesty. I know you were scheduled to leave this morning, but I figured you'd want to know."

I pivot on my heel, facing the cell on my right. "Yes. When did he start showing symptoms?"

"Last night. His pinky started twitching, and then this morning his breathing picked up."

I tilt my head, watching the man, a servant from my kitchens, sitting in the center of his cell. His eyes are unfocused, and his body is utterly still other than the occasional twitch in his fingers.

He's pulling out of the mind loop I trapped him in.

Two weeks ago, when my soldiers brought the servant before me, he could barely stand, arm wrapped around an already bruising waist, jaw swollen, and nose bleeding. The soldier had caught him in the birdhouse with a note in his hand, and the bird master, Jurel, dead at his feet. He had been trying to send out a messenger bird to an uncle of his. The message revealed the two planned to follow Lucaryn and his party when they went on the hunt for the Heart Stone, and if they found it, the servant and his uncle planned to ambush Luc and take the Stone.

My soldiers beat the servant to near unconsciousness before dragging him before me. Everyone in my kingdom knows betrayal is the fastest way to find yourself in an existence of sheer agony ... or an early grave, if you're lucky.

But I prefer to make examples of those who cross me. So, I had the uncle hunted down, and he was quickly and publicly executed in the town square of his village. And the servant? I looped him, not in a memory, but in a fear. For the past two weeks, he's been falling over and over through a crack in a frozen-over lake, trapped in the freezing water while struggling to find a break in the ice to take the tiniest of breaths.

The prisoner's finger twitches again, and I take in his thin form.

Broth is poured down all the prisoners' throats once a day, but some are so deep within the magic, the liquid simply dribbles from their mouths. Starvation can overpower the magic, but not always. Sometimes my prisoners die within their minds. But it seems overwhelming hunger is pulling this man out of his nightmare.

The Stone warms in my back, and I welcome the sensation in the cold of the dungeons as I release him from the loop. His eyes blink faster, and his body shakes as he tries to focus. A sob bubbles from his lips, and he gasps with great inhales of air while wrapping his arms around his stomach.

I shift my weight to my right leg, sliding my right hand into my pocket while my left hand plays with my dagger.

The prisoner startles when I speak. "You made it two whole weeks."

His voice cracks from disuse. "Please. Kill me. Don't send me back."

The guard to my left chuckles, and I turn my head, grinning at him. "Why do they think they can get away with such things?"

His big shoulders lift in a shrug. "No idea, your Majesty."

"Am I not clear when I allow you to join my service?"

"Extremely."

"And yet ..." I wave a hand at the prisoner.

My gaze returns to the shriveled prisoner before I look down the long hall of cells. I think a reminder of my power and the consequences of crossing me is in order. Baring my teeth in a cruel smile, I turn back to the guard.

"Tomorrow, bring down a few of the Sagas. Shackle every prisoner, then bring them to The North Wind."

The guard tilts his head. "The tavern in the center of town, your Majesty?"

"Yes. And make sure it's during the lunch rush. Let each prisoner eat their fill. Let everyone witness their desperation, their fear, their broken spirits. Make sure the people witness and are reminded of what happens when you betray me. Bring the prisoners back down here once the lunch hour is over."

The guard nods, a slight frown on his face. "Some of 'em might try to escape or take their own lives to avoid coming back down here. A fork, or knife, or even a broken plate can sever an artery."

I look back at the prisoner to my right. His panicked eyes bounce between the guard and me. I shrug. "Keep them alive if you can, but don't go out of your way. Once back in their cells, they may receive normal rations until I return."

The guard snaps his fist over his heart. "Yes, your Majesty."

Making my way back down the line of cells, the prisoner's sobs follow me, and when I reach the staircase, I release the magic from all the prisoners' minds with a smile.

Groans, screams, sobs, curses, and begging follow me up the stairs, and I slow my pace to enjoy their suffering. A shiver spills down my spine, and I grow hard as the screams bounce off the stone walls. This is power, and with the power comes pain, but also pleasure—the pleasure of knowing I'm in control, that I am untouchable. I shiver again.

I push back through the iron door and into the light of the main floor of the castle. Pausing, I adjust myself, glancing out a window, noticing the morning light brightening toward midday. I adjust myself again, and Luc's teasing words come back to me. Maybe I *was* trying to scratch the wrong itch. With a smile, I head to the kitchens. Luc is going to be in a huff, but I'm going to be a bit later.

The smell of fresh bread hits me on a blast of warm air as I pass through the archway leading into the kitchens. It's controlled chaos, and the clatter of pans, the snick of knives, and the clink of utensils rings through the air. I snag a small tart off a tray as I round a table, the flavors of butter, sugar, and apple dancing on my tongue. A few servants look my way before nodding and going back to work, but one pauses.

Asha's brown eyes meet mine. A band holds back her flour-dusted brown hair. The heat of the kitchens adds a pretty flush to her brown skin, so similar in tone to Luc's. Her gaze travels down my body, stalling at my groin, pulling a smile to her lips as she meets my gaze.

I raise an eyebrow in question, and she turns, her hips swaying with the movement. I grab another tart with a grin, stuffing it in my mouth as I follow her.

Asha grew up in these kitchens, learning from her mother, who learned from her father. We have fucked a few times over the years since I took the throne. The first time was at my celebration dinner a few days after I killed King Ammeryn. I had not yet had Luc put the Stone in my back, and Ammeryn's gaudy necklace was sitting on the table before me, the green stone shining like a beautiful curse. My head throbbed with the chaos of thoughts pressing against my mind, mixing with the sounds of revelry bouncing around the dining hall.

I wanted to retreat to my rooms, to try and find some quiet, some relief, but my army deserved that celebration, and I resolved to stay as long as I could. I pasted a smile on my face, but Luc kept glancing at me with a worried frown, knowing I was close to my limit.

That's when Asha's arm brushed against mine as she leaned over to place a plate of food in front of me. Her lust-filled thoughts flared through my mind—simple, aroused thoughts of a woman who found her new King attractive. Her thoughts were so clear they overshadowed all the other mental noise, and I almost came right there in my chair at the images spilling from her mind into mine. I pulled her down into my lap and kissed her neck, eager for the distraction from the pain.

I can still recall how she tasted that night—sweat and spice.

The party was already well past rowdy at that point. Several playful fights had busted a few chairs, and more than a few people were enjoying the pleasures of the flesh in darkened corners or right out in the open.

My hand slid up her torso, cupping her breast over her dress, and she arched into me. I bit her ear before whispering, "Your thoughts are delicious."

She moaned as I continued to knead her breast while my other hand gathered her skirts, bunching them around her waist. Her voice came out on a husky breath. "Indeed?" Images of my cock in her mouth, in her ass, in her pussy flooded my mind. She imagined riding my face to orgasm and being tied up and subjected to my dominance.

I groaned when I slid a finger into her pussy, and she gasped, grinding her ample ass against my cock. My lips trailed her ear. "Dirty girl. All in good time. For now, I'm going to take you right here."

Her desire screamed through my mind as she whispered, "Yes."

I inserted a second finger, curling them with a single pump before withdrawing. Unfastening my pants, I shifted her, lining her up before thrusting into her heat.

Her moan caught Luc's attention from farther down the table, and he saluted me with his glass. I grinned back before snaking my arm around her curvy waist, reaching back under her skirts to flick her clit. Her breath quickened to little pants of pleasure as I rocked my hips into her.

I followed the trail of her thoughts, rubbing her clit in circles, and when her climax was right at the edge, I yanked her bodice down, pinching her nipple and her clit ... hard, just as she wanted. She came with a whimper, biting her lip to keep from screaming in front of everyone. Her pussy clamped around my cock, sending me over the edge as well.

That had been the quietest moment I had experienced with the Stone since claiming it. I pulled out of her and straightened her dress, but when she moved to get up, I held her tight, keeping her in my lap, letting her simple, honest thoughts drown out the rest of the mental noise. Her mind was calm, easy, bright, and happy. No ulterior motives, no scheming—what you see is what you get with Asha. She was a godsend in that moment, and her uncomplicated presence allowed me to enjoy the rest of the evening.

Now, in the warmth of the kitchens, I've already unfastened my pants as I push through a pantry door, enclosing us in the cramped, dark room lit only by the weak light of a small window high in the wall. Asha slides the sleeves of her servant's dress over her shoulders and pulls her bodice down, freeing her large breasts.

With a smile, she reaches for me, tugging my pants down my thighs. "What's got you all worked up, my King?"

Her words flutter her breath over my stomach as she kneels before me, grasping my cock before sliding her tongue over the tip.

I groan, running my fingers along her scalp before fisting her hair. "I had some business in the dungeons."

Her eyes rise to meet mine. "You *do* love the power." I shove her face down my cock until her nose hits my stomach. Drawing her back, her lips pop from my shaft, and she smiles. "And I like that you know what you want, and you take it."

Her lips curl around the head of my cock before her teeth draw down my length. I hiss at the combined pain and pleasure. I grip her shoulders, hauling her up and slam her against a wall. Jars rattle with the impact, and I wrap a hand around her throat. My other hand cups her breast before I bow, sucking one brown nipple into my mouth before moving to the other. She grinds against me, but I hold her firmly against the wall.

"Take me, your Majesty."

"Oh, I will, sweet Asha."

She gathers her skirts, and I grip her undergarment, shoving it down her legs, and she steps free. Her mind is a flurry of pleasure and desire. The second I see the image in her head, I slam my cock into her wet pussy as I scrape my nails over her nipple. She tries to hold back her scream, biting her lip.

With a grin, I whisper against her lips, "Can you keep quiet, my sweet?"

Her body jerks under my hold with every thrust, and she shakes her head with a moan. "Make me."

My grin widens, and I press my palm to her mouth as I slam even harder into her. My hand muffles her screams, and I hitch her leg higher over my hip, adjusting the angle to go deeper. I grab her ass, loving how much there is to hold on to. My grip is so hard, I know there will be bruises, but I don't care. And neither does she.

My hand continues to press firmly against her lips, her moans and screams trying to push past my fingers. Her arm thrashes out, slamming her palm against the shelves to my left, sending sacks and jars tumbling to the floor. Her other hand grips the leather straps of my chest harness, heedless of the sharp knives strapped there.

Agonizing pleasure builds in my lower back, wrapping around to my cock, ready to send me into an orgasm. My hips pump into her tight pussy, the slap of skin meeting skin keeping time with the thunk of her body being thrust into the wood wall at her back.

I wait for her thoughts to shatter with her own pleasure, and right as her orgasm crests, she fists my hair so hard, pain erupts across my scalp, and that sends me over the edge. I spill into her, pleasure driving my hips between her spread thighs until we both sag with release.

I shift back so she can set her feet on the floor, straightening her skirts as I pull up and fasten my pants. Before she pulls her sleeves back up, I run my thumb over one nipple, the peak still pebbled.

"The tarts were good."

She smiles, pulling her dress up to cover herself. "Apple *is* your favorite. Take a few to go." She undoes her hair tie, pulling the stands back in a tidy tail before tying them up again. Bending over, she begins to clean up the fallen items, setting each back in its place on the shelves. "Have a good journey, your Majesty."

This is what I like about Asha. No complications.

I run a hand over her skirt, palming her ass before giving her a little smack. "I'll miss your cooking."

She snorts, glancing over her shoulder. "You could stand to miss a bit of my cooking."

I laugh. "Are you implying I'm getting soft?"

Her eyes flit to my groin, then travel up my body with a sigh. "No, despite my best efforts, you keep that royal body fit for battle."

"Well, you keep trying. If anyone can make me soft and fat, it'd be you."

She snorts again, turning back to her task, and I push out of the pantry. No one looks up as I pass back through the kitchens, but a few thoughts flicker through my mind.

'*That last batch of bread didn't rise as it should have. I'll have to check our stores of yeast.*' ... '*When will that wretched boy be back from the orchard? I need those apples.*' ... '*How can Asha just let the King use her like that? If he were fucking me ... and I wish he would ... I'd ask for jewels or gold or something. At the very least, I'd get myself out of these sweltering kitchens.*' I smirk at that thought. That's why I've never fucked her, despite her pretty face. I use, I am not used.

The thoughts continue to float through my mind. '*The meat from the last hunt is almost gone. I'll salt the rest and tell the game master to arrange another hunt or two before the snows move in.*' ... '*I wonder if Lila will let me come to her bed again tonight?' ... 'I can't wait for the winter solstice party.'*

I leave the thoughts and the kitchens behind, striding through the castle, and once I'm outside, I pick up into a jog toward the stables.

Luc is standing at the edge of one of the horse pens talking with a Sagas; Kahar packed and tied next to him. When Luc sees me, he turns, and the Sagas walks off, retrieving his own horse. Luc crosses his arms, his broad chest straining with the movement. I take him in, and for a fleeting moment I wish it had been him I had just fucked. I shake the thought away as I draw up to him, and he frowns.

"We're behind schedule."

I grin. "I'm the King, so we're right on time."

Luc smiles just as I feel a tug from behind. Another tug brings the sound of seams ripping, and I crane my neck to see Luc's horse, Kahar clenching my cloak between his teeth. With every toss of his head, I'm jerked back and forward. I tug my shoulder, trying to free myself. "Luc, get your horse off me."

He just chuckles, and I feel another seam strain, on the verge of ripping, so I shake out of my cloak, stepping away from the big black beast.

Kahar looks pleased with himself as he tosses his head, my cloak flying through the air like a flag. I wave a frustrated hand at the horse, glaring at Luc who just laughs again before walking over to the giant steed. He shoves his thumb in the space at the back of his mouth, pressing down. "Come on, Kahar. Give Ry back his cloak."

Kahar tries to toss his head again, but Luc holds his muzzle, keeping pressure in his mouth until my cloak slips from between his teeth. Luc strokes his hand over the horse's face before bending down, picking up my slobbery cloak, and handing it back to me.

"There you go."

I snatch it from his hands, trying to swallow the smile that wants to escape. "That horse is a menace."

Luc just shakes his head, smiling as he swings onto his horse. Kahar pins his ears back and stomps in anger as Luc settles into the saddle.

A stable hand brings out a blue roan mare, packed and saddled with my tack. Gripping a fistful of her mane, I swing up and into the saddle, gathering the reins and nudging the mare forward. She's one of my favorites in my stable. I named her Yara, after my sister, Yareen —though this horse is too sweet-natured to carry my sister's name. It's more of a reminder than an homage.

I give Yara a quick pat on her neck. "Se'ausiy sa sre'asz iyais se'afr?" *Ready to stretch your legs?*

The royal horses are all trained in the old language—a language no longer used. A language spoken when magic was commonplace, so much so that excess magic was fed into objects, like the Mind Stone. Luc and I taught ourselves the language from ancient scrolls and texts, putting together our own codex of the language as we learned it. With the old language no longer spoken, we are the only ones who can command our horses. The horse master has a copy of the codex, and the soldiers are taught basic commands ... Surs *Stand,* E'auriy *Easy,* Se'ausiy *Steady,* Fa *Go,* Iye'ar *Yes,* Uss *halt,* and a few others.

Luc and I are fluent in the old tongue, basically able to converse in code if needed.

Luc pulls up beside me as we move into a controlled canter, Kahar snapping his teeth at Yara before Luc pulls him back. I glare at him, but he shrugs. "He'll calm down in a bit."

I roll my eyes.

Four of the five soldiers Luc picked for this journey trail behind us and the fifth rides ahead as scout. The sun is already fairly high in the sky, and I'm grateful for its weak warmth as we head to the coast. The temperature is going to drop quickly as we ride toward the arctic winds coming off the sea.

We fall into an easy rhythm as we quickly leave the capital city of Farden behind, and the mountains grow shorter as we head west and south.

I t's a week's-ride to our border with Adren, and we've made good time the past two days, but the days are shorter this time of year. The nights are quickly becoming brutally cold—nothing us northerners can't handle—and traveling at night can be dangerous along the coast with hidden crags that drop far to the sea below. Glancing at the dark sky with only a hint of color remaining on the horizon, I think we should arrive at a spot suitable enough for camping within the hour.

We end up single file on a narrow path that leads through large rock outcroppings, and I'm grateful for the cover from the brutal winds, especially with night cloaked around us, the soft glow of the crescent of the child moon giving us only a sliver of light.

The scout is too far ahead to see. Luc is in front, and I'm trailing him with the rest on my flank.

Just before we round a bend, whispered thoughts not within our group touch my mind.

I whistle, mimicking a gray thrasher bird. Luc pulls back his reins, and Kahar tosses his head with annoyance. Luc twists, looking at me, and I touch my finger to my temple, then point to our right.

We're being followed.

7

Our group quickly dismounts, and Kahar stomps with impatience but stands firm with the other horses, all trained to hold their ground, even without being tethered. Yara stands calm like the angel she is.

Luc holds up one finger, pointing at a soldier behind me, then to himself. He then holds up three fingers and points at me. A soldier slides past me, following Luc as they track back and around a small bend in the rocks to circle our prey.

The other three soldiers shift so two stand before me, and one covers my flank. My steps are soft and deliberate as I move forward, right toward my enemies, the soldiers keeping pace silently.

The Stone is hot in my back as I isolate the thoughts of those who have followed us. I pick out twelve voices, and I tilt my head as I pause behind a particularly large outcropping before I climb the large boulder on my right, the three soldiers moving to follow me.

The group stalking us is from the kingdom of Trislen. Queen Rava sent them to trail me if I were ever to leave the capital. Their minds sharpen with fear and excitement as the leader pauses their advance with a raised hand. His whispered words carry on the wind. "They've stopped. He may have caught our thoughts. Remember your training."

I smirk as images of rippling water, blank paper, black fabric, a blanket of snow, and a clear blue sky flicker through my mind. They're trying to shield their thoughts.

I almost laugh out loud.

Luc pushes his thoughts at me to let me know he's in position. I grin, glancing down and purposely kick a small rock at my feet. The clack of stone tumbling over stone reverberates through the silence, and the Trislenian soldier's minds erupt with fear.

Too easy.

I walk down the slope of the boulder, landing on the ground as I move to bring myself into their view, my soldiers on my flank. Luc and the soldier with him round the bend, coming up behind the group with swords raised.

Just as I'm about to say a hearty hello, I catch a thought, *'Take him out.'* Panic spikes my heart rate until it feels like my chest is going to break open. My soldiers raise their swords at my sudden stiff posture and are already advancing on the Trislenians, but I grab at the mind of the female Trislenian soldier at the back of the pack, ready to drop her.

I'm too slow. The woman has already launched her arrow. I watch in horror as it soars, not toward me, but straight at Luc. I yell in his mind, the mental communication nearly driving me to my knees, but he hears me and lunges to the side. The arrow sinks into his shoulder instead of his heart, and I sigh before a pleased thought from the archer caresses my mind. *'It's done. The poison will finish him.'*

I slam into Luc's mind, finding it already dimming at the edges as he struggles to stay focused. Fury is too mild a word for what I feel. My vision bleeds white as the soldier at Luc's side charges the Trislenians, quickly cutting down the archer before clashing swords with a man on his left. Blood soaks the archers' clothes, but it's not enough. I want to rip her head from her shoulders. I want to tear her rib cage apart and yank her heart from her chest. I want to feed that heart to Queen Ravaxina until she's choking on the blood of the one she sent to kill my captain.

I jerk my head, and the three soldiers at my side sprint into the fray as I run to Luc's side.

He drops to a knee, sweat already coating his skin, and his eyes are too bright as they meet mine. My hands shake as I grab the shaft of the arrow and brace my palm on his chest.

"One, two," I yank it from his flesh, and he grunts through clenched teeth.

"I can't believe,"—his hand comes to my shoulder to steady himself—"I didn't see ... that coming. Thanks ... for the ... warning."

"Fuck, Luc, we need to get you to a healer."

He doesn't respond as he falls to the side, landing on his hip, curling his leg under him to keep himself in a sitting position. His sword thuds to the ground as his fingers go numb.

Blades clashing, flesh tearing, and cries of pain reach my ears. I don't have time for this.

I stand, spinning, noting one of my soldiers is dead, but the other three are desperately holding their own. There's no sign of our scout.

A glance at Luc, flushed with fever from the poison, sends another flash of white rage across my vision. I brace my feet and shove my magic into the minds of the remaining eight Trislenian soldiers. A scream rips from my throat as my muscles immediately start shaking, and pain explodes in my head, shooting down my spine.

I tear their minds apart, pressing the magic against their skulls. Every single one falls to the ground, some kneeling, but most falling flat, grabbing their heads.

Clear brain fluid seeps out of their ears and noses as their screams join mine, tearing through the night. I draw my dagger as I approach the first few soldiers, slicing it across the throat of one, then stabbing it into the heart of the next. I slam my blade into the back of the neck of the third before stepping over her to sink my blood coated dagger into the soft spot under the jaw of the fourth. Another two throats open on my blade before I'm standing over the final two.

Over my shoulder, I say, "One of you, go find our scout."

A man peels away from the group, running back to our horses. The sound of pounding hooves fades away in the darkness.

I kneel in the dirt, blood coating the knees of my pants as I stare into the pain-filled eyes of a moaning Trislenian soldier. "What was the poison?"

He shakes his head, lips pressed so tight they turn white, but the word '*Cathis*' flashes through his mind.

Shit, Luc doesn't have much time.

Flicking my eyes to my soldiers, I command, "You two, take these two back to the capital. Throw them in the dungeons. I'll deal with them when I return." As my soldiers bend down, binding then lifting the near-catatonic Trislenian men over their shoulders, I face the last soldier of my group. "Help me get the captain to the horses. He needs a healer. Now."

He nods as we run through the bodies scattered around us to Luc's side. He's still upright, but his breaths are shallow, and the front of his shirt is stuck to his body from sweat. The soldier at my side hoists Luc over his shoulder, and I pat my friend's back before we race to the horses.

I swing onto Yara before reaching down to haul Luc off the soldier's shoulder into the saddle in front of me. I wrap an arm around Luc's waist, shocked at the heat coming off his skin, even through his clothes.

Kahar makes no protest as the soldier grabs his reins. Mounting his own horse, the soldier leads Kahar into a canter, and I kick Yara to follow. We push through the rock outcroppings into open land, racing through the night with as much speed as Luc can handle.

His head lolls against my shoulder, and I grip him tighter. There's a war happening in my body. The thought of losing Luc has my stomach roiling to the point I might vomit. But my anger at this attack has my blood boiling. It's taking everything I have to keep from handing Luc off and storming into Trislen.

As we ride, my mind stays with Luc, monitoring his thoughts. Panic and fear, the likes of which I haven't known since childhood, grip my chest as Luc's thoughts become quieter and more scattered.

I whisper in his mind, ignoring the stabbing pain in my head from using so much power. The shaking in my muscles threatens to loosen my grip on both the reins and Luc's waist. My eyes burn with the threat of tears, and my throat constricts as I try to swallow the bile that's churning in my gut.

Mind to mind communication is the hardest power for me to wield, but I will endure, for Luc. *'Please hold on Luc. Stay with me. All this means nothing without you. Ze'aure'a.'* Please.

His hand lightly clutches mine, his words quiet in my mind. *'Uh'n siyuhr. Uh'n rassiy. Uh'n siyuhr.'* I'm sorry. I'm trying. I'm sorry.

I feel myself shattering. I chant in his mind, *hold on, hold on, hold on*. Finally, we approach a small village that skirts the western territory of Lieren a day's ride north of the border we share with Adren.

I don't care that it's now the dead of night. I yell into the darkness down the quiet streets. "Healer! I need a healer!"

Orange light flickers behind a few covered windows as I pull Yara to a stop. The soldier dismounts, sword drawn just in case.

I call out again. "Healer!"

A few people poke their heads out of their homes, their thoughts annoyed at the late-night disturbance in their village. A small, hunched man with gray hair haloing his bald head shuffles from a small house. "Bring him here." His eyes are on Luc, but as his gaze flicks to me, his eyes widen, and he bows. "Your Majesty."

The soldier takes Luc from me, draping him over his shoulder, and ducks through the doorway. I press a hand to my chest, my shirt damp from Luc's fevered skin. I can't breathe around my fear, but I force myself to jump off Yara to follow the soldier into the house, the old man on my heels, his voice commanding as he points across the room. "Place him on that table."

The soldier flops Luc onto the wood table. A tin plate clatters, and a porcelain cup shatters when they topple to the floor. The healer doesn't react to the destruction of his wares as he moves to the back of the kitchen, retrieving a satchel.

"Cathis." I bark the word, and the old man's eyes widen again before he nods his head.

"How long ago?"

I run my hands through my hair, the shoulder-length strands falling around my face as they escape the tie. "An hour, maybe a little more."

The healer moves around the room, gathering jars and cloth, water and powders. As he mixes a tonic, I place a hand on Luc's forehead. It's hot, but at my touch, his eyes flutter open. His pupils are mere pinpricks, making the vibrant blue even more startling.

I lean down, pressing my forehead to his. "I'll kill her for this."

He chuckles, but it comes out on a weak cough. "You can't, Ry."

"Watch me."

Luc opens his mouth to respond, but the healer grips his chin, tilting his face up, forcing me to step back. He pours a white liquid down Luc's throat before he cuts Luc's shirt, stripping it back and starts poking at the bleeding arrow wound, veins turning black around the edges. Luc coughs, then groans, and my fingers tighten on his forearm. With a murmur, the healer turns. The clinking of bottles and the sloshing of liquid resume as he mixes up something else.

I turn to the soldier. "Your name."

"Runic, your Majesty."

"Keep watch."

He nods and steps outside, closing the door behind him.

As the healer pours something over the arrow wound, Luc's head falls to the side. Pained eyes find mine as agonized grunts pass his lips. "What about ..." He mumbles something, and I lean in closer. " ... about Erathan?"

I know what he's really asking, and I don't care about the Heart Stone right now. I force my hands to unclench and shake my head. "It can wait."

He's about to protest, but I shake my head again. "Luc. It can wait."

The healer pokes the arrow hole, sinking his finger into Luc's flesh. Luc screams, and I shoot the healer a look that promises death, but he doesn't look up as he speaks. "I need to feel if the poison has started eating the muscle." His thoughts are determined and focused on saving Luc, so I calm the need to kill and leave him to his ministrations.

The hours pass slowly as the healer monitors Luc, wiping sweat from his skin, turning Luc's head every time he vomits, then pours more tonics down his throat. The healer occasionally checks Luc's pupils, and presses his fingers to Luc's neck to feel his pulse ...

I incessantly pace the small space, five steps across and back. My dagger dances in my hand, but it's not calming me in the least. I pause my pacing to brace my hands on the back of a chair, eyes combing over Luc looking for any sign that he's improving, but he still looks pale and sweaty.

Luc grunts and heaves again. I rush to his side, grabbing him by the shoulder and rolling him so he's on his side. Vomit splatters on the wood floor at my feet, and my stomach drops at the sight of blood. Luc flops back and ... stops breathing.

"Luc!" My voice roars through the small house, probably waking everyone in this small town.

The healer lunges forward, pressing a surprisingly firm hand to my chest. "Stay back. Give me room." He stacks his palms on Luc's chest and begins punching his hands downward. My own chest aches with every compression, and at one point, I swear I hear a rib crack. I must have made a sound, because without stopping, the healer says, "A broken rib is a small price to pay if I can bring him back."

Fuck! I can't take this. Luc's lips are turning blue, and his body jerks lifelessly with every press of the old man's hands. A tear escapes, gliding down my cheek just as the healer swears, fisting his hands. He raises them over his head and slams them down on Luc's chest with a hollow thud.

The room is silent. I'm pretty sure my heart might stop right here. How can it keep beating if Luc is gone?

A loud intake of breath collapses my knees, and I hit the floor as Luc coughs. His voice is weak as he tries to lift his arm but fails. "Has Kahar kicked me in the chest again?"

I laugh through my tears as I shakily get to my feet. The healer mops Luc's head, then his own with a nod. "No, that was me. Don't make me do it again."

Luc closes his eyes, but there's a faint smile on his lips, and I just want to kiss him.

The healer slides his hands over Luc, once again checking his eyes, tongue, pulse, and stomach before setting a glass of water next to me. "I think I've countered all the poison. He will sleep for a few hours, and it would be best if you or someone you trust continues to monitor him. I'm going to rest. Wake me if anything changes. Drink the water, your Majesty."

I nod, keeping my eyes on my friend, and the old man turns, quiet footsteps taking him to a back room where I hear the groan of a mattress as he lays down.

I drag out a chair and drop into it, watching my friend's slow breaths. The glass is cool against my dry lips, and I gulp the water down. My whispered words float around the room with a promise. "She will die for this."

Another hour passes quietly, then another. The longer I sit at Luc's side, my fear melts back into a burning rage. *How dare she?* My knee bounces in agitation, and my dagger plays in my left hand. *Luc was almost taken from me.* My hand reaches out, gripping Luc's fingers, rubbing my thumb over his knuckles. *I can't ... I ... I.*

My eyes fall from Luc, landing on the edge of the table where my dagger has dug a hole in the wood. I sheath the blade, but my leg begins bouncing again. My fingers drag through my hair, gripping the ends and pulling ... hard.

Finally, my anger drives me out of my chair, toppling it to the floor with a muted thud. I stand there for a moment, breathing deep before bending down and righting the chair. I press my palm to the table, my thumb brushing Luc's sweaty hair. Staring at him, my knees tremble and my insides melt. The world slows down as I lean over. My lips are a breath away from his. I shift, pressing a kiss to his cheek, whispering, "I lo—" My eyes close on my stalled words before saying, "I'll return to you soon."

Turning, I stride across the wood floor. The first time I kiss Luc—really kiss him—he's going to be aware of it.

I throw open the door, step outside, and quietly close it behind me. Runic snaps his fist over his heart, and I glance at the door through which my friend sleeps.

"Continue to watch over him. When the healer says he's well enough to move, get him back to the capital as quickly as possible." I stare him down, ignoring the sweat beading on my face as I scan his thoughts. Runic is loyal, if a little scared of me, and he's concerned for his captain. His hands ball into fists the longer I stay in his mind, but when dots dance across my vision, I pull away, cracking my neck.

My eyes narrow, but I nod, sufficiently satisfied with what I see in Runic's mind. "Once the captain is home and in the healer's care, gather half our forces, half from each unit, and go to the Foothill Forest five miles north of the Trislenian border. Wait there for me." I push past him, skirting the side of the small house to where our horses are tethered.

"What will you do, your Majesty?"

My hands grip the leather of Kahar's girth, and I tug, tightening the saddle. The great war horse huffs with a stomp but doesn't try to kill me, yet. I glance over my shoulder with a wicked grin.

"I'm going to pay Queen Ravaxina a visit."

I lift myself onto Kahar's back. I prefer Yara, but Kahar is much faster and has better endurance, which will come in handy on the long journey to the southernmost kingdom of Imoria. It's a full day's ride to the Adren border and another four days, maybe five, to the capital of Trislen. I could make it there in four if I push.

"Alone, your Majesty?"

His thoughts are a tangle of contradiction. He wants to follow my order and watch over his captain, but he doesn't want to let his King go unprotected into enemy territory. I dig my heels into Kahar's sides, and he jumps forward, but I hold back the reins.

"Don't worry, soldier. I'll be fine. Your only task is to take care of your captain, then come south." I lean over, eyes narrowing again. "I'm trusting you."

His skin leeches of color before he recovers and salutes. "Yes, your Majesty."

I give Kahar his head, and he bolts, the thuds of his hooves thundering in time with the rage in my heart.

Once I'm a few miles outside the small village, I pull Kahar into a more controlled canter. I skirt east, hugging the foothills through Adren, planning to pass into Trislen at the border crossing nearest the capital. The villages of Adren are few this far east, and I should be able to travel quickly through King Erathan's territory. I'll deal with him and the Heart Stone later.

The difficult part will come when I cross into Trislen. The capital is vast and heavily populated, but I have an idea of how to get to Rava. Though, it will test the magic of the Stone and my fortitude.

I roll my head again, cracking my neck, trying to shake off the tension and pain from ... everything. My fingers are a bit numb, and the exhaustion from the magic threatens to make me drop the reins. But the image of Luc's pale face, blue lips, chest still and without breath, tightens my muscles. I grin, a shiver tickling down my spine as I picture Rava's face when she realizes she's finally pushed me too far.

Kahar senses my excitement and tosses his head, his black mane slapping me in the face. Leaning over his neck, I whisper to the snorting steed. "Sir sie'a, Kahar, irs sir se'ausiy." *Run true, Kahar, but run steady.* "We have a long way to go until we can unleash our rage."

8

I run out of packed provisions two days after I leave Lucaryn at that healer's house. I've been lucky and snared some rabbits and other small vermin along the way, eating them as I catch them since winter is moving in fast and carrying meat would attract wolves.

The mountains stick to my left as I travel the foothills for cover, and the nights become a little milder the farther south I get. I track back west as I get closer to Trislen, and now, as I approach the border, my blood almost hums with anticipation.

This old path, nothing more than a barely-there track in the grass and hard-packed ground, is seldom traveled, and I have yet to pass a soul today. I know all the ways through Imoria. I know how to travel quickly or unseen, or both or neither.

I leave the cover of the woods and now ride in fairly open country with the short stone border wall between Adren and Trislen undulating across the landscape on my left. It needs repair; the stone crumbling in places, and Kahar could easily leap the wall. It wouldn't be all that hard to climb it on foot either, but if someone were traveling by wagon or cart, they wouldn't be getting across the border unless they used a designated crossing station.

I make a mental note to send out a team of grunts to inspect our southern border with Adren. The letters of concern from my southern villages seem more valid right now. With recent events, I should shore up my border. I must protect my own.

Kahar walks steadily beneath me. I've given him plenty of rein over the past five days, and I think I've run some of the crazy out of him. With a grin, I pat his neck, his hair course but warm under my palm, his muscles firm. My lips slide into a frown as I think of Luc. He's been a constant worry in my mind, and I want nothing more than to reach out with my magic and hear a string of annoyed thoughts from his mind. But I'm too far—the magic only reaches a mile at most.

At least he's alive. Or he was when I left.

And he better be when I return.

Leather creaks as I grip the reins, my rage and worry pushing against my skin, making it hard to breathe. Kahar tosses his head, and I loosen my grip, arching my back. My spine pops, and I roll my shoulders.

I'm nearing a crossing station, which means Queen Rava's retribution is close at hand.

Absently, my fingers slide under the collar of my shirt, rubbing over the thin scar that slices across the top of my right chest near my collar bone. This scar is a reminder, a lesson. Several years after *that* night, Luc and I were living in an abandoned bookbinder building in Farden, the Leiren's capital city. I was nine at the time, and we had assembled a little team of orphans—kids desperate and alone. They were our network of thieves and spies, running the streets, giving Luc and me a cut of what they stole in exchange for a safe space to sleep in our building, consistent meals, and the protection of the group.

Sinclair, or Sin, was an older boy, maybe thirteen. I never asked. The other kids looked up to him, followed his lead, and he followed Luc and me. Until he didn't.

I found a stash of money in the small space of the bookbinder building that he had claimed for himself, and it was obvious he wasn't giving up his entire cut of what he was stealing. When I confronted him, he smirked, eyeing me up and down. His chuckle made a few of the other kids shift uncomfortably, but a few quietly laughed with him. In that moment, I felt Luc's and my hold on the group slipping, but Sin just shrugged, handing over the money owed.

I should have kicked him out. I should have killed him. But I was still young, still naive, still learning.

Not a week later, Luc, Sin, and I were walking down a dark street, headed to the tightly packed area of the city that held the rowdier taverns and pleasure houses. Easy pickings. But before we cleared the narrow street, Sin fell back a few paces, and when I turned, he held a sword to my throat.

I didn't give him a chance to explain, I just ducked to the side, the blade slicing across the top of my shoulder. When he swung at me again, I rolled, and the distraction allowed Luc to step in and land a heavy punch to Sin's face. I grabbed Sin's wrist, and with another quick spin, pulled his arm over my bleeding shoulder and yanked down with all my strength.

I wasn't a big nine-year-old, but I knew how to leverage my body weight.

Sin's arm snapped, and his scream echoed off the stone street. His sword fell to the ground with a metallic clatter, and Luc punched him again, hitting his temple. Sin crumpled to the street, and I glanced at Luc. He nodded, his lips pressed in a tight line, and I bent down to retrieve the fallen sword. With one smooth thrust, the blade slid between Sin's ribs and into his heart.

Now, as I crest a small rise, I pull my hand away from the small scar and smile. It was a lesson I needed to learn. Unless you have a use for them, never let your enemies live.

A small stone hut with a thatched roof comes into view where the trail I'm traveling intersects with a wider maintained road. My eyes follow the path of the larger road to the northwest, spotting a few travelers dotting the landscape either on horse, carriage, cart, or foot. The road is fairly free of traffic, despite it being the principal thoroughfare between Adren and Trislen.

I roll my shoulders, and the Stone warms under my skin. Reaching back, my fingers grip the soft fabric of my hood, pulling it low over my head.

Here we go. A small test before I get any closer to the Trislenian capital.

Kahar prances, his body tense, ready for action, and I grin. I get why Luc likes him. As I get closer to the hut, I brush against each mind. There's a short line, five deep, waiting to cross from Adren to Trislen, and I can't see if anyone is waiting on the other side of the hut to cross from the other direction. Four soldiers pass bored looks over the travelers, checking bags and wagons before collecting the coin required to cross the border.

A family stands at the end of the line, the two men's heads bowed in exhaustion, their dusty boots and clothes telling the tale of a long journey. One man—his shaved head gleaming with sweat even though the sun is setting, and the air is cooling slightly—holds the hand of a small girl who dances in place.

I press my lips in a tight line, thinking ... did my mother or father ever hold my hand? Not that I can remember.

The little girl's brown hair floats around her face as she watches her dress twirl around her knees. The man's thoughts are slow, tired, ready to get home. The children have been well behaved, but traveling with young ones is exhausting, even for the most patient of men. The girl is growing restless but is content to make little swirling designs in the dirt with the toes of her shoes as she twists side to side.

The other man, a bit taller than his partner, shifts to hoist another small girl farther up his hip. His thoughts are on the verge of anger. He's over traveling, he's over waiting in line, and he's over carrying his daughter, wondering how a two-year-old could be so heavy. Her fist is in her mouth, and drool coats her knuckles and drips down her chin.

I steer Kahar around the family. The men don't even bother to look up when the two girls lift their heads. I wipe myself from the dancing girl's mind, like painting over my image in a painting, and she keeps swaying. Amused, I wave at the toddler as she points her slobbery hand at me.

"Big horsie."

The man shifts, following her gesture, but I've wiped myself from his mind before he can even register I'm here. He tilts his head at his daughter, and with a shake of his head, heaves her to his other hip. I wave again before passing them, enjoying the confused looks the men give their cooing daughter.

Making my way along the line, I wipe Kahar and myself from everyone's minds, moving like a wraith from another dimension. Pinpricks of pain bloom behind my eyes as a soldier glances up, squinting his dark eyes, scanning the area. The Stone grows hot as I fight to keep myself hidden. After a tense moment, my muscles bunched tighter than Kahar's, the soldier shifts his attention to the next group in line, holding out a hand to halt them for inspection.

My back trembles with exertion, and my teeth grind against the pain that feels like an electric charge along my skull, but I grin with the power of passing unseen right into the kingdom of Trislen. I've never used the Stone like this, and despite the toll it's already taking on me, I can't help but feel excited to discover how far I can push the magic.

As I continue to travel south, it doesn't take long for the road to clear of travelers. I take the time to push down the magic of the Stone, releasing some of the tension in my head. I'm only an hour away from the capital, and I spend that time building my anger, cultivating my rage. Images of Luc's pale, sweating face flash through my mind. I'm haunted by the mental vision of his still, breathless body. My hands tremble at the memory, and I roll my head, cracking my neck. It doesn't help. My chest still feels too tight, and my stomach feels like it's a pit of writhing snakes. If Rava was aiming to push me into action by coming after Luc, she succeeded. Her fate is sealed.

Forcing my thoughts away from Luc, I chuckle, and Kahar's ears twitch at the sound. I'm sure Rava has some sort of trap set for me, but little does she know, she's poked the evil monster that lives inside me. I've done truly terrible things in my quest for power, but this ... this is going to be a masterpiece.

The capital sprouts obtrusively from the countryside. There's open space, grass and rocky earth spreading to the north and east, then houses rise, clustered tightly, their walls and low-pitched roofs huddled tightly together as if afraid of what lies beyond. The road soon becomes clogged with travelers as the capital comes into view, and I melt into the crowd approaching the edge of the city.

I take a deep breath as a grin spreads across my face. This is going to be painful, but oh, so much fun.

As I ride through the shadow-cloaked streets, the occasional shaft of sunlight breaks through to break up the gloom looming around what is obviously the poorer section of the city. Pools of liquid, most of which I'm quite sure are not water, stand stagnant in the streets. There are cracks in several windows of homes and businesses. A few buildings slant so far to one side or the other that the neighboring structures struggle to hold them up.

This place is too reminiscent of my childhood home. Anger stiffens my spine as a man stumbles between the narrow opening between two buildings. His eyes are glassy, his skin pale and glistening with sweat. He licks his lips several times before rubbing his teeth with a dirty finger. I can practically smell the too-sweet scent of the street drug he's obviously addicted to, and my mother's empty smile flashes unbidden across my mind.

I shake my head, my hood brushing my cheeks, as I watch people move with their heads down, clothes clutched around hunched shoulders. That is, until my magic washes over them.

Magic pulses off me like a giant rock thrown into a pond, sending huge ripples in its wake. Today, Rava will learn what it means to go against someone with actual power.

Every person who's hit by my magic goes wide-eyed before their gaze goes blank, and they crumple to the ground. A woman gasps before she collapses on the steps of the building she just exited, her head smacking hard against the stone. A couple, hands still clasped, fall against the large, dirty window of a cobbler's building. One woman hits the ground, pulling her partner down on top of her where their sightless gazes stare into the street as I pass. A boy lands in a large puddle of ... something, splashing dirty water over his face and soaking his clothes.

The pain snakes down my spine, spreading across my back, and I fight the urge to slump in the saddle. Squeezing Kahar's sides, I urge him to move faster as a horse trots past with a man slumped over his neck. With every stride, the shadowy slums slowly transform to moderate districts until I'm passing large, opulent homes, two and three stories tall with fresh paint and gleaming windows.

My clothes stick to my skin with sweat as bodies continue to drop. Here, the space between buildings doesn't impede the sunlight at all, and the streets and walkways are bright and clean, showcasing the collapsed Trislenians all around me. My head throbs with every pulse of power, and it feels like it might burn a hole in my shoulder blade, but at the same time I'm exhilarated as person after person falls to my power. The Stone's magic is truly amazing.

A woman clothed in a deep red dress clutches the arm of a man wearing impeccably tailored pants and a gold trimmed sleeveless tunic. Her eyes widen as Kahar stomps toward her. The couple falls in opposite directions, like a log split in two, their fine clothes creating a bright contrast against the pale stone walkway.

Ahead, a man lies in the street, his body curled in on itself, and as Kahar prances past, I notice the toddler clutched to the man's chest. The man's vacant eyes stare across the street, but the boy's glazed eyes are aimed at the sky as if watching the puffy clouds.

Rounding a corner, I look down the straight shot of the stone street. A woman snaps her head in my direction before saying something to the man behind her. The man's eyes go wide, and he fumbles before nocking an arrow that's blazing with phosphorus fire. As he angles the bow toward the sky, I chuckle then wince as another strong pulse of magic ripples from me, dropping everyone in sight, including the two who I assume were trying to send a warning or alert.

I mock a bow at the pair as Kahar prances past, his hooves clopping loudly in the silence. Bodies litter the streets, walkways, and doorways, lying blank and unconscious as I continue toward the palace. I have no idea how long the effects will last. Some minds are so vacant, I wonder if I've killed them.

Wiping a hand across my face to keep the sweat out of my eyes, I clench the reins with the next pulse of power, stiffening my spine against the pain. If necessary, this entire city will pay the price for their Queen's misstep.

At the next turn, the scrolling metal gates of the palace stand before me. Soldiers patrol the perimeter, guarding the massive gates, which stand open.

My skin pebbles as pain wars with excitement, and I bite the inside of my cheek to keep the building chuckle from escaping. The magic is pulsing strong, and though it's bordering on agony, I push it, curious to see what I can get this power to do for me ... for Luc.

This is going to be So. Much. Fun.

I take a deep breath as a wave of magic hits the soldiers before me. Each one goes stiff before folding into a heap of leather, armor, and weapons. Some minds float in the gray fog of unconsciousness, but a few are black nothingness.

I stride right through the gates like a vengeful King, which I am. Kahar's hooves crunch on the gravel that leads us through the courtyard to the main entrance of Queen Ravaxina's palace. The cloudless blue sky smiles down at me as birds chirp happily in the sculpted trees and flowering bushes lining the path. Pain, adrenaline, excitement, and arousal courses through my body until the cloying scent of roses hits me, and my nose wrinkles, bringing thoughts of my mother to my mind. She always smelled of dying roses, the useless woman.

I don't bother to dismount as I draw up to the wide marble steps, urging Kahar forward. He storms up each level, stomping over or on fallen soldiers, and once we reach the top, I yank his reins to the left to allow me to lean over and shove open the two-story carved wood doors of the palace. They crash into the interior walls, startling the soldiers standing guard and turning the heads of a few people of Rava's court who are milling about the expansive receiving area.

They all collapse with the next agonizing pulse of magic. The edges of my vision throb in time with my heartbeat, but I keep coaxing the magic outward.

Kahar's metal shoes ring out with every step on the polished white marble floor. Thoughts from deeper in the palace scatter into fear and chaos, mixing with audible screams as they come across fallen bodies. I swallow around the sheer elation humming through my blood as I bathe in their terror before they fall as well.

The radius of my power expands. My back feels like it's on fire.

A woman clutches her chest with a gasp before she crumples,

hitting the side of her face against a small table on the way down. Blood pools around her head, soaking into her tight black curls.

Metal sings as several soldiers draw their swords, eyes bouncing between the fallen and me. The magic thrums from me, and one man actually manages to make it two steps in my direction before he falls to his knees, body swaying while he fights to keep his sword lifted. Kahar knocks into him, flattening him to the marble floor before stomping his sharp hooves into his torso for good measure. Luc's war horse is out for vengeance as well. A moment later, the rest of the soldiers fall like autumn leaves scattered at my feet.

The closed double doors to the throne room loom before me. The pain is so intense I'm either going to scream or laugh, so I laugh, the sound manic even to my own ears. I squeeze Kahar's sides, pulling back on his reins. The black horse rears back, kicking his front legs, striking the doors, splintering the wood and crashing them open with a deafening crack.

Every eye turns to me as my hood falls back. The room goes silent for a long moment before screams erupt from the courtiers. Soldiers posted around the room and near the dais draw their swords. Their terror is like the sweetest wine, tempering the pain of the magic scorching my body. Kahar's hooves echo around the soaring chamber as I press him into a canter, sending people scrambling to the edges of the room, clinging to the walls with fear, some fleeing through side doors. They all drop with the next wave of pulsing magic, falling in piles of bodies in fine clothing, armor, and weapons.

I don't let the power hit Rava, though, pushing the magic around her like water rushing past a rock. Our eyes clash. Her hazel eyes sparkle with rage, her teeth grinding. '*He made it all the way here undetected and unharmed.*' Images flash through my mind of soldiers dressed as citizens stationed throughout the capital, even in the slums. Weapons dipped in a paralyzing toxin hidden but at the ready, arrows tipped with phosphorus ready to raise the alert. Every street corner watched, every soldier trained to act without thought or hesitation. Overwhelming numbers was her strategy. As soon as any soldier sighted me, I was to be fired upon. A signal shot into the sky would have drawn every soldier to my location—her thoughts confirming my suspicions.

Her eyes track me, and fear expands her pupils as her thoughts scramble. She knew I'd come, but not like this—strolling through her kingdom, her castle, unimpeded by the numerous traps she set for me along the way. She underestimated the power that emanates from a single point in my back.

And honestly, so did I. The magic ... *my* magic ... my power is intoxicating.

She aimed to take the Stone and the kingdom of Leiren from me, using Luc's death to draw me to her, giving her the home advantage. And while it was a good try, she really should have known better.

I've struck first. I've struck hard. But I'm not done yet.

As her thoughts fray with panic, I pull Kahar to a stop at the foot of the steps leading to her dais. A smile draws up my lips as she struggles to comprehend the power I wield while scrambling to find a way to escape. But there's nowhere for her to go. She's mine now.

As her thoughts spin toward hysteria, I dismount and let the silence drive her mad. Kahar seems to enjoy the panicked energy because he stands as still as I've ever seen him, and I grin, patting the black warhorse's neck.

Rava's terrified thoughts caress my mind like a lover as she glances at the ring on my right middle finger. '*I can't be the only one without power. Erathan most likely has the Heart Stone, but at least he can be reasonable. But Rydel ... I needed to take him out, take his magic.*' Her eyes desperately search the room looking for help, for an escape, her hands gripping the arms of her throne so tightly her knuckles are white. All around Rava, her soldiers lay in heaps, their swords scattered on the floor and down the steps.

My foot hits the first step, the small thud sounding overly loud in the quiet, vaulted chamber. I hit the second step and pause, raising an eyebrow. When I climb the third step, my lips peel up into a wider grin. I mount the final step, eyes glued to the Queen before me.

Hope blossoms in her thoughts as more soldiers pour into the room, weapons drawn. I see it in my mind before it's loosed. I lean to the left without breaking eye contact with Rava, and the arrow sails past me. The soldiers rush toward the dais, but I throw back a hand, directing the magic in a wave behind me, dropping every soldier.

I take a second to assess the room, making note of each door and window that I can use as an exit. While I plan to go out the way I came, through the front door, it's always good to have backup plans.

The magic clings to me like a cloud. My skin feels raw, like the coarse bristles of a horse brush have repeatedly scraped over my body. Spots dance in my vision, and I swallow the bile that's trying to claw its way up my throat—all while dealing with a blissful thrill that keeps my grin pulling at my lips like a madman. The magic coaxes out every emotion from pain to pleasure, to the point I'm worried I might pass out. But I grit my teeth, straighten my spine, and laugh at Rava.

My dagger flashes in my hand as I step over a soldier, then another whose mind is black and empty, probably dead. I stalk Rava as she rises and unsteadily steps back, trying to move around the fallen soldiers, her bright, colorful skirt tripping her up.

She steadies herself, and her hand presses to her chest, her dark skin beautiful against the cheerful yellow and red print of her bodice. The layered gold necklaces tinkle together prettily, matching the dangling gold earrings hanging down the long arch of her slender neck. Her voice is poised, and I'm surprised at how well she masks the fear that tumbles through her mind. "Rydel. Come to avenge your fallen friend?"

My rage flares, pressing in on my vision, but my expression doesn't change. I keep advancing, and with every step, she backs up.

Her bravado melts to fear, then panic. "What do you want? Money? Territory? The rights to the spice trade?"

That last one almost gives me pause. Controlling the spice trade would add significant wealth to my kingdom and leaving her alive to witness me strip away her main source of wealth would be delicious, but Sin's lesson is well ingrained. I don't need her to take control. I don't need her for anything.

My legs shake with the magic pulsing from the Stone, and I almost stumble with my next step, but I lock my knees and keep going.

My eyes travel down her body and back up again. Her back stiffens, and she fists her hands at her sides. I chuckle as she recalls the sunny afternoon three years ago at her summer solstice celebration, which she hosts every year. I host the winter solstice, and Erathan hosts the spring harvest festival. That year it wasn't even midday, and I was drunk and bored. Luc had wandered off with a woman, and I was looking for similar entertainment. It was easy enough to seduce the Queen, luring her to the gardens with a whispered word in her ear of promised pleasure.

I laugh louder as Rava's skin flushes, recalling how she got on her knees for me. How I pumped my cock into her mouth before spinning her around and sliding into her wet heat. She couldn't contain her moans of pleasure, and when those moans turned to screams, my name ripping from her lips as she came on my cock, my orgasm slammed through me as I bucked my hips against the Queen's ass.

I lick my lips, smirking at her. "Hoping a repeat will stay your punishment? That *was* a fun afternoon."

"Maybe for you." Her skin practically shimmers in the light from the sweat dotting her flesh.

I tsk at her. "So you say"—I tap my temple—"but I *know* how turned on you were from being taken, being dominated. It delighted you knowing your guests and members of your court were milling about and could have caught us at any moment. I *know* that when you came on my cock, screaming my name, it was the most powerful orgasm you've had." I shrug. "But we're off topic. You were offering me the keys to your kingdom for … your life?"

Flexing her jaw, she clenches her teeth. Her hair, shaved on the sides with tight curls kept short on top, adds an intensity to her fierce posture and her sharp cheekbones. Her lean, muscled arms flex with the desire to fight or flee. She can't pick which to do, so she remains still.

With my next step, she rolls her shoulders down her back, standing tall, her delicate gold crown glinting in the light. She faces me with her chin lifted, every inch a Queen. She sighs, the sound coming out more annoyed than resigned. "I underestimated your power, but are you really prepared to take on absorbing Trislen? Don't be brash."

I tap my dagger to my bottom lip, pretending to consider as I stare at the swell of her small breasts. I let the silence build as she shifts under my scrutiny. A few moans and groans float around the room as a couple of soldiers fight their way to consciousness. Rava's thoughts reveal one of the rousing men is her captain, and she struggles to come up with ways to stall until he can come to her side.

I could strike the rousing soldiers back down, but I don't. I let Rava have her moment of hope.

She tilts her head as if death is not staring her down. "Rumors have reached me that Erathan might have possession of the Heart Stone." I keep my face blank as she continues. "We could form an alliance. I'm sure you have your own people in place, but so do I, as close as Erathan's advisors. I can get to him as soon as tonight."

That *is* interesting, and I find myself impressed with her cunning, but it won't save her. This isn't about land, expansion, or even the Stones. This is about Lucaryn.

Rava takes a step toward me. "Let's talk, Rydel." She lifts her hand with a small smile. "It wasn't personal."

She stumbles back, her hand flying to her chest where the hilt of my thrown dagger protrudes. Blood seeps between her fingers, and she takes another step back. I stalk her until I'm in her space, gripping the hilt, pressing my face nose to nose with hers.

"It was fucking personal."

9

R ava gasps, pressing her hand over the wound as I rip the
dagger from her chest. "You should have known better."
Driving the dagger into her gut, I twist it, sinking it deeper. My skin
tingles with the pleasure of her scream. "I can ignore quite a lot,
Rava." Pressing my hand to her breasts, I shove, and she falls back,
her crown toppling from her brow and clattering to the floor with a
faint metallic clang. Maintaining my grip on my dagger, it tears from
her stomach. "But coming after Lucaryn is unforgivable." I straddle
her, her legs kicking in a feeble attempt to unseat me, her sandals
scraping with a whisper of sound against the marble floor. I tilt my
head, gripping her chin to force her to meet my gaze. "You brought
this on yourself."

Rava's eyes go wide as I slowly slice my blade over her throat. Her
cry comes out in a gurgle of pain as I'm painted with her blood. I sit
there, watching the light fade in her green-brown eyes until her body
goes slack under mine.

Reaching over, I pick up her crown. Gripping it between my
hands, I flex, bending the gold until it snaps. I am the crown breaker
once more.

I stand, tossing the pieces on the floor in front of her throne—

now mine. The tinny sound of gold clanging against marble acts like a herald to my new reign.

The captain groans—still fighting the magic—as I grab him by his collar and drag him through and over the scattered bodies to the busted throne room doors. Kahar snorts and dances to the side as I pass him.

A servant woman, who must have been outside the reach of my power, pushes through a side door. Her eyes go wide as she trips to a stop, taking in the room. A second later she screams and runs off, her black braid flying behind her.

I don't even pause. I drop the captain between the doors before leaning down and slicing my dagger up each of his forearms. A weak moan is his only response, and I dip my fingers into his blood, bringing them to the doors over and over, painting my message.

Stepping back, I smile at my work.

"Long live King Rydel Wescaryn."

I leave the captain to bleed out as I turn back to survey the throne room. It's so quiet with only the occasional intake of breath or moan from those trying to climb their way back to consciousness.

I make my way back to the dais, sliding my dagger between the ribs and across the throats of the semi-conscious. The metallic scent of blood hangs heavy in the air, and my skin and clothes are sticky with the thick substance.

I smile, patting Kahar's neck, leaving bloody prints on his midnight hair before I climb to the throne. Despite my exhaustion, I turn with a flourish and slowly lower myself onto the opulent wood-carved monstrosity. Crossing an ankle over my knee, I lean to the side, propping myself with an elbow against the chair arm.

Kahar stomps with impatience, and I smirk at the warhorse. He pins his ears back but stands firm, just as he was trained to do.

I wait.

My finger taps a steady rhythm on the chair, and only a minute passes before the sound of clattering armor reaches my ears. I stay relaxed, settling deeper into my new throne. When the first few soldiers burst through the open doors, I smile as their steps stutter, causing their comrades to bump comically into their backs. Some mouths drop open, others grit their teeth as they take in the scene. It doesn't take long before every eye lands on me.

Metal sings as twenty or so soldiers draw their swords and slowly advance. A woman in the front, well muscled and the steadiest of the group, lifts her sword. "This is an act of war."

I tilt my head, keeping my smile firmly in place. Her pale skin blanches at my silence, but the grip on her blade is steady. She takes another step toward me, lifting her boot to step over a body, the other soldiers advancing behind her.

I sit back, interlacing my fingers and resting my hands on my stomach. "You're right. It was an act of war when your Queen gave the order to kill my captain." I sweep my hand around the room. "And this was the consequence."

"This will not stand."

I lean forward, bracing my elbows on my knees. "Oh, but it will." We stare at each other for a moment. The other soldiers shuffle with unease. The creaking of leather and armor bounces around the room, making the tense moment seem alive.

With a deep breath, I flex my hands, knowing this will take a lot of effort. With every shift, I feel my shirt sticking to my skin with my sweat. My head feels like the magic might crack my skull. Spots dance across my vision, but they clear with my next deep breath.

The leader takes another step. "Take hi—"

I flick my wrist, and she stumbles back, her sword arm lowering as her other hand reaches for her neck. Blood coats her fingers as she touches my dagger that's lodged hilt deep in her skin. Her mouth opens and closes as she tries to speak around the blade in her throat.

Over half the soldiers swarm around her and rush me. I stand and almost sway as I throw out a hand, swallowing the scream that wants to rip from my chest at the pain of using so much magic. The charging soldiers fall like puppets cut from their strings before they even make it to the bottom step of the dais. The marble floor is becoming hard to see under the piles of bodies.

I chuckle as those remaining standing back up, swords raised, but fear dances in their eyes. "Those of you still thinking to avenge your Queen, you have three seconds to stand down and submit."

The thump of my boots counts down as I descend the dais, swiping a sword from a fallen soldier in my right hand, and as I pass the now dead female soldier, I palm my dagger, ripping it from her throat, relishing the feel of my favorite blade back in my left hand.

The weight of the soldier's sword is heavy but familiar. I didn't take the throne of Leiren with magic. I took it *for* magic. I claimed my throne through might and cunning and skill with weapons, and though my head is pounding, and my muscles are shaking, adrenaline fires through my blood, itching for a physical fight.

I land on the last step. "Time's up."

Three lower their swords and step back, five advance. I shove my magic outward, but the soldier's merely shake their heads, and a few stumble. The power has taken its toll, and I fail to bring them down. So, I square my shoulders with a grin and meet them head-on. Steel clashes, mixing with grunts and shuffling feet. Kahar tosses his head and stomps his hooves into the marble floor, adding his own melody to the battle sounds.

The bodies scattered around the room make it hard to maneuver, and while my opponents try to skirt and step around the fallen, I simply step on or over them. As I strike down one soldier, I plant my foot into the back of a body, launching myself into the air, driving my dagger down through the skull of the soldier before me.

I spin, and my sword slides through flesh between the joints in a man's armor, and his cry of pain rings through the room. I shove him into a soldier to his right, and the two stumble back, limbs and weapons flailing as they trip over the fallen. There's a hiss in the air, and I move just in time to raise my dagger and deflect the crossbow bolt aimed for my chest.

I sprint straight at the crossbow wielder, her eyes wide and panicked as she tries to load another bolt. Metal meets wood, and I knock the crossbow from her hands with my sword before running her through.

Flesh tears with a wet sound as I rip my sword from her chest. I'm sweating even more now, and a few strands of my hair have worked free of their tie, falling into my face. I toss my head as I duck the swing of a sword, thrusting my dagger forward. It scrapes off armor, but I follow through with a slash across the soldier's arm, severing tendons.

I kick out behind me, knocking the blade from an attacker that has circled to my flank, then I plant my foot, spin, and arc my sword across his neck. Shifting the grip of my dagger, blood explodes across my knuckles as I punch a soldier's nose, his cartilage crunching under my fist. As he stumbles back, he lands against Kahar, who whips his head around, ears pinned to his head, and bites the soldier on his forearm. He shrieks, ripping his arm from Kahar's teeth. I grab the soldier's head, ramming it down on my knee before shoving him to the ground. I slam my dagger into the back of his neck, leaving it there for a moment as I stand, gripping my sword two handed and throwing it end over end. It lodges in the last soldier's chest, right through his armor.

My lungs heave as I catch my breath. The magic shows me myself through the eyes of the surrendered soldiers, and I look like a demon. Blood and sweat pastes my clothes to my body. Blood also coats my hair which hangs in dark ribbons around my face.

I lean down, retrieving my dagger before I stand facing the silent room. My dagger flicks through my hand, the habitual movement calming me from my fighting rage. I look around. More soldiers have filed in, spreading around to cover the edges of the room. Through the open doorway, servants peek in, trying to see what the commotion is about without getting themselves involved.

I do a quick mental scan of the soldiers in the room, doing my best to ignore the knife-like pain slicing through my temple. My legs feel like they're going to give out, but I keep my stride strong and steady as I turn my back on the room and once again, climb back up the dais, my boots toeing the broken crown, sending a light tinkling sound through the room. With measured slowness, I lower myself onto the throne, sitting tall but resting my right hand on the armrest while my left hand absently plays with my dagger.

Everyone holds their breath, and I keep my face blank, ticking out the seconds of silence. Finally, I grip the hilt of my dagger and point it at a female soldier standing by the door. Resignation floats through her mind, and I almost smile at her thoughts. *'Regimes change. I need this job, so I'll serve whoever sits on that throne.'*

"You." My voice rings out, and even I'm shocked with how commanding it sounds, because honestly, I feel like shit.

She steps forward, bowing. "Yes, your Majesty."

I do smile now. She's smart—a survivor. "Take my dagger"—I have to force my fingers to release my beloved blade as she crosses the room—"and ride north into the forest beyond the Trislenian border. You will find a contingent of my army there. Give the one in charge my dagger and tell them to come here." She bows again, and before she can turn to leave, I add, "And if you meet resistance bringing my soldiers into the capital, which I'm sure you will, I have ordered my army to cut down any who bar their way to me."

I haven't given such an order, but she doesn't know that, and my soldiers will indeed slash and trample whomever they need to get to me.

Lifting her gaze to meet mine, I notice the gold rimming her chestnut brown eyes, which are narrowed slightly. Her pupils are dilated, her dark skin damp with nervous sweat. Her thoughts betray her fear. *'I've heard the rumors of this King. I'll need to watch myself,'* a flash of panic whites out her thoughts for a moment before I hear, *'and my thoughts.'* She stands taller, keeping her eyes on mine. *'Are you reading me right now?'*

I nod, and after a moment, she nods back.

I wave my achingly empty left hand in dismissal. "Go. And if there are any comrades you wish to save, I'd warn them to allow my soldiers to pass."

With a salute, she spins and leaves the room on quick feet. A few of the other soldiers track her retreat before turning back to me. I point to another soldier, my arm feeling like it's weighed down by water-logged dock ropes. The man is only a few steps from the dais on my left. He bows. "Gather every soldier in your 1st unit. I want them all here within the hour."

I know almost everything about the Trislenian army thanks to my spies, including their numbers, ranks, and skill. *My* southern army is about to get a bit of a shake-up.

He salutes, head bowed, and, without making eye contact, rushes from the room.

I glance around. "All other soldiers are sequestered to your barracks until I send for you." Wide eyes, some clenched fists, a few smirks, and some shocked, blank stares meet my gaze. "Dismissed."

A heartbeat passes before some soldiers turn, filing from the room, but more than a few stay where they stand. A voice pushes through the others in my head. '*How dare he command us with our Queen lying dead, and her crown—*'

His scream rips through the silence as he grips his head and falls to his knees. I tear at his mind, overloading his thoughts, pushing pain against his skull, making an example of him. He slumps to the ground as clear fluid drips from his ears and nose. His mind goes dark, dead.

The soldiers around the room back away, sheathing weapons, holding out empty hands in fear. A few hunch in on themselves, hoping to make themselves a smaller target against my wrath.

I raise a hand, shrugging. "I know your thoughts, your desires. Anyone else have a problem with my orders?"

The eyes of the soldiers flick between me, the fallen man, and the carnage of the throne room. My muscles quiver, and my back spasms as I struggle to quiet the magic, to quiet the panic and fear and anger coming at me from every mind in the room. I want nothing more than to find silence, yet at the same time, their terror is like a drug, and I want more.

The remaining soldiers file out quickly, wanting to escape the power of the Mind Stone—to escape me. I slump against the back of the throne, breathing in through my nose and out of my mouth. Every muscle aches, and the edges of my vision waver like I'm looking through imperfect glass. I press my thumb between my brows, closing my eyes. The pain, the exhaustion, is overwhelming, and I'm not sure I'll be able to open my eyes again. My pulse pounds against my skull. I can't keep my hands from trembling slightly as I rub my fingers through my hair, pressing into my scalp.

Fuck, my body feels like it's on the verge of shutting down.

But despite the agony, I love the magic. I love the power. I'll pay the price every time. I'll endure what I must. This was for Luc. I could leave Trislen to the wolves and watch as the high families and political leaders clamor for the throne. There might even be civil war ...

But, no. I'll take this kingdom, and eventually Adren. I'll rule all of Imoria one day, and this, though unplanned, brings me that much closer.

Eventually, the 1st unit of the Trislenian army files in, and I peel my eyes open. They line up in neat rows, standing shoulder to shoulder. A man approaches Kahar, reaching for his reins, but the warhorse spins, kicking out his muscled hind leg. The sound of his hoof meeting flesh is like iron striking the anvil, and the soldier flies back, crumpling to the ground with a moan.

I chuckle. That horse is a menace, but he's definitely growing on me. "I'd leave him be."

The soldiers give Kahar a wide berth as they fill the room. I count almost one hundred and twenty soldiers before the last two pull the busted doors closed behind them with a deafening scrape of wood against stone. All these are in the 1st unit—the top ranked soldiers? We'll see. I have high standards, as they will soon find out.

I give myself a little mental talk of encouragement before rising from the throne. Bracing my feet, I lift my chin, looking down at the gathered Trislenians. "I am King Rydel Wescaryn, and I am now your sovereign. I wield the power of the Mind Stone. I will know the truth of your thoughts. I understand your anger and commend loyalty, but your Queen is dead"—I gesture at her bloody body—"and your loyalty now belongs to me."

The room is silent, but the barrage of angry, confused, resigned, scared, and rebellious thoughts almost drives me to my knees. I have to make this quick before I pass out. "Your fidelity will be tested over the coming days. I'm starting with you because you are supposed to be the elite of the Trislenian army. If I ask you to stay, to continue your service, to join my army, you will all be expected to follow my rule."

I pause, and in the suspense, the rush of thoughts calm slightly as they wait for me to continue.

"Don't betray me." I pause, my gaze flowing over the lines of soldiers. "My commands are law, no matter what I ask of you. You will serve with loyalty, and if you don't ..." I grit my teeth, pushing out a painful burst of power so my voice echoes in their minds as well as around the vast room. "You will die."

Every soldier grabs their heads, a few hunching in on themselves. I sit before my legs collapse, but I keep my posture tall, not showing them any sign of weakness. "You are dismissed to the courtyard." I don't want these soldiers sequestered with the rest of the army. If these are the elite fighters, I don't need them influencing any of the others one way or the other. Divide and conquer is the game here. "A contingent of my northern army will arrive shortly, and when I'm ready, you will be retrieved. Until then, stand down and await my orders."

In a shockingly orderly manner, the soldiers file out of the room. Sighing as the last soldiers disappear through the doors, I bring my shaking fingers to my temples, attempting to rub away the piercing pain. My eyes close, and I vaguely register my hands falling away into my lap.

I crack my eyes open at the sound of footsteps approaching the throne room. My eyes widen in shock as I take in the sun's position through the windows. I could have sworn it had only been a few minutes, but it appears at least two hours have passed.

Shifting in the uncomfortable throne, I manage to sit straight just as the female Trislenian I sent after my soldiers comes into the throne room. Runic is hot on her heels, and one hundred members of my army file in. They don't stand in neat rows or shoulder to shoulder. They spread out, covering windows and doors, their attention sharp and focused in defense of their King.

I sigh as the female stops at the base of the dais, but Runic climbs two steps, bowing. "Your Majesty. Captain Lucaryn is secure in the castle. He's resting and recovering under the healer's care."

I have to swallow a few times to keep the tears clawing up my throat from falling. The female Trislenian soldier's thoughts whisper through my mind. *'He cares. That's ... that's surprising, but good to know.'*

I curse myself for letting my relief show on my face but make a note that this one appreciates empathy. I can use that to gain her loyalty.

I nod at Runic. "Secure the soldiers in the courtyard, as well as the barracks. Send patrols into the cities and villages. There's going to be riots and looting. Ignore the opportunistic thievery and fighting. Focus on acts of rebellion or insurrection. Crush any who think to move against us—quickly and brutally. We need to control the capital with an iron fist until I can sort out their army." I pause with a grin. "And whoever is brave enough, bring Kahar to the stables. Make sure he's well looked after."

A few chuckles ring out around the room as my soldiers shake their heads. I even see a few flipping a coin. Eventually, a soldier steps forward, dodging Kahar's snapping teeth to grab his reins, and leads him from the throne room. The warhorse prances and stomps the entire way. I can't help but laugh.

Runic turns to face the room, his voice snapping out. "Baldred, take twenty to the courtyard. Tyra, take ten to the barracks. The rest hit the streets. Once the capital is secure, I'll divide you among the other cities and villages. You have your orders."

I look at the female Trislenian standing still at the base of the dais. I'm too exhausted to waste power. "Your name."

"Reena, your Majesty."

"Where are Queen Ravaxina's chambers?"

Without hesitation, she turns. "This way, your Majesty."

I stand, but my leg buckles as I descend the first step, and Runic subtly grabs my arm. He stays silent, and his thoughts hold nothing but concern. I let myself lean on him until I hit the last step, then forcing myself to walk under my own power, I push away from Runic's firm grip and follow Reena through the busted doors, down a gilded hall.

My head pounds, and I have to clench my hands to keep from rubbing my eyes as sunlight streams through the windows lining the left wall of the hallway, the bright light bouncing and reflecting off the gilded mirrors hanging down the right wall.

I almost come to a standstill when a staircase comes into view, but I force the shaking muscles in my back to hold strong as I grip the banister and climb step after step. I'm drenched with a new layer of sweat by the time we reach the top, and I almost weep when Reena stops in front of the first door on the right. "Here, your Majesty."

Runic sweeps past her, opening the door to clear the room before me. I pause on the threshold, quickly scanning her thoughts. Her skin pales and sweat dots her forehead. I find determination and resignation, so I release the magic, and she huffs a small sigh of relief. I need to build loyalty within my new South Leiren army, and I'll start with her.

Leaning over, I pitch my voice low in Reena's ear. "This is your station. No one comes through this door but Runic. I'm trusting you with quite a lot. Don't betray me."

She swallows, and even through my exhaustion, her fear is delicious. She nods, and I step into the room. Runic will keep an eye on Reena.

I close the door and collapse. Runic rushes to my side, gripping me under my arms to haul me over his shoulder. I'm placed on a bed, the scent of roses nauseating as I close my eyes.

"Do you need anything, your Majesty?" Runic's voice is close but quiet.

I rub my fingers into my eyes, trying to escape the pain. The craving for the mind-numbing street drug flits through my mind, but I shake it off. I haven't used it in years. "No, thank you, Runic."

"It's my honor to watch over you. On my life, you will be safe."

I can't respond. The world around me floats away, and I sigh, ready for some peace, some quiet. But the image of blood and carnage in the throne room connects me to my childhood, and I'm unable to keep the dream from building as my battered and drained mind takes me to *that* night in my childhood home where I crouch in a corner, holding my bruised ribs as my father advances on me.

10

T he wood of the wall presses into my back as I try to make myself smaller. One arm wraps around my waist, protecting my aching ribs as the other wraps around my shins. The heavy footsteps of my father seem to echo around our small house. The slow thump, thump, thump sounds like a drumbeat that's announcing the pain to come.

My father clenches his fist at his side, one hand holding a book as he stares at me. His green eyes are too bright against the red coloring the whites of his eyes. He's been drinking ... again, and he still wears the royal armor of King Ammeryn from his day's work.

"You're old enough to be earning your keep, boy." His deep voice grates over my nerves, sending shocks of fear tingling across my skin. "But instead, I come home from a hard day's work to find you ... reading." He sneers the word as he hurls the book at my head.

I try to duck, but wedged in the corner like I am, there isn't much space to move. The edge of the book hits the side of my face before thudding onto the floor at my feet.

I know better than to talk back, but the only thing stronger than my fear is my anger. "I worked all day! I checked and reset all tha traps and brought home two rabbits. I made stew, baked bread, planted tha winter vegetables, traded our goat's milk for fabric for a new dress for Yareen—"

My scalp bursts with pain as my father fists my hair and hauls me up *from my crouched position. My ribs scream in agony, and dots dance across my vision as I try to hold back a cry. As he drags me across the room to the kitchen, my eyes find my mother. I don't know why I hope that this time will be different from any other time. It's not. My mother's gaze goes right through me from where she sits slumped in a chair by the cold fireplace. A flush colors her pale cheeks and the small, drug-induced smile on her face mocks me.*

I'm not sure if my father abused my mother before my sister or I were born, but in my seven years of life, I've never known a day where either of my parents were sober. My mother hordes coin she thinks my father doesn't know she takes from his purse to pay for her drugs. Father allows her to steal from him because the drug makes mother malleable. He likes a silent, submissive, near-unconscious fuck.

Father tosses me in a chair before grabbing both my arms in a bruising grip and slamming them on the table. "Stay there, boy."

He stalks off, heading toward the one bedroom in our house, the one he sleeps in, the one he fucks my mother in. My sister usually sleeps on the floor by the fireplace. I prefer to sleep outside, away from the stink of alcohol clinging to my father, and the cloying, rotting-rose scent of my mother's drugs.

A small creaking noise draws my attention to the back door of the kitchen. My sister stands in the shadows, her brows pinched, a frown pulling down her lips. She looks so much like my mother, it's hard not to hate her on principle. Two years older than me, she's a quiet soul and somehow escapes the abuse of our father. Which is good. I'd hate to have to defend her as well as take care of her. I'm the one who makes sure she has warm clothes, food to eat, and books to read. Yarren loves to read. It's the only thing we share.

My fingers scrape on the table as I think about bolting past Yarra into the night, but she shakes her head, whispering, "Just do as he says, and it'll be over."

And that's the crux. No one in my family cares, not even Yarra. Not enough to help me. But even if I ran away, who else would help? My father is in the royal army. No one would take the word of a dirty seven-year-old boy over a soldier in the king's army. I've tried. So many times, I've tried, but I'm always dragged back home to my father's smirk and, later, his fists.

Father storms back into the room with his sheathed sword. "Stand up and keep your hands on the table."

My legs tremble, and I'm not sure if they will support me. I know what's coming. Somehow, I press myself to standing, using the table for support. I'm almost yanked backward as my father rips the shirt off my back.

"This will teach you to waste time. You will never be a proper man if you bury your nose in books."

I don't feel the pain, not right away, as my father brings the flat of his scabbard down on my small back. But with my next inhale, the pain flashes, and I bite my lip.

"I'm disappointed that I have to teach you this lesson, boy. Again!"

The slap of the scabbard meeting my skin again sounds loud in our tiny house, and I claw my fingers into the scarred wood of the table.

"You should be training to become a soldier."

More pain compounds with the third strike.

"You should be trying to make me proud!"

The strikes are getting harder, and a silent tear falls down my cheek with the next hit as I feel my skin split. Blood drips down my back.

"You are a weak," he strikes again, "useless," and another, "boy, and—"

"Stop it!"

Lucaryn's voice halts my father's blows. I whip my head around, seeing my friend standing in the open doorway. His fists are clenched, and his face is red with anger.

"Luc, no." I mean for my words to come out as a command, but a whimper is all I can manage around the agony.

My father chuckles. "Ah, your little friend is here to save you, boy."

Luc stands tall. Even at only ten years old, he has defined muscles. He's always been braver than me, stronger than me.

I wince as my father tsks. "You're little boys. You know nothing of this world. You know nothing of true pain. But you will."

Two of my fingernails split and crack as I dig them into the table, my anger clawing at my chest like it might rip through my skin and consume everyone around me. I wish it would. "Do ya worst old ma—"

Pain explodes, like I was hit in the side of the face with a hammer as my father's fist connects. The room goes dark for a handful of moments. The *blackness recedes slowly, and the room spins. As my father reaches for me, he knocks over a chair; the sound muted in my buzzing head.*

His hand wraps around my throat, hauling me off the floor. Agony consumes me as he punches me over and over. My nose crunches, and my left cheek collapses. My left eye swells shut, and I can feel the hot drip of blood sliding down my face, but the pain is fading. Even I know that's not a good sign.

I see Luc behind my father, his fists pounding on his back. His lips are moving in a scream, but I can't hear him. I can't hear anything.

I feel myself slipping toward unconsciousness, but I fight to stay awake. Where's his sword? He dropped it at some point.

Between hits, I'm able to glance down. It's there! Right at my feet. Can I reach it?

My body is shutting down, and I'm afraid my father is going to kill me this time. And what then? Will he turn on my sister? Or Luc?

No!

I let my anger free. It's like a burst of hot air that sets my body on fire. My arm snaps up, and I punch my father in the throat. Hard.

I crumble to the floor as he releases me, his choking gasps satisfying, but I know I have little time. My palms pat the floor, searching for the sword. It's hard to see through the blood and my tunneling vision, and panic is making my movements erratic.

"Nice try, you ... little shit." A cough stutters my father's words. "But you are ... not strong enough to go against me. You'll never be strong enough."

Fuck, fuck, fuck. Where is it?

My fingers brush leather and steel, and I wrap my hand around the hilt of his sword triumphantly. Desperation, fear, and anger tremble through my body. My hands are shaking so badly, I can't get the sword free of its scabbard.

A movement behind my father catches my fuzzy vision. Luc attempts to pick himself up off the floor, and I assume my father struck him to get him out of the way so he could focus on me. He's always focused on me.

The metallic scrape of steel is like a song from the heavens as I finally get the sword free. I look up at my father's grinning face as he says, "You think you can use my sword against me, boy?"

I grit my teeth against the pain and lift the sword with shaky arms. I've never been so angry. My rage blends with the pain. My breathing speeds up, and the world around me slows down.

And then there's nothing.

Darkness.

The next thing I know, I'm blinking open my eyes, unsure why my body feels so strange.

I'm kneeling, and at first, I think there's something wrong with my vision, but then I reach up, my arm feeling like it's filled with lead, and wipe my hand over my face. I stare at my hand for several long moments.

Blood. Lots of blood. I'm covered in it. The strange sensation I couldn't place was hot blood drying on my clothes and skin. I'm gripping the sword in my other hand, and it too is covered in blood as well as pieces of flesh, muscle, and other things I don't want to know.

"Ry?"

Luc's voice is quiet, but it startles me like a clap of thunder. I look up at my best friend. He has a black eye, and blood also splatters him from head to toe.

I swallow, tasting copper. "What happened?"

Luc bites his lip, a frown pulling at his brows. "It had to be done."

I'm scared to look beyond my friend, but I peel my gaze away from his bright blue eyes and scan the room. Cooling blood paints almost every surface, the bright red quickly turning dark, almost black, almost as dark as the stain I feel spreading across my soul.

My father lays before me, blood pooling under and around his still body.

The kitchen table is on its side, and all four chairs are scattered around the room.

My mother still sits in her chair, her eyes staring straight ahead. She looks the same except for the long slash across her throat. I don't think she even moved when the blade cut through her skin.

And there, in the kitchen doorway, lies my sister's body. She's face down, her upper body halfway out the door like she had tried to run.

My eyes crawl back to Luc. "What happened?"

"You don't remember anything?"

I shake my head, and he kneels, pressing his hand to my shoulder. "You screamed. It was a sound like I've never heard. It stopped us all in our tracks." He pauses, swallowing. "You don't remember?"

I shake my head, searching for the memory but coming up empty.

Luc bites his lip. "You shoved the sword into your father's stomach before ripping it out and slashing at him over and over. When he fell, Yareen screamed. She yelled for help, Ry. She yelled for the guards. I tried to grab her, but she kept screaming. The next thing I knew, you slid the sword between her ribs. It was so quiet, so quick, and she just fell."

Luc takes a deep breath, folding his legs under him, blood squishing as he sits next to me.

"Then you calmly walked across the room, stared at your mother for a few seconds and sliced the blade over her throat."

Luc waves a hand at my father's body. "You came back, slashed him over and over until you collapsed here." He pauses a moment, tilting his head at me. "You really don't remember?"

I shake my head, licking my lips, forgetting they're covered in blood.

"I'm sorry, Ry."

I shift to face him. "Why?"

"I didn't stop you. I didn't want to stop you. Should I have stopped you?"

I glance at Yara. She shouldn't have had to die, but when I brace for the jolt of guilt or sadness, they don't come. I just feel … relieved. I don't have to take care of her any more. I don't have to take care of either of them. I don't have to fear my father. I look at my useless mother, then at my father. I smile. I don't have to fear anyone. Look what I did! The smile grows to an outright grin, and then I'm laughing.

"Ry?"

I throw back my head and laugh louder. I'm free! I've never felt this light, this happy. "No, Luc. You shouldn't a stopped me."

I laugh again as I plant my hands on the floor, blood oozing between my fingers. I stand, looking around. Luc nods at me. "You did this, Ry." He stares at my father a moment before looking back at me. "You're strong. Stronger than you ever gave yourself credit. We're strong. Together."

I glance around the house again. My fingers squelch with blood against the leather of the sword hilt. "Together. You and me, Luc. I'll never be powerless again. I'm gonna rise to tha top. I'll be untouchable. We'll be untouchable." *I wave around the house.* "We're getting outta here." *I lock eyes with Luc.* "You'll come with me, right?"

He smiles and sighs. "Of course. It's always been you and me, Ry. And it always will be. Together."

We spend a few minutes trying to figure out how best to clean up, and in the end, we just set the place on fire. We watch from a block away as my house goes up with the raging flames, spreading to the houses on either side. People scream and run into the night as thick, black smoke chokes the air.

Three streets have burned by the time Luc and I have cleaned ourselves in the frozen river, but the fire is still hungry, resisting the desperate efforts of the people throwing buckets of water at the flames. Luc and I leave without a glance back, heading toward the capital. We travel under the brilliant white light of the mother moon, the weaker blue light of the child moon trailing her across the sky. I lead my goat, and Luc holds the reins of his old mare, who is sway backed and slow, but carries us for short stretches. The goat gives us milk and then brings us decent coin when we sell her in Farden.

We find an abandoned book binder's store, and the irony is not lost on me as we set up our meager possessions and make ourselves a little home surrounded by musty, loose pages and disintegrating books.

The first night in our new 'home,' we huddle under a canvas sheet, pressing our bodies together for warmth and comfort.

Luc's scent, the soft smell of the air right before a rainfall, relaxes me. I'm safe with Luc. I've always been safe with Luc.

11

Reality pulls at my mind, trying to suck me up from my dream, and the dredges of pain start to register. I resist as much as I can, holding onto the petrichor scent, trying to hold the memory of Luc and me as children navigating our way through life in the capital. But my mind has other plans, and I'm ripped from sleep with a groan.

"Your Majesty." The vaguely familiar voice sounds from my left, and when I crack open my eyes, I find myself in a strange room. Midday sunlight streams through a large window, bathing the room in bright light, revealing a palate of cream, gold, and green. I roll to the side, breathing through the dizzying spin that brings bile up my throat. A glass with a milky liquid is shoved into my view, and I follow the hand up a corded arm.

Runic. The name flashes through my mind, and I take a moment to assess him as I take the glass from his hand, the crystal cool and heavy in my grip. He's average height, muscled but lean. His pale shaved head shines slightly in the bright sunlight, and the shadow of a beard dusting his face is dark, almost black. His brown eyes look me over with concern, and I hold up the glass.

"What's this?" My voice is raspy, and I try to swallow, but my mouth feels like it's filled with cotton.

"A tonic from the royal healer. She said I was to have you drink it as soon as you awoke."

I swirl the liquid, watching it coat the inside of the glass. I lift my gaze back to Runic with a raised brow, and he mirrors the expression which emphasizes the scar that splits his right eyebrow. "She's been monitoring you under my watchful eye." He pats the sword on his hip with a smile. "And she seems genuine enough, but ..."

I nod. "We all know how easy it is to hide fear and anger behind a pair of seemingly eager-to-please eyes."

I lick my lips and swallow again, trying to ease my dry throat. Runic passes me another glass, so I set the healer's tonic on the side table. "Water." I take a thankful sip as he crosses his arms. "Luckily, you have your mind-reading thing."

I almost spit out the water.

Coughing, I wipe my chin with a grin. "Mind-reading thing?"

Embarrassed, he scratches the back of his neck, bicep flexing. "I mean, I know it's magic, but beyond that ... how else am I supposed to describe it?"

I shake my head with a chuckle, sending my hair dancing around my face. "No. No, you're right. It's fortunate I have my mind-reading thing." I take another small sip of the water and set the glass down, feeling much better despite the continuous pounding in my head. "How long have I been out?"

"A little over two days."

Well, that's not great.

"How is captain Lucaryn?"

Runic crosses his arms. "According to his messages, he's feeling better, but if I were to read between the lines, he's mighty angry he was left out of"—Runic sweeps his arm in an arc—"all the fun."

I laugh as I once again wrap my hand over the top of the glass containing the tonic, holding it by the rim. I notice someone has washed me, and I am wearing soft, loose-fitting pants and a tunic. Rubbing my hand down my left shoulder, my fingers absently trace the scrolling ink on my skin. "Send for the healer and a scribe. I need to send word to the captain and make sure he stays in Leiren. I'll meet you in the courtyard once I've ... talked with the healer."

Runic smiles, nodding. "I can't imagine the captain will be too happy to be told to stay put."

Another laugh bubbles from my chest. Luc's going to be a little more than unhappy. But I need him there, watching over my kingdom —*our* kingdom, our home. I shrug, continuing to swirl the glass in lazy circles. "Any news from Adren?"

"Captain Lucaryn's message from two days ago mentioned updates from Adren, but no confirmation either way on the information you're waiting for."

I sigh. Rumors spread fast, but until I have confirmation, that's all I have ... rumors and conjecture. "Come to me immediately with any new information on that front." He nods, and I shift focus to what's been happening here. "Has there been much resistance?"

"Surprisingly, no." My brows lift, and his left shoulder hitches. "I mean, there were a few small skirmishes in the barracks, but they were easily subdued. There were two attempts by small civilian groups to storm the gates, but again, we quickly brought them under control. A few minor riots broke out in the slums, people trying to take advantage of what they assumed would be a lawless transition. But overall, so far, it seems everyone is just waiting to see what is going to happen next."

I nod along with his telling before setting the glass back down. "Casualties on our side?"

"Minimal, your Majesty. Only three dead, half a dozen wounded."

"Have the families been notified?"

"Two of the three had no family. A message was sent to the only living relative, a grandparent of the third."

My legs don't tremble as I stand with a nod, and I'm bolstered by that small sign of strength. My head still pounds, but I'll endure it. It's all part of using the power of the Mind Stone—a price I gladly pay. "You're dismissed."

Runic salutes, striding purposefully from the room. I circle the bed, not bothering to straighten the rumpled cream bedding. There's no carpet under foot leaving the dark wood floors exposed, lending warmth in color and texture to the room. The fireplace is clean, telling me it hasn't been lit, even this late in the year, yet the room is comfortable. Living in the south has its privileges, but I miss the mountains towering outside my bedroom window back home.

I splash some water from a basin in the washroom on my face, and I hear a knock, followed by the quiet opening of the door. Turning, I find a small woman with deep brown skin standing in the doorway. She has pulled her tight curls into a knot on the top of her head, and a white linen apron covers most of her plain green dress. She bows her head, clasping her hands in front of her. "You sent for me, your Majesty?"

"Runic told me you've been tending to me."

She keeps her head down. "Tending is too kind a word. I've simply been monitoring your breaths, heart rate, and pupils. I've never dealt with magical fatigue ... magical anything, so I wasn't sure what to watch for, but I did what I could, at your man's insistence."

There's no bite to her words. In fact, she seems almost amused, and an image flits through my mind. *Runic standing at the side of the bed, sword raised, aimed at the healer as she holds her fingers to the pulse point in my neck.* Her thoughts bleed into the image. *'It's sweet how Runic cares for his king. Though the sword was a little much. Like I would refuse a patient. Silly man. Beautiful, but silly. I hope he stays.'* A quick flash of skin, lips on lips, and hands tunneling through hair, brings a slight flush to her face as her fantasies continue to spool in her mind, thus in mine. *'Soldiers are so often in need of tending. I'd like to tend that one.'*

I try to keep the smile from my lips, but I must not do a very good job of it because her eyes go wide, and her flush turns scarlet as she quickly averts her gaze. Runic is going to have his hands full with this one, especially since I plan on stationing him here permanently, installing him as captain of my South Leiren army.

A young black man enters, standing in the doorway, one hand gripping several sheets of paper, the other balancing a pen and inkpot. I meet his dark brown eyes. "I'll be with you in a moment."

I glance at the glass sitting on the bedside table, turning my attention back to the healer. "And this tonic?"

She frowns, snapping her eyes back to my face. "You haven't taken it?"

"Obviously not. I am an enemy king, in an enemy kingdom. I'm not going to throw back whatever is handed to me without suspicion."

"I guess I can understand that." She crosses the room, picking up the glass, bringing it to me with an outstretched arm. "But I need you to drink this, your Majesty. It will help with the pain in your head and will boost your energy."

"How do you know I have pain?"

She smirks, actually smirks, placing her free hand on her hip. "What kind of healer do you take me for?" My brows shoot up, and she bows her head. "Sorry. Sorry. My mother always said my mouth would get me in trouble. I just figured you can read my thoughts, so I might as well speak my mind. There's no sense in you making that headache worse trying to separate the words on my tongue from the words in my head."

My head falls back as I bark a laugh. The move sends pain down my neck, but I don't care. This woman is a delightful break in the tension I've held for the past several weeks.

When my laughter dies off, I find her still standing there, still holding the glass. I sigh. "Despite your candor, I can't trust you. Not yet."

She stands taller, though even at full height only comes up to my chin. "Do what you must, then take the tonic."

I push into her mind with no warning, with no hesitation. She gasps softly but stands strong. There's nothing in her mind other than the desire to heal, to help, no matter the patient. I catch her frustration that I didn't take the tonic as soon as I woke, but only because my pain could have subsided by now if I had followed her instructions through Runic. There's a quick thought of telling off the handsome soldier with a pointed finger in his chest.

Her shoulders relax down her back ever so slightly, and I laugh as I release her mind. "Don't give my man too much trouble, he could not have forced me to take the tonic any more than you could have."

Her lips quirk in a half frown, but she nods. "Just drink." She shakes the glass, and I take it, throwing it back in one gulp. A mineral taste coats my tongue and throat, but a honey aftertaste soothes the bitterness.

The healer nods again. "Good. I'll make you another for this evening that will help with any residual pain and help you sleep." She holds up a hand before I can object. "It won't send you too deep. It will simply relax you enough to fall more easily into sleep."

"Fine then ... ?"

"Rannae, your Majesy."

"Rannae, you are dismissed."

Without pause, she turns and quietly leaves the room. I like her, and I like that I like someone right now, because today is going to be hard ... the next month is going to be hard.

Before turning to the scribe, I notice my bags leaning against the wall near the bed. I bend down and have to brace my hand on the wall to keep from toppling over, but I manage to rummage through the bags until I find the small pouch. Using my forefinger and thumb, I pinch a small amount of the powder and drop it in the glass of water. I stir it up with my finger before swallowing down the contraceptive. I don't plan on fucking anyone anytime soon, but it's a habit, and doing something normal settles me.

I turn to the scribe, waving a hand at a small desk standing delicately in the corner. He crosses the room on hurried feet, sitting with a straight spine, stacking the papers neatly before dipping the pen into the ink and holding it poised over the paper.

I dictate a brief letter to Luc, explaining the situation, leaving out everything I truly want to tell him—that I miss him, that I've gone nearly mad worrying about him, and that I wish he was here with me.

The scribe sprinkles sand over the wet ink, efficiently folding the papers before dripping melted wax over the folds. I don't have my royal ring with the crown breaker seal, so I press the moldavite ring into the wax. The shape of the stone is fairly unique, and Luc knows it well.

As the scribe slips from the room to hand off the letter to a runner, I roll my shoulders. Time to inspect and start whittling down my Trislenian army, now the army of South Leiren.

The last two weeks have been grueling, but honestly not as bad as I thought it would be. It's taken some time getting used to the warmer climate. I feel like I sweat through my clothes before each day even begins. I've worked my way through the Trislenian army in groups of ten, scouring thoughts. I've picked through the 1st, 2nd, and 3rd units, keeping who I could, killing those I couldn't trust.

Now, I'm almost through the final unit, the 4th, but I'm still waiting on some soldiers to arrive from outlying cities and towns around Trislen. There were a few who refused to come to the capital, but my soldiers took care of them.

The latest group of ten soldiers stands before me … well, eight now. Sunlight beats down on us as Runic wipes the blood off his blade with the shirt of the soldier crumpled at his feet. The remaining eight soldiers bounce their gazes from me to Runic and back again. Their thoughts range from shocked and fearful to resigned, but no one moves, and the courtyard remains silent.

My dagger dances in my left hand as I roll my shoulders down my back. "You all may return to the barracks. Report to Reena for your new assignments."

The group walks away wordlessly, but their thoughts still hammer against my skull. *'Thank god that's over.'* … *'I can't believe Iva and Marc still held loyalty to Queen Ravaxina. She's gone. Why fight? Especially against the King of the Mind Stone.'* … *'I just want to get back to work.'* … *'I'm going to ask for a transfer out of the capital. I've wanted a quieter posting for years now. Maybe this is my chance.'* … *'Our new king is brutal. But it's what I would do. Why keep anyone from the court of your competition that you can't trust?'* … *'I've been stressed about meeting the king for over a week. I'm glad that's over.'*

Four Trislenian soldiers peel away from where they've been stationed at the edge of the courtyard. The guards change every day, soldiers from the newly formed 5th, those under a trial period of sorts, picked to witness the culling. Today's guards lift the two bodies, one's grip slipping on a blood-soaked leg, almost dropping the corpse but manages to keep a hold. They silently haul the bodies out of the courtyard to be added to the near-constant burning pyres.

I turn, walking a few paces to the chair set up at the edge of the gravel courtyard on the south side of the palace grounds. Combing my fingers through my hair, I sit with a sigh, shifting to try to find some comfortable position in the rigid chair.

I grit my teeth as the next group draws near, though they are still out of sight, and faint voices build in my mind. I press my fingers into my temples, circling slowly.

"We can take a small break, your Majesty." Sympathy fills Runic's eyes, and his thoughts reveal his own exhaustion, and his concern for me using so much magic for so long.

I shake my head, and sit taller, annoyed I let any weakness show enough for Runic to feel the need to comment. He presses his lips into a thin line before nodding. "Then, before the next group arrives, you should know we caught three from the group of soldiers who ran two days ago."

"Bring them."

Runic nods and slips away, returning quickly with another guard and the three prisoners. Their chained wrists clank loudly as they file in front of me, their feet shuffling, heads bowed. There's a bruise blooming on the female's cheek, the shirt of one of the males is torn, dirt caking his nails, and the last male has dried blood around his nose.

Their thoughts are a low rumble of noise that hums against my skull. That hum becomes a growl as the next group of ten from the 4th comes through the door. They stand in a line, shoulder to shoulder. Each salutes with a fist over their heart before bowing their heads. The four guards slip back to the outer edges of the courtyard, waiting to see if they'll need to haul away any bodies from this group.

The silence fills the air, and no one moves, each head staying bowed. But there's no such thing as silence for me. Voices scrape the inside of my head like a spoon trying to scour the last remnants of jam from a jar.

I grip the worn leather hilt of my dagger for a moment, grounding myself before letting it play back through my fingers. I face the prisoners first. The magic heats in my back, and I grit my teeth as I send the power screaming into their minds, sending the message that their brains are swelling, pressing against their skulls. All three drop to their knees, hunched over, gripping their heads. The female screams, her cries of pain echoing through the vaulted ceiling, and I smile as their bodies react to what their minds believe to be real and excruciating agony.

The group of ten soldiers shift nervously, eyes darting. One of the male prisoners lifts his head, tears leaking from his eyes, his hands pressed to his temples. "Please, your Majesty."

I look at the ten soldiers, then down at the prisoners. "I have no need for cowards."

The magic seeks the light in their minds, and with a single thought, I snuff it out. The three crumple to the floor, eyes blank.

I crack my neck. Well, that's three less minds crowding my own.

Stepping over the dead prisoners, I approach the first soldier in line, a man with gray painting his black hair along his temples. "Stand."

He lifts his head, and I notice his black skin is smooth, with a few wrinkles at the edges of his eyes and around his mouth. It's hard to guess his age, but I'd wager he's older than most of the soldiers in his unit. I can't help but wonder why he hasn't risen in the ranks, but when I focus the magic on him, the Stone practically burning in my back, I see contentment. He's grown up in the Trislenian military. No family. No aspirations beyond keeping his job, earning a living, and being left alone. I can work with that.

I release him. "Will you swear loyalty to me?"

His lips press in a hard line, and I barely keep my sigh from sliding from my lips. But his eyes hold mine as he nods. "Yes, your Majesty."

A breath puffs from his lips, and he rubs a hand against the back of his neck as I shift my attention to the next soldier. I smirk. He thinks it's bad having me in his head? Try having everyone in your head ... all the time.

"Rise." The next man lifts his head, giving me an unobstructed view of his brown skin with his long locs pulled back in a tie. His gold eyes meet mine, and I notice his hands clenched tight at his sides. "Will you swear loyalty to me?"

His mind and voice ring out at the same time. "Yes."

Well, that was ... eager. Interested, I focus on his mind. Ah, yes. There's anger, but not at me. He did not like the late Queen, and he's frustrated on the verge of hatred at his superiors. His opinion of himself is quite inflated, and he believes he's been held back from promotions. The 1st unit is his ambition, and yet he's been stuck in the 4th for years, only getting small village assignments. Bored. He's been bored.

"You want the 1st unit." It's not a question, and his eyes widen as I respond to his thoughts. Why are people still so shocked when I display my power?

"Yes, your Majesty."

I tilt my head, and a grin pulls at my lips. Let's see how badly he wants it. "I'm going to send you to Leiren to join the grunt unit." His eyes narrow, and his fists clench even tighter to the point I'm surprised I don't see blood dripping from his palms. "You will spend the next year with them, and at the end of the year you will run the mountain trial."

His thoughts are practically screaming inside my mind, and I resist cracking my neck to alleviate some of the pain. He voices his thoughts, and I let him. I let him make an example of himself. *How dare he dangle the 1st unit ...* "How dare you demote me! And to the North?" *I've never been to Leiren, and I don't want to go. This prick.* "You come here, throwing around your power, thinking you're special. You're not. You're just some guy who managed to get his hands on a magic stone." *I'm not starting back at the bottom.*

I smile, spinning my dagger at his chest as I lift my right hand, middle finger raised, the fake green stone shimmering dully in my ring. "Fuck yes, I'm special. I have the Mind Stone. I see you. I see your parents, your sister and her family. I see the boy who used to beat you until you wet your pants." His cheeks flush as his eyes widen. "I see the coin you stole to pay for your entry into the army. I see what you think about when you stroke yourself off." The other soldiers shuffle, putting distance between him and them.

I grin. "So, you will do whatever the hell I tell you to do because I have plenty of soldiers. In fact, I have too many. The Trislenian army is much too large, especially for such a small kingdom. If I don't have use for you, I have no problem eliminating you." I gesture to the pools of blood cooling to a dark red on the gravel. "The question is, are you going to be useful to me?"

He reins in his anger before nodding, his mind still buzzing but resolved. "Yes, your Majesty."

I lean in. "Good news. If you survive and do well during the trial, you'll have your pick of units." His eyes flare, making the gold sparkle, and I chuckle with no warmth behind the sound. "*If* you survive."

His expression sobers, and his thoughts turn determined.

I step to the right, my boots squishing in the sticky blood, facing the next in line. "Stand."

She lifts her shaved head with tight curls at the top, styled like her late Queen. Her dark eyes meet mine, and before I can open my mouth or focus on her thoughts, she says, "I'll swear my oath to you, your Majesty."

Her thoughts are true. She's bored with all the waiting for the past few weeks. Annoyed with the change of sovereign, but only because it disrupts her routine. She doesn't care who's on the throne. She has a job to do, protect her city and protect her fellow soldiers. What is someone like her doing in the 4th?

I nod, seeing her aspiration. "The lieutenant of the 4th did not want to serve under my rule ... so ..." I gesture at the blood at my feet, and she glances down before looking back at me with hunger in her eyes. "Congratulations, lieutenant."

Her lips twitch as she fights to hold back a smile. She salutes and bows her head again. "Thank you, your Majesty."

I finish the group, each loyal enough for me to spare their lives, and as they file out of the throne room, I still the dagger in my hand, looking at Runic. His beard is a little fuller since the night Luc nearly died, and his eyes are tired. It feels like a lifetime since the attempt on

Luc's life, and Runic has been a solid presence as I've *dealt* with Trislen.

"How many more groups?"

His long strides take him to the edge of the courtyard, where he picks up a piece of paper from a rickety wood table standing under a tree with dark green leaves and small white blooms. He scans the paper before setting it back down. "Six."

"Shit." Sixty more soldiers to go through. "And how many are we still waiting on from the outlying villages?"

"Only a dozen, your Majesty. My reports indicate the last will be here the day after tomorrow."

Okay. Almost done. I can do this. I did it in Leiren, granted that was ten years ago, and I haven't taxed my magic so hard since then. Luckily, I went through Rava's advisors, her foreign minister, her treasury staff, her trade master, and the rest of her servants and staff the day I woke up. Most didn't make the cut, and I replaced them with my people. A few of the spies in Rava's network came forward of their own volition, offering their services to me, but others had to be hunted down and killed.

The sweet burning scent of the pyres has constantly filled my nose, and I can't wait for the day they finally run out of 'fuel.'

I also met with all the Trislenian high families, vetting them against my magic, tossing a few spouses and children in the dungeons with the promise of release once loyalty has been proven. I killed one high lord's son in front of him when he thought to take me by surprise by drawing a 'hidden' blade from his boot. I saw it coming a mile away, and had my own dagger at his son's throat, slicing through his skin before he could blink.

I smile at the memory of the boy's parents' screams as my soldiers dragged the father off to the dungeons. His wife fainted, her fancy dress pooled around her on the blood-stained floor. The other high families in attendance kept their distance from her and her dead son, each falling in line, swearing loyalty, which I weighed against their thoughts.

My smile fades as the new group of ten soldiers arrive, and a thought from a soldier shifts my own thoughts. '*Will we be invading*

Adren? Rumors say King Erathan has the Heart Stone, and everyone knows King Rydel is obsessed with owning both Stones. I wouldn't mind wetting my blade on the Adren army. If we won, maybe I could be re-stationed at one of the port cities. I miss the sea.'

Yes. The Heart Stone.

I know my limits, and conquering two kingdoms in a month may well kill me. Now's not the time to make that move. I *can* be patient. But maybe there's another way.

I want that Stone. I *need* that power. It might be so close, within my reach, just a day's ride to the northwest. Just a day's ride. I need to know if Erathan has it, and I think I can find out without starting a war ... maybe. The Heart Stone is the key to my supreme sovereignty. And Luc and I will be that much more protected—we will be untouchable.

Luc.

It's time to go see a man about a Stone.

12

During the long days of culling and reorganizing, whispers reach my ears of a man who calls himself The Shadow Lord. Digging deeper, I find a vast underground operation with quite a bit of influence and power within Trislen. This Shadow Lord runs black market merchandise, beggars' rings, fight clubs, protection services, gambling dens, and more. He even had some of his people placed in the palace as servants—until I removed them.

My spies tracked him down three days ago, but I waited to summon him, giving him a false sense of security, leading him to believe he might have avoided my notice. But this morning I sent one of my people to fetch him.

I sit on the throne, the chair still uncomfortable and unfamiliar to the point I want to squirm, but I remain still. The Shadow Lord stands before me with a cunning smile on his face and intelligence in his eyes. His thoughts reveal his name to me, Mica, as well as his willingness to serve under my rule, as long as he doesn't lose too much in the transition. I grin at him, appreciating his ambition.

"Shadow Lord, Mica Kafir." His smile falters slightly as I use his name. "You have quite the operation here in Trislen."

"I've done okay for myself, your Majesty." He is shorter than average, but lean with a build that hints at speed and strength. His short, chin-length hair hangs around his face, and his black skin seems to fuse with his famed black-on-black clothes, leaning into his title of Shadow Lord. Brown eyes shrewdly observe the room, and though his posture looks relaxed enough, I notice he keeps his hands within easy reach of his thigh sheaths that hold his daggers. His thoughts are shocked that I allowed him to keep his weapons, but this man does not pose a threat to me, and I want him to know that.

But a part of me realizes I *should* fear him, at least a little. I was this man, years ago in Leiren as Luc and I were working our way up through the slums, aiming for the throne—but I have magic now, and I'm not as careless as King Ammeryn was with me. Trust will get you killed, with or without magic.

I wave a hand absently. "I don't care about most of your dealings. In fact, I encourage you to continue business as usual. Your 'services' will help maintain a sense of normalcy during this time of transition."

His brows raise, and his thoughts betray his relief. "As you wish, your Majesty."

"However. I will collect a tax from your 'earnings.' Nothing that will hurt you. Twenty-five percent." I laugh at his panicked thoughts. "Well, it might hurt in the beginning, but you'll adjust. Also, you will cease your protection services. My new army will see to keeping order in the capital and beyond." This is what Luc would do. He'd want complete control of the city, and so I plan to extend that task to Runic.

I hear his protest before he opens his mouth, so I hold up a hand to stall his words. "I will not be moved on this point."

'*Shit. What am I going to do with my enforcers?*'

I grin. "Feel free to send your enforcers my way. If they prove true, they'll be more than welcome to join my army."

His eyes widen. "It's going to take some getting used to that power of yours, your Majesty." A small smile curves his lips. "But I doubt many of my enforcers would be too happy serving in such a struc-tured organization."

I shrug. "You never know. But I'm not concerned with what they do, as long as they are no longer collecting coin to run off thieves and rival gangs. Starting today, if I hear of your enforcers, enforcing, they will be arrested and thrown into the dungeons." My grin widens as his thoughts flit from one option to the next with lightning speed—the mind of a survivor. "And trust me, nobody wants to end up in my dungeons, caught inside the most painful memory or fear I can find in their mind."

I wave a hand, snapping him out of his thoughts and bringing his attention back to me. "I'll also require you to compile reports on what is happening in my new kingdom. Weekly. You will be my eyes and ears."

He frowns. "You have your own spy network as well as that power of yours. Why do you need me?" I raise an eyebrow, and sweat dots his forehead. "Your Majesty."

"I don't *need* you. But you have a unique position to feed me insights from a different perspective, and I will use all my resources to my advantage ... until they are no longer an advantage. And then ..."

I let the statement hang, and he presses his lips together, bowing. "Yes, your Majesty. How shall I deliver your reports?"

"In person for the next few weeks. If I'm not available, you will report to Captain Runic. After you've proven yourself, you may deliver your reports by messenger bird, in code."

Annoyance coats his thoughts with having to personally attend me, but he is already mentally shifting his schedule to accommodate my command.

I jerk my head to the throne room doors behind him, repaired since my takeover. "You're dismissed."

He bows again. "Until next week, your Majesty."

He leaves with quick steps, his black hair swaying with his retreat.

Another piece of controlling my new kingdom falls into place with the Shadow Lord under my thumb, and I finally feel comfortable enough to leave Trislen ... South Leiren for a short while.

After a few more quick meetings, checks on stores of food and weapons, and a hasty review of the updated budgets with the adjusted taxes, I make my way to the stables. Reena, the female Trislenian soldier I sent to retrieve Runic that first night, falls into step with me. "Your Majesty, are you—?" Her head snaps to the right, her finger jabbing toward a soldier crossing the large yard spanning between the palace and the barracks. "You!" The man pauses, a look of annoyance crossing his face before he does his best to school his features. I glance at Reena, catching the flex along her jaw as she grinds her teeth. "Aren't you supposed to be with the rest of your unit on patrols in the city?

The man's eyes flick to me, and I notice the mark of the 2nd unit on the sleeve of his right arm. I just stare at him, letting Reena handle her new job as Runic's second in command, overseeing the 2nd, 3rd, and 4th units. He fixes his gaze over Reena's shoulder, standing at attention. "There was a slight scuffle with some ... protesters. We got everything under control, but Hilden sprained his ankle, so I helped him to the healers bay."

Reena nods. "Any other signs of unrest?"

"Not today. Not so far." His voice pitches low, his next words barely a mumbled whisper, but his thoughts are loud and clear.

I take a single step, and his eyes snap to me, sweat breaking out on his forehead. "What was that, soldier?"

I smile as he looks between Reena and me, knowing I've heard him, knowing there's no escape from his insubordinate thoughts. "I, um ..."

Reena's eyes narrow. "Speak up, soldier, your King asked you a question."

His hands clench. "I said, we wouldn't have 'unrest' in the city if *he* had just stayed in his own kingdom."

I nod, amused at the warring anger and fear flooding his thoughts. But I want him to voice his thoughts. I want him to admit the secret parts of himself. "And ...?"

He swallows, his arms trembling as his gaze meets Reena. "And you just do as he says, like his little puppy."

And, there it is. I swallow a laugh, hearing Reena's calm thoughts before she says, "I'm doing my job, soldier. But your statement makes me believe you don't have a need for this job. Are you independently wealthy?"

His brows scrunch. "No."

"Have you been moonlighting on another job?"

His shoulders slump. "No."

"Then I'm astonished you would be so careless as to let your emotions threaten your only source of income."

He remains still, having no response, and his thoughts spin through options if he loses his job right now. There's a long pause while Reena lets the man sweat. My temples are starting to throb, so my mind wanders, simply to keep their thoughts out of my head as much as possible.

I have culled my South Leiren army. Some ran, but my soldiers hunted them down and killed the deserters. Some fought and were also killed. And some relented and now work in my service. So goes the conquering of a kingdom. This isn't my first time. But descent and malcontent always slip through or build with time—like with his man.

Finally, Reena puts her hands on her hips. "I'm demoting you to the 3nd unit, and you are on the dawn shift until further notice."

I scratch my beard to hide my smirk. The dreaded dawn shift— the poor souls relegated to patrols three hours after midnight until three hours after the break of dawn. It's a boring, tiresome shift, and no one wants it. Reena is smart. Her thoughts reveal she plans to pair him with one of the trusted soldiers from the 1st unit ... with Runi's permission. This soldier will be watched, and if his attitude remains a problem, he'll be dismissed.

Between Reena and Runic, things are handled here in the south.

Reena nods. "Go report to the 3rd's troop leader."

The soldier snaps to attention before hurrying down the crushed-stone path.

Reena sighs. "Sorry about that, Sire." We turn back toward the stables, and she continues. "I originally came to ask you if—"

"I am going north for a bit. Not too far, and I don't expect to be long, but I see you have things well in hand."

"Thank you, your Majesty. Shall I assign a few soldiers to gear up to travel with you?"

I like that she asked. Luc would have just sent soldiers to stick to me like honey.

"No. That's not necessary for this trip."

Her thoughts are doubtful, but she doesn't argue. "Then I wish you safe travels. I—" Something catches her attention, and she turns. "Nira!" A female soldier with close-cropped black hair turns at Reena's shout. "I have a job for you."

From Reena's thoughts, I realize this is the soldier she wants to pair with that belligerent soldier. Reena turns to me as Nira makes her way over to where we're standing. "I'm sorry, your Majesty, I just need to—"

I wave her off. "Go. You're doing your job." The words are on my tongue to thank her, but they get stuck, and I swallow them down. Platitudes and praise don't come naturally to me.

She salutes, then rushes forward, meeting Nira halfway. The two women talk in quiet voices as they turn and walk around a bend in the path.

Continuing my way to the stables, the scent of hay, dust, and horses greets me a moment before the long building comes into view. I walk down the center hall, waving off the stable hands, stroking soft muzzles as the horses lean over their stall doors in greeting.

A loud crack of hoof meeting wood brings a smile to my face, and Kahar's giant head lunges over his door, ears pinned.

"Hello, you grump."

He huffs, but steps back as I enter his stall. I brush Kahar down to the sound of his teeth crunching on the fresh hay in the metal holder along the side wall of his stall.

Leading the war horse from the stables, I absently saddle Kahar. I check his girth, stepping back just in time as he lunges into my space to try to knock me over. Grinning, I pat his neck. "Nice try. I'm figuring you out, e'ass asre'a." *hell horse.* He snorts but stands still as I grip his reins and a fist full of his mane, swinging up into the saddle. Smiling, I turn Kahar away from the stables and nudge him up the northern road, my eyes burning slightly at the hint of smoke still hanging in the air.

The day I stormed into the Trislinean capital, most of the people who fell under my magic didn't wake up for a full day. Some never did. Soldiers and citizens cleared the streets of the dead, their bodies adding fuel to the pyre fires. Even all these weeks later, the sickly, sweet scent still permeates the city.

I nod at a group of soldiers on patrol in the city, a mix of North and South Leiren. They all salute, and though there is still some tension and anger, their thoughts remain loyal to me—or at the very least, resigned.

As I make my way through the city, occasional glances from citizens flit my way, most too concerned with their day that they don't look too closely, not recognizing their new King in their midst.

A woman with a baby in her arms looks up at the sound of Kahar's hooves. She goes to continue on her way, but does a double take before bowing, quickly stepping back and pressing herself against the wall of a clothing shop. Her mind is a cloud of fear as she inhales, blanching around the stench of burned flesh that clings to the air.

A group of three men, dressed sharply in airy fabrics with bright colors, draw close. They pitch their voices low, heads tilted down. One looks at me as I approach, and his green eyes go wide. He stops, catching his friends off guard as they continue a few steps beyond him. They turn with a question on their faces until they follow his line of sight. All three bow and step back, sliding into a darkened alley and beyond my view, but I still *hear* them. Their minds flood with images of the day I came through the capital, of the bodies littering the streets, of the many who never woke.

As I continue on, I can feel my back stiffening with tension, but I can't stop the thoughts pushing through my defenses and into my mind.

'That's him. King Rydel.' ... *'I need three bolts of fabric to finish my orders by the end of this week.'* ... *'I wonder if the rumors are true. Did the king take out everyone that was in the throne room with just his magic?'* ... *'I wonder if there will be a funeral for the Queen? Though why would there be?'* ... *'I'm so tired. The baby didn't sleep last night, and Sinar was up all night coughing.'* ... *'Maybe I'll visit the brothel tonight to take the edge off before I go home. I can't think about him, his body in the street, how he wouldn't wake up.'* ... *'I wonder how the new king will deal with the Shadow Lord? I'm tired of paying him for protection from the thieves and rival gangs. But what else am I supposed to do?'*

Finally, I break through the slums and out of the city. I give Kahar his head, and he takes off, stretching his muscled legs. I lean over his neck, and tears stream from my eyes at the speed, but I relish it—the freedom, the wind, and yes, the bit of fear that comes with knowing this powerful beast could take me down.

After a few minutes, my mind is free of others' thoughts. I slow Kahar to a gentle canter. I miss Luc. In these moments when the magic quiets, the space left by the silence is filled with him. I hope he really is okay. I wish he could be here with me ... but I don't think he'd like it here in the south. The weather is too warm, too sticky. The mountains, if you can call them that, are small, and the people are too bright in their colorful clothes.

No, he wouldn't like it here ... Or maybe that's just me projecting.

As I move west, the landscape bleeds from open, tree-studded countryside to the scattering of dwellings that tell me I'm nearing the city. I pull myself from my thoughts, trying to shake Luc from my mind, and focus on what lies ahead—the capital of Adren.

King Erathan Bryrel and I are going to have a little chat.

13

Unlike my entrance into Trislen, I keep my power leashed as I ride into the capital city of Adren. I want to be seen. I don't have my crown, and not many commoners know me on sight, but Kahar is obviously a royal horse with a blanket from Rava's cavalry sitting brightly under the saddle. That, combined with my clothes, hastily but finely crafted by the new South Leiren royal tailor, identifies me as someone important, or at least someone with money.

I'm curious what Erathan's reaction will be to my unannounced arrival. The sea-salt and fish scent of the coast carries on the breeze, mixing with the smells of a large city—too many bodies, fresh and stale food, booze, and sewage.

The moldavite ring glints at me from my right hand, and as I flex my fingers, straining them straight, several people's gazes flick to the stone before darting away, minds flaring with shock, suspicion, fear, and skepticism. Heads bow, whispered murmurs float behind raised hands. Most people have only heard rumors of the Stone and what it can do. And honestly, until you've had someone pluck your thoughts and memories from your head and use them against you, it's quite unbelievable to imagine magic like that still exists.

What no one understands, no one except Luc, is that I'm a slave to the magic—not that I'm complaining, but even *I* have my moments. I try to dull the noise, but it's never completely gone, and for a second, exhaustion threatens to tumble me from Kahar's back. But I need the magic. I need to protect what Luc and I have conquered, what we have fought and bled for. Luc and I will stand above them all. We will be unstoppable, unbreakable, unreachable. We will be Gods.

The 'slums' of Adren's capital are not as run down as Trislen's, probably due to the fact that Adren is wealthier than both Trislen and Leiren combined. I have one port city in my kingdom that does fine, but the freeze comes in earlier and earlier each year, cutting our trading seasons short.

Trislen has one port as well, but it's so far south, most traders from the west don't waste the time or coin it takes to extend their journey, not when they can dock in Adren. The only reason the Trislenian port continues to survive is because of their extensive spice trade, and the few traders who brave the long voyage around Imoria from the east.

The capital city of Adren is itself a port city, one of five large ports in Adren. The weather here is temperate and trade happens all year. I have a decent amount of spies in Adren just to keep track of what is coming and going through the ports.

A pair of soldiers pause on a corner, eyes watching me, hands gripping the hilts of their swords but not drawing their weapons ... yet. I tilt my head down with a small smile as I pass, practically feeling their tension as their thoughts scramble for reasons I'm here —here alone—and what they should do.

Not a block later, and I go through the same response with another pair of soldiers. And again. And again. I'm sure by now, King Erathan has been notified of my presence, and if not, he needs to overhaul his security.

I hold Kahar to a slow pace as I keep my eyes and mind open to any threats, seen or unseen. I'm distracted by a tangle of angry thoughts to my right when Kahar, never one to waste an opportunity, drops his head and arches his back with a quick hop. "Shit." I tighten my hold on the reins as I squeeze my thighs to keep my seat and prevent him from shifting the bit forward to get the bit between his teeth.

That's the third time today he's done that. Hell horse.

I'm surprised I make it all the way through the city without being stopped. In fact, I'm not approached until I reach the gates of Erathan's castle. I catch a glimpse of crashing waves beyond the stone and glass of the king's home, and I take a deep breath of fresh sea air.

Pulling Kahar to a stop, four soldiers draw close, blocking my way —not that Kahar couldn't take them all down with one lunge. Three of them bow as the fourth steps forward. "Your Majesty, I am to escort you inside. The king is waiting."

I hide a smirk at his wording. *The* king. He's waiting, as if he summoned *me*.

I swing my leg over Kahar, dropping to the ground as a second soldier steps forward. "I'll take your horse to be brushed down, watered, and fed."

I step back, releasing Kahar's reins to hang to the ground. With a grin, I sweep my hand toward the warhorse. "If you dare."

The man only pauses for a second before reaching for the dangling reins. As soon as he comes within range, Kahar flattens his ears and bites the man's hand. The man swears, snagging his hand back, shaking it out, and I see a bruise already forming around a trickle of blood.

I shake my head with a laugh. "Good luck." I gesture through the gates, looking at the first soldier. "After you."

He takes off at a quick pace, the last two soldiers stepping in behind me. I feel renewed by the quiet ride here. The magic thrums from my shoulder, down my back, ready to drop anyone and everyone at the first sign of trouble. The energy of anticipation tingles through my blood.

I allow the soldiers flanking me their false sense of security even as I pick through their thoughts with ease. I don't dive deep enough to alert them to the intrusion, just enough to warn me of what is coming.

The problem is, they don't know, so neither do I. But as annoying as that is, I'm ready for anything. My magic is ready. Even if Erathan has the Heart Stone, the magic will be new to him. I am seasoned. I will take what I want.

The clomp of cobblestone gives way to the crunch of gravel before changing to the soft snap of stone underfoot. The sand-colored lime-stone carries into the castle as I'm led through towering double doors and into a receiving area, which is empty.

I almost stumble. The entrance is not just empty, it's quiet, mentally, and it remains silent even as we travel down a window-lined hall, up a short set of stairs, down another hall lined with portraits of the Bryrel royal family, and toward a pair of open doors that showcase the throne room.

Beyond the soldiers escorting me, I don't see a soul, but more importantly, I don't *hear* anyone.

My shoulders pinch together slightly, and I fight the urge to look over my shoulder for some unseen foe. I shove my left hand in my pocket to keep from grabbing my dagger as I cross over the threshold of the grand room. The beamed ceiling towers overhead, twenty feet at least. The western wall is mostly windows that climb all the way to the ceiling, and there are doors leading to a stone balcony.

Erathan doesn't sit on his throne, but stands off to the left, staring out one of the windows at the sea beyond. The sun's setting rays dance and sparkle over the waves, casting the room in hues of gold and white.

The king turns with a smile on his face, which crinkles the edges of his warm, brown eyes. He's a little older than me, in his late forties. His large hand runs over his shaved head which is smooth and tanned, revealing he spends a decent amount of time outside. Combed neatly, his long reddish-blond beard spills to just below his collar bones. There are two small braids that trail down the right side of his beard. He's a few inches shorter than me and is bulkier than Luc, his bulging arms a testament to his preferred weapon, his double-sided ax. It takes enormous strength and stamina to lift such a weapon, nonetheless wield it for any extended amount of time.

His deep voice is calm, light even, almost comforting. "Thank you, you are dismissed."

The soldiers bow, turn, and retreat until I can no longer hear them with my ears or my magic.

I smile back as Erathan approaches, bracing myself to notice any change to my feelings and ready to retaliate. But all feels ... normal, unless that's what he wants me to feel.

His large hand clasps my forearm, and I relax just a fraction as his thoughts spill into my mind. '*This meeting, though unexpected, could mark a great alliance between Leiren and Adren, if you allow it, King Rydel.*'

I grin as I return his clasp. "I'm interested to see what we can achieve today."

He nods, releasing me. "Good." He gestures to the door to my left. "I have arranged for some food and drink. Let us dispense with formality and talk over a meal."

I follow him through the door, reaching up to tie back my hair in a knot to keep it from whipping me in the face as sea-spray cools my skin. A half-wall of limestone blocks us from the jagged rocks below, and there's a table set off to the right behind a screen of climbing greenery that shields us from the worst of the wind and spray.

I slide into a seat that's built into the limestone wall and piled with cushions, and Erathan takes a seat to my right at the end of the table before gesturing at the food. "Please, help yourself." He places brightly colored fruit and wedges of salty cheese onto his plate, and I do the same before cutting off a piece of honeycomb to spread on a slice of fresh bread.

I take a few bites, and we sit in silence. His thoughts are calm, appreciating his food, enjoying the sound of the waves and the warmth of the sun. His mind doesn't turn to me at all, not once, and it's ... unsettling. He's content with where he is and what he's doing. I might as well not even be here for all the attention he's giving me.

Finally, I say, "You've emptied your castle. Quite a bold move."

He lifts a brow and nods with a smile. "I figured it would allow you to more fully concentrate on what you came to discuss with me today."

Erathan and I haven't had many run-ins in the past. He's mostly kept to himself as long as I did the same. I have my spies in place in his kingdom, as does he in mine, but other than that, he's seemed content to rule his slice of Imoria and to leave me to mine. He's definitely never been the thorn in my side that Ravaxina was.

I didn't plan on broaching the subject so soon, or at all, but I take a chance. "And your empty castle has nothing to do with needing space now that you have the Heart Stone?"

His chewing slows, and as his thoughts surface, he voices them. *I can't hide.* "I know I cannot hide from you, Rydel, so I shall not even try." *I shouldn't tell him this, but he'll find out. He'll know. And well, what else can I do?* "I don't know why, but I can't call the magic." *Hear me out.*

My heart stalls, and I hold my breath as he reaches inside his shirt, pulling out a pendant on a simple silver chain. Dangling from his fingers sits the object of my obsession. The Heart Stone.

The pink Rhodonite stone, about the size of the pad of my thumb, is speckled with black. The rock is raw, unpolished, and housed in a silver claw. I almost have to sit on my hands to keep from reaching out and snatching the Stone from around his neck, but I have a suspicion that I want to play out.

He tucks the pendant back into his shirt before continuing to eat, but with less gusto. "I've read what histories I could find on the power of the Stones ... as I'm sure you have as well."

I clench my hands, knowing full well what those texts said, for I have most of the originals in my study. I'm nothing if not thorough when it comes to the last vestiges of magic in Imoria.

"I also have the reports on how you ... wrestled with the power when you first obtained it."

He presses his hand to his chest over the pendant before picking up a mug and taking a large gulp. "I *know* this is the Stone. It was exactly where the ancient texts said it would be." He glances at me with a smirk. "You had people there as well."

I shrug with a smile but say nothing, keeping my face blank. I figured he'd bring this up, but I'm going to wait him out ... see how much he reveals and how much he wants for my breach in our tentative 'peace.' It may have been Luc who killed Erathan's scouts at those caves, but the blame and repercussions fall to me. As it should.

He continues. "It's the correct shape and size, and it even warms at my touch." *This is the Stone. I know it. I just need to access the magic somehow.*

His eyes meet mine. "Your man killed five of my soldiers on Adren soil."

I shrug. "And?"

"And if I didn't need your help, I'd be inclined to do something about it."

I smile, licking honey from my finger. "But you *do* need my help. Besides, hunting the Stone is a dangerous endeavor. It's a life and death matter when it comes to claiming the very last piece of magic in Imoria—maybe in the world."

Once my fingers are clean of honey, I palm my dagger with a lightning quick move, dancing the blade in my left hand. Erathan's eyes pinch slightly, and my smile widens. "My question is, why allow me into your country, your city, your home? And practically empty your castle as well?" I nod at where the pendant sits under his shirt. "Especially since you don't have the power to stop me from taking the Stone from you."

'Calm. I need him.' "Like I said, I need you."

"Why? Say it plainly."

Help me, and we can do great things together. "I would like you to tell me how to access the power of the Heart Stone." *Rydel has more knowledge of the Stones and their power than anyone else in Imoria.*

I smirk. I don't think so. Raising an eyebrow, I go to deny him and 'offer' to just take it from him, but he holds up a hand, shaking his head. "I know what I ask will require something monumental in return. So, I offer you a deeper alliance between our kingdoms. We will share the burden of wielding the last magic of Imoria. Our combined forces will better protect our kingdoms from any invasion from across the sea." *Not that the kingdoms overseas have attacked us in over fifty years.* "And I will grant your ships access to our ports."

Now that is interesting.

He continues, "I will fund the expansion of the spice trade out of Trislen ... sorry, South Leiren, I presume, with only a small percentage of the take in return." I raise an eyebrow, and he taps a finger on the table. "We can work out specifics later."

I remain silent. Picking a green grape off its stem before biting it in half. I chew slowly.

Erathan watches me with a neutral expression, but his thoughts stay focused on his tapping finger. I smile, popping the other half of the grape into my mouth, the skin bursting between my teeth. Mentally, he sighs. *Fine.* "I've even been considering expanding east, seeing what it would take to reclaim part of the Varyen Desert. It's been long enough, and though superstition still exists around the empty lands, I think it's time to expand. And I will share this expansion with you. We can redraw Imoria. You have Leiren and now Trislen ... sorry, South Leiren. Let us bring Imoria together in an alliance under the combined power of the Stones." *Yes, I know.* "I know you want the Heart Stone, but the power comes at a cost, as you well know."

"A cost you have yet to experience."

He frowns. *I'm trying to do what's best for my kingdom, my people.* "Let us share the burden and not throw our kingdoms into any more turmoil."

Very interesting.

I sit back. "But you don't have the power, not yet." Crossing my ankle over my knee, I bring the mug of ale with me. I take a sip as I consider. There are several avenues before me, but which one should I take? I let the silence stretch, relishing the power of my position as Erathan's thoughts once again focus on the food-laden table, his mind solely on the piece of thinly sliced meat he wraps around a piece of melon before taking a slow bite.

The fact he can focus so intently and keep his thoughts from me when he wants, sets my teeth on edge, but I let the silence drag on, keeping my ring on display with little taps of the gold band against the table. I wrap my long fingers around my mug to showcase the stone.

Erathan's eyes flick to my ring before he sits back, his mind mapping the shape and texture of the fake stone. "I heard what you did to Rava's people."

I shrug, popping a date into my mouth, chewing slowly.

"And now that you know the magic is eluding me, you're in the position to take my kingdom, if that's what you wanted."

Again, I shrug, letting my lips pull up into a grin before I take another small sip of ale.

"I'd prefer to keep my throne and for my people to be spared your particular method of conquest."

That draws a laugh from me, and I spin the ring around my finger with my thumb. "It's an effective method."

Erathan watches the ring twirl around my finger before he meets my gaze. "Indeed. But there's another way."

I set the mug on the table, tapping my ring against its rim. "Peace?" The single word comes out on a sneer.

"Yes."

An image slips through his focus, and I see the dagger hidden under the table.

I grin, relaxing back into the cushions before glancing at the spot on the table where the blade hides. "You can try."

He stills, holding his breath. Finally, he sighs and sits back.

I raise the mug again, taking another sip of ale, enjoying the lemon undertone. "Peace, hmm?" His mind settles on the leaves of the vine swaying with the sea breeze, but hope lights up his brain. I drink it in. "Peace is good, but boring."

I lift my dagger, letting it twirl between my fingers, and his eyes and mind follow the fluid movement. His control is ... impressive. Infuriating, but impressive.

I wave a hand at him. "But all things considered, your timing will work in your favor ... for now." I finish the ale and set the mug on the table, sheathing my dagger and folding my hands across my stomach. "I have a lot on my plate right now, and an alliance with Adren will go a long way to stabilizing South Leiren and bringing needed funds into my northern kingdom."

I now rule more than half of Imoria. How ... surreal. A flicker of unease tightens my gut. I can't help but wonder what Luc's reaction is to all this? Our brief correspondences have given me nothing of his thoughts or feelings on the sudden expansion of our kingdom. Knowing him as I do, I'm sure he's frustrated at my brash behavior, but beyond that ...

Erathan takes a bite of bread; the crust crunching between his teeth, his thoughts intent on the slightly sour taste. "I think this will be a great move on both our parts." A thought leaks through. *This will all work out.* "Imoria will prosper like never before."

Erathan's voice raises slightly, and his words come faster. I recognize the ploy for what it is. He's hoping to hide his thoughts. And it ... works. My eyes widen slightly as his thoughts stay hidden behind his stream of words.

"We will be revered the world over. Our legacy will be talked about for centuries. All I'm asking for is help. You have nothing to lose. You have nothing to fear from me, my friend."

Friend. That word burns in my chest. I don't have friends. Just Luc. That's the safest way to live, to win.

I know I'm staring at him, but his control is unlike any I've come up against. All these years, I've thought Erathan uninterested or unwilling to come after the Mind Stone. Has he spent all this time learning and building defenses against my magic?

My dagger twirls again, the movement instinctual, trying to calm my rising fear. What does he really want? Is it as simple as peace?

I still my dagger, leaning forward. "You say I have nothing to lose, that there's nothing for me to fear. But what happens *if* you access the magic?"

He smiles, rubbing a hand over his shaved head. "Once I have the power of the Heart Stone, your Mind Stone will warn you if I intend to alter your feelings—not that I would as your trusted ally."

I nod, forcing my face to stay neutral, swallowing the frown that wants to turn my lips down. He's strong enough to hide his thoughts. Would I be able to see an attack coming?

It doesn't matter. I continue playing my part. Taking a measured breath, I smile. "Then let us ally."

He smiles, genuine and relieved. And that's when his focus cracks, just for a moment. '*Imoria.*'

It's just one word whispered in the back of his mind, but the intent behind it shivers down my spine. He wants Imoria. He wants it all. I down the last of the ale in my mug as he stands. I stay seated, holding up a hand. "But I'll be honest with you, Erathan." Doubt clouds his mind in a yellow fog. "I do not know why the Stone is denying you its power, and I don't know how to access it."

'*Lie!*'

That I hear loud and clear. I smile, hiding my glee under a look of false sympathy. "I'm not lying." He strokes his beard before tugging on one of the small braids in frustration before his thoughts follow the movement of his hand as he tugs the pendant free of his shirt, playing with the small stone between his fingers.

I play with my ring, smiling. "I feel I must warn you."

A frown pulls his brows together, but his mind stays on the pink stone between his fingers.

"The accounts of my initial ... struggles with the Stone are underwhelming. In truth, it was agony. There were times I didn't think I'd survive the magic. And ten years later, I still deal with the power's effects."

His eyes flick to my ring, and a single eyebrow lifts.

"I'm alone, Erathan. Truly alone. It's necessary, lest I go mad."

He chuckles, startling me. "Rydel, I have a feeling you've always been closed off."

I smirk, relaxing slightly. "Fair enough, but understand, I hear thoughts. *All* of them. Especially the ones people don't want me to hear." I don't know why I'm telling him this, but something is slowly unraveling within me as I unburden myself. "I hear the thoughts that have no intent behind them. Hearing someone think that you're weak, or wish you'd just go away, or cringe every time you enter a room tears apart your soul until you're afraid you might not have one any longer." I'm pretty sure I lost my soul long ago. I lift a shoulder, rolling it back with a sigh. "It's painful as fuck."

His face has fallen serious, and his thoughts are clear with the intent for me to hear them. *Magic comes at a cost. Maybe it's too high a price.*

I nod, letting my face fall into a frown, playing the part of martyr to the cruel magic. "I hate the magic, but I LOVE the power. I'll *never* give it up. Just be prepared to experience feelings you don't want to know about. The feelings of your enemies are expected. It's the people you trust, the ones you rely on—It's their thoughts that blind-side you and wound you the most."

My finger traces the scar on my right forefinger as I recall my early years with the Stone. A 'friend,' Dashe, helped Luc and me gain our positions in Ammeryn's army, then the execution of our hostile takeover. Several months after I took the throne, Dashe sat to my left one evening at dinner. We had been drinking, and my buzz was beginning to dull the power of the Stone, dampening the screaming thoughts of everyone around me. I was thinking of retiring for the evening, maybe taking a small pinch of the mind-numbing street drug to help me sleep, when Dashe's drunk thoughts invaded my mind. *'It should have been me. I should be king. I should have the Stone.'* He took a swig of ale, lifting his mug with a smile and a salute as he caught my eye. I knew he was drunk, but his thoughts behind his smile still sliced through my heart. *'He's pretty drunk, and if he takes that drug tonight, it would be so easy to slip into his room, slit his throat, and take the Stone. It would all be mine for the taking.'* The knife in my hand scraped across my plate, slicing into my finger, mimicking the pain in my heart. Hearing a friend's thoughts can be the worst sort of torture. I finished my meal in silence, ignoring my beer before climbing the steps to my rooms. I left my guards explicit instructions to keep everyone out of my rooms, no matter who they were or what they wanted. The next morning, Dashe's drunken thoughts were non-existent. He didn't even remember harboring those thoughts. But I did. And I couldn't let it go. I reassigned Dashe to Joxsis with the excuse that I needed someone I 'trusted' in charge of Leiren's only port city.

Even the smallest of innocent words or thoughts can create a pretty deep fissure in my soul. I don't know how many more cracks I can handle before I shatter.

After that experience, I never used the drug again. I couldn't afford that weakness of temporary oblivion, no matter how much I craved it at times.

I bring myself back to Erathan. "So, if you're sure you're prepared for what the magic will do to you, I have extensive notes on the Stones and their lore, some of which I'm quite sure you do not have. I'm willing to share, in the name of peace."

"Thank you, Rydel."

"In fact, I'll have my library set up for you when you come to Leiren for the winter solstice celebration. You are coming, yes?"

His eyes burn with the desire to go through my library. "I wasn't sure if you were going to hold the celebration this year, what with everything ..."

I grin, relaxing into the cushions. "What better time than now to celebrate?" He warily returns my smile as I take a sip of water before setting the glass back on the table. "I would love to have the famed Adren fire dancers perform at my castle."

He tugs his beard again. "I'll arrange it."

"Excellent!"

We finish our meal over discussions of trade, seasons, the mysteries of the Varyen Desert, and for a short while, I let him drone on about his extensive family legacy. The Bryrel family has ruled Adren for hundreds of years, and Erathan was determined to tell me about each generation. According to him, his family even had natural magic centuries ago. But all the high families claim to have magic in their lineage. It's a hard thing to prove or disprove.

Finally, we move back inside. A scribe is called, and we work for a few hours on the treaty before each signing two identical copies of our agreement, him with his royal ring, me with my fake Mind Stone ring, binding our two kingdoms together, effectively tying Imoria together for the first time in known history.

My heart skips a beat as I sink my ring into the melted wax, and my palms sweat as I step back and clasp Erathan's forearm.

The country is as good as mine.

I send my copy off with a runner to be sent to Luc with a short note from me explaining our new situation. Erathan offers me a room for the night, and it is tempting, or rather, the silence of his castle is tempting. Even though the capital of Trislen—no, South Leiren—is a full day's ride away to the southeast, I decline his offer and step out into the night to a tacked and waiting Kahar. The soldier practically throws the reins at me, and I chuckle as I grab them and swing onto the warhorse's back. Digging my heels in as he rears back, Kahar barely misses clipping the soldier in the face with his hoof.

I turn south, even though my heart pulls me north, toward Luc. I'll spend one more week, two if necessary, in South Leiren making sure everything is fairly settled, and announce the treaty with Adren. Then I'm going home.

I set Kahar at a fast walk through the city, then a bouncy trot through the outskirts. Once we hit open country, I let him open up, and when he reaches top speed, the air whistles past my ears, and I laugh into the wind.

It's a fake. Erathan doesn't have the Heart Stone. He's so sure the power is just being elusive. He's not willing to acknowledge it's not real. It's the size and shape it's supposed to be. It was even hidden where a reliable source led both of us to search. I imagine the warming sensation he feels is just his mind playing into his desperation.

But it's not real. I know the power of the Stone. There's no coaxing it out, no chant or spell. The power owns you as soon as you own the Stone. The Stone is my master much more than I'm its master. The texts never describe the power or even how to use it, but I know, in my soul, that the Heart Stone will work just the same as the Mind Stone. The natural magic of a powerful mage created both Stones over a thousand years ago. Both forms of magic were born from the same source.

My laugh becomes almost manic as Kahar screams across the landscape, the sea rolling and crashing on our right.

It cost me nothing to sign that agreement other than some books and the effort to feed Erathan some convincing false hope. But it gained me quite a bit. I now have access to the riches of Adren's ports, and I have funds to expand the already lucrative spice trade in South Leiren, all without having to take over and restructure yet another kingdom. That will come in time, but right now, I just want to ride and enjoy my time away from the tedious pressures of ruling.

I smile, thinking of Erathan, my new 'ally' who is no longer looking for the Heart Stone because he thinks he has it, as do most magic hunters in Imoria. *And* I walked away knowing that I still hold all the power. The Heart Stone is still out there, it's still in play, and now I'm the only one looking for it.

The note I sent Luc said nothing of the Heart Stone being fake. That's something I want to tell him in person. I want to see his face light up. I want to see him throw back his head with laughter. I want to celebrate with him.

Imoria is ours.

14

'He's going to pay. I've watched. I've waited. I've followed. And now, I will avenge my Queen.'

I'm only two hours from the capital of Trislen—ugh, South Leiren—when the thoughts slide into my mind. My back warms as I glance at the fake ring on my hand. Rolling my eyes, annoyance bunches my already tight muscles. I'm in no mood for a delay. My hands flex as I lean over, patting Kahar's neck. "I'll make quick work of this, my friend. Then we can be on our way. Iyai'ss e'a sire'as urs e'as uhr ra suhnea." *You'll be brushed and fed in no time.* He shakes his head, his long mane tossing through the air as if to tell me to hurry.

I smile as I pull him to a stop and swing to the ground. My feet tingle as I hit the dirt, and I take a moment to shake out the pain in my legs from the long day of riding. I lean against Kahar's side, his warmth penetrating my clothes, adding heat to the already warm day. Palming my dagger, the feel of the hilt is calming as I let it dance in my hand and around my fingers.

I wait.

The voice in my mind gets stronger. 'He will pay. Trislen will rise in remembrance of our great Queen.' I roll my eyes again. His memories reveal him to be a soldier that was stationed in one of the smaller villages of Trislen. When my men showed up, he ran, biding his time.

I see myself in his mind, painted as the villain of his story, something I'm quite used to. His image of me is distorted, my face harsher, and there's almost a shadowy quality to my figure. A word attaches to the image. 'Evil.' My green eyes are black, my hair is greasy. He was nowhere near the palace when I killed Rava, but he's painted his own version of the events. As I stand over Queen Ravaxina's dead body, my crooked grin reveals black teeth behind my sneering lips.

Quite the imagination. This man really hates me.

And then it's all gone, and I find myself watching crashing waves over an endless sea as he readies himself to face me. Too late.

He comes into view. Cresting a small rise, he aims his horse right at me. He's no longer trying to hide, aching to play the valiant knight and challenge the monster who murdered his Queen. He tries to hold on to the image of the sea, but as he draws closer, the sight of me ignites his anger, and a speech that he's obviously put a lot of thought into starts marching through his mind.

'King Rydel. I am Salhin Jum, and I am here to avenge my Queen. Your evil will no longer walk this earth ..."

I remain relaxed against Kahar, shutting out his diatribe as best I can. I've heard such speeches many times. It's like these 'heroes,' full of righteousness and self-importance, all have a script they work off of. I chuckle as I stroke Kahar's muzzle with my free hand, and he snorts, the air puffing against my hand. "I know, my friend. It's absurd."

Salhin draws his horse to a stop several strides away. He drops to the ground and unsheathes his sword as he faces me. He holds his blade steady, and his stance tells me he's well trained, but it won't help him, not against me.

A grin pulls up at my cheeks for a moment, but I quickly smooth my face into a more serious expression, lips pressed together, eyes watching but bored, keeping a casual stance, leaning against Kahar.

He strides toward me with a spin of his sword. "King Rydel. I am—"

My dagger thuds into his stomach, and his practiced speech dies as he stumbles back. I shove off Kahar and sprint across the short distance between us. I'm on him before he's even realized I moved. Gripping the hilt of my dagger, I twist as I knock him onto his back. His head thumps loudly against the rocky ground, and his sword clatters free of his grip. I rip the dagger upward, scraping against ribs, ripping a scream from his throat.

I lean forward, staring into his dying eyes. "I appreciate your loyalty to your Queen, and your speech was, well, I won't lie, it was predictable." His eyes go wide, and then I tear another scream from him as I twist the blade again. "I'm sorry I can't give you the duel you were hoping for. I have a very busy schedule, you see." I slide the dagger from his chest, my thighs warming with his blood before I shift my blade to my right hand and press the tip to his ribs right over his heart. The heels of his boots dig into the ground as he tries to shuffle away, but every movement wrenches his wound and brings out delicious groans of pain. I could get lost in his agony, but I force myself to focus.

I slide the dagger between his ribs, relishing the feel of the blade slipping through skin and muscle and between bone before piercing his heart. His mouth opens on a silent scream, and his back arches before slumping to the ground. Once the spark of life has left his eyes, I stand, wiping my dagger clean on his pants. I give my blade one last twirl before sheathing it and swing back onto Kahar.

"Se'as'r fa." *Let's go.*

I squeeze his sides with my thighs, now sticky as the blood cools, and Kahar leaps into a fast canter. A couple hours later, after passing through the city, Ravaxina's—no, *my* palace looms before me. The guards hail me as I ride through the gates. Stopping at the stables, I swing to the ground with a frown on my face when no one comes to take Kahar. I mean, I get not wanting to come near the warhorse, but still. I expect to be tended to.

The seconds tick by before I lead Kahar into the stable. A mare on the right sticks her head over her stall door, curious, but Kahar's ears flatten against his head as he snaps his teeth at her. She squeals, tossing her head as she backs up, slamming into the back wall of her stall.

I chuckle. "Kahar, iyai'se'a riz ur urr." *You're such an ass.*

He shakes his head, his long mane tossing in the air. I lead him past two empty stalls and put him in the third, giving him some space and keeping him from the other horses. Closing myself in the stall with him, I remove his bridle, reaching over the door to hang it from a hook. My fingers slide between leather and his sweaty hide to loosen the girth with a tug. I grab the saddle and blanket together, letting it slide from his back before hooking it over my left forearm. I toss it onto the stall door, horse hair sticking to my skin.

The wood handle of a coarse brush fits perfectly in the curve of my palm, and I get lost in the gentle strokes as I brush Kahar down. I press deeply against the sweaty marks where the saddle blanket sat on his back, where the girth wrapped under his belly, and where the leather of his bridle sat behind his ears and over his muzzle.

Kahar's tail swishes, slapping me now and then, but his head is low, and I almost chuckle when I notice his bottom lip is drooping. I've almost put the fearsome warhorse to sleep. Setting the brush down, I pat his neck, whispering, "Ras iye'as niy suhe'ars." *Not yet, my friend.*

I grab a pick, standing shoulder to shoulder with Kahar before I bend down, pressing my fingers into the soft flesh at the base of his hoof as I push my elbow into the crook of his knee. "Don't maul me like you did to Luc or ra suhrre'as as iyai." *No dinner for you.*

The threat is empty, and I'm pretty sure he knows it, but he calmly lifts his hoof, and I go about cleaning it, then the other three without incident.

Tossing the brush and pick in a bucket outside the door, I pat Kahar and run my hands through his thick mane. "Don't tell Luc, but I think you might be my favorite horse now." His head turns, pushing me slightly with the side of his face. "Okay, okay. I'll get your dinner."

I push out of the stall, scooping feed into a bucket, inhaling the sweet scent of molasses and oats. Hooking the bucket to a peg inside the stall door, I grab the large pail, the metal handle cold against my flesh. Stepping out the back doors of the stables, I set the pail down and watch the splash of clean water as I pump it from the well.

The bucket is so large, I have to lift it with both hands, my forearms and shoulders heaving, but I haul it to Kahar's stall. I set it down, swing the door open, place the bucket inside, and with a last pat, I leave Kahar to his evening.

This was nice. Time to myself. Menial tasks that busy my hands while clearing my head.

I lean over each stall I pass on the way out, making sure they are clean and that the horses have water. Satisfied, I leave the stables and head to the palace. It's been almost an hour since I arrived, and I never saw a stable hand. It's a small thing, but I'll have to get that sorted.

Soldiers and servants salute and bow as I pass through the halls. When I come to the stairs that lead to Ravaxina's—damn it, no—to my rooms, I stop a servant coming down the steps with arms laden with linens.

"Have a meal sent to my rooms."

He nods, ducking his head as he finishes descending the stairs and hurries down the hall.

I push into my rooms, my boots thudding on the dark wood floor as I pull my shirt from my pants and over my head. I'm toeing off my boots when a knock sounds at my door.

"Enter."

Renna comes in, leaving the door open, standing at attention right inside the doorway. I manage to hold back my smile as her eyes flick to my bare chest, admiring the scrolling tattoo over my left chest and shoulder before snapping her gaze to the middle distance. But her aversion is out of respect, not embarrassment or arousal. She prefers women, appreciating the male form, though it does nothing for her. "Your Majesty, welcome back."

I run a hand through my hair, noticing it's getting too long for my liking as the dirty-blond strands fall well past my shoulders. "Update."

"The transition is moving fairly smoothly, all things considered. There's still the occasional push-back among the soldiers, but nearly all are just happy to have a job and have jumped back into work. The citizens have settled. The slums are still occasionally looting, and we've had several requests from the high families to, and I quote, 'curb the lowlife violence'."

I smirk. "How many civilian deaths?"

"Eighty three."

I spy a glass with a light blue liquid in it on my bedside table. Another tonic from the healer, if I were to guess, but I won't drink it until I know for sure. I haven't made it this far by making stupid mistakes.

"Keep an eye on the situation, but allowing the people to have a little push-back is good. It makes the lower populace feel powerful, if even for a moment." I know this from first-hand experience. It always comes back to hope. And I *love* crushing it. "We'll handle it if it gets any worse."

"Yes, your Majesty."

"Where are the stable hands?"

A frown pulls at her lips. "I'm sorry, your Majesty. I didn't think. The stable master died last night—A nasty fall from a new stud. His sons run the stables, but the funeral was today. I didn't think to find replacements for the day."

I wave a hand. "Don't worry about it."

An old man with dark wrinkled skin, short silver hair, and slightly cloudy brown eyes, sticks his head around the corner of the door. "Excuse me, ma'am." Reena steps out of the way as the man shuffles into the room carrying a tray of food. A small boy with pale skin follows on his heels, carrying a pitcher and a mug. The old man bows. "Where would you like to dine, your Majesty?"

I glance around, pointing at the small table with three chairs in front of the large windows of the sitting area. "There."

The tray clinks against the wood as he sets it down. He turns, taking the mug and pitcher from the boy, setting them down as well. "Trislenian, I mean South Leiren wine, your Majesty. But I can get anything else you'd like."

"No, that's fine."

I quickly sift through their thoughts to check my meal while the man and boy bow before shuffling quickly out the door.

I want nothing more than to change out of these ruined pants. I cross the room and pull out a chair, but remain standing, not wanting to sit in my bloody, sticky clothes.

"Where's Runic?"

"He's attending the horse master's family."

I take a bite of bread, the flavor slightly sweet and so different from the malty bread of the north. "Any news from Leiren?"

She reaches into her pocket, holding out a crumpled letter. "Only that captain Lucaryn has everything well in hand."

I take the paper, turning my back on Reena to stride toward the windows. As I open the single folded sheet of paper, a waft of petrichor, Luc's scent of rain on dust, reaches my nose and my shoulders slump.

> *Your Majesty,*
> *All is well in Leiren. Applications are filing in for vendors*
>   *and entertainers to set up at the solstice celebration.*
> *The first of the soldiers from South Leiren arrived yesterday*
>   *and are finding their place amongst our ranks. Fresh*
>   *soldiers from the north should reach you a few days*
>   *after this letter.*
> *The taxes from the south-east villages were short, so I've*
>   *sent a collector to assess the situation and collect the*
>   *necessary coin or commodity.*
> *Your kingdom will be here when you return.*
> *Captain Lucaryn*

I take a sip of the wine, tasting chocolate, oak, anise, and cherries. My kingdom awaits me. Lucaryn is waiting for me, probably to yell at me for invading a kingdom without him.

I smile, looking forward to seeing him again, even if we fight ... at first.

My smile falls to a neutral expression as I turn back around, setting Luc's letter on the table. I nod at Reena. "When you report to Runic, tell him to come see me in the morning."

"Yes, your Majesty."

"I'm going to make an announcement tomorrow, so prepare the

scribes, runners, and bird master. There's going to be a bit more shifting here in South Leiren." Her lips press together, and I smile. "For the better, I assure you."

She nods, dipping her head.

I spear a greasy piece of meat with my fork and take a bite. It's slightly chewy, and it squeaks between my teeth, but at least it's flavorful, several spices dancing across my tongue.

"You're dismissed."

Without another word, Reena turns, leaving the room and closing the door quietly behind her. Looking around at the sun-soaked room, I take in the neutral tones of wood and cream linens interrupted by bright pops of green, orange, red, and yellow. This room, this palace, does not feel like me, and I can't imagine spending a lot of time here in the south once things settle. I might just make this my Summer Palace. Make the trip for the summer solstice, but otherwise, my castle in the north will be the seat of power for all of Leiren.

I finish the meal, refill my mug with wine, and grab Luc's letter before heading to the washroom. Setting the mug on the marble counter, I undo my pants, shoving them to my ankles, kicking them free. There's no shower, but the bath is filled, and when I dip a finger in the water, I find it warm. I press my palm to the outside of the tub and heat tingles against my skin. Leaning down, I see a bed of coals under the tub, glowing red, their heat shimmering in waves against the bottom of the tub. Smart.

I slide into the tub with a groan, resting my head against the raised back. I close my eyes, letting my muscles relax one by one, one hand floating along the top of the water. Keeping my eyes closed, I bring the letter to my face, taking a deep breath, drawing the comfort of Luc's scent into my lungs. It's faint, but enough to conjure his smiling face to my mind.

I place the letter on the ledge before taking a breath and sliding under the water. The world goes quiet. Blissfully silent.

Stars dance behind my closed eyelids before I push up, inhaling deeply. I shove my hair out of my face and grab the bar of soap sitting on a ledge to my right next to the letter. I clean quickly, dunking myself under the water for another long moment before standing, stepping out, and drying myself off, grabbing the letter on the way out.

I pad naked to the bedroom, throwing back the covers. I climb into the bed, laying on my back, propping my arm behind my head so I can watch the setting sun through the glass doors that lead to a small balcony.

I read the letter again, practically hearing Luc's voice in the written words. I miss him, and it's thoughts of his warm, brown skin, and bright blue eyes that lull me to sleep. My dreams are calm, just Luc and me. No magic, no Stones, no kingdoms. Just us. I let myself sink into the dream.

The fantasy of Luc's strong arm banding my waist, his warm breath fanning my cheek, blooms in my dream as we spend hours in my bed reminiscing about the years we lived in that abandoned bookbinding store. He props himself up on an elbow, running his hand up my arm, my muscles flexing, my skin pebbling under his touch. He presses a kiss to my shoulder before leaning over, lips brushing against my ear, whispering, "It's time to get up." He raps his knuckles against the headboard, and I frown at him as he says, "Your Majesty," knocking his knuckles against the headboard again.

My eyes peel open, shifting slightly to try and subdue my painfully hard erection. I blink as the late morning sun streams through the glass doors right into my eyes. The knocking on my door continues, and Runic's muffled voice calls from the other side of the door. "Your Majesty. I'm sorry to wake you, but I've received some information you need to be aware of."

I grumble as I push myself up, wrinkling my nose at the faint rose scent that Rava loved so much. The smell still clings to the sheets. That sickly-sweet scent is enough to wilt my erection. "Give me a minute." The knocking stops, and I stand, ripping the bedding from the mattress before crossing to the double doors, flinging them open to air out the room.

I pull on a clean pair of dark-brown pants, a cream sleeveless shirt, and my leather chest harness, securing my throwing knives. My fingers absently buckle my thigh sheath in place, and I call out as I lower myself to a chair in the sitting area, shoving my foot into a boot. "Come in."

Runic strides in, a few pieces of paper in his hand. I pull on my other boot and stand. Runic opens his mouth, but I hold up a hand, walking across the room. A guard salutes as I poke my head out the door. "Coffee. I need coffee."

She bows, her long black hair that's pulled back in a neat tie, falls over her shoulder. As she stands, flicking her hair down her back, she nods. "I'll have it brought up immediately."

Turning back into my rooms, I sit in the same chair, letting the warmth of the sun hit my back. I wave a hand at Runic. "Okay."

He shifts from foot to foot, glancing between the papers in his hand and me. "Well, um." His forefinger flips through the papers in a nervous gesture. "Apparently, Queen Ravaxina has a distant cousin, many times removed. He lives in Eshena across the eastern sea."

I've heard of Eshena but know little about it. If I recall, it's a small kingdom in a large country with dozens of kingdoms. I reach out as a servant comes in, walking quietly around Runic. I take the porcelain cup, breathing in the deep coffee scent, before taking a sip. It's strong and hot and just what I need. The servant places a carafe on the table next to me and leaves without a word.

After another sip, I tilt my head. "And why do I care about this distant cousin?"

Runic glances at the papers again before meeting my gaze, his brown eyes filled with uncertainty. "He is claiming the right to the Trislenian throne. He has demanded you step down and take your army and leave Trislen. Or else, he claims he will bring the might of Eshena and take his throne from you."

15

I almost spill my coffee as I throw my head back and laugh. Runic relaxes as my laughter dies off, and I grin, topping up my cup. "Even if this cousin had left last week, he wouldn't arrive for another month, at least." I frown. "Which begs the question, how did he find out so quickly? How did the message arrive?"

"Sea bird."

I tap my ring on the cup in thought. "Messenger sea birds are rare. Still, for word to get to him and then for him to respond and send this message ... someone here is feeding him information."

"It would seem so, your Majesty."

I take a slow sip of coffee, thinking it through. Should I take the time to ferret out the person or persons in league with this cousin? Even if I found them and eliminated them, Rava's cousin would still be able to get information on what is happening in Trislen. Information can always be bought. Everyone has a price. The real question is, will a resistance rise up in his name? Have they already started? Probably. It's what I'd do.

"Keep a watch out for secret gatherings. Post a soldier at every messenger station."

Runic's brows furrow.

"Yes, every single one. I'm not going to make this easy for them. I want every message coming and going to be monitored."

Privately owned messenger birds are becoming more common, but sea birds capable of traversing the eastern sea are very expensive and much rarer.

"Send word to the Shadow Lord. Don't tell him the details, though he might already know." I'm amazed at the information Kafir is able to scrape up. "Just have him look for more than the usual activity from overseas, or secret gatherings or rumblings of insurrection. Even if they're not coming from Eshena, it's good to know if people are thinking of rising against me."

Runic nods. "If the cousin *does* follow through, how do you think he'll try to invade?"

I rub the cup between my palms. "The eastern sea is vast and not easily crossed, especially at this time of year with the winter storms and ice flows. Then there's the Varyen Desert. It's the most direct route but getting an army across the scorching sand dunes that turn freezing at night is a feat very few have accomplished. Going through the mountains is ... impossible."

Runic frowns. "He could sail around."

I tap my finger against the cup again, the metal of the ring clinking softly. "Even if he sailed all the way around the south of Imoria, that would add another month, figuring conservatively. Then he would have to find a place to dock, and with my new alliance with Erathan, I have every port along the entire western coastline of Imoria covered. I mean, he can try—"

"Alliance?"

I smirk, crossing an ankle over my knee. "King Erathan and I have signed an alliance." Runic's brows rise, showcasing the scar slicing his right eyebrow in half. "I won't bore you with the details, but it works in our favor. Very much in our favor."

My grin spreads, and Runic smiles in return. "Shall I gather the scribes and runners?"

There's a bit of surprise in Runic's thoughts that I would agree to an alliance. I smile, following his thoughts and agreeing, "Yeah, I'm usually more prone to violence and displays of power." I sweep my arm around the room suggestively. "But trust me, this was the best course of action."

"I'm sure it was, your Majesty." He chuckles. "The scribes?"

"Reena is taking care of that. I'll outline the basics of the treaty, and we can have runners and birds on their way before lunch." My ring clinks against the cup again. "Have our spies that are still in the capital report here after lunch. I'll send a few to Eshena via the next ship leaving Adren, and we should put some eyes on the Varyen Desert passes, just in case."

Runic clasps his hands behind his back, papers and all. "May I suggest you send your ... hmm"—he gestures between himself and me—"your more light-skinned spies."

I tilt my head in question. He shrugs. "I actually have a relative, Eraln Vranna, who lives in Alara." He pauses, and when I don't respond, he continues. "Alara is the kingdom bordering the south of Eshena. Erlan doesn't see many dark-skinned people over there, and those few she does are usually servants." He grimaces. "Or slaves."

I frown, unable to imagine living somewhere where everyone has the same skin color. How boring. How unfortunate. But I nod. "This Erlan, do you speak often?"

Runic frowns. "I haven't heard from her in a few years, but she'd be happy to hear from her favorite nephew." I raise an eyebrow, and he shrugs. "Okay, her only nephew, but still." He crosses the room, rifling through stacks of papers before pulling a map out, using his palms to flatten it on the desk. I cross the room to stand on the other side of the desk as he runs a finger across the eastern sea to Alara. He keeps his eyes on the map as his finger traces north. "My aunt lives within a two-day ride to the capital of Eshena. She could provide our spies with a base of operation and help them get the lay of the land. I can draft a coded letter of introduction for your spies to take with them."

I set the empty cup on the table, slapping my thighs before standing. "Done." I crack my back, pressing my hands to the base of my spine. "I'm going back to Leiren in a week."

Runic shakes his head. "Calling Trislen 'South Leiren' is going to take a while to get used to."

I nod with a smile. "Is there anything pressing or of concern that I should address before I leave?"

Runic takes a moment to think before he shakes his head. "Nothing off the top of my head, but I'll compile a list for you to review in a few days. I think we have everything well in hand, considering."

"How *is* the Shadow Lord's operation doing?"

He shrugs. "Business as usual. The fighting rings are seeing more than the usual action, and we have had no run-ins with the enforcers. Kafir seems to have abided by his word and shut that part of his operation down."

I nod, heading out of the room, Runic on my heels. As we walk down the long staircase, I say, "I need to meet with the trade council. My new agreement with Erathan gives us free access to all the Adren ports, so we will need to make adjustments accordingly."

Runic's eyes go wide. "What did we have to give up for that?"

I chuckle. "Nothing, Runic. Absolutely nothing."

I've spent the last week shifting details to take full advantage of our alliance with Adren. South Leiren will increase the spice production for the harvest this coming spring, then will up production even more through the summer. That will allow us to charge premium prices to ship our spice during the winter months.

We're working on a route that Lieren's can use to travel between the north and south of our kingdom that isn't too intrusive through Adren.

I also had the throne removed from the palace and repurposed the space into a second, large dining hall for the 1st unit similar to what I have set up in Leiren. Now, the 1st unit of my South Leiren army has the same dining benefit as my Sagas back in the North.

With the southern throne gone, I've officially established my seat of power in the North. That is where I will rule my territory. Eventually, when I've conquered Adren, it too will be absorbed as West Leiren.

All in good time.

Runic and Reena have things well in hand, and the members of my southern court have their orders. Knowing that they are too afraid of me to betray me, I feel reasonably confident about leaving and returning home—at least until after the winter solstice. I'm not naïve enough to believe there won't be acts of rebellion once I leave, but Runic and my Southern army will keep things in relative order. I'll come back south after the celebration if necessary.

I take the reins from Reena, giving Kahar a pat, earning an angry stomp from the warhorse. "Sar's e'a ra rais. Ze'a'se'a fauhr anea." *Don't be so sour. We're going home.*

I swing onto his back, his hooves clomp loudly against the cobblestones as he prances in place. Gathering the reins, I look down. Reena backs up several paces, giving Kahar room as he does a small buck, hopping in a tight circle. My thighs squeeze his sides. "Saz e'auhr ur urr." *Stop being an ass.*

Reena jumps back as Kahar kicks his back legs, and I grin. "Reena, I'm trusting you to keep things in order. Runic has a lot on his shoulders, and you are to help him however he needs."

She nods. "Yes, your Majesty." *'This is such a big opportunity. I will be captain some day.'*

I like her ambition. Swiveling my head, I look over my other shoulder to keep Reena in view as Kahar spins again. "We have the runners and birds in place. Keep me constantly informed. I want to be annoyed by the amount of messages you send." She nods, returning my smile, but it quickly falls from my face. "And you know what to do if there is trouble."

She nods again. Her orders are to act swiftly and without mercy. It's the Leiren way. It's my way. A frown pulls at her lips. "Your Majesty, can I not persuade you to take an escort with you? Even just two soldiers? You traveling on your own, your Majesty... I don't think..."

I'm shaking my head with a grin before she can finish, and she snaps her mouth closed. "I'll be fine, Reena. I enjoy traveling alone." I tap my temple. "Less noisy." Though, I promised Luc I'd be more careful. But it's over a week of travel to the north, and I just can't pass up the opportunity to find some peace during that time.

Her face relaxes, and pity fills her large eyes. I hate that look. I wield the magic of the Mind Stone, and yes, it can be burdensome, but I wouldn't trade the pain and intrusive thoughts for all the gold in the world. The pain equates to power, and the power is mine.

Turning from her annoyingly empathetic look, I pull Kahar around, aiming him out of the courtyard and into the wealthy section of the city. Sparks kick up from Kahar's metal shoes as he prances through the streets, flattening his ears against his head at anyone he thinks is too close, which seems to be everyone.

I leave the city through the western gates, avoiding the slums. It's not as direct, but this way gets me into open country much faster. And as soon as we hit dirt—patchy grass spreading around us, the expanse dotted with trees—I let Kahar have his head.

As his mane whips me in the face and my hair streams behind me, I think of Luc. We've been exchanging regular correspondence since I took the Trislenian throne. One such letter sits in my pocket, the rest tucked into my pack. Like my habit of playing with my dagger, I've taken to unfolding and folding Luc's letters to the point the papers are practically disintegrating.

As Kahar settles into a steady rhythm, I recall Luc's words in his latest letter.

> *Your Majesty,*
> *All is fairly quiet here in the North. The surviving soldiers*
> *returned from the mountain trial a few days ago. Eleven*
> *dead. The one you sent to re-run the trial actually*
> *survived and has been training extra hours since his*
> *return.*

I could practically hear the amusement in the words, and each time I read them, I smiled.

> *I'm continuing to recover from the poison, feeling stronger*

every day, though I wish vengeance was dealt by my
own hand.

The ink was darker over that sentence, and I felt his rage in the words he didn't say. He's furious that I went off on my own. He's furious at himself for being caught off guard and taking that arrow.

All the high families in North and South Leiren have been
sent invitations to the solstice celebration.
I've set aside time to discuss and arrange further shifts as
we continue to integrate Trislen, as well as what needs
to be addressed with our alliance with Erathan.
There's a lot to talk about.
Captain Lucaryn

Those last few short sentences were concise and informative, but I could read between the lines. He's outraged that I ordered him to stay back home. I'm not sure how much of that rage has died down in the past few weeks, but if he's still angry with me when I get home ... a smile pulls up my lips. I will let him take his anger out on me, gladly.

I skirt a small town, keeping Kahar a mile outside the edge of the outermost houses, avoiding the thoughts and images of the residents, and as the town shrinks behind me, the sun reaches the top of the sky.

Leather creaks in my hands as I pull the reins back, slowing Kahar to a walk, aiming him slightly to the east. A long while later, the forest thickens, the foothills come into view, and we stop at a stream that flows from the river that is fed by the snows of the Imorain mountains far to the north.

"Se'as, Kahar." *Rest, Kahar.* My palms press to this coat, the hairs somehow both rough and soft as I stroke his neck. He dips his head, slurping water from the shallow stream. Bending over, cool water flows over my fingers. Cupping my hand, I scoop water up before I let it drip between my fingers.

I imagine bringing my wet hands to Luc's face, pressing my thumb between his brows, smoothing the scowl from his face, watching the water cling to his brown skin, holding on at his chin like it can't bear to let him go. I know the feeling. My imagination paints a sly smile on his face as he shakes his head with exasperation—a gesture I know well, the one that says he wants to stay mad at me, but can't.

I smile into the water, reaching down to untie my boots when Kahar's head jolts upright and pain erupts across the left side of my back. A quick glance reveals an arrow shaft sticking out of my shoulder.

Shit.

16

The sound of running feet erupts through the woods as a cacophony of thoughts bounce around in my mind.

Fucking great.

Six men break through the trees, and Kahar spins, lunging before me, rearing back, pawing his front hooves at them. One man is not fast enough and catches a hoof to the shoulder, which spins him and knocks him back several steps. I draw my sword, but the action feels slow, like I'm moving through sand.

Shit. Poison or paralytic?

I deflect a downward swing but catch a blade on my right arm. I flick a throwing knife at a man on my left, and it sinks into his right eye. His scream bellows between the trees as he falls, gripping the knife, blood slicking between his fingers.

Kahar lunges between me and another man, slamming his giant head into the man's chest. The warhorse earns a shallow slash across his front shoulder, but he pins his ears back, snapping and kicking at anyone who comes close.

I duck and sidestep two more attacks, hearing their moves in my mind before they make them, but their mental voices are growing quieter, and I feel myself getting slower. As two men lunge at me, three advance on Kahar, who turns, fast as lightning, and kicks his back legs out, snapping them at full extension, keeping the men at a distance.

The man closest to me, his long blond hair pulled back into a knot, a jagged scar cleaving across his left cheek and down his neck, calls out. "Kill the horse. Take the king."

My heart rate spikes, speeding the spread of whatever coats the arrow.

"Kahar, sa'ase'aus!" *Kahar, retreat!* I jump back to avoid a blade, and Kahar unleashes one more kick with his hind legs before he takes off through the trees.

"Leave it." The blond's orders keep the three from chasing down Kahar, not that they could.

I flick two more throwing knives, one finding its mark in the throat of one man, but the other flies wide. I try to sort through their thoughts, but it sounds like I'm trying to listen to a conversation from under water.

I catch the glint of a sword a split-second before it falls, giving me time to raise my blade, but the blow knocks it out of my hands. I stagger back, landing against the trunk of a tree, my shoulder screaming in protest as the arrow shaft catches on a low-hanging branch.

The blond, who seems to be the leader, gestures to the man on his left. "Tie him up." He's smaller than the leader, but their coloring and features are so similar they must be related.

I sway, stumbling a little more than needed to hide my left hand gripping my dagger. The smaller blond steps forward with a sneer. I want to sneer back, but I keep my face relaxed and my eyes listless. He draws near, bringing the stench of sweat and unwashed bodies with him. Air rushes from my chest as he lands a punch to my gut, but that puts him right in my face.

"Mistake," I whisper in his ear as I slide my dagger between his ribs. I twist the blade before shoving him to the ground.

"Killan!" The big blond rushes forward, kneeling at the dead man's side. He grips my dagger, pulling it from the body, knuckles white around the hilt as his blue eyes rise to mine.

I lift my arms from my sides with a grin. The two remaining men move to charge me, but the big blond holds up a hand, stopping them. With a deep breath that expands his broad chest, he commands, "Just take him down."

"You can try." I feel the drug or poison pulling at my strength, and he shrugs, tucking my dagger into a sheath on his chest, and I nod at it. "I'm going to take that back from your cold, dead body."

I fall to one knee, the edges of my vision going dark, and he smirks. "How the mighty Rydel has fallen." The three men chuckle as the leader grips my left hand, pulling the ring from my finger, slipping it onto his own.

I want to laugh at his false triumph, but my body isn't cooperating. I fall onto my side, oddly noticing the tickle of leaves against my face before fists and boots rain down on my body. Darkness closes in around me, and my mind goes blessedly blank.

I know I'm dreaming because Luc is here, and he's in my bed. His fingers comb through my hair, and I sigh. His voice is soft, close. "What trouble have you gotten yourself into?" I shrug, not willing to think about it. "You should get up."

"But it's so quiet here."

"I know, but—"

Cutting him off, I give his head a little shove, and he smirks at me before kissing his way down my chest, fingers trailing lightly over my skin. My cock twitches as it rubs against the short hairs of Luc's beard. I press my head into the bed as his lips close around my shaft, and he sucks me into the heat of his mouth until I hit the back of his throat. Our moans float through the air, and I buck my hips, making him take me deeper.

"Fuck, Luc. You feel so good. I've wanted you for so long. Don't stop."

He pulls back, his teeth scraping my flesh with a delicious bite of pain before he licks me like I'm his favorite treat. But when he looks up at me, he's frowning. "Ry, you're in trouble. You need to wake up."

I grip his hair, trying to shove him back down, but he vanishes, appearing at the side of the bed. He leans down, pressing his lips to my forehead. "You need to wake up. You need to come home."

I groan in frustration, screwing my eyes tighter as pain flares in my back ... my arm, my face, my ribs. Luc's voice whispers across the shell of my ear. "Remember, you were strong before the Stone."

I don't know what that has to do with anything, but I want to call out as his touch fades, the darkness recedes, and consciousness returns with a deep sucking sensation.

The chill in the air, as well as the lack of light beyond my closed eyelids tells me it's night. My body feels stiff, and pain blooms in ever-increasing intensity from the beating these men must have continued to give me after I passed out.

But for some reason, I'm alive.

I reach for the magic, waiting for the heat in my back and the invasion of the thoughts of my captors, but the heat doesn't come. The woods are quiet around me, and that silence extends into my mind.

I jolt, finding my arms and legs bound, pain pulling at my muscles. I force myself to keep my breathing even as I work myself into a sitting position. A quick glance reminds me my ring is gone, as are all my weapons, including my dagger. Adrenaline rises, filling me with comforting rage. I shift and roll awkwardly until I find a rock sharp enough to saw slowly through the ropes around my wrists. My skin rubs raw, then bleeds with every pass of the ropes over the rock until finally, my arms are free. My numb fingers fumble at the ties at my ankles, and once I'm free, I lean against a tree, the rough bark pressing painfully into my skin, grounding me.

The ache in my shoulder terrifies me, and I'm afraid to reach back, but I grit my teeth, pressing my fingers to the gaping wound the arrow left behind. The arrow is gone. So is the Stone. The bleeding wound is right over my scar. What a fucking lucky shot. If they'd just left the arrow, they never would have found the Mind Stone.

Fuck that. I took it once, I'll take it again.

Pressing a hand to the tree at my back, I grunt, standing as I look around. I have no idea how long I've been out, and Kahar is nowhere in sight. The bright light of the large mother moon filters through the trees and I notice the ground around me is disturbed from my fight with my attackers, but as I work my way to the outer edges of the evidenced struggle, I find a few small drops of blood and several sets of boot prints leading north.

I pick up my pace, heading north then turn slightly west as the trail of my prey angles decidedly toward Farden.

Ignoring the aching in my ribs, I roll my shoulders, missing the warm tingle of power in my back as the arrow wound burns over my shoulder blade. I slide my hand into my pocket, not knowing what to do with my hands without my dagger. Without the Stone and my blade, I feel naked, on edge ... angry. I'm so gods damned angry.

Clenching and unclenching my hands, I start to jog as the surrounding trees thin out. The soft tread of my boots and the occasional scurry of night creatures are the only sounds that reach my ears.

It's too quiet. I swivel my head side-to-side, waiting for some unknown foe to spring at me from the shadows without the warning of my stolen magic.

I'm not sure if Kahar's in range, but I let loose three short, shrill whistles. I keep walking, repeating the whistles again after a few minutes.

I resign myself to tracking the thieves on foot, but the faint sound of thundering hooves brings a smile to my face. I whistle again just as I break from the woods, and Kahar canters toward me from the south like a shadow of death through the night. He slows to a trot before reaching me, tossing his head, his reins torn from where he stepped on them.

I reach out a hand, patting his shoulder, careful of the thin cut that's bleeding down his leg. "Se'ausiy, Kahar." *Steady, Kahar.* I lean into his warmth, moving with his breaths. "We have enemies to hunt." He huffs, pawing the ground. "Ze'a zuhss se'asuhe'as se'an se'aus." *We will deliver them death.*

The scent of leather wafts down my nose as I flip up the flap of a saddlebag, rooting around until I find the small coil of thin rope I use to make snares. Unfastening the broken reins from Kahar's bridle, I thread the thin rope through the rings. These makeshift reins will tear my hands to shreds, so I retrieve my gloves from the other saddlebag.

Kahar's ears flick, and I swing onto his back, grunting with the pain. We head west, following the trail of my prey ... a few boot prints, snapped branches, crushed grass. My back aches with tension as, for almost an hour, I lose the trail, but a few drops of blood on the rocky path sets me on their heels again.

The ground is hard, the grass stiff with frost. The sky has lightened from midnight black, to deep purple, to smoky blue. The sun is on its way, and the bleating of sheep greets me. I jerk in the saddle in shock as a boy and his flock approach us. I didn't *hear* him. The only sounds spilling through my head are the sheep, the soft tinkling of a bell around one of their necks, and Kahar's snorting breaths. I should feel relief at the absence of pain and intrusive thoughts, but my lungs burn and my skin feels too tight as unease courses through me.

The boy directs the sheep off the road, skirting around Kahar and me.

I pull Kahar to a halt, leaning down toward the boy. "Have you seen three men come this way?"

His eyes widen as he takes in my bruised face and dirty clothes before he glances north, then back at me. "Lots a folks been coming this way, especially with solstice comin."

I scratch my beard, Kahar prancing in place under me. "They might have been in a hurry, maybe a little roughed up?"

He bites his lip. "I mighta seen who ya lookin for, about a day ago. They passed through the village headin' north. Overheard 'em saying something about getting to the capital before solstice."

I nod toward the supposed village hidden over a small rise in the landscape. "What village is that?"

The boy startles, but smiles. "Fairlond, sir."

I nod back with a smile of my own, kicking Kahar into an easy canter. Fairlond. We are only a few miles from the southern border of

Leiren. I lean over Kahar's neck. "We'll clean up real quick and get something to eat before we continue the hunt."

I could easily eat on the road, but Kahar needs fuel. He pulls at the short rope, trying to take control. "E'auriy, Kahar." *Easy, Kahar.* "Not too much. Not yet. Pace yourself."

He tosses his head again, but settles into a steady canter, steam rising off his warm body, shrouding me, and I imagine we look like a specter from hell as the sun crests the horizon, painting us with streamers of red and gold.

I grin, patting his neck. "E'ass asre'a." *Hell horse.*

17

The village is small; the houses spread out with a small cluster of businesses in the center. I quickly clean myself from a pump in someone's yard, scooping water into my hand and wiping the dirt and blood from my skin. I wash and tend to Kahar's wound as well, relieved the cut is not too deep.

Leading Kahar down the dirt road, I spy a wood sign with an anvil. I search for the thoughts of whomever might be inside, pausing with a start as I remember I no longer have the magic. I'm going to have to go in blind.

I duck my head as I pass through the open door, the heat of the forge hitting me in the face, drying out my eyes. Blinking several times, it takes me a moment to find the man in the back corner digging through what looks like a toolbox.

His blond hair is pulled back away from his angular face, his sleeveless shirt revealing arms roped with muscle, his skin shiny with sweat. He doesn't lift his head as his voice carries across the open space between us.

"I'll be right with ya."

I use the delay to take in the rest of the building, which is nothing more than one large open room. The forge glows red-hot against the back wall, several anvils stand around it, and three large drums of what I assume is water stand near the anvils. My boots scuff the dirt floor as I move to stand before one of the four open windows that run down the sides of the building. The slight winter breeze doesn't do much to alleviate the heat, but it's something.

The blacksmith turns, glancing at me before setting a tool on a table next to the forge.

"How can I help ya?"

He either doesn't recognize me, or he's pretending not to know who I am. I have no idea which. "I'm in need of a set of reins."

He leans to the side, looking out the door behind me, before smiling. "For that giant warhorse out there? You been ridin him with"—he glances out at Kahar again—"rope?"

I shrug, trying to keep the tension of not being able to hear his thoughts from my muscles. My speech easily slides into the cadence from my childhood spent on the streets. "Gotta do what ya gotta do."

He chuckles, turning to walk to the far wall on the left. As he bends over to rifle through a large wood box, I can't help but appreciate the way his back muscles flex beneath his shirt, and the backs of his legs ripple under his tight-fitting pants. He stands, striding over with a set of thick leather reins in his hand.

"They're used, but that means the leather's been broke in. They won't last more than a season, especially with a horse like that, but they're cheap and a far sight better than that rope."

I take the reins with a nod, appreciating the soft slide of the leather against my fingers. "Do ya happen to have any horse feed, or know of somewhere I can buy some? He could use a meal before I move on."

He nods, walking past me out the front door, and I follow. We round the building to a small shed in the back. The door creaks as he swings it open, and he disappears inside.

As I wait for him to come back out, I look around at the small houses, the open space between them, the naked trees ready for the first snow. It's ... so quiet. I know there are people in their homes and the businesses crowded in the center of town, but I don't know how many there are, and what they're thinking.

I nearly jump out of my skin, and my head whips around as the blacksmith shuts the door behind him with a great screech. I hadn't heard him come out. Gods, this is exhausting.

He shoves a bag into my arms. I shift the slight weight, and the smell of molasses hits me. As we walk back around to the front, he shakes his head at Kahar, who snorts at him. "That won't be much for a beast that size, but it's somethin."

I set the bag down on the ground with a thud and pull Kahar's bridle off before opening the sack of feed and rolling the top back. It's probably less than two pounds, but like the man said, it's something.

As I work at replacing the reins on the bridle, I describe the men I'm looking for, but he shakes his head. "Can't say I've seen anyone like that, but I'm in my shop most of the time. I'd go see Lina at the tavern. She knows everything and everyone in this village."

I pay him from the stash of coins I have hidden in Kahar's saddlebags, noticing Kahar has already finished his meal. Chuckling, I walk in the direction the blacksmith points me, Kahar following along like a puppy ... a giant puppy who pins his ears back at anyone who gets too close.

No one seems to recognize me, which is just fine with me. I'm on edge, and passing through with some anonymity has its benefits. Still, I can't keep from swiveling my head at every sound. I'm jumpy and ... lost without the magic.

Kahar stops outside the tavern when I do, his head held high, dark eyes scanning the few passersby, as if he feels my anxiety. And he probably does.

It takes a moment for my eyes to adjust as I step into the tavern, the dark room lit only by the ambient light coming through the open door and one grimy window. A quick scan of the room reveals one patron sitting slumped over at a table near the bar. The marriage ink crawling up his hand stands stark against his pale skin. I keep an eye on him, wary of a surprise attack, as I cross the room, my boots sounding overly loud against the worn wood floor.

The woman behind the bar eyes me as I shove a stool to the side to stand before her.

"You Lina?"

"That's me." Her voice is gruff, like she's spent a lifetime shouting over the noise of the tavern.

"I'm looking for three men. They mighta passed through here a day or so ago. Mighta been in a hurry. One mighta been sick."

Her breasts nearly spill from her blouse as she crosses her arms, resting them on top of the bar, her eyes trailing down my body before climbing back to my eyes. When she remains silent, I slap a coin on the bar, but keep it pressed under my finger.

She eyes the coin before looking back at me. "Yeah, I saw em. Nervous bunch, glancing over their shoulders every couple a minutes. The big fella kept clutchin' his head, sweatin' a lot. I thought he was gonna be sick all over my floor. The other two ate fast, tryin' to get their friend to eat, but he kept shakin' his head. They had ta practically carry him out."

I grin, knowing the pain the man is dealing with. I shift, my boots sticking slightly to the floor as I slide the coin across the bar, nearly brushing her breast.

"Were they on foot or horseback?"

"On foot."

"How long ago was this?"

She fingers the coin, sliding it into her cleavage. "Last night."

A grin pulls my lips back as I slide another coin across the shiny wood surface of the bar. "For your time."

She taps the coin's edge against the wood, eyeing me. I may not be able to read her thoughts, but I know the look in her eyes all too well.

No marriage ink on her.

I wink, tracing a finger lightly across the swell of one breast, delighting in the way her flesh prickles at my touch.

"I'm in a bit of a rush, but if I wasn't ..."

She leans into my touch, her blond hair falling over her shoulder, her curvy hips canting to the side. "Next time you're in town, then."

Pulling away, I step back, adjusting myself, drawing her eyes to the growing bulge in my pants. "Sure, sweetness. Next time."

The half-drunk patron huffs a wet chuckle that turns into a cough. The crack of wood hitting wood spins me around, my left hand reflexively reaching for my missing dagger at my thigh. I swear under my breath, my muscles tense, my body ready to spring.

A small woman is bent over, picking up a chair she must have knocked over, and Lina sighs behind me. "Child, you're as clumsy as a newborn foal."

I relax slightly, trying to slow my racing heart, as the girl blushes, eyes averted as she hurries around the bar, disappearing into a back room.

I turn back to Lina, whose brows are raised. "You're a jumpy fella. Got someone after ya?"

Struggling to release my shoulders down my back, I shrug. "Ya never know. Ya got a messenger station in this town?"

She eyes my pockets before raising a brow again. Smirking, I toss another coin at her, though I could have easily found out the information for free.

"Follow the main road north through the village. It's the small building on the right at the edge of town."

I push through the doors, grabbing Kahar's reins, the heavy thuds of his hooves keeping time as we walk to the bird house—though 'house' is a generous term. It's more of a crumbling hut.

Stepping over the threshold, I'm wound tight with tension, waiting for the unknown. Sunlight spills through the gaping holes in the roof, and the cooing of three pigeons greets me.

I glance around, double-checking the dark corners for anyone who might be hiding. The space is so small I could brush the side walls with my fingers if I stretched my arms out, but my paranoia in the wake of losing my magic has me in a firm grip, and I can't help but see enemies in every dark, shadowy corner.

The moldy structure is empty, besides the birds in their cages. The first cage has a torn piece of paper tied to the front with Joxsis written in dark script. The middle cage is labeled Farden. The one next to it, labeled Sanhold, is empty, and the last holds the final bird with Malnar written on the paper.

I scribble a quick note to Luc.

Captain Lucaryn,

> *Met some trouble on the road. Some things were stolen.*
> *Everything is quiet. I'm on the hunt. I'll be home once*
> *I've recovered what was taken.*

I pause, the pen poised over the paper, a spot of ink splashing on the waiting parchment. My fingers tremble, but I press the pen down, the scratch of hollow bone over paper overly loud.

> *I know you're going to worry. Please don't. Trust me. I can*
> *handle this, and I'll be home ~~to you~~ soon.*

I try to scratch out 'to you,' but mockingly, the words seem to hold on to the page. Tightly rolling the paper, I slide it into a threadbare leather tube. Rifling through the various implements and seals, I find the royal stamp, pressing it to the tube so that no matter which station this bird lands at in the capital, the message will be brought to the castle.

Downy feathers caress my hand as I gently lift the pigeon from its cage, securing the message to its thin leg. Stepping outside, I take a deep breath, cleansing myself of the stuffy, dusty air from the cramped building. My finger lightly trails over the bird's head as I glance over my shoulder at the shack.

Leaning down, I whisper to the fragile creature sitting docile in my large hand. "I wouldn't come back if I were you. Stay in Farden. It's a little colder up there, but the capital is nice." My mind wanders to my home, conjuring images of my looming stone castle, the towering mountains almost always capped with snow, the crowded city crouched at the base of the mountains, rock and trees shielding us from the rest of the country. The bird's feathers ruffle as my whispered words fan over its head. "Fly true. Someone very important to me is waiting at the other end."

Raising my arms, the bird flaps its wings, feathers and air brushing against my skin as it takes flight. I peer into the sky, squinting my eyes as its small body grows smaller, and its pale color blends into the clouds.

With a sigh, I turn, swinging onto Kahar, squeezing my thighs as he side steps, tossing his head.

I turn us northwest, toward the capital, and keep the warhorse at a contained canter—fast enough to gain ground, but slow enough to watch for signs of my prey.

Two hours later, I yank back on the reins, maybe a little too hard. Kahar squeals, rearing back slightly, then bucking twice, trying to unseat me. I pat his neck before swinging down. "Rassiy, niy suhe'ars." *Sorry, my friend.*

My stiff knee pops as I kneel off the side of the road, but a smile peels my lips up my face. The sour stench of vomit coats the back of my throat, and my eyes track the trail of sick leading away from the road. I stand, my gaze drawn to a copse of trees in the distance, bordered by a towering rock outcropping.

Kahar paws the dirt, tossing his head before I lead him in the opposite direction, finding him a small patch of grass beyond a small knoll that hides him from the road. "Suiy." *Stay.*

I slide his bridle over his massive head, hooking it to a strap on the saddle before I give his rump a pat, dust and dander flying up around my hand.

Crossing the dirt road, I easily follow the trail of my prey, knowing the magic has driven the thief to his limits, the vomit trail pointing the way, and crushed grass leading me on.

I skirt to the right, holding back a chuckle as the sound of low voices reaches me. I may not have the power of the Stone, but I'm still a hunter, and my body vibrates with anticipation.

I keep my breathing even as I draw closer, trying to listen to what they're saying. The absence of their thoughts is jarring, but a groan floats across the air to me, and I grin. I rise on the balls of my feet, ready for action. That magic is MINE.

Stalking closer, I hide in the shadow of a large tree, and as I peer around the trunk, I see two men pacing a tight circle around a third person, sitting in the dirt, hunched in on himself.

One of the men, thick and burly, curses, running his fingers through his black hair. "We have to keep moving."

The sitting man groans, retching. "Can you think quieter!"

189

"How am I supposed to thin—"

"Shut up." His head spins in my direction, and the other two turn, searching the shadows.

I step around the tree, my steps light but steady, my feral grin expressing the lightness within my chest. I don't have the power of the Stone to give me the advantage of their thoughts, but I also don't have the distraction of the pain of the magic. The only pain I feel is an almost comforting lingering soreness from the beating these men gave me a couple days ago.

Holding my arms out, I stop at the edge of the small clearing within this grouping of trees. "Good effort, gentlemen, but you should have killed me. I'm going to take back what you stole now."

The big man takes a step forward, shielding the man on the ground while glancing at him. "You're right. We shoulda."

Hmmm. Dissent in the ranks over the decision to leave me alive.

I grin, and the big man smiles back. "But now that you're here, I'll be happy to beat you down again, your Majesty."

His voice is deep and gravelly, and I shrug. Nothing drives these tough-types over the edge like indifference. His eyes narrow, his jaw flexing as he takes another step toward me. The third smaller man steps to the big man's side, his eyes pinched with what I interpret as worry. "How did you control the Stone?"

My eyes flick to the leader, who's clutching his head, his shoulders shaking slightly, and I just make out the fine sheen of sweat beading on his face.

A laugh peels from my throat, startling all three men and scaring up a couple of birds. I ignore the two men advancing on me, keeping my eyes on the prone leader. "Horrifyingly painful, isn't it?" He scowls at me, his fists clenched. I can practically feel the Stone sitting hot in his hand. "I'm surprised you were able to remain conscious in the village back there." I chuckle, and the big man charges. I stand still, relaxed, cataloging his movements, catching a small hitch in his left knee, and his right shoulder sits slightly higher than his left, revealing he's most likely right handed.

A second before he winds back to throw his first punch, the leader staggers to his feet. "Eras, stop."

The big man's fist stalls mid punch, and he grits his teeth at me before dropping his hand to his side.

I keep my eyes on the leader as he spits in the dirt at his feet before pressing his hands to his shaking thighs, standing slowly. As he walks toward me, he sways slightly, and I don't bother to keep my laugh from bubbling up. "This is just with three people around. You had months, maybe years of pain and suffering ahead of you, so ... you're welcome. I'll take that burden back from you."

His pale face goes even paler, and I expect him to throw up, but he keeps his composure. "Does Erathan have the Heart Stone?"

His teeth grind together as he picks out my amused thought, '*No.*' But I don't care that he knows. It doesn't matter since he'll be dead soon. I laugh louder. "You're ambitious. I like you. But you can't even handle the Mind Stone right now, nonetheless the Heart Stone. Pace yourself, boy."

He bristles at that. "This *boy* took what no one else has been able to take from you."

I shrug. "By sheer luck. Besides, I'm not worried about that. I'll have it back soon enough, and you'll be dead."

The third man takes a step back, bending down, gripping a bow and casually nocking an arrow. He holds it low before him at the ready. I nod at him. "I guess I have you to thank for the arrow in my back."

His face remains blank. I roll my shoulder, feeling the tight pull of pain.

A fucking lucky shot.

The leader takes another step toward me. "How many guard your castle right now?"

"Which one?"

I picture legions of soldiers, all wearing the armor of Leiren, and the leader smirks. "I think you exaggerate."

The image in my mind shifts, and I picture Luc and my Sagas unit standing at the gates. '*That's more than enough to keep you out.*' His breath speeds up, and his arms start shaking. '*Painful, isn't it? And it doesn't get better, it doesn't get easier. You can't escape it. The power will always be there, even if you hide the Stone away.*'

The big blond rolls his eyes, fingers pressing to his temples. "Enough. I have the Stone. That's all that matters. Your army, your kingdom, will bow to me." His blue eyes meet mine. "You did it, so can I. I don't need you. Your reign is over."

"Why didn't you kill me?"

The young archer sneers at me. "We're not monst—"

The leader speaks over him. "A mistake I'll now fix. Kill him."

The dark-haired man, Eras, reaches for his blade, which is a stupid mistake. He's almost toe-to-toe with me. He could have just snapped my neck, but by going for his weapon, he's giving me an opening.

The leader shouts, "Watch ou—" but my hands are already snapping out, connecting with his throat. Eras chokes, eyes wide, as I grab his shoulder, pulling him in front of me. His eyes go even wider when his comrade's arrow slams into his back. I snatch his sword from the sheath at his hip, shoving him back, and driving his blade into his stomach.

Eras goes limp, and I let him slide from the blade. I duck a sloppy sword slash from the leader before rising to meet his gaze. '*That Stone is mine!*' I scream in his mind, relishing his pain as he stumbles back, clenching his jaw, squeezing his eyes shut before retching at his feet.

I drop to the ground, sword and all, rolling over my aching shoulder as another arrow flies over my head. As I come around to kneeling, I whip the sword overhead. It lands with a wet thud into the archer's chest. I don't spare him another look, turning instead to the last man standing—the leader, the one who took my Stone and my dagger.

I hold up my fists, guarding my face, grinning at the big blond. "There. I silenced two voices for you. Now it's just you and me."

He unsheathes my dagger from his chest strap with a smirk. "I'm going to kill you with your own blade."

My hand physically aches with the desire to hold my dagger again. I sneer. "You missed your chance when I was unconscious."

He grins, but there's pain behind the expression as he stuffs the Stone into his pant's pocket. "I'm about to rectify that."

I roll my eyes. Why do people like to talk so much about violence and death? *Just do it.*

With a grin, I charge, adrenaline and fury momentarily driving the pain from my body. I duck his slash and land a double-fisted punch to his ribs. He slices the blade across my back, but I push back quick enough to keep it from going too deep. I step into his space again, but he dips away from my awkward swing at his temple, landing one of his own against my jaw. My head snaps back, but I reach out, gripping his throat with both hands.

I squeeze, and he slices my dagger over my forearms, cutting deep, but I tighten my grip with a roar. He thrusts the dagger up toward my gut, but I twist away, releasing his throat to grab his wrist as I spin. I bring his arm over my shoulder, yanking downward.

He punches me in the kidney, and my vision goes dark for a second. He steps back, slicing the dagger through the thick muscle where my shoulder meets my neck. A roar of pain punches from my lips as I spin back to face him just as he thrusts at my stomach. I grab his hand, halting the blade an inch from piercing my skin. We stand like that for several seconds, both grunting with effort to move the other.

'*Let go. Step into the blade.*' His command echoes through my mind, and I smile, our noses nearly brushing.

"Nice try. But you're not strong enough."

That phrase snaps the image of my father into my mind, and the blond grins. He grasps the memories of my father beating me day after day and holds them in my mind. My jaw clenches as the blade sinks an inch into my skin through my shirt.

He leans in. "How's this for strong enough?"

My eyes travel back up his chest until I meet his gaze. "Good try." I grip his wrists tighter. "You want to know a secret?" I smile as I wrestle his grip back, and the tip of the blade slides out of my stomach. "I live with these memories every day. I live with worse nightmares each night. I'm always trapped in the pain of my past." Squeezing his wrists, I feel his bones grind under my fingers. "You can't trap me there." Slowly, I overpower him, turning his hand back until the blade is pointing at his stomach. I hold him there as I think about slamming the blade into his stomach. He jerks in my hold, trying to find leverage to yank himself free as he sees his death in my thoughts.

I grin, a shiver of excitement stealing down my spine. "The trick to beating the Stone is knowing your truth, knowing your fears, and not bowing to them." The blade slams through his skin, sinking to the hilt. "Ironically, the truth really does set you free." I shove him back, ripping my dagger from his gut. Leaves billow out around him as he falls to his back, and I stalk him, looking down as he clutches his bleeding stomach with one hand, fumbling in his pocket with the other as he sees my intentions.

I chuckle as I bend down. "Hold this." He screams as I plant my dagger in his thigh. I pry his fist open with my fingers, plucking the small green stone from his grasp. Immediately, his thoughts flood my mind, and I tense with the rush of power, but a grin lifts my lips.

"How—" a cough racks his body, "How can you stand it?"

"You had the Stone for all of ...?"

'*Two days. I only held the power for two measly days.*'

Ahhh. That's better. I welcome back the magic and this man's thoughts with a shiver.

"I've had it for ten years. And I'm quite ... creative with its power." He grunts as I rip my dagger from his thigh, cleaning it on his other pant leg. "Let me give you a little taste of what magic you could have wielded."

His eyes go wide as he struggles to swat at his skin. I plant the image of stinging ants streaming from the ground, covering his body, biting his flesh. If he took a second to calm his mind, he would realize that the stinging ants don't live this far north, but he's caught up in the pain and fear. His screams ring out as he slaps and brushes at his skin. Blood wells from his wound, running in thin streams down his sides as he rips his shirt off, smacking every inch of his exposed skin. Welts appear as if he was indeed bitten, his mind telling him the ants are eating his flesh, and his body physically reacting to that information.

I take a moment to search his thoughts and memories, looking for any hint that them finding the Stone wasn't dumb luck—that they knew where to look. But no. As I watch the scene in his memories, the pure shock of finding the Stone eases my concerns.

Gripping his hand, I interrupt his desperate attempts to knock the imaginary ants from his skin. Sliding my ring from his finger, I put it back on mine before I slice my dagger up his inner thigh, severing the artery.

I turn from his writhing, screaming body.

The mind is a powerful thing, and I control the mind.

I slide the real Stone in my pocket. I'll have to have Luc sew it back into my back. I peek at the sky through the branches of the trees, noticing the deepening blue announcing the coming of evening. The small crescent of the child moon barely peeks over the horizon.

The man's screams die off as I limp away. Kahar's nicker greets me as I grunt, sliding his bridle back over his head. Every punch and cut screams at me as I haul myself into the saddle, but I smile around the pain.

"Se'as'r fa anea." *Let's go home.*

18

It's been three days. The trek home has taken longer than I anticipated. Trudging one foot in front of the other, I huddle into my cloak, chin tucked into my chest as the frozen winds from the snow-covered northern mountains, and the freezing gusts coming in from the sea to the west tries to rip my clothing from my body. My boots crunch in the fine dusting of frozen snow underfoot. Kahar has his massive head bowed, his powerful neck arched, trying to shield himself from the wind and the cold. My gloved hands grip his reins as I lead Kahar over the tree-studded rocky terrain.

Yesterday, he started favoring his front leg, and I knew the wound, though shallow, was bothering him. I've kept it clean, tending both our wounds with packed snow and crushed medicinal herbs I found along the banks of the nearly frozen river, but we're both sore and tired.

Hazy clouds shroud the sun as it kisses the horizon, tucking itself into bed for the night. The temperature drops, and Kahar's puffing breaths steaming from his muzzle mix with my clouded exhales. I stop, leaning over, pressing gentle fingers to the cut on Kahar's shoulder. His muscles twitch, but he stands still. There's a little swelling, but it's nicely scabbed over.

I swing onto Kahar's back, draping my cloak over his flank,

capturing his heat. I know he's tired, he's pushed himself hard these past few days, but he wants to get home as badly as I do. Still, I monitor his breaths and his stride, making sure he doesn't push himself too hard on this last stretch.

After an hour, the spires of my castle peek into view, the great mountain range, blanketed in snow, stands sentinel at its back. The first big snow has not hit the city yet, but it's coming.

I can't keep the grin from my face. Sporadic firelight flickers with a soft glow throughout the city that lies to the east of the castle. Thin columns of smoke curl up from several chimneys, and a lone dog's bark echoes through the otherwise quiet night.

As welcoming as my city looks nestled at the base of the mountains, I skirt the capital, aiming for the western gate.

Drawing close, I hold my posture tall, though I want to weep at the thought of my soft bed. My temples are pounding with the buzz of mental activity—that incoherent rumble of noise—but I'm thankful for the pain. I feel settled with the magic once again humming through my mind.

An arrow wizzes past my right side, thudding into the ground. A warning shot. I wheel Kahar to the left and stop. I sit taller, looking over my shoulder toward the castle. A deep voice rings out into the quickly darkening night. "Declare yourself!"

"It is your King."

There's a pause, the silence choking me with impatience, before I hear. "Approach slowly."

I swallow back my annoyance. My soldiers are doing their job. If I had ridden right up to the gates, I would have killed whoever was on watch. Thankfully, that lesson doesn't need to be made tonight.

I nudge Kahar into a walk, having to hold tight to the worn reins to keep him from racing home. I pat his neck as he dances with short, hopping strides. "Uh hraz, niy suhe'ars." *I know, my friend.*

As I draw nearer, the voice rings out. "Open the gates! Our King has returned."

I allow Kahar to canter, and I sigh as the thud of his hooves on dirt changes to the sharp crack of iron shoes on cobblestone, and the metallic whine of the gates closing behind me rends the air. I circle toward the stables, soldiers and servants quickly stepping out of my way with a bowed head or a salute. As soon as we come to the stables, a young girl with pale, freckled skin, thin, but strong arms, and short curly red hair, runs out, gripping the reins without fear, and surprisingly Kahar stands still for her. I almost fall from his back in shock when he nuzzles her hand.

Dismounting, I pull my gloves off before patting Kahar's sweaty neck. I wrap my fingers through his long mane, looking at the stable hand holding tight to the reins, stroking his nose. "Are you a witch?"

Her startled eyes snap to mine, and I chuckle. "I jest. It's just, Kahar doesn't like anyone."

She smiles, dipping her head, continuing her strokes. "I've always been good with horses, your Majesty. I had to beg the stable master for a month straight to allow me to apprentice. He told me the hell horse would be my test." She scratches the soft fuzz of his muzzle, whispering into his face, "But you're not a hell horse, are you, E'ara-suhis?" *Beautiful.*

A single brow climbs my forehead. "You know the old language?"

I'm impressed. She can't be more than fourteen.

She nods, continuing her gentle strokes as Kahar's bottom lip flutters. "I knew the royal horses are trained in the old tongue, so I ... found *stole* a text that contained a few words and taught myself."

I hide my smirk at the guilt clouding her mind when she recalls slipping from the large house she used to clean for money, the old book tucked under her cleaning supplies. But her excitement and desire to gain knowledge that might land her a job in the royal stables bolstered her bravery.

"Well, I'd say you've passed your test. But keep your guard up. He finds pleasure in catching people by surprise."

She nods, her flaming hair bouncing around her face. "I'll be careful. I always am, your Majesty. Horses are majestic, wonderful animals, but they are powerful and should always be respected." Love and passion fill her, and I can't help but smile. I can easily see her becoming the stable master one day.

I grip Kahar's mane, shaking him slightly before stepping back and leaving him in ...

"What's your name?"

"Shana, your Majesty."

"Well, Shana, I leave Kahar in your capable hands. He's worked very hard for the past few days."

"I'll make sure he's well taken care of, your Majesty."

She takes the black steed into the stables before clipping him into a lead tied to the wall. As small as she is, she has to stand on a stool, but deftly undoes the tack before rubbing him down, taking extra care on his sweat-slicked skin where the saddle and bridle sat.

I turn with a grin and break into a jog into the castle, barely registering the bows, salutes, and whispered, "Welcome home, your Majesty."

I stride into the dining hall, glancing around. Conversation halts, and the clink of plates and silverware quiets as everyone bows or salutes, eyes wide as they take in my battered appearance. But Luc isn't here, so I turn, the sounds of meal time picking back up as I leave.

Taking the stairs two at a time, I rush down the hall of my wing until I'm standing before Luc's door. Without pausing, I push in, quickly skimming the mess before my eyes land on the rumpled bed. It's empty. I spin, jogging down the hall, and when I come to my door, the soldiers salute, eyes catching on my fading bruises and wounds.

I have to fight to keep the bark from my voice. "Where's the captain?"

One gestures over his shoulder. "In your rooms, your Majesty. He said he needed some books."

I relax slightly. "How is he?"

"I'm fine." Luc's voice, filled with annoyance, calls through the closed door.

I grin and push into my rooms, closing the door behind me. I take a second just to watch Luc, bent over my desk, picking up and discarding books. His brown skin looks healthy, and his posture seems strong. I have the urge to find his thoughts, to make sure he is okay, but his presence is a slice of peace for me, and invading his mind seems ... wrong. So I ask instead. "You really are fine?"

He turns at the concern I tried to hide from my voice, but his shoulders hitch up, and anger tinged with worry pinches at the corner of his bright blue eyes as he takes in my torn clothing and the bruises and cuts on my skin. "What the hell happened?"

I try to wave off his concern. "It's a long story. They're all dead. I'll see the healer later." I can practically feel his eyes caressing my skin as he takes an inventory of each mark. The deep cut across my right shoulder burns, and every breath I take sends a twinge of pain through the open wound in my back where my Stone was cut away. The twin slices in my forearms have streaked my sleeves with red ribbons of blood, and my face still feels swollen. The left side of my jaw is sore and blinking my left eye is painful. But none of that matters. "Luc, tell me the truth."

He holds his hands out at his sides with a smile that steals my breath. I can't believe I almost lost him. "Yes, Ry, I'm fine." He waves a hand at me. "Much better than you, it seems. I'm going to need that entire story ... later." He crosses his muscled arms over his chest. "You went out on your own."

"I know I promised, but it was over a week of traveling. I couldn't pass it up, I mean, the quiet, I ..."

He holds up a hand. "I know, Ry. It's just seeing you like this—it tears at me."

"And seeing you stop breathing on the healer's table nearly killed me."

He rubs his chest, a frown on his face. "I guess we both need to do better."

I take a single step forward, hands clenched. "I didn't mean it like that, Luc." Why are we arguing? This is not how I wanted my homecoming to go. "You did nothing wrong. You couldn't have avoided that arrow."

He shrugs, rubbing his chest again. "So you're back from conquering the world?"

I smirk, letting him change the subject. "Just expanding our little slice of Imoria." My eyes travel down his body and back up again.

"And you survived the hell horse."

I laugh, and Luc joins in, the sound giving me life. "I get it now. He's ... well, he's Kahar."

He chuckles, shaking his head. "At long last, my best friend and my trusted steed, coming to terms with each other. I can die happy."

His choice of words brings a frown to my face, and he sighs. "Truly, Ry, I'm fine. I still tire easily, but the wound has closed and is healing nicely." He grips the collar of his shirt, pulling it down to reveal the stitched wound below his right collarbone. "I've been training with the Sagas the past few weeks, and I'm getting stronger every day." He notices the skeptical tilt to my brows and laughs, the sound once again loosening more tension from my chest. "I had to do *something* to keep myself occupied, otherwise I would have raced to Trislen, no matter how many messages you sent commanding me to stay here."

I grin. "South Leiren."

He shakes his head with a chuckle. "That's going to take some getting used to."

"Tell me about it. I've caught myself saying Trislen more than a dozen times."

"I guess that comes with the territory of claiming a kingdom on a whim."

"It wasn't a whim, Luc. I couldn't let her live. Not after ..."

"I know." He rubs his chest again, the gesture seemingly becoming more habitual, but then he drops his hand, crossing the room. Glass clicks as he pours whiskey into two glasses.

As he crosses the room, I say, "I wanted you with me, Luc. But I *needed* you here to watch our home, to hold it, to keep it safe."

"I know, Ry. But we could have gone together if you had just waited, if we had talked about it."

"I couldn't wait. She ha—"

"Why isn't Leiren enough? Why aren't ..."

I take a step back. "Leiren was *never* enough, Luc. Don't you remember talking through the night in that book binders about being the strongest, the most powerful?"

"Of course I remember."

"Well, that means conquering, Luc. Conquering it all! Being untouchable!"

He rubs his chest yet again, and my fingers literally itch to pull his hand away and ease whatever ache he's experiencing. "I just wish ..."

"Luc, Rava went too far, so I delivered a message. 'Don't fuck with us'."

He sighs. "I know, Ry. And you acted swiftly and ruthlessly. It's the Leiren way." He shrugs, the liquid swirling in the glasses with the movement, and a smile lifts his face. "I guess I'm just pissed off you went without me." He raises an eyebrow, passing me a glass. "Look what happens when you go out on your own." He nods at my battered body. "You come back looking like that."

"But I come back. I always will."

Luc laughs quietly. "Fuck, Ry. You always have an answer. Just say you're sorry and drink."

I shove my hand in my pocket, playing with the Mind Stone, letting its warmth tickle my fingers. "Yes, you're right. I'm reckless, brash, and unreliable. I got myself into a spot of trouble, but I managed alright." I stare at the amber liquid gently sloshing in the crystal glass to avoid meeting Luc's eyes. "I'm sorry none of this is happening as planned, but I'm doing my best, Luc."

His silence draws my gaze, and he drops his eyes with a dip of his head, causing his black hair to catch the light. "Thank you."

"For what?"

"For saving me."

I take a step, clenching my hands. "Was that ever a question?" He remains silent, and I'm so tense, my muscles shake. "Luc. I would never leave you."

He frowns, rolling his left shoulder.

"What?" Anger snaps my voice across the space between us. "Did you think I would, what? Leave? Let you die?" My heart breaks at his silence. How can he question me? How can he question *us*? I close the space between us, gripping his shoulders, ignoring his wince.

His voice is quiet. "No, not really. But the Heart Stone. We were so close. You—"

I shake him, and I catch his scent, the scent of rain falling on the dry earth. "Fuck the Heart Stone, Luc. You're the only reason I was strong enough to face my father. You're the only reason I can tolerate the agonizing power of the Mind Stone."

He shakes his head, about to object, but I press on. "No, Luc! No. If I lost you, this entire country would burn." His bright blue eyes meet mine, startlingly brilliant against his brown skin and dark hair. "I don't want the Stones if it means losing you. I don't want any of this without you. Tell me you're with me."

One heartbeat, two, three. The silence stretches, our breaths mingling, our chests nearly brushing with each inhale. My eyes catch on his mouth, and I nearly groan as his tongue darts out, licking his lips. I'm painfully hard, and I don't need to read his thoughts to guess what he wants. I can feel it in the slight tremor of his body under my hands, in the catch to each of his breaths, in the dilation of his pupils. I'm not sure when our friendship shifted for him ... but I've wanted this for a long time. I want him so desperately.

My lips are a whisper away from his. "Tell me you want this. I need to hear you say it—that you want us. That you want *me*."

His nostrils flare, his muscles bunching under my hands, and I wait for his response ... for the words that will change my life.

19

A loud knock on my door snaps the spell, and Luc groans. I keep my eyes on his as I yell, "Go away."

Luc chuckles, and a voice calls out from the other side of my door. "I'm sorry, your Majesty, but the captain asked to be notified when word returned from Malnar."

Luc sighs, closing his eyes as he presses his forehead to mine. "I'm sorry. There was a cave-in at the mine two days ago. I need to talk to the soldiers."

I take a deep breath, nodding. "Never apologize for taking care of our kingdom."

Turning toward the door, I have to clear my throat before calling out, "Enter."

I cross toward my washroom as Luc picks up a few books, stacking them in his arms. The soldier strides across the room, saluting. "Your Majesty. Captain."

Luc's deep voice tightens my core. "Report."

I step into the washroom, and I shiver as I peel my ruined shirt over my head, the crackling fire from my bedroom doing hardly anything against the cold. I hear the soldier through the open door between us. "Twenty-three dead, ten still trapped." I shudder, imagining being stuck within the mountain, waiting for air to run out.

"They're still attempting to dig them out, but the threat of a second collapse is slowing the work."

I kick off my boots, shove my pants to my ankles, and kick them free. My cock is still semi-erect and aching from being so close to Luc just moments ago. Facing the large mirror leaning against the far wall, I quickly assess my injuries as the conversation in the next room continues.

Luc asks, "How much ore did they extract this month?"

"A little over half the quota."

"The east mine is completely tapped?"

There's a pause before the soldier answers. "Not completely. There's a few veins that still have ore, but they are deep within the mountain and will require weeks of labor-intensive tunneling."

"Do they need additional forces to help try to get the trapped miners out?"

"I'm not sure we'll be able to get them out alive, but if we mean to make a decent effort at it, yes."

Grabbing a small towel, I wet it in the filled basin, quickly washing the dried blood oozing from reopened wounds from the ride today. I gently poke at my still-tender face, wincing at the green and yellow coloring around my eye, cheek, and jaw. I'll have the healer bring me some salve and a tonic for sleeping tonight. I think I could sleep a full week.

I bend down to fish the Stone from my pant's pocket and snag a large towel, wrapping it around my waist. I take a few deep breaths before heading back into the sitting room.

Both men turn to me as I place my fists on my hips. "Take as many soldiers as you need. And have the head of the city's builder's guild accompany you as well. Maybe he can help assess structural implements."

Luc and the soldier nod, and the soldier looks between Luc and me before Luc flicks his hand toward the door. "Go. Leave as soon as you can. I'll join you in Malnar in two days."

I frown. Luc's presence is not necessarily needed in Malnar, but I stay silent.

The soldier salutes to us both before turning on his heel, quickly leaving my suite, the door clicking shut behind him. Luc hefts the stack of books higher in his arms and moves to leave, but I call out, stopping him with an outstretched hand.

"I need your help before you go."

His eyes catch on the green stone sitting in my open palm before they jump back to my face. "Did you take it out, or did someone find it somehow?"

"The second."

He bends down, setting the books on the floor, then steps forward, taking the small Stone between his forefinger and thumb. "How the hell, Ry? Did they know?"

I turn, shaking my head as I give him my back. He hisses at the torn wound in my right shoulder. "Dumb luck. I was ... distracted, and an arrow landed in just the right spot. It was a million-to-one shot. They took the ring before I passed out. They worked me over while I was unconscious, but when they yanked the arrow free, it must have exposed the Stone."

"And?"

"And I tracked them, killed them, and took it back. I made sure"— I tap my temple—"they didn't know the Stone's location beforehand."

I can't help but jump a little at his touch, even though his fingers are gentle as he prods the edges of the wound. His voice is quiet and ... close. "So, it really was luck."

I nod, and he crosses in front of me, disappearing into the washroom, and after some rustling around, he emerges with a threaded needle. He passes by, and light footfalls move away from me before I hear the door of my liquor cabinet open. A glass bottle scrapes over the wood shelf before Luc crosses back to me. I hear the telltale pop of the cork being pulled from the bottle, and without warning, Luc splashes liquid fire onto the wound.

"Fuck!"

Luc grabs my shoulder. "Stay still." I grit my teeth so hard, I'm surprised my teeth don't crack as Luc pushes the Stone into my open flesh. "Breathe." His voice, so close, so deep, it sends a shiver down my back, and my towel tents again. Then pain shoots from my shoulder all the way to my hip as he sews me up. I count each one, the needle stabbing me eight times before Luc ties it off. I hiss as he cuts the excess with his teeth.

I roll my shoulder as I turn. "Thanks."

"Just try not to lose it again."

I smirk. "I'll do my best. Though once in ten years is not that bad of a record."

Luc just shakes his head as he retrieves his books. "I have a full day tomorrow." He glances out the window, and I follow his gaze, noticing the moons are low against the horizon. He sighs. "Today. I have a full day today, and I'll leave for Malnar the next. But we need to talk. I have updates for you, and you need to catch me up on ... everything."

I nod. "Dinner tomorrow?"

His lips pull down in a frown, shaking his head. "Can't. New soldiers from Trislen, damn it, South Leiren will be here tomorrow evening."

I want to ask about his plans for integrating our new army, but if I ask, the questions won't stop. "Breakfast before you leave?"

"Maybe. Though I don't want to be rushed in our talk, and I can't delay getting to Malnar."

My shoulders bunch. Why do I feel like he's suddenly avoiding me? I could check. I could fan that little spark of doubt and let the magic find his thoughts. But I refuse. I've always trusted Luc, and I won't stop now. Still, I ask, "Why is it so important for you to go to Malnar?"

He shifts the books from one arm to the other, rubbing his chest twice before dropping his free hand. "There's a possibility the cave-in wasn't an accident."

Well, if that's true, that's very serious. "Sabotage?"

"Not sure. Maybe. Maybe from Adren or South Leiren. Maybe from within. Maybe nothing at all. Maybe it was just an accident."

"What led you to think there was a possibility of foul play?"

He drums his fingers against the spine of a book. "Some reports of score marks on the main supports in the back of the cave."

"I can go. I can ferret out the truth with ease."

Luc shakes his head. "No need. I can handle it. You have plenty to do here."

My eyes narrow. "I wasn't implying you couldn't handle it. But I—"

"Ry, I've got it."

I bite the inside of my cheek at his frustrated tone. Why is he pulling away?

Luc turns to leave. "I'll try to carve out some time for us to sit down together, but it might have to wait until I get back."

I nod at his back, knowing he can't see me, and I don't bother to answer aloud. Something is off. Did my advances make him uncomfortable?

Shaking my head, I call out before my door closes, watching Luc stride down the hall. "Guard, send for the healer."

A second before the door clicks shut, she answers, "At once, your Majesty."

I turn on the shower, stepping under the hot spray, but I barely register the pain as water sluices over each cut and slash in my battered skin. I absentmindedly run the bar of oatmeal soap over my body, replaying everything with Luc over and over, trying to find the cause of his ... mood.

Did he meet my eyes when I asked him if he was with me? Was he avoiding eye contact? No. I remember the blue of his eyes, right? Were his muscles tense under my grip on his shoulders? Was he tense from desire or was he uncomfortable? Or was he angry?

Shit. I rub my hand over my face, the hot water flushing my skin.

His lips had been a breath from mine, and I know what I saw, what I felt. But then his distance, his anger ... I—

A high-pitched male voice rings out from my main room. "I'm here to attend you, your Majesty."

The healer.

I quickly scrub my scalp with the soap, combing my fingers through my tangled hair until the water runs clear. I turn the water off, grabbing a fresh towel. Patting myself dry, I walk into my bedroom, missing the warmth of the wood floors of my southern palace.

A smile curves my lips at that thought until the healer tsks at me. "Your Majesty, you should have come to me as soon as you arrived."

"As king, I set my own priorities."

He bows, his pale scalp showing through his thin brown hair. "Of course, your Majesty. I only meant—"

"I know what you meant. Just stitch me up and fix me one of your pain tonics as well as one for sleep. Not too strong, just enough to take the edge off." And hopefully dull the buzz of mental noise.

I glance at the table next to my bed, knowing the street drug isn't in that top drawer. I haven't bought the drug in years, but I can't seem to stop my mind from craving it still.

The healer's hands twist the leather handles of his bag for a second before he crosses to me and sets the bag down with a soft clink of the bottles within.

Little hums of displeasure, and tsks of disapproval accompany the pokes of his needle as he sews up my other wounds. His fingers are rough and cold as he smears a thick, green mud-like substance over the worse of my bruises.

After what feels like an hour, he stands, cracking his back. "I'm going to return to my workroom to mix you a tonic for the pain and for sleep. I'll bring it to you when it's ready. It's best taken with food, so I recommend you take it with breakfast." He closes and picks up his bag. "Can I convince you to rest until I return?"

Sleep sounds heavenly, but I should get started on the pile of correspondence I'm sure covers my desk in the library. He sighs at my silence. "Well then, this is all I can do for now. You need rest, but if you won't listen to me, you'll have to deal with the prolonged healing time."

He has never been the gentlest of healers, but I find his gruff demeanor entertaining. I smile at him. "I'll take the tonic tonight. I'll deal with the pain till then."

He purses his lips at me before he leaves.

I run a hand through my hair, glancing at my bed. What I would give to be wrapped up in Luc right now. I yank on the ends of my hair to clear my head. Moving slowly from my aches and pains, I dress as quickly as possible.

I'm about to leave my rooms when I spy the books and papers stacked neatly on my desk. I cross the room, running my finger over the spines, recalling specific lore on the Heart Stone contained within each book. Now that I know Erathan's stone is a fake, I need to discreetly resume my hunt for the real one.

Leather presses against my palm as I stack a few books in my arms, topping them with a few papers. These books and passages are ones I don't want Erathan getting his hands on.

Crossing the room, I stand on the left side of my bed and press my hand against the wood-paneled wall. A quiet click sounds before a section of the wall bumps out. I work my fingers into the small crack, opening the hidden door. There are a few shelves, mostly empty, and I brush aside some old papers to make room for the books in my arms. Once they're neatly stacked, I run my hands over the spine of a book on the next shelf down. "Adventures of Allerian" is stamped in black down the cream spine. It's the tale of a boy who finds a magic sword, and through trial and tribulation, he saves his kingdom, becomes the glorious hero of his country, and lives in wealth and happiness for the rest of his life.

It's a fanciful story. Idyllic, meant to teach children to be brave and true. Luc and I used to take turns reading this book aloud to each other when we lived in that abandoned bookbinders shop.

Picking it up, I carefully open the book, breathing in the stale paper smell, transporting myself to that dark building. Luc and I had very little, but we had each other, and that was enough. It's still enough.

I bite my cheek again. Does Luc really believe he is less important to me than the Stones? I need to fix that. I need him to know ... I thought he knew. Shit, staying out of Luc's head is the right thing, but not knowing is tearing me apart.

I close the book with a little whisper of leather and paper, setting it in its place before pressing the hidden panel closed and heading out of my rooms toward the library.

Just as I assumed, a pile of papers and sealed letters greets me as I sit in the cushioned chair. I read through each piece of news and information, vaguely aware of the room brightening as the day dawns.

My spies in Adren confirm the ports are in a state of slight chaos as they shift to get ready to accommodate my needs. A letter from Erathan asks for more specific numbers on the spice tonnage for this summer, and if he needs to make arrangements for my logging exports through his ports.

I chuckle. Why yes, yes he should.

He also informs me a small passage is being planned along his eastern border along the foothills, which will allow free travel between North and South Leiren. How accommodating he's being.

I smile, pausing in my reading of his letter as I think about my papers, scrolls, and books upstairs in my room. I'll need to gather several items to send to Erathan today. There are a few books I have in mind—texts that have specific lore tied to the Stones. I've already ruled out those leads, but they will serve the purpose of keeping Erathan busy. The information will give him ... hope.

I chuckle again as I focus back on the paper in my hand, but I frown as I reach the end of Erathan's letter.

'Word has reached me that a cousin is making claim to the Trislenian throne. I'm sure you are monitoring this threat, but per our treaty, I'm ready to shore up my ports and my eastern borders. I await your first delivery of what was promised.'

I need to send my spies across the sea to Alara as soon as possible. Today, when I'm done here, I'll select a few spies and send them to Adren. It will take them a minimum of two months to get to the continent across the eastern sea, so the sooner the better. In the meantime, I'll ask the new bird master if we have any sea birds capable of making the journey to Alara. If so, I'll get a message to Runic's relative, Eraln Vranna, and see if I can't get more information about the situation in Eshena.

Runic's report from the South says nothing much has changed since I left. The Shadow Lord is still delivering his reports on the underbelly workings of the capital, but he has uncovered nothing on the mysterious cousin.

I craft a letter to Runic, telling him to up the patrols through the capital and larger cities of South Leiren, and to put more pressure on our Shadow Lord. If anyone can find a hidden person or persons bent on insurrection, it's Mica Kafir.

I leaf through the remaining letters, the woodsy scent of paper coating my nose as my fingers darken with the stain of ink. A high family to the east wants to send their son to court. The port city of Joxsis has officially closed for the winter season. A small village along our southern border is requesting an extension on their winter taxes —the same villages who were short on their autumn taxes. I'll have to find out what's going on down there … hard times or corruption or …

There's another letter from Runic with a list of soldiers asking for a transfer to my Northern army, along with his recommendations on who to accept. I set that letter aside for Luc.

There are at least three letters with invitations to court high family daughters, both from North and South Leiren. With the winter solstice fast approaching, I'm sure families are hoping I will finally take a bride and announce her at my annual celebration. Now it seems South Leiren families are already ready to throw their daughters at me.

I frown. I will need an heir, someday. I want Luc as my consort, but I have no idea how he would feel about that. Somehow, I think he would object. And I wouldn't blame him. Consort sounds so … useless.

If I developed feelings for a woman, I guess I could entertain the idea of making her my consort, but the more I think about it, the more the muscles in my back bunch up with tension. I doubt any proper high lady would be willing to share me with Luc—if Luc even wants me. Maybe Luc and I could adopt an orphan from the church outside our home village—if Luc wants kids. But I'll need an heir.

I shake my head, trying to dislodge my rambling thoughts. This is all conjecture. I'm getting ahead of myself. I need to talk to Luc and figure out … us. I can worry about the rest later.

I toss all the letters of courting proposals in the fire, watching the flames eagerly eat the paper, the edges turning black before curling into the flames.

I spend all day working at my desk, and when I stand, stretching my arms overhead, my eyes are burning. Each wound pulls and stings with the movement, but it feels good to stretch.

I make neat little stacks, tapping paper on the wood of my desk, tidying my space, and just as I'm ready to head out, there's a rap against the open door.

Looking over my shoulder, I smile as Asha comes into the room, her curvy hips swaying, sending the hem of her skirt dancing around her ankles. The smells of roasted meat and vegetables, baked bread, and apple tarts, carries across the room from the large tray in her hands.

"I hear you had an eventful journey." Her voice is light and happy, though there's a little concern over my bruises. Her thoughts are simple, tracking along with everything she says. Asha is always a breath of fresh air.

"Indeed." I place my hands on my hips as she sets down the tray on a cleared space on my desk. "Though you wouldn't be thinking of asking to move to the south, are you? I know the spice is plentiful down there, but I own the spice mines now. I can have anything you desire brought to you."

She chuckles, bending over to pour white wine from a bottle into a glass. "I'm happy enough where I am, your Majesty."

I frown, coming up along her side. My palm rests on her shoulder, feeling her strength built by years working in the kitchens hauling heavy pots, kneading dough, and endlessly cutting, grating, and rolling. "Happy enough is not happy."

She tilts her head at me with a small frown. "I'm happy, your Majesty." *I like it here. Sure the winters are harsh, but the cold just gives me an excuse to curl up in my blankets, drink hot spiced wine, and enjoy a lover or two.* "I would miss the winters, the bite in the air, the frost and snows."

"And the hot wine."

She laughs. "And the hot wine." She nibbles on her bottom lip, and I smile at her thoughts. She leans down, taking a tart between her fingers, holding my favorite treat before my lips. "Besides, no one would feed you like I do."

I chuckle, enjoying the way her pupils dilate at the sound. "That's true." I part my lips and allow Asha to slide the tart into my mouth. Spiced apple and buttery pastry dances on my tongue before I close my lips around her fingers, tasting her along with the tart. Her lips part on a gasp as I pull back, swallowing. I pick up the glass of wine, taking a sip as I turn, cross the room, and close and lock the door.

As I stalk back to her, I'm well aware I just had Luc in my arms earlier today. I'm aware that I'm using Asha to take the edge off—and I don't care. Well, maybe I do, but it's not going to stop me. This month has been ... a lot, and Luc left this morning. He could have told the soldier to wait. He could have dealt with the mining situation *after* we talked. But he didn't. He left. And I let him.

Asha smiles as she slides one sleeve down her shoulder, then the other. I snap my hand around her throat, holding her still. Setting the glass on the desk behind her, I brush my nose along her neck, sending a shiver down her spine. I crush my lips to hers, and she opens to me immediately. Our tongues dance, pulling a groan from my throat. But when she moans into my mouth, anger floods my body. Her lips are too soft, her skin too pale, her moans too ... feminine.

On a frustrated growl, I spin her around, moving my grip to the back of her neck before shoving her down on the desk. The tray of food clatters to the floor, the wine bottle and my glass shatter, soaking the thick carpet.

She braces her hands with a loud slap of flesh against wood as I bunch up her skirt, tossing it around her waist. With my free hand, I grip her undergarment and slide it down her thighs, and she kicks free of them. Sliding my hand down her large ass, I trail my touch along the inside of her thigh before sinking one finger between her wet folds. She groans, trying to shove herself back so she can ride my fingers, but my grip on her neck holds her still.

Her mind is a tangle of arousal and frustration, and she lets out a little shout as I insert a second finger, curling them up with my harsh thrusts. She's soaking my fingers, and her wet heat is intoxicating, but her breathy moans are not what I want. I want Luc's deep growl of lust. I want his brown skin pressed against mine. I want his masculine moans floating around the room from the pleasure I give him.

With a growl, I rip my fingers from her, ignoring her whimper of protest as I quickly undo my pants, freeing myself to plunge into her. I sink to the hilt with a curse on my lips, and her hips jerk back against my balls. I pull back, watching my cock slide from her body, glistening with her arousal, imagining it's Luc's ass.

But it's not.

I press my soaked finger to her ass, sliding it past the tight entrance. Slamming my cock back into her, I keep my hold on her neck while my other hand pumps my finger into her ass. Relentlessly, I pound into her, pleasure building, but frustration and anger holding my orgasm at bay. So I go harder.

Inserting a second finger, she gasps as I stretch her, the pain mingling with the pleasure. I've never been this rough with Asha before. Sure, I've tied her up, blindfolded her, and deprived her, but never have I been this rough. Yet, her pleasured moans drive me on, and her thoughts let me know she's enjoying this. But with every thrust, my anger builds. Her skin is too soft, her curves that I normally love to grip, and bite, and squeeze are not satisfying. Her little pants and groans are lovely, but too delicate.

I need muscle, and grunts, and growling. I need hard edges, and scars, and the scrape of a beard against my skin. Fuck. I need Luc.

I move the hand from her neck and snake it around her waist, finding her clit and circling my thumb against her nub. She screams, bucking against my touch, slamming her hips back with every rough thrust I give her. I feel her letting go, her mind erupting into pleasure as her orgasm crashes through her. Her pussy contracts around my cock, and her ass squeezes my fingers. And fuck, it feels good, but it's not enough.

A whimpered sigh slides from her lips as she comes down, and the purely feminine sounds snaps my control. I can't listen to her anymore. Beyond frustrated, I pull out of her as I claw my hand up her scalp, gripping her hair and spinning her around. My voice comes out in a gravelly growl. "Kneel."

She drops to her knees, eyes wide. Without warning, I shove my cock between her lips and down her throat. She gags, and her mind startles at my brutality, but her lips close around my base as she grips my hip with one hand and my ass with the other.

I use her mouth, guiding her head down my cock again and again. Spit leaks from the edges of her mouth, and tears gather at the corners of her eyes. The wet sound of her sucking me off is accompanied by her thoughts. *'Yes. Use me. Take what you need.'*

What I need is to stop hearing her feminine voice. I shut my eyes, painting the image of Luc's lips wrapped around my cock, of his bright blue eyes looking up at me with love as he swallows me down.

I almost shout his name as I come, releasing down Asha's throat with hard thrusts against her mouth. The buzzing pleasure shoots down my spine, curling my toes. When my hips stop pumping, I loosen my grip, sliding from her red and swollen mouth. She swallows, licking her lips, but the smile on her face doesn't quite reach her eyes. She stands, straightening her clothes, and I tuck myself back into my pants. I feel I should say something, but I'm not great at being nice. What do I say? I know she enjoyed it, even if my fucking her mouth was a little startling to her.

"Asha, I—"

She shakes her head. "Don't, your Majesty. I enjoyed that very much. In fact, I wouldn't mind more rough play in the future." She averts her gaze. *"If there are future times." I don't know if I can give him what he wants any longer.* "I enjoy our fun together, and I'm always happy to ... serve my king." She looks up at me with a wink, and I can't help but smile at her. "But I don't think I'm who you really want."

I don't know what to do or say, so I gesture at the mess of food and shattered glass. "I should clean that up."

"I'll do it."

We both kneel, reaching for the tray at the same time, and we pause. She places her hand over mine, and I fight to keep from pulling away. I don't like that she seems to see me so well.

She squeezes my hand. "Talk to him."

I jerk back, and she turns, picking up the mess, placing everything on the tray before standing. "The rug will need a bit of cleaning. I can send someone up."

I nod, a frown pulling at my lips. She leaves without another word, shutting the door behind her, closing me in the library with my thoughts.

I want nothing more than to talk to Luc, but it felt like he ran from me this morning. But maybe I misread him. I'm tired, and hurting, and nearly always aroused at even the thought of him. I can't let him leave for the mines before I have a chance to talk to him.

With my meal ruined, I sigh, resigned that I'll have to go to the dining hall. But before that, I'm finding Luc. We've been best friends all our lives, and we've never let anger, or frustration, or misunderstanding come between us—at least not for too long.

Leaving the library, I stop the first person I come across. The servant bows, his pale fingers smudged black with soot, his hands clutching a large pail of coals. He must be tending the baths. I had small coal reservoirs put under each tub in all the bathing rooms, like in my Trisl ... my South Leiren palace.

His hands grip the handle of the pail tightly. "I'm on the way to your rooms, your Majesty. I will draw your bath momentarily, and it will be kept hot."

I shake my head in annoyance. "Fine. Where's Captain Lucaryn?"

"I haven't seen him since this morning, your Majesty."

I brush past him without another word, and his mind actually sighs with relief at my departure. I ask three more people with no luck until I end up storming out the main doors of my castle into the freezing late afternoon. The guards standing to either side salute.

"Where is Captain Lucaryn?"

There's a pause, and panic scatters through both their minds. '*Did the captain not tell him? Shit.*' ... '*Oh fuck. Did the captain not tell him?*'

"For fuck's sake. Where is he!"

Their faces drain of blood, and one actually takes a step away from me. The other swallows before stuttering, "H-he, he left this af-afternoon for Malnar, y-your Majesty."

20

My body goes still, and a strange rushing silence pushes all outside thoughts from my mind for a single heartbeat. My voice comes out surprisingly even. "What do you mean, he left?"

The other soldier steps back forward, giving his comrade backup. "He left for Malnar with twenty of our soldiers from the Sioastr unit. Said he wasn't sure when he'd be returning, that the situation at the mines might keep him there for a time, and that with Runic now in Trisl ... I mean South Leiren, that Casin was in charge until he returned."

He left. He left without telling me. I feel like I've been punched in the chest as I turn without a word, walking back into the castle. What the hell is going on? The sound of my boots striking the stone floors sounds distant, and the cold seeping off the walls matches the chill in my heart.

I find myself in one of the many unused rooms of my castle. The wall before me is almost all windows, and the setting sun has painted the sky orange and pink. There's a roaring fire to my right, and as I walk farther into the room, I brush my hand over a forest-green velvet chair. A glance around reveals more plush chairs and sofas scattered in small sitting groups with little tables nearby.

Sinking into the high-backed chair, I lean forward as it hugs me, and I brace my forearms on my thighs. Why did Luc leave? Was he still angry that I went off on my own? Was it that I got myself captured and injured? Were my advances not as wanted as I thought? Or does it have nothing to do with me?

I flop back, resting my head against the velvet as I absently palm my dagger, twirling it around in my left hand. This is not at all how I pictured things going. I expected him to welcome me back with a smile—that we would drink in celebration of an enemy eliminated and a kingdom conquered. But here I am, alone and confused. And I still haven't told him about the Heart Stone being a fake.

The flat side of the blade taps my thigh as I watch the sky turn to soft purples and blues. I still trust Luc, always. So, no matter the reason he left, I'll respect him, and when he returns, we'll talk.

To take my mind off Luc, I consider the upcoming winter solstice. I imagine Erathan's beside himself with the desire to read through my research, and I'd bet this month's lumber shipment that he will spend the entire celebration with his nose buried in my books. If he wants to waste his time, not that he knows it's wasted time, I'll be happy to let him. Besides, the items I don't want him looking through are safe in my hidden compartment.

I cross my ankle over my knee, dagger dancing in my hand. With the amount of responses we've received, this year's winter solstice looks to be one of the largest attended events so far. In two and a half weeks, high families from all over Imoria will invade my home, packing it full of annoying people and unwanted thoughts. Commoners too, will flood the streets of Farden to revel around the giant bonfires, and hopefully spend a lot of coin on drink, wares, and food.

I'm having spices and fruits brought up from South Leiren, and hunting parties are on a near constant rotation in the eastern forests and even in the mountains to provide meat for the celebration. The circus troupe here in Farden will perform throughout the city all day. Extra wine is being brought from South Leiren, and we'll have the Adren fire dancers, which is sure to draw a large crowd. I'll have them perform in the city square the morning of the solstice, then they can perform in the evening once the sun has set in the castle gardens. It should be quite spectacular.

I focus back on the window before me, the view spilling out to the south. There are no mountains to view in this direction, and the sea is too far to catch a glimpse. Instead, raised as the castle is, I can see the long buildings of the barracks below, and people milling about, going about their day. A large store house sits beyond the barracks, its low roof hunched over the walls as if it's protecting the food stores inside.

Orderly blocks of houses and businesses sprawl beyond the walls of my castle, giving me a view of a small corner of the capital city. The shadows have crawled through the streets, hiding the people moving about from my view. Soft firelight flickers behind windows and in street torches.

It's all mine. Mine and Luc's. With a smile, I watch the sky as it turns indigo, a few stars pushing their light into the fast approaching night.

Sliding my dagger into its sheath, I stand, looking around the empty room. It's a shame, really. It's a pleasant room, comfortable, quiet. I wonder what other rooms are standing unused, waiting for someone to spend a few moments within their walls?

As I walk, I barely register the hum of voices in my mind beyond the slight tension in my temples. I manage to keep coherent words from punching through until I draw near the dining hall.

It's not as busy since the dinner hour has passed, but there's still a decent crowd of about thirty in different stages of their meals. I absently place a few things on my plate, distracted by the thoughts now crowding for dominance in my mind.

'He doesn't seem upset. Maybe the rumor is wrong.' ... 'I can't believe we now own Trislen. And he took their kingdom all by himself. Shit. He can probably hear me now. If you can, I'm sorry, your Majesty. I'll try to keep quiet.' Her mind focuses sharply on the potatoes on her plate, blanking out her thoughts. I take a seat on an empty bench, nodding with a small smile at the soldier staring at her potatoes sitting on the other side of the table down to my right. But the distraction is short-lived as other thoughts ping around my skull.

'I wonder how long the Captain will be in Malnar? Such a mess out

there. And what if it was sabotage?' ... 'Do I have everything packed that I'll need on the hunt tomorrow? I'm hoping for a boar or two for the festival.' ... 'I'm so tired, but I still need to clean my weapons and sew up that shirt I ripped yesterday.'

On and on, the thoughts crowd my mind. I vaguely taste the stew as I scoop it into my mouth—vegetable and ... rabbit, I think. A wood cup lands with a thud on the table to my left. Looking up over my shoulder, I meet Casin's brown eyes. "May I join you, your Majesty?"

I nod, sweeping my hand to the empty space, and he folds his excessively tall form onto the bench. He sets his plate and another cup next to the one he set down earlier. The marriage ink scrolling down the back of his hand flexes with the movement as he slides the cup toward me. "I brought you some ale. Looked like you could use a little something to take the edge off."

I chuckle, taking a gulp of the dark ale. "Indeed." I can't help myself. "Any news from the Captain?"

He shakes his head as he tears off a bite from a roasted chicken leg with his teeth, grease coating his lips. "Nothing new anyway. It'll probably be another day, possibly two before they arrive in Malnar. The latest report from the mines doesn't sound good."

I can't release the tension in my neck and shoulders, but I say, "I'm sure the Captain will have everything well in hand."

"Aye. He's a good man."

I nod, swallowing my fast-rising emotions with a mouthful of roasted carrot.

Casin continues between bites. "In the event the Captain isn't back for solstice, I've come up with some plans."

I bristle at the thought that Luc won't be back for solstice, but I shove another spoonful of stew into my mouth before waving for Casin to continue.

He takes a sip of ale before wiping his lips. "I was thinking of stationing the Annarr unit at the border crossings to help with the influx for the celebration. The week leading up to the solstice, I planned on having the Prioi and Annarr units take shifts. And for the night itself, the Annarr unit will be on duty first, with the Prioi taking over halfway through the evening. I wanted to make sure all the soldiers have a chance to enjoy the festivities, but I have ordered them all to refrain from drinking until *after* their shifts. Unless you think we'd need additional soldiers that night, I figured even with our reduced numbers after sending ranks down to South Leiren, that will be plenty of security."

"The Prioi and Annarr, even at half their numbers, will suffice."

He nods, taking another sip of his ale. "The Sagas will patrol the castle grounds."

"It sounds like you have everything well in hand." I swallow, hiding my clenched hand under the table. "Even if the Captain doesn't make it back in time, I trust you will have our city well looked after."

"Thank you, your Majesty."

A sudden thought pops into my mind. "How did the little meal time with the prisoners go after I left?"

His brows furrow for a second before he realizes what I'm asking about. "It was actually the talk of the city for a few days. It was chilling watching those prisoners' haunted faces walking single-file through the streets to the tavern."

"You were there?"

He nods, rubbing his hand over the back of his neck. "I didn't feel like that was something that should be delegated."

I nod. "Show me."

His back stiffens ever so slightly, but he nods. I focus the magic on his mind, and the scene snaps to life. I close my eyes to better see the tavern come to a slow standstill as a soldier brings in the prisoners. The metal clank of the manacles seemed to ring around the room, filling the ceilings with the sound. A few of the prisoner's eyes darted around, silently pleading for help. Others kept their eyes downcast, their shoulders slumped, their thin bodies barely holding them up. I recognize Silas, and I smirk at a tear tracking down his cheek. The guard leading the line pointed to an empty bench. "Sit."

Each prisoner awkwardly lowered themselves to the bench, swinging their chained feet up and over.

The guard at the back of the line shouted, "Hands on the table. Your food will be brought to you."

Manacled hands landed on the scarred wood table with another clatter of sound, and a few minutes later, plates of food were placed before each prisoner. The rest of the room was silent as the soldiers watched the prisoners stare at their plates before a few started shoveling food into their mouths with their hands, their hunger driving them to take as much as they could. Others continued to stare, either at their food or at the soldiers or the patrons openly staring at the scene before them. Through Casin's memory, I feel the tension building. Casin knows something is about to happen.

The prisoner I had gone to see that morning, the one I had mentally falling into an iced-over lake over and over, grabbed his plate, tossing the food in the air before slamming the tin plate on the edge of the table trying to break an edge sharp enough to do damage. It dented but didn't break. "I won't go back!" He continued to beat the plate on the table as everyone stopped eating to watch.

A guard approached, wrestling the ruined plate from the prisoner's weak fingers. He moaned, reaching for the plate like a child reaching for a toy being taken away from them. "No! I won't go back. I can't." His desperate eyes bounced around the room. "Please! Don't let them take me back! Please, help me. Kill me. Someone! Please!"

No one moved, but as the guard moved away to carry off the battered plate, Silas, the prisoner who tried to steal my Stone at the spring waters, jerked forward, swiping a short sword from the guard's hip. Without a word, Silas sliced the blade across the screaming prisoner's throat before plunging the sword into his own chest, right into his heart.

I shake my head, watching the memory. Fucking hero-types.

I thought the room was quiet before, but after that, the silence of shock hung heavy in the room. But it lasted all of a few heartbeats before the guard swore, "Well, shit." He gripped Silas' shoulder, pulling him back from where he landed slumped over the table, yanking his sword from his chest. After wiping it off, he sheathed it and gestured to the other guard. "Get someone to help you haul these two out of here."

As they moved, he looked down the line of prisoners. A few

resumed eating, their hunger so great, even the death of two other prisoners right in front of them didn't curb their appetite.

The guard put his hands on his hips with a frown, eyeing the prisoner's ignoring their food. "Finish eating. You have five minutes."

From where Casin was observing the scene, propped against a far wall, he called out to the room. "Everyone go about your business. Finish your meals, then head off to your families or your work. Show's over."

Slowly, the room moved into action, side glances aimed at the prisoners until they were ordered to their feet and paraded from the room.

The vision fades, and I open my eyes. Casin's eyes pinch at the edges, and his breathing comes out deep and controlled to stave off the worst of the pain from having me in his head.

I take another drink. "The rest made it back to the dungeons without further incident?"

Casin nods.

I'll need to go down there at some point and put them back into the magic, continuing their punishments. Maybe I'll even be nice and find them a new memory or fear to trap them within, you know, to keep things fresh. I can't have them conquering their fears.

I smile, and Casin shakes his head with a chuckle, throwing back the rest of his ale. "I don't like that look."

I nod. "Now's as good a time as any to go check on the prisoners, see how they've enjoyed their break from my magic."

Casin stands, taking his cup and empty plate with him. "I'll never understand people who think you won't know."

I shrug. "Hope can be a very dangerous thing." I swing one leg over the bench, cup in hand. "Keep me apprised on any news from the mines."

He bows his head slightly. "Of course, your Majesty."

He walks off, dropping his plate and cup in the large bin of soapy water. I follow shortly after, tucking in my shirt where it had come loose. The magic goes back to an indiscriminate rumble of noise as I leave the dining hall behind and make my way to the dungeons.

As my foot hits the last step, I flex my frozen fingers. The air down here bites with the cold of winter. While there's been a few light dust-ings, the first big snowfall hasn't come yet. I lift my head in a small nod at the guard at the end of the row of cells, and he bows in return.

"How are our guests?"

"Quiet for the most part, your Majesty."

I turn to the first prisoner, tilting my head as I meet a pair of blue eyes. A tie holds back her blond hair, the cold tinting her full cheeks. Her arms wrap around her thick waist, but she meets my gaze with a scowl.

"You're new. Who are you?"

Her eyes narrow, but she presses her lips together. I laugh, the sound startling several prisoners down the line. "You think keeping that pretty mouth of yours closed will keep the answers from me?"

The guard strides toward me, stopping to stand on my right. "She's a new guest. She was caught in the stables last week putting poison in the horse feed. None were harmed. We caught her in time."

My entire body goes rigid. The horses? Why? I clench my teeth at the thought of Yara or Kahar or any of the magnificent steeds dying in writhing pain. I look down at the prisoner, and what she sees in my eyes frightens her. She scrambles back, pressing her back to the stone wall, hugging her knees. "M-m-more will c-come."

I glance at the guard, who shrugs. "After some ... prodding, she named one coconspirator. He didn't come quietly, put up quite the fight. He's dead. We've got nothing else from her."

I aim my stare back at the prisoner. "Why the horses?"

She narrows her eyes at me before glancing through the bars to the other prisoners. *'How strong is the magic?'*

"Strong enough to know if you lie to me. Powerful enough to tear apart your mind if I so desire." Her eyes go wide, and I smile. "Yesss. My magic is very real, and very powerful."

Her hands start shaking, and she grips them tighter around her legs. *Adastra is coming.* "With your horses gone, the response time of your army would be crippled."

"Who is Adastra?"

She jerks in surprise but tries to cover it with a smirk, the fear in her eyes gone in an instant. "The one coming to kill you."

I shift my weight to my right foot, kicking out my hip as I grab my dagger. The blade taps rhythmically against the bars as I ponder her words. A second later, realization hits. "The cousin?"

She rocks forward, spit flicking over her lips. "The Lurona family will take back what you stole."

Ravaxina Lurona was the daughter of King Axis Lurona, and he married into the title, so the Luronas had not held the throne for long, but it seems the family is determined to hold on to Trislen.

Well, too fucking late.

I shove into her mind, digging up any crumb of information about this Adastra. Disappointingly, there's very little, and most of her information is vague. She doesn't even know what he looks like. From what I can tell, Adastra has been eyeing the throne for a while, long before I took it. It seems he's using me and my ... reputation to gain support from those still loyal to the Lurona name.

This prisoner was part of a small group sent north shortly after my takeover to try to cripple my army and make it easier for this cousin to infiltrate my kingdom.

I glance at the guard. "There were six sent with her. All different missions. We need to find them."

The guard glances at the woman before looking back at me. "What do they look like? What were their missions?"

The woman grits her teeth but is unable to hold back the moan of pain as I push for deeper details in her mind.

"There are four males, including the one who was killed, and one other female." I close my eyes and shiver as the woman screams a short bark of pain. "Male: short, balding, older than me, stub nose. Male: tall, thin, blond, young, maybe twenty, pock scars on his cheeks. Male: tall, average build, brown hair, my age." My dagger scraps across the metal bars as I fight the pain of the magic to see more details. My eyes pop open at the thought that slips from the woman and I laugh at her stricken expression. "Apparently, this male smells like cinnamon and has soft, tempting skin."

The guard chuckles, and the woman tries to hide her blush with a scowl. She can't hold it though as I close my eyes once again and shove back into her mind. "Female: average height, short blond hair shaved on one side, green eyes, but her left eye has a sliver of blue."

I search for more before pulling away from her mind and resuming the twirling of my dagger.

"As to their missions and where they might be right now, she doesn't know. They were given their assignments individually and separated once they arrived here in Farden."

The woman retches, spitting on the stone floor. The guard crosses his arms. "Smart. Shift change happens in the morning. I will put together a search party."

I tap my blade to the bars again, eventually shaking my head. "No. I'll send out a team tonight."

Wiping her mouth, the woman smiles around the pain. "Adastra will defeat you, despite your *magic*."

She scoffs around the word, and I shove down my anger reminding myself she hasn't been subjected to my power long enough to break her, not yet.

What I find most concerning is her expectation that Adastra will make his move soon. How soon? There hasn't been enough time since Rava's death for him to get here any sooner than two months' time. Unless I'm missing something.

I slam back into her mind, not trying to hide my grin as she topples over into a fetal position. But no matter how deep I dig through her memories, the answers aren't here. However, along the way, I find a delicious memory, and my grin grows through the strain of the magic as I bring it to life within her mind.

She screams as she sinks into the scene, "No! Please, no! Not that!"

21

The prisoner, a young girl in this memory, kneels on the floor, her grandmother towering over her. The old woman's gray hair sits at the nape of her neck in a tight bun and hatred sparks in her blue eyes. The girl hates her just as much. Her parents died the year before, and her grandmother reluctantly took her in.

The old woman's voice barks out. "How many times do I have to tell you that your nice dresses are not meant to be played in?" The girl tries to wipe away the grass stains on her skirt, her small hands shaking under her grandmother's wrath. "I told you if you ruined another dress, you would be punished."

A tear leaks from the corner of the girl's eye as she rolls up her sleeves, holding out her arms, palms up. Stripes still mark the skin of her forearms from the last lashing she received.

Her grandmother tsks. "No. The lashes are no longer enough. You keep disobeying." She shifts, bringing her hands from behind her back. The old woman drops a white and brown animal on the floor, and the girl chokes on a cry. Her small hands reach for the cat, and when her fingers meet cold, hard flesh, she screams, her chest constricting with pain ... too much pain.

The grandmother turns, her voice carrying over her shoulder as she leaves the room. "I told you not to disobey. Now that you don't have anyone to play with, maybe you can manage to keep your clothes clean."

The door slams, and the girl scoops the dead cat into her arms, her tears wetting the fur, its small, stiff body laying ridged in her lap.

I pull away from her mind as I loop the memory. A fitting one, since she aimed to do the same to my horses.

I need to find out more about this Adastra, but first, the rest of the prisoners.

I roll my shoulders as the guard shifts next to me. "It's always slightly terrifying to watch you do that. The way their faces go blank, but there's somehow still terror behind their eyes. It's … unnerving."

It's meant to be unsettling. The entire point of hunting down the Stones was so people would fear me, so they would think twice before crossing me … or Luc. I wear others' fear like a layer of armor.

I take a few steps down the line, passing an empty cell before turning to one on my right. A man sits in the far corner, one leg extended along the floor, the other bent with his forearm resting on his knee. Hunger has drawn his pale skin over his bones, and his cheeks are hollow. "Go on then, send me back to the woods."

Ah yes, this one has a fear of the dark, so I had sent his mind into a dark wood, the shadows so deep he couldn't see past his outstretched hand. The howls of wolves drove him, stumbling through the trees. The snap of their teeth keeping him running, the brush of fur against his legs sending him darting in all directions.

But it seems this nightmare has gotten old. I tap the bars of his cell with my dagger. "Not this time." His eyes go wide as his mind gets shut in a box. There's no room for him to move in any direction in the coffin he believes himself to be trapped in. The darkness is complete as his palms slap the wood a mere inch above his nose. His mental screams tingle down my spine, and as I slip from his mind, I grin at the well of tears shining in his vacant eyes.

The guard shifts again. "I'm just going to go stand at my post if that's okay, your Majesty."

I dismiss him with a wave, and he hurries to the end of the cells, sitting in the wood chair against the wall, drumming his fingers nervously on the scarred table to his right. The torch flickers light and shadow across his face.

One step to my left brings me to the next prisoner, then the next, and the next. Before long, I've sent each prisoner into their own version of hell, and I'm striding back up the winding stairs. My head aches, but the flush of power has my blood racing. It's always been a heady combination—the pain and the pleasure.

I don't bother going back to the library or my rooms, instead heading out of the castle and straight to the bird house. The soft crunch of boots on gravel trails me as a guard follows, his mind focused on my back, on keeping me in sight but staying far enough back to allow me perceived space. He stays outside as I push through the old wooden door. The sour scent of bird droppings and the cooing of birds greets me. Dust motes dance in the air, and as I cross the dimly lit room, feathers kick up and dance around my feet. Cages of all sizes, set into the side walls, poke halfway outside to allow the birds access to the sun and sky. But most have the leather flap closed, blocking some of the cold, and the birds are nestled in their downy feathers.

Many cages are empty, and the bird master is not in this main building, so I pass through, absently running my fingers along the long wooden table stretching down the center of the room. Neat stacks of paper, message tubes, writing implements, and such are all in their places in their little nooks built under the table.

Pushing aside a split drape of heavy leather, I step into the large structure off the back of the room. The heavy acidic scent lifts as the space opens up, and I'm surrounded by glass. The walls climb two stories, letting the starlight twinkle through the large tree in the center of the aviary. Smaller shrubs dot the perimeter, and various perches hang at different heights around the glass room. The occasional flap of wings is accompanied by a whispered voice.

I round the tree, finding the new bird master lifted on his toes, arms stretched overhead, adjusting a perch. A large gray pigeon swoops down, flapping its wings to land on the bird master's head. He chuckles, the sound soft, before lowering himself and turning.

He's younger than I thought, maybe early twenties, and his pale skin seems overly bright under the starlit night. His hair is black, curling around his ears, and his stained shirt billows around muscled arms, his pants hugging lean legs.

His green eyes go wide, and he presses a hand to his chest upon seeing me. "Oh! Your Majesty. I'm so sorry. I didn't hear you come in."

I wave him off. "You are the new master?"

A small frown pulls at his lips, a bit of the light dimming from his eyes. "Aye." *'I miss poor old master Jurel. He was a kind man, and he loved the birds. He didn't deserve such a cruel death. If only I had been here...'*

"I need several messages sent out tonight, right now."

He rubs his hands down his pants, which are stained with dirt and bird shit. "Of course, your Majesty."

He passes me with a hurried pace, and I glance at his hands. No marriage ink.

I shake off the thought, reining in the heated rush of lust, knowing this man would just be a substitute. And a substitute won't do. Not this time.

The bird master leads the way back into the smaller primary structure. Leaning down, he pulls out small strips of papers and sets an ink pot to his left, pen poised in his left hand.

With a little cough, I clear my throat. "I need a message sent to South Leiren:

> *Captain Runic—Need information on Adastra. Possibly the cousin. Ask Shadow Lord. Rumors of movement against the throne happening soon."*

The master's pen scratches quickly with neat, tiny letters before setting it aside.

"Next, send this one to Adren:

> *King Erathan—Possible trouble from Eshena. Need any and all information on Adastra. Possible movement happening soon... Be prepared."*

As soon as he sets that note aside, he looks at me expectantly. I rest a hand on the worn wood table, glancing around the stacked cages. "Are there any birds capable of making the journey to Alara?"

His brows furrow as he crouches, pulling a rolled, waxed paper from its slot. As he smooths it out, I notice it's a map. His dirty finger traces a line from Leiren, over the Varyen Desert, across the eastern sea, landing on Alara. I notice Alara is one of the larger kingdoms of that country, with the tiny kingdom of Eshena perched on its northern border—where this supposed cousin, Adastra, is plotting against me.

The master's finger taps over Alara before raising his head, looking around the room. "I think my Amur Falcon could make it." He bites his lips. "Though, this time of year, with the freezing winds … I'd hate to lose her."

I tap a finger against the wood. "I need a message sent now if you can make it happen."

He nods. "Yes, your Majesty. I'm sure she can make it."

"It's going to Craxid, a small town in Alara." The master runs his finger over the map until it stills over the word Craxid fairly close to the Eshena border. "The message is:

> *Erlan Vranna—Runic sends his regards and assures me you*
> *could be of assistance. I have people on the way who*
> *should arrive in two months time. Any movement in*
> *Eshena? Need information on Adastra."*

As soon as his pen stops scratching, my hand grips the edge of the table, and I force myself to peel my fingers from the wood, placing my right hand in my pocket, my left hand absently gripping my dagger. "Final message. Going to Malnar:

> *Captain Lucaryn—Status? May have uncovered new infor-*
> *mation on the cousin."*

The master deftly sets the last message next to the others before lifting a hand, waving his forefinger in the air. "That reminds me, there was a message from the mines that arrived at dusk. I had it set aside to be brought to you, but, well ... here you are." He shuffles past me, kicking up feathers and dust. He reaches into a box, retrieving a slip of paper, quickly bringing it back.

I sheath my dagger, taking the message, knowing I should wait to read it until I'm alone in my rooms, but I can't stop my fingers from unrolling the paper.

> *Rydel - The snows have stalled our efforts in getting the*
> *trapped miners free. We have not given up, but things*
> *don't look good. The eastern mine is being opened, but*
> *ore extraction won't happen for at least a month, maybe*
> *more. I don't know how long I'll be here, but I'll do my*
> *best to be home for solstice.*

I want to crush the paper in my hand, but I still my fingers, swallowing my frustration, fear, and anger. I shouldn't be mad at Luc. He's doing his job. But my mind can't help but stitch together the coincidences that have occurred since I made that small advance toward him in my rooms.

I shove Luc's message in my pocket, nodding to the master. He nods back, his hands rolling the messages without looking at the papers. "These will go out presently, your Majesty."

I push out of the building, taking a deep breath of air not heavy with bird shit. I tap my thigh in time with my steps, boots crunching through the thin layer of snow. My breath puffs before me, hitting me in the face. I glance towards the stables, itching to ride hard to the coast until the voices drift away and the freezing sea spray chases away my emotions.

But Luc took Kahar to Malnar, and Yara is too tame for the kind of ride I'm looking for. Besides, I promised the healer I would get some rest. My battered body could certainly use a break. If only I could turn off my mind.

Luc. Why did he leave? Without telling me?

I pause on the steps of the castle, watching my breath drift away on the breeze.

Luc.

I fight the urges I haven't indulged in since the early days and weeks with the Stone.

I shouldn't.

Luc.

I can't. Memories of my mother's empty smile bring a grimace to my face, and I scrub my hand through my beard, sighing. I am not my mother. I'm stronger. I don't need the drug.

As I draw closer to the castle, the mental rumble in my head gets louder, and I pause again.

Luc.

Maybe I'm not.

22

Climbing the stairs, I stop the first servant I come across. "I need a runner into the city."

The young man, maybe seventeen, bows. "I can go, your Majesty."

"Is that your job, boy?"

He keeps his head bowed, shaking it, sending his blond hair swinging across the top of his head. "No, your Majesty. I'm a food runner from the kitchens, but I just finished for the night and am happy to run for you."

"Follow me."

I climb the stairs, hearing his light footfalls close on my heels. Striding quickly down the hallway, I ignore the guards posted at my door as I push into my rooms. The boy follows and stops inside the doorway.

He stays where he is as I disappear into my bedroom and return, a few coins clinking softly in my hand, along with a note. I pass both to him.

"Go to The Broken Mountain." His eyes widen slightly, and he swallows before he nods. The Broken Mountain is a pleasure house deep within the city. "Ask for Hillan. Tell her the king sent you. She'll know what I need."

He nods again and runs off as I dismiss him with a wave.

I kick off my boots as I swipe up the glass on my bedside table. Downing the pain tonic in one swallow, I set the empty glass on the counter of my washroom as I peel off the rest of my clothes. My tub is full—and by the steam rising off the top—was filled not all that long ago. I bend over to see the newly-constructed trench under the tub filled with glowing coals.

Sliding into the tub, I take a deep breath and let my head sink below the surface. The rush of water over my ears drowns out the mental noise, and I watch bubbles from my lips dance to the surface. My chest burns, my lungs desperate for air, but I hold myself under, needing the silence more than I need air at this moment.

The edges of my vision close in, and my limbs go limp. I almost inhale the water, but before I can open my mouth, my body protests and shoves me above the water. I take a big inhale, gasping as my lungs greedily suck down air.

I drop my head against the raised edge of the tub, tapping my ring against the side. Luc, Erathan, South Leiren, Adastra, the solstice, Luc, Luc, Luc ... it's a parade of problems and responsibilities marching through my mind.

After a while, my ass and the backs of my legs actually start burning from the heat of the coals. My fingers are getting wrinkly anyway, so I drag myself out of the tub, sloshing water over the floor as I dry myself off and fall naked into my bed, draping my blanket over my hips.

I rub my temples, counting my breaths until light footsteps cross my room. The boy has returned, his lips pinched, a small pouch clutched in his hand. I almost smile at his thoughts, his mind reeling at what he just saw in the pleasure house, but I hold out my hand. He drops the silk pouch in my palm without a word before turning and fleeing from the room, my door clicking shut behind him.

I loosen the string, the sweet decaying-rose scent of the powder inside hitting my nose, and I shudder in disgust even as my pulse races with the desire to taste it—to fall into oblivion. I take a pinch, dropping the drug on my tongue, swallowing the bitter powder. One pinch is more than enough, but I'm not looking for 'enough.' I take another, licking the white residue from my fingers before I bend an arm behind my head, resting my other hand on my chest.

It doesn't take long for the drug to take effect as the mental noise softens, like the rumble of a cart's wheels over dirt far in the distance. My skin tingles, and the shadows in the room shift, dancing across the ceiling. The walls seem to bend before they melt, then solidify again. When I wave my fingers in front of my face, they leave little trails of light. The ink on my shoulder crawls across my skin, painting my entire arm black.

The hallucinations are dizzying, but the slide of the sheets over my skin grounds me. It feels like water, or better yet, if I concentrate, like Luc's fingers trailing up my thighs.

I crawl my fingers down my chest, wrapping my hand around my cock, spreading the pre-cum down my hard length, gritting my teeth, forcing the image of Luc kneeling above me to come to life behind my closed lids.

I don't remember if I actually got myself off, but the next time I become aware, the room spins, and the rush of mental noise rips a groan from my dry lips. The pouch is in my hand, and I'm dipping my finger into the powder before I even register what I'm doing.

Every time I start to come down, my hand reaches for the small bag, and the drug once more coats my tongue, sending me into oblivion for a few more blissful minutes, or hours—I'm not sure.

Morning sunlight spills across the ceiling, my drugged mind turning the light into winged fairies. I watch them dance around my room before everything goes dark again.

My pounding head pulls me from the quiet, and a knock on my door shoots pain through my skull. With a groan, I ignore it, reaching for the pouch once more. It's much lighter than it should be, and I wonder for a moment how long I've been riding the drug. I'm pretty sure it's only been a night. My eyes roll back as I sprinkle a bit more on my tongue. I fumble with the drawer in the table next to the bed, My fingers are slightly numb, but I manage to grab the bottle of oil, ripping the cork from the lid with my teeth before pouring it over my chest and stomach. The bottle falls to the bed, lost somewhere in the tangled sheets, but I don't care as my palm slicks through the oil. I grab my cock, imagining it's Luc's mouth wrapped around me. I pump into my fist. The room spins from the effects of the drug, so I shut my eyes tight, picturing Luc's muscled body, his flexing arms, his straining abs, his flexing thighs, his tight ass, his thick cock.

I come hard, painting my hand and stomach with my release, but the drug keeps my cock hard, or maybe it's the thoughts of Luc—or both. My hand keeps stroking. I come again, my body jerking as pleasure shoots down my spine, tingling across my body.

But as soon as the orgasm dies, pain shoots through my skull, pulling an actual shout of pain from my throat. I grab the pouch with sticky fingers, licking the drug and my own cum from my hand

I need just a little more. Just a little while longer.

The shadows close in around me, and I sink into nothingness.

I'm deep in the darkness when my body jerks with the pain of lightning striking my skin. My entire body fires up in agony. I gasp, sitting upright, clutching my chest, my heart racing.

"Fuck!"

The grumble of mental noise comes barreling back. My mouth feels like it's filled with sand, and my head feels like Kahar has kicked me straight in the forehead. I groan, reaching for the pouch, only to find it gone.

"No more of that, for now, your Majesty." I turn, facing the healer who is packing up his bag. "Solstice is fast approaching. Casin came to me, desperate to help you. You need to get up."

"How long have I been out?" My voice is gravelly, and the healer hands me a glass of water. It hits my tongue and slides down my throat, and I nearly sigh with relief.

"Four days, your Majesty."

Well, shit. Only a week until solstice.

"Has the Captain returned?"

"Not that I know of, your Majesty."

What the hell. I will go to Malnar and drag him back if I have to.

"Where is Casin?"

"The war room, your Majesty."

I swing my legs over the edge of the bed, disconcerted by the tremble in my legs as I shove myself to my feet. I rub my aching chest, reminded of Luc's new habit. An image of his large palm pressed to his broad chest flits through my mind. When did he start doing that?

My fingers flex. "What the hell did you give me?"

He smiles, though he tries to hide it, tilting his head down to fasten his bag. "A concentrated stimulant. A drug that has the opposite effect of the one you've been taking."

"No wonder I feel like I could run all the way to the coast."

"I wouldn't recommend that, your Majesty."

I smirk, padding naked to my washroom, hearing the door open and close as the healer leaves. I wash quickly before dressing in black pants, a black shirt, my black boots, and my chest harness and thigh sheath. My clothes feel rough, and my skin is itchy from whatever the healer gave me.

Striding through the castle, everyone who sees me quickly changes direction, giving me a wide berth. I know from the thoughts that flow in and out of my mind what everyone is thinking of me—the rumors of the drug-addled king that have spread like fire through the castle—and I just don't care.

A glance out a window reveals a thick blanket of snow on the ground, and the midday sun hides behind low, heavy gray clouds. Walking through the open doors of the war room, I spy Casin standing at the far end of the rectangular marble table. He's hunched over, hands braced on either side of a messy stack of papers and a map.

My voice carries across the room. "We're not at war, Casin." Adastra jumps to mind. "Not yet."

He keeps his muscled arms braced on the table but lifts his head. "Always good to be prepared, your Majesty."

I stop at the other side of the table, looking over the map. "I sent messages out"—I rub a hand over the scruff of my beard—"four days ago. Any responses?"

He nods his head at the end of the table where a few stacks of letters sit next to three small tubes. "There's a message with Erathan's seal, one with the Captain's seal, and one from Runic in South Leiren. The others are mostly pertaining to the solstice celebration."

I let my fingers trail along the cool table, the sensation tingling along my still sensitive skin. I literally itch with the desire to open Luc's message first, but I force myself to run my finger under Erathan's seal. The tiny drop of wax pops, and I flip the lid of the small tube, shaking out the tightly rolled paper.

> *Rydel-*
> *I look forward to researching your library during the*
> *solstice celebration. I'm sorry, I don't know of this Adas-*
> *tra, but I will see what I can find. The ports are secure.*
> *My army is ready to defend.*

Erathan is more than likely already on his way here, so there's no use in sending a response.

I pick up Runic's tube next.

> *Your Majesty-*
> *I have not heard of this Adastra, but my relative might*
> *have. I'll send a bird today if I can find one that can*
> *make the journey. I went to The Shadow Lord myself*
> *and asked about Adastra. He claims to have never heard*
> *the name, but I suspect he knows something. Please*
> *advise - detain him for further questioning, or put one of*
> *our spies on him?*
> *As for an imminent threat, we are as prepared as we can be.*
> *Erathan sent word that he is ready to act in our defense,*
> *and with his forces only a hard day's ride away, they*
> *can come to our aid fairly quickly if needed.*

I place the paper on the table, the ends immediately curling. I stare at Luc's seal on the small tube. I don't know why my palms are sweating as I take it in my hand, popping the wax, shaking the paper free.

> *Your Majesty-*
> *We managed to open a small shoot to the pocket where the*
> *miners are trapped. Two have been extracted. Eight*

remain. It's slow going with the snows and the constant
threat of further collapse, but with a little luck,
everyone will be cleared by the end of the week.
I'm still investigating if this was sabotage or an accident,
but at this time, I believe it was an accident.
I'll be back by solstice, solstice evening at the latest.

My eyes travel over 'your Majesty' again and again. I hate when Luc uses formality with me, especially after what happened between us and his sudden departure.

But he'll be home soon. We'll talk. Everything will be fine.

It has to be.

23

The Solstice has arrived. I swallow down a pain tonic, the third of the day, as my long legs quickly carry me out of my rooms and through the castle. A group of three—their thoughts revealing them to be father, mother, and son—approach. They all bow and press themselves to the wall to allow me to pass in the narrow hall. A servant, back hunched with the pile of linens stacked in their arms, comes from a room on my right, but upon seeing me, she scurries back through the door, head bowed and buried in the fabric.

The press of the mental noise vibrates in my teeth. I take a sharp left, hoping to cut through the small gathering room to escape the castle. People fill this room as well. Eyes turn my way and every head bows. The room goes silent, like everyone is holding their breath, but the voices in my head are a rushing waterfall of noise.

A sea of colorful dresses and dark pantsuits shift with the desire to approach me, but I raise my hand, halting everyone where they stand. "Happy solstice. I will see you all at the festivities tonight." And with that, I cross the room with long strides, eager to be away from my guests. It feels like every high family as well as any family of any importance is in my castle right now.

I enjoy a good celebration as much as the next person, but the press of bodies is ... uncomfortable. I feel like my brain is melting, and I've been drinking four or more pain tonics a day for the headaches, but I haven't touched the drug again.

As I continue through the castle, I marvel at its warmth. It's almost too warm. Fires blaze in every hearth, candles are everywhere, and torches flicker even though it's not yet midday. The servants have been working non-stop, and everything has been set up to stun and delight my guests. Evergreens drape over every tapestry, mirror, portrait, banister, and table. The scents of cut pine, cinnamon, and vanilla permeate the air, and festive red ribbons adorn the evergreens.

A servant rushes past, a tray of flaky pastries in his arms, and I realize how hungry I am. One can't live on tonics alone, so I snag a tart, popping it in my mouth without breaking stride. I lick my fingers, swallowing the buttery, sugary bread before grabbing my cloak draped over my forearm. With a flutter of fabric, I swing it over my shoulders, securing its fur-lined warmth around my shoulders. The movement only brings a twinge of pain from my injuries, and the bruises on my face have finally faded.

As soon as I step outside, the freezing air steals my breath, biting my skin. But the mountains almost glow where they tower beyond the city, and despite the pain in my head, I smile. Snow has whited out the skies the past few days, but today, the late morning sun shines bright, not a cloud in sight. A perfect day to celebrate solstice.

A thin layer of stubborn snow crunches and squeaks under my boots as I walk down the cleared path, the snow piled above my knees on either side. A familiar squeal trumpets through the air, and I chuckle, rounding a hedge that brings the stables into view. Kahar tosses his head, his long mane flaring. The stable hand almost drops the reins as he backs up to avoid being struck by Kahar's flying front hooves.

The young stable hand, Shana, comes running from inside the stables.

"Idiot! Move aside."

She grabs the reins, careful not to yank them, practically shoving the man aside even though he's more than twice her size. Kahar drops his front hooves, settling with a snort. Shana turns, leading the giant black horse into the stables while mumbling, "Aanea, Kahar. Se'as'r fe'as iyai zse'aur urs e'as." *Come, Kahar. Let's get you clean and fed.*

I shake my head as the warhorse follows the small girl like a docile puppy. She requested access to old scripts and texts, the eager glow in her eyes hard to resist, so I gave in, and she's picked up even more of the old tongue. I suspect she'll be as fluent as Luc and me soon.

But then my smile freezes as Luc strides out of the stables. His black hair is messy, like he's been running his hands through it, and his facial hair has gone from scruff to a full-on beard. He has thrown one side of his cloak over a shoulder, exposing the black shirt he wears covering his broad chest. His face is in profile, talking with a soldier to his left, and as she walks off, Luc's eyes snap to mine, like he knew I was here.

The intensity of his blue eyes stops me in my tracks for a moment, but I recover quickly enough, striding to meet him halfway. Our forearms clasp, and I feel the warmth of his hand through my clothes.

"Your Majesty."

I smirk. "Captain." We let go of each other, heading back toward the castle. "Were you able to save everyone?"

He keeps his gaze straight forward, rubbing his chest before dropping his hand at his side. "All but two. The small passage we created collapsed before we could get the last ones out."

I nod. "You did the best you could. How does continued ore extraction look?"

Luc shoves his hands in his pockets. "A month, maybe more depending on the snows, before they will be back to regular production, but they are going to have to find a new vein soon. The current mines are almost tapped."

"And the investigation?"

"We found no evidence of sabotage. The marks in the supports were old, probably created when the posts were first constructed."

"You're sure?"

He runs his fingers through his dark hair. "As sure as I can be, Ry. I questioned everyone personally. Unless the saboteur was one of those who died in the cave-in, I didn't find anyone at fault."

"I should have gone with you."

I can't help but smile as he tsks at me. "I can handle things just fine without your almighty magic trick."

"I know. I know. It just would have saved you some time if I were there."

He shrugs. "I would have been there just as long. I wasn't leaving until we got them out, or all hope was lost."

Silence hangs heavy as silvery snow sparkles around us. We stomp our boots on the steps to dislodge the packed snow before entering the castle. Now, the almost overbearing warmth is nice. Luc heads toward the stairs that lead to our wing. "I'm going to get cleaned up. I'll come find you later, and we can talk before the festivities ramp up."

He pulls ahead of me, but I press my lips together, fighting the urge to reach for my dagger. I follow, catching the slight bunching of his shoulders as he hears me climbing the stairs behind him. He doesn't turn around. He doesn't object. But he's not inviting me either.

I shove my clenched fist in my pocket. I don't need to be invited anywhere within my castle, but it would be nice to know that I'm welcome in Luc's presence right now. I have no idea what's going on with him, but I'm going to find out. This strain between us, real or imagined on my part, is driving me mad.

Luc's large hand grips the metal handle to his door. His knuckles are white as he turns the lever, and I almost snap at him, needing to know what has made him so tense around me. But I hold it in, following him through the door, not quite succeeding in keeping the door from slamming shut.

Luc's powerful legs carry him across his sitting area into his bedroom without a glance in my direction. As I follow, he leans down, grabbing a handful of clothes—clean or dirty, I don't know—from a chair, dropping them to the floor before sitting to take his boots off.

Leaning against a wall, I prop myself on a shoulder, crossing my arms over my chest and one ankle over the other. I have a million questions, but none make it past my lips. I just stare at him as he keeps his head bowed, concentrating too hard on his boot laces.

Without looking up, he asks, "What's with this Adastra fellow?"

This is not what I want to talk about. "I'm not sure. I haven't heard from Runic's relative in Alara. Erathan claims to have never heard of him, and the Shadow Lord is claiming ignorance as well, though Runic seems to think he might know something."

Luc stands, facing away from me as he pulls his shirt over his head, his back flexing with the movement. "It's good to keep digging, but it'll probably end up being nothing. A nobody trying to throw their title around. I can't imagine a no-name cousin of Ravaxina crossing the sea to take on the Crown Breaker, The feared King of the Mind Stone."

I tilt my head at the slight tinge of bitterness in his voice.

"I wouldn't normally be worried about this cousin, but there's a woman in the dungeons. A soldier caught her trying to poison the royal horses, supposedly on Adastra's orders."

Luc finally turns to face me, his brows raised, his bright blue eyes surprised.

I continue, "She was one of a group sent to sabotage our army. One of her co-conspirators is dead, two others have been captured, and according to the prisoner's memories, there's four more out there —from her group. She didn't know much else, other than the belief that Adastra would make his move soon. I'm moving forward under the assumption that there are other rebels and spies working for Adastra here in Farden."

Luc stands still for a second, thinking through what I said before turning again, running his hand through his dark hair. "How soon could Adastra reasonably get here? We should have two months at the very least to gather more information and hunt down his supporters."

"That's what I figured, but I have a bad feeling about this, Luc. Something feels off with this whole thing. Adastra acted too quickly. He knows too much."

Luc turns, actually taking a step toward me before pausing. "If you're concerned, we'll put as many people as we can spare on it. We'll figure it out. We always do."

He rubs his chest, and I drop my arms to my sides, sliding my hands in my pockets. "What's going on, Luc?"

His eyes drop to the floor.

"Should I have not said what I did? It's okay if our relationship is not … that. You're my best friend, Luc. I just need you by my side, as my friend."

His hand continues to rub his chest as his head slowly lifts, his dark hair falling around his forehead, his beard adding a ruggedness to his already striking features. A corner of his lip lifts in a weak half-smile. "You really never read my mind, do you?"

My eyes go wide, and I gasp in surprise. "No. I trust you. The magic is quiet around you, only you. Besides, I wouldn't betray you that way. We share a lot, Luc, practically everything, but your thoughts—your mind, is your own."

His hand stills, fingers splayed across his chest, pressing into his flesh. I take a step toward him, pulling my hands from my pockets, holding them out slightly at my sides. "What is it, Luc?"

His deep mental voice slides into my mind. He's only ever pushed his thoughts at me a handful of times, mostly in times of danger, when knowing each other's thoughts would sway the situation to our side. But now, it feels … intimate. His voice caresses my mind like cool water on heated skin. *'I've thought long and hard about this, and I'm still not sure it's the right time.'*

I take another step, that cursed feeling spreading through my chest … hope. "For what?"

'I was glad you said what you did, Ry, though I'm conflicted. I'm your Captain.'

I think my heart might ram right out of my chest. "How so?"

'How can I protect you? How can I protect your kingdom when I'm so consumed by you?'

My heart stops—it actually stops before I take a small breath. "Who better to protect *our* kingdom? Who better to protect me than you?"

'You mean so much to me, Ry. Maybe too much.' His gaze holds mine. "Uh sahe'a iyai." *I love you.*

24

His gaze jumps between my eyes, searching for my reaction to his whispered declaration.

I take the three strides that bring me before him, gripping his shoulders, closing my eyes as I press my forehead to his. "I have always loved you, Luc. That love has simply changed, become more. It's hard to breathe when I look at you, but it's hard to function when you're gone."

His silence draws out, and I lift my head, taking a step back, but before I can pull away, he grips the back of my neck, and my cock jumps at the possession in his eyes. "For the record, yes."

My brows pinch together in question as his hand travels up my torso, over my shoulder, and down my arm until he grips my wrist. "What you asked me before I left." He presses my hand to the front of his pants, bucking his hard cock into my palm. "I want this." His voice is deep and gravelly, spooling desire between my thighs. "I want us."

I grip him through his pants, pulling a groan from both of us before I pull him to me and crush my lips to his.

Our tongues dance, and my palm strokes over him, and I'm desperate for our clothes to be gone. He shares his thoughts with me, and ... shit, the imagery. We both growl with world-shattering desire. His moan reverberates against my chest, and I'm painfully hard, pressing against my suddenly too-tight pants. My hands curl around his neck before combing up the back of his scalp, gripping his short hair to tilt his head so I can take the kiss deeper.

A slice of pain lances through my bottom lip as he bites me before sucking my lip between his. My heart is racing, trying to escape my rib cage. But even if it did burst from my chest, I know it would be safe in Luc's hands, and that thought alone almost buckles my knees.

I back him up, quickly unfastening my harness before dropping it to the floor with a thud. Pulling my shirt from the waist of my pants, Luc helps me rip it over my head, and it flutters to the floor, lost to the mess of Luc's room.

The back of his legs hit his chair, and he almost topples into it, but he slaps a palm to the back of the chair to push himself upright. He pauses, lightly trailing his fingers over the tattoo that crawls from my shoulder down my chest, my skin pebbling at his touch. Then his hand wraps around my neck, pulling me closer as his other hand runs over my stomach, causing my muscles to clench.

I shiver as he grips the waist of my pants, tugging while our tongues duel, thrusting, wrestling in the motion my hips want to make against his. I need something to ease the aching pleasure straining at my lower back and pulsing through my cock. As my hands travel up his muscled torso, my hips rock forward, and I can feel his arousal against my stomach.

"Gods, Luc." My words are a mere whisper as I run my fingers through his beard, cupping his jaw, fingers pressing to either side of his ear. "Tell me to stop now if you're still conflicted. I don't want you to feel uncomfortable with me, ever."

His hand grips my hair, yanking my head back. His piercing blue eyes clash with mine. "I've wanted you forever, and I'm damn well going to have you."

I bite my lip, drawing it between my teeth, feeling the scrape of my own beard against my tongue. Luc holds my head immobile, but I reach for his pants. He yanks my head back even farther, baring my neck for his teeth to scrape across my skin.

I groan, my hips thrusting toward him. "Fuck, Luc."

His eyes slowly crawl back to my face, and his wicked smile

almost has me coming right here. "You are always in charge, Ry. You wield control like a weapon." He leans in, his lips brushing my earlobe. "Don't you want to give up control for a while?" His tongue slides up behind my ear, and I'm helpless to do anything but hold on to his broad shoulders. "*Can* you give up control, Ry?"

Honestly, I don't know, but if I can let go for anyone, it would be Luc.

I grin, snapping my teeth at him. "Do your worst."

Before I can take another breath, Luc uses his grip on my hair to spin me at the same time his other hand snaps around to grab my throat. He squeezes before trailing his hand down my chest and over my stomach before pressing his palm against my cock over my pants. I groan, and his voice purrs against my ear. "Don't. Move."

His touch feathers over my inner thigh as he shifts to undo my thigh sheath, gently setting my beloved dagger on a small table. His heat presses against my back once more, his teeth nipping my ear. "Now, lose the pants."

I hesitate, prickling at the commands, even though I want nothing more than to comply. When I don't immediately reach for my pants, Luc tightens his grip on my throat. "Now, Rydel. Be good, and I promise to reward you."

My fingers fumble as my cock pulses with desire, but I manage to undo the clasps and get my pants halfway down my thighs. Luc's grip doesn't ease, so I have to work them the rest of the way off by kicking and stepping on the pant legs, but finally I'm bare, my back pressed against the front of Luc's body.

"Your turn." My voice comes out gravely with desire, and his nose brushes the back of my neck, his breath teasing my skin until I'm shaking.

"Don't move, Ry."

I clench my hands at my sides but can't keep the snark from my voice. "Yes, sir."

His answering chuckle is deep and guttural, the sound shooting right to my cock, and I grip it, stroking myself once. He steps away from my body, tsking, leaving me cold without his body warmth.

"Immediate disobedience. I said"—he grips my arms, pulling them behind my back—"don't move, Rydel."

I grip my wrists behind my back, shaking with the effort to stay still. The shuffling of clothes reaches my ears before he steps back into my space. The hard steel of his cock presses at my ass, and I rock back into him.

His hand scrapes back up my scalp, gripping my hair at the base. "Turn around."

I turn slowly, his grip moving with me. My breath leaves my lungs at the intensity in his eyes. His lips are slightly parted and swollen from our kiss, and as his gaze travels down my body, my insides turn to molten liquid.

He licks his lips. "I've seen you naked so many times before, but not like this, Ry, not for me." He leans in, brushing a gentle kiss against my lips. "You are glorious."

I swallow, taking down his taste. "I am yours, Luc."

"Kneel."

I raise a single eyebrow. I haven't knelt to anyone in ten years, and even though this is for Luc, the thought still rankles.

His abs flex as he yanks on my hair, and his cock bobs with his chuckle. "Rydel, do as you're told."

I step into his space. My stomach clenches with pleasure as our cocks press together. "I had no idea you were so bossy."

His lips quirk up in a smile that steals my breath. "I am your c]Captain. I give orders for a living."

His grip is still firm in my hair, but I don't need to bend to reach his cock. I wrap my fingers around his shaft, sliding the bead of pre-cum down his velvet length. We both groan as I squeeze him at the base. "I am King. I also give orders for a living."

I pump him again, and the grip on my hair tightens before he releases me and steps out of my grasp. His eyes travel back down my body, snagging on my cock before rising back to my eyes. "Kneel."

We stand facing each other for a moment before I bend first one knee, then the other.

"Touch yourself. Show me."

I wrap my hand around my aching cock, needing it to be Luc

touching me, but I yield. I stroke myself, grip strong and slow, pre-cum slicking over the head and down my shaft. After a few more pumps, Luc steps forward, lacing his fingers back into my hair.

"Open."

I lick my lips, staring at his glorious cock before me. "Yes, sir." His cock twitches, and I grin. "You like me calling you, sir."

His grip tightens as he presses the head of his cock against my lips. "Open."

I part my lips, letting the strong length of him slowly slide past my lips, over my tongue, and down my throat. I groan when I hit his base, and the vibrations have him moaning, and his head falls back. "Fuck, Ry."

I slowly slide back, curling my lips over my teeth as I suck. My tongue swirls around the head of his cock before I wrap my hand around him and take him deep again, and his soft dark curls brush my nose. Squeezing him with my fingers and lips, I start slowly, then pick up the pace before moving slowly again. Before long, he takes control, hips thrusting his thick length into my mouth, his hand shoving me harder and harder onto his cock until saliva drips from the corners of my lips.

Just when I think he's going to come, he pulls back. "On the bed."

"Thank Voluptas."

Luc chuckles. "The goddess of pleasure isn't here, Ry. I am. Your pleasure is mine."

I stand and cross to the bed in three long strides. The drawer of his side table rumbles with the low sound of wood scraping wood as I pull on the knob. Extracting the small bottle of oil, I move to upend some into my hands when Luc grabs it. Grabbing his wrist, I twist until the bottle drops to the bed. I spin, bringing his arm up behind his back, and I press his chest down. "I think I'm done submitting, for now."

He kicks out a leg, knocking me off balance before spinning. His hand reverses my grip so that he now has my thumb in his fist. He wrenches it back as his other hand grips my throat. "Are you sure about that?"

His grin threatens to stop my heart, and I grin back. I lean into his hand that's pressing against my throat. "Yes, sir."

I shove him onto his back, following him down on the bed. He releases my thumb to keep from hurting me, and I spread his thighs. I pick up the bottle, plucking the stopper and dripping the oil into my hands. Rubbing them together, I stroke my cock, watching his hungry eyes dilate, then I stroke his cock, causing his hips to buck beautifully into my hand. I trail my oil coated hand over his balls, cupping him for a moment before I probe lower.

His knees bend deeper, spread wider, as I circle one finger around his entrance before slowly sliding it inside him. Our breaths match my small pumps as I press into him, adding a second finger.

Luc's chest is gleaming with sweat as his hips buck in time with my hand until I pull out of him and line myself up between his firm ass cheeks. Grabbing the bottle again, I re-coat my hand, smearing the slick oil over my shaft and swirl it at his entrance. He lifts his hips, meeting me as I slide into him, one glorious, tight inch at a time.

"Fuck, Ry."

I grip his thigh with one hand and his cock in my other. "I intend to, sir."

I slide to the hilt, pressing my hips against his ass before slowly drawing back, keeping the stroke of my hand on his cock in time with my hips. The head of my cock catches at his entrance, and I slam back to the base, squeezing my hand down his shaft.

My gaze finds his still-raw arrow wound where the poison nearly took him from me, and the fingers of my free hand climb his chest, fluttering over the stitches. His hand presses over mine, and his face wavers before me as tears rim my eyes. His hand presses mine more firmly to his chest. "I'm okay, Ry. I'm here. We're here. Stay with me."

I blink back my tears and pick up the pace, watching his muscles flex with my every thrust, reassured by the strength of his body under mine.

My cock feels like it grows impossibly more rigid as I watch it slide in and out of Luc's perfect ass. As the sound of our flesh meeting over and over carries around the room, Luc reaches his arms over his head, gripping the edge of the bed. His biceps flex, and the extra leverage allows him to buck into my thrusts.

"Gods, Luc." I throw my head back as I work his cock with my hand, slamming into his ass as I grip his thigh to pull myself closer to him and him closer to me.

The pleasure is beyond anything I have ever felt. It builds in the muscles of my lower back, spilling around to my stomach and pulsing down my cock.

Luc releases one of his hands from the mattress, gripping my bicep and pulling me down. When I'm within reach, his fingers grip my chin, pulling my mouth to his. Our teeth clash before our tongues spear against each other.

He releases my lips with a growl, his eyes blazing, hips bucking against my desperate thrusts. "Come. Come for me, Ry. I want to see you undone from being inside me."

"Fuck!" My entire body is tingling, pinpricks of pleasure so intense it's almost painful.

"Right now, Ry. Come."

And I do. Fiery pleasure floods my body as I pump into Luc, and as my climax rips through me, I *feel* Luc's orgasm building—not from his thoughts, but his actual feelings. His pleasure, his love, floods my chest until his bliss is so mixed with mine that I can't tell us apart.

Before I can wonder about what I'm experiencing, his climax rips through him, pumping into my fist. His pleasure is so intense it takes me with him, drawing my orgasm out, on and on with his, like we're sharing each other's pleasure, the other's orgasm enhancing our own.

Finally, my hips slow, then stop before I collapse onto my side, sliding out of Luc. My sweaty skin sticks to the bedding as I try to slow my breaths. My hand rests on Luc's stomach, and I feel his ragged breathing as well.

I turn my head, watching his profile before he turns to me with a grin. I grin back. "Well, that was ..."

"Overdue."

I chuckle, propping myself on an elbow to lean in. Brushing my lips against his, he tugs on a strand of my sweaty hair in a teasing pull. I lean away and flop onto my back.

We lay in silence for a few moments before I jerk upright. "Luc!"

He jumps out of bed, scanning each window and door. I grin as I take him in, ready to fight. He really is a specimen of a man. "Calm down, Captain. I just remembered something."

He rolls his shoulders, then his eyes before laying back on the bed on his side, propping himself on his elbow.

My grin widens. "It's fake."

He frowns and sits up. "What?"

"Erathan's Heart Stone. It's fake."

25

His frown deepens, carving lines between his brows. "Fake? How do you know?"

"That alliance ...?"

"Yeah, I was wondering about that. I read through those signed documents you sent me three times. I couldn't figure out what you gave up for all those nice terms he gave you."

I laugh, and it feels good. This feels good, with Luc.

"Nothing, Luc. We gave up nothing. He gave us near unfettered access to his kingdom as well as his aid should we need it—which might end up being fortuitous, but we'll talk about that later. All that in exchange for my help in figuring out how he can access the power."

"He can't use the magic?"

I spring up and start pacing at the foot of the bed, his eyes tracking me with a small frown on his face. "No." I pause, my laugh bouncing around the room again. "Because it's not real. It can't be." I reach across my body, fingers trailing over the tattoos on my shoulder, sliding toward the back of my shoulder, just out of reach to the almost healed scar hiding my Stone. "I know the magic, Luc. The Stones are twins born of the same mage's magic. There's no way Erathan would feel *nothing* if the Stone was real."

Luc absently rubs his chest. I flex the fingers of my left hand as he bends one leg before him; the sheets pooling around his waist as he leans a forearm on his knee. "Are you sure he's not lying?"

Shrugging, I start pacing again. "I'm sure, Luc." I tap my temple. "He's well trained against the Mind Stone, but I would have found a lie. He wouldn't have been able to hide that." I stop before Luc, smiling. "He's convinced his Stone is real. And I'm going to feed him as much hope as I can. I'm going to shove every text, scroll, map, book, and scrap I can find on the Stone's lore—seemingly begrudgingly, of course."

Luc smiles. "Of course. Always with the dramatics with you."

I lean over, bracing a hand on his arm that rests on his knee. "Don't you see? It's still out there. It's out there waiting to be found and everyone in Imoria believes Erathan has it."

I stand, picking my way through the piles of clothes, random weapons, stacks of books, and empty cups. I retrieve my shirt, pulling it over my head before grabbing his and throwing it to him. "We are now the only ones looking for the Heart Stone." As soon as Luc's head pops through his shirt, I grin at him. "Imoria is ours, Luc."

A small smile lifts the edges of his beautiful lips, and I can't help but cross back to him, leaning over to take his mouth in a quick kiss.

He moves to stand, so I step back, and we both finish dressing quickly. As Luc tucks his shirt in his pants, and I buckle my harness and thigh sheath back in place, he turns to me. "I have a few things to attend to with Casin and the soldiers, but it shouldn't take me longer than an hour or two. Then I'll be back here, patrolling the castle and the gardens."

"Casin did well in your absence."

Luc nods as he looks around for his boots, and I shake my head with a chuckle. "Well, I'm going into the city. I want to watch the fire dancers." I glance out the windows, seeing there's still at least two hours until midday. "Then it'll be time to light the bonfires."

It's tradition for the solstice fires to be lit at midday, fed and kept burning until midday the next day. Ever since my first year as ruler of Leiren, I've lit the first fire in the city square.

Luc stands, buckling his leather armor down his chest. I don't know where his leathers were hiding, but damn, he looks good in them.

He tsks. "Would you consider skipping the fire dancers and waiting for me before you go to the square? The dancers are performing in the royal gardens later, so you won't be missing anything."

I take a deep breath, filling my lungs before slowly releasing it. Luc frowns, shaking his head as he straps a dagger to his forearm, knowing I'm going to object.

I smile. "Come find me when you can."

He sighs, crossing the room, placing a hand on the bed, kneeling to draw a sheathed sword from under the bed.

I laugh as he fixes it in place across his back. "Gods, Luc. Under your bed?"

He smiles, rubbing his chest. "It's sharp, clean, and oiled. It may seem careless, but I take care of my weapons. You know that, Ry."

I palm my dagger, the steel flashing as it catches the light streaming through the window. "Aye, I know."

He glances around the room as if looking for something. "When do you want to further discuss this cousin, Adastra? I'm sure you have measures in place, but I need to be fully briefed on everything you know, and we need to have several plans and contingencies set up."

I nod. "Later, Luc. Let's enjoy solstice. I know I said I'm worried, and I am, but the threat is still across the sea, and even if he has set sail with some kind of force, he would still be on the far side of the eastern sea. We have time."

His hand rubs the back of his neck, his bicep flexing through his leathers. "I don't like it, Ry. This all feels ..."

"I know. I'm unsettled too. But I'm determined to enjoy the here and now." I cross the room as he drops his hand. I squeeze his shoulder. "And who knows? Maybe his ship will sink in the freezing sea." Luc grins as I chuckle. "The North is ours. The South is now ours." He winces, rolling his shoulder, rubbing the arrow wound, but the pain quickly leaves his face, and I continue, "Erathan is our lap dog." I grin. "Let's celebrate, Luc."

"Aye, let's celebrate." He pokes me in the chest with a finger. "But be careful."

"Yes, Sir."

His eyes darken as he smirks at me. "Keep playing, Ry. We'll see who ends up on top next time."

I chuckle, my cock hardening, and I can't help the flutter in my heart that there will be a next time. Hopefully, many next-times.

As Luc moves to the door, I almost stumble as a wave of anxiousness bordering on pain spears through my chest. I rub a hand over my breastbone, reminiscent of Luc's habitual movement, but as quickly as the feeling hits, it's gone.

What the hell?

My eyes follow Luc's back as he disappears through the door. He's worried about me, and it's nice having someone to worry over me. I think I love Lucaryn, as much as I can love someone. I wasn't sure I was capable of love. I certainly never loved my family. But Luc is my family. He's all I need.

26

Laughter and scattered conversation floats through the sun-drenched air. The buzz of the crowds of people mixes with the grumble of noise in my mind. I took another pain tonic before leaving the castle, and it's taking the edge off, but I can't help the tension that pinches my shoulders.

I'm jostled, my hood falling back slightly as a man bumps into my shoulder, his laughter ringing out loudly. "Apologies, friend." He holds out a hand to steady me, but freezes, his eyes going wide as he recognizes me. His smile falls from his pale face before he quickly bows his head. "Your Majesty. I'm sorry. I didn't see you."

My guard has moved forward, but I shake my head before clapping the man's back with a smile. "The streets are full. The revelry has begun. We are all here to celebrate the winter as only Northerners can."

Relief spills through his mind as he looks up. "Indeed, your Majesty. Happy solstice."

I nod, walking off, letting whispers of my presence, both verbal and mental, bleed into the swamp of noise. A child runs past me, her arm brushing my thigh as she squeals with laughter. A taller girl races on her heels. "Amara, slow down!"

Two men clasp forearms in greeting before they begin to trade gossip. A third man joins them, passing around mugs of foamy ale.

I slide my hand in my pocket, fingers brushing the cold disks of coins. I pass one to a young woman standing at one of many tables that have been pulled out into the streets. She takes the coin with wide eyes but with a sweet smile, handing me a length of paper wrapped into a cone with spiced nuts inside.

Cinnamon, cardamom, salt, and sugar coat my tongue as the nuts crunch between my teeth. The biting wind hits my face, sending a shiver down my body.

I finish the nuts, balling up the paper, tossing it in a bin, and slapping my hands together to brush them clean. A couple shares a kiss under a sprig of mistletoe that's strung up across the street. Her hand wraps around her partner's waist, her partner threading her hand through her hair, holding her tight. I can't help but wish Luc was here.

A small crowd to my left claps and a chorus of ooohs float through the air. I move toward the action, standing at the back to the right of where the Adren fire dancers have leapt from the back of a brightly covered wagon. Their skin-tight black outfits have shiny red threads on the cuffs, making it look like their feet and hands are on fire. A woman dancer does a front somersault toward the crowd, and a coil of rope with a dart on its end flies from her hand. With a big sweep of her upper body in a large arc, the rope swings out to the crowd, backing them up, creating a semicircle of space for the performers.

She wraps a section of the rope under her arm, around her elbow, and snatches back the dart, fast as a cobra strike. It spins in a circle as the rest of the troupe joins her—six in all, with the woman with the twirling rope in the middle. Fire blazes from the hands of the man on the end. The sleight of hand is so seamless, I can't tell where the fire came from, but his palms are alight, and the crowd ahhhh's, a few standing on tiptoe to see better.

The performer lunges to the side, sweeping his flaming hands in a wide circle, and once his arms reach the performer to his right, he claps his hands. Flames and sparks fly away from him, catching on a ball the next performer throws in the air.

The crowd claps as the man catches the ball and starts juggling it with three others. One by one, each ball catches fire as he tosses them up in increasingly difficult patterns. On his next throw, a ball flies over the rope dancer, who is still coiling and slinging the rope and dart around her body. The woman on her right catches the flaming ball, rolling it up one arm, over her shoulders and down the other arm, dropping the ball to the ground. The path the flaming ball took ignites streamers of fabric that flow from her arms, and she dances, her arms trailing fire as she spins, flips, and kicks with the flames dancing around her.

She's getting ready to pass on the flame to the man on her right when a voice whispers over my shoulder.

"Enjoying the show?"

I don't turn, but a small grin pulls at my lips as Luc's arm slides under my cloak and around my waist, pulling me back against his chest.

I place my hand over his. "Indeed. They seem to top themselves every year. I can't figure out how they're doing half of that."

He chuckles, the sound sending a shiver down my spine. "You could find out easy enough."

I shrug. Sure, I could focus the magic and pull out the secrets of their art, but it's hard enough to keep all but the closest voices out of my head. "Sometimes it's nice to live in a bit of mystery."

I glance over my shoulder. Luc's cloak drapes casually over his broad shoulders, and his hood hides his face in shadow. I feel more than see his smile as he leans in. "You'll see a variation of this show later at the castle."

I raise an eyebrow as he steps back, taking my hand and pulling me between two buildings. The crowd quickly moves forward to fill our vacated spaces, stretching to see over the heads in front of them.

A little girl with a green cloak drags a man through the narrow space Luc is leading me down. "Hurry, papa. We'll miss it. Hurry."

They skirt past us without a glance, and I resent the flutter of jealousy that skips through my heart. How different I might be if my father had ...

No! I love my life. The pain, the pleasure, the magic ... Luc. My eyes travel down his body. I'm where I'm meant to be.

Once the girl and her father reach the edge of the crowd, the man hoists her on his shoulders, and she squeals in delight, clapping her hands as her father looks up at her with a smile.

Luc tugs me to the left, between two other buildings, until he stops in front of a wood door. He releases me, drawing a pick set from somewhere in his cloak. He quickly glances up and down the narrow cobblestone street, and I smirk. "Let's see if you've still got it."

"You know I do." He grins over his shoulder at me as he slides the pick into the door.

"You sure we won't have to explain why the king and his captain are breaking into this place?"

He chuckles. "I watched them lock up and leave a few minutes ago."

And with that, the lock snicks, and Luc turns the handle, stashing his tools before grabbing my hand and pulling me through the door, closing it behind us and locking us in.

I freeze on the spot as the scent of paper, glue, and leather fills my lungs. I look around, taking in the shelves of books and stacks of paper, both blank and printed. The press stands open in the center of the room, and though it's almost midday, the closeness of the buildings on either side only allows weak winter light to filter through the windows. Dust motes dance in the pale light, and as I turn to face Luc, he drops his cloak, the dark fabric pooling at his feet.

I smile, lifting my arms. "This brings back memories."

He nods. "Sometimes I wish that old building we'd lived in hadn't been converted into a tavern. I would have liked to buy it for you."

My heart squeezes as if he had reached into my chest and wrapped his fingers around it. I chuckle to dispel the intensity of my feelings.

I recall our old home in the abandoned book binder building. One day we went out to steal what we could, and when we came home, there was a horde of people chucking the press and books into the back alley, some prick standing right where we'd been sleeping for several years, pointing at the back wall, yelling to get the space cleared so he could bring in his barrels and start constructing his bar. We'd had to scramble that evening to find somewhere reasonably warm and dry to sleep, finding shelter in the loft of an inn's barn.

Luc's voice snaps me out of my memories. "But look at us now."

I smile. "Look at us now."

He steps into my space, cupping his hands to my face. "I missed you."

My heart stutters. "It's only been an hour."

He brushes his lips over mine, whispering against my mouth, "So?"

I wrap my hand around the back of his neck, pulling him to me, my tongue stroking the seam of his lips before he opens for me. Our tongues dance with heated desire, and when we pull back, we're both breathing heavily.

I grin, tugging his hair. "I was right. You are going to be a very needy lover."

He throws his head back, laughing to the vaulted ceiling, and I can't help but laugh with him. When we both quiet, his bright blue eyes find mine. We stare at each other for a moment before he glances out a window. "There's still a little time before midday strikes and you'll be needed to light the first bonfire."

My hand snakes down his torso, over the waist of his pants, drawing his eyes back to mine. I cup him over his clothes, and his jaw flexes as he grits his teeth. My fingers quickly start undoing his pants as he reaches for mine.

"Time enough."

27

Luc backs me up until I hit a wall with a thump. My head strikes the wood behind me as Luc unfastens my thigh sheath before shoving my pants down.

"Boots. Off."

I kick free of my boots, and Luc scrambles to get my pants all the way off. I only get his pants down his thighs before he reaches into his pocket, drawing out a small bottle of oil.

I smirk as the small popping sound echoes, and the top of the bottle falls to the floor. "You came prepared."

He deposits a small amount of oil in his hand and rubs it over my straining cock. "It seems that now I've had you, I'm going to be consumed with wanting you. So, yes. I'm prepared." We both groan as the oil mixes with my pre cum, his tight fist gliding down to my base and back up again. His mouth crushes to mine, our teeth scraping as I wrap my hand around his cock and squeeze. He bucks into my grip. "Fuck, Ry. I want you so much."

"Yes, Luc. Gods, yes."

He wraps a hand under my right thigh, hooking the back of my knee over his elbow. He awkwardly dumps the rest of the oil in his hand before sliding it over my balls and between my cheeks. His finger presses against my entrance, and I bear down on him as he slides one finger, then two, into me.

A bead of pre-cum shimmers on the end of his cock, and I pump my dick twice, gathering some of the oil in my palm before I press small circles around the head of his cock. His hips jerk as I slide my fist down to his base.

Luc removes his fingers, and I release him, watching as he fists himself, lining himself up at my entrance before slowly sliding into me, inch by inch. His girth stretches me, and I press my head into the wood wall, a gasp on my lips as he fills me.

"Shit, Ry. Gods. You feel so good. So good. So much better than I ever imagined."

I thrust myself downward, shoving him to the hilt inside me before drawing up slightly. "You imagined fucking me, Luc?"

His hips thrust with my next one, our skin slapping together. "Yes. Fuck, Ry. So many times. So many ways."

I grip my cock, pumping in time with our thrusts. My other hand pulls him to me, and our kiss fuels the passion between us. I pull back, biting his lip, growling, "I want to hear about each and every way you imagined us." He groans, pumping his hips into me even harder. "But for now, I need to get your shirt off, because I plan to paint your chest with my cum."

His hips never stop their assault as he leans back slightly, one hand gripping my ass to lift me on my toes to allow him to hit even deeper, while his other hand helps me unclasp his leathers before unbuttoning his shirt enough to pull it over his head.

He grabs my wrist, running his tongue against the base of my hand, licking all the way up my middle finger before releasing me. I grip my cock, pumping it hard, grunting, "I'll have that tongue on my balls and around my shaft next time."

"Yes, your Majesty." I chuckle at his smirk, driving myself down hard on his dick with his next thrust. "Fuck, Ry, I'm so close."

I pump my cock faster, watching his abs flex with each thrust. "I'm there too, Luc. Gods!"

My head thumps against the wall as he rams into me, his orgasm throwing his own head back, and the sight of him lost in me sends me over the edge. My fist tightens. I'm so full of him. I feel his cock twitching against my inner walls as he fills me, and shuttering pleasure erupts from my core, my cum coating Luc's heaving chest.

We stay like that for a few moments before he releases my leg. I lean against the wall to keep myself upright, oil and cum sliding down my legs. Wiping away what I can, I bend down to pull on my pants. Luc does up his pants before looking around. He crosses to a workbench, snatching up a rag and wiping off his hands and chest while I just wipe my hands down my pants.

I laugh, buckling my thigh sheath back on as Luc holds the rag, looking around the room before shoving it in his pocket. He pulls his shirt on, his dark head of hair poking through the neck followed by his sparkling eyes and chiseled face.

He grins at me while buckling his leathers. "I'll toss the rag in a bonfire later on. It'll be my sacrifice to the gods. Embers of the solstice fires will carry the evidence of your desire for me up to the heavens."

He whirls his cloak around his shoulders, fastening it and settling the hood over his head, and I smirk. "Needy *and* romantic. What am I supposed to do with you?"

"Don't know, but it's much too late now. You've got me. You've always had me."

I cross to him, wrapping my hand around his throat, leaning into the darkness of his hood. "And I thank the gods for you. I would have died in that shithole under my father's fists if it weren't for you. You've always been my strength."

He shakes his head, but I squeeze his throat as he whispers, "You've always been strong, Ry. But we're stronger together."

"Aye." I press my lips to his, just breathing him in—the scent of dust mixing with the first drops of a rain shower.

We pull away, straightening our clothes before slipping out of the bookbinders, locking the door behind us.

"Oh, hold on." Luc reaches into the folds of his cloak, drawing my crown out from somewhere.

I laugh, taking the crown and placing its heavy weight on my head. "What else do you have in there?"

"I'll let you search me later." I laugh as he walks to the edge of the building to a piled drift of snow. Grabbing a handful, he holds the packed snow toward me. "Wipe off your hands and pants. The King can't walk around with our cum staining his clothes."

I take the snow, and it starts to melt. Brushing my wet hands down my thighs, I manage to clean up most of the mess. "For the record, I like having our combined releases on my skin. I want you to lick it off me later."

"Fuck, Ry." He grabs my shirt, and my cock kicks in my pants as he presses his lips to mine. It's a slow, leisurely kiss, our bodies pressed against each other. I'm reluctant to pull away, but finally we part, his fingers lingering on my body before he steps away, and I stride down the narrow lane. Luc falls into step behind me, immediately slipping back into his soldier stance, once again my Captain.

I glance at the sky, noticing midday is upon us. Angling toward the square, I lead us through the winding streets until the buzz, both vocal and mental, of a large crowd reaches me. I square my shoulders, glancing back, catching Luc rubbing at his chest.

He grins at me. "Time for the king to start the celebration, officially."

I roll my eyes but face forward just as we break into the square. I have to blink a few times to adjust from stepping out of the shadows of the buildings into the open brightness of the square.

Luc calls out from behind me. "His Majesty, King Rydel Wescaryn!"

The crowd parts, heads bowing. I clench my fist in my pocket as I struggle to keep the voices in my head to a murmur. The scent of freshly-chopped wood and pine reaches me as I approach the large, unlit bonfire in the center of the square. The gathered people move, creating a circle of space around Luc and me. At my back stands the church of atonement where worshipers of any god or goddess can come to ask forgiveness for perceived sins.

I wait as I stare out at the crowd.

Planting my feet onto the cobblestones to keep from fidgeting, the thoughts of those closest to me solidify in my mind despite my effort to keep them out.

'I can't wait for the fires to be lit, then the real party begins.' ... 'He looks

tired.'... 'I'm going to have to work my way through this crowd quickly after the lighting to get the first servings of Alice's spiced wine. I'd hate to get the stuff at the bottom of the barrel.' ... 'I'm hungry.' ...'I wonder how much the king actually hears in his mind with that Stone?' ... 'The sun may be out, but I'm cold. Wish I had brought my other cloak.'

Finally, the bells of the church ring out, signaling the midday hour, and all eyes turn to me.

My voice carries, seeming to bounce off the stones of the streets and buildings of the city. "As the earth grows colder, the winds blow faster, the fire dwindles smaller, and the snows fall harder. Let the light of the sun find its way home."

A man steps forward, handing a lit torch to Luc, who bows his head as he hands it to me. Our hands brush as I take it from him, and a small smile tugs at my lips. Quickly pressing my face into a more serious expression, I raise the torch overhead, slowly lowering it to the base of the large pile of wood that stands almost twice my height.

I whip my head around, leaning to the side as an arrow flies over my left shoulder. "The false king should not be leading us in this sacred right!" A male voice yells out from the back of the crowd. Heads turn, and bodies part to reveal a cloaked figure striding forward, crossbow loaded and aimed at my chest. "This man killed Queen Ravaxina in cold blood." Several more black-cloaked figures push through the crowd, shoving people aside, making their way toward me. Some hold bows and arrows, others hold blades. "He stole our kingdom and has the audacity to stand before us with his head held high."

Luc has unsheathed his sword, and he steps in front of me. I notice people peeling from the crowd, moving toward the rebels, and upon closer inspection, I recognize my soldiers in plain clothes.

Of course, Luc was prepared for something like this.

I step forward, placing a hand on Luc's chest, shaking my head as I whisper, "I want the leader." He nods.

The man continues. "Adastra will rise! This false king's blood will run this day in payment for the atroci—"

I aim the magic at his mind, and his body crumples to the ground in a heap, unconscious. I'll question him later. A few of those advancing pause, while others break and charge forward, several calling out, "For Trislen!"

I sidestep another arrow as Luc's sword clashes against the first rebel to reach us. I look at the flaming torch in my hand, and a grin exposes my teeth in a feral expression as I turn my attention back to my enemies. Bystanders scramble back, bumping and jostling to get out of the way, pressing their bodies against the buildings, eyes wide, watching the drama unfold. A small portion of the crowd runs off down the streets, not wanting to chance getting caught in the crossfire.

My magic pulses, heating the skin of my back as I latch onto the mind of the closest rebel. I tell his mind that he's caught fire, and his body responds. He screams, slapping at the non-existent flames before falling to the ground, head thrown back as he rolls back and forth. The man fighting Luc falls, blood pooling from the wound in his gut, and Luc advances on the next two charging him.

I make eye contact with another rebel, her green eyes flaring wide as my magic convinces her the flames have caught her clothes. She stops, peeling her clothes off, but I tell her it's too late, her skin is already on fire. Her skin reddens and blisters, her body reacting to what her mind believes is happening. Her screams rip from her throat. On and on, I make eye contact with each rebel, my magic controlling their minds, and their bodies fall flailing to the ground as the onlookers watch them scream and rip at their clothing, their hands desperately trying to put out flames that aren't there.

I look over my shoulder, seeing both of the rebels Luc was fighting dead on the ground. Luc's breathing hard and sweat beads on his beautiful brown skin. I look him over, catching blood on his arm. There's a tear on his shirt sleeve, and I see his cut flesh. He flexes his hand, turning his arm to check his wound.

"Are you okay, Captain?"

"Fine, your Majesty."

I nod before turning back to the small crowd that stuck around. The screams have died off, and the bodies have stilled. "Now that's been settled, let us celebrate!" I toss the torch on the bonfire, and after a few moments, smoke curls from the wood before flames lick their way up the pile. Before long, more people have come back into the square. The bonfire is raging, and the people clap and cheer, skirting the dead bodies, doing their best to ignore them.

I turn to Luc. "Have that one"—I nod to the leader—"brought to the dungeons. The others need to be removed and burned."

He nods, his long strides taking him through the press of people until he stands before a pair of men. I recognize Casin and another of my soldiers. They nod at whatever Luc tells them before peeling off to their left. They speak with two more people who nod. Their heads swivel as they scan the crowd, meeting the eyes of several more plain-dressed soldiers across the square, all nodding before heading toward the bodies. They heft each up, dragging them from the square.

Luc returns to my side, and I smirk. "A bit of overkill, don't you think?"

"Never where your safety is concerned."

I roll my eyes, clapping him on the back. "Let's have a drink before we head back to the castle and I'm forced to deal with the high families and Erathan's endless questions about his faulty stone."

Luc laughs as we head to the nearest table. There's a small crowd, three or four deep, waiting to purchase ale at this booth, but as they see Luc and me approach, they part. The woman behind the table grabs two mugs with one hand, holding them out to us. "It sure is something watching that magic of yours, your Majesty."

I smile, taking both mugs, passing one to Luc, who takes the opportunity to brush his fingers against mine again. "It was a bit of unexpected entertainment."

Several chuckles sound out around us as I drop a few coins on the table before turning and striding away. The woman's voice calls after us. "Your Majesty! This is too much. I owe you change!"

I wave her off over my shoulder, taking a sip of the cold, dark ale, its bitter bite soothed by velvety tastes of chocolate, nuts, and cherry.

Luc holds his mug up, and I click mine to his. "Happy solstice, Lucaryn."

"Happy solstice, Rydel."

The soldiers have cleared all but two of the bodies. Luc and I leave the square behind us, the shadows of a narrow street closing in as we make our way west, toward the castle.

The snow has not been cleared here as well as the main streets, and our boots crunch and squeak with each step as we kick our way through the gathered snow that's as high as my knees in some places.

I attempt to high-step through the snow, glancing at Luc. "We need to find out who these rebels are, how many, and how the fuck they got into Leiren."

"I know. I've already sent the soldiers from the square to gather small squads and hunt down information. But I imagine we'll get the most information from the leader."

I nod, smiling. "I'll find a moment after tonight's toast to steal down to the dungeons and see what he knows."

My pants are soaked through from the thighs down, and I'm shivering as we break from the winding streets of the city, the sun back on our faces, the gates before us. As we pass through, I catch movement to the right, and turning, I see the fire dancers setting up for their performance later tonight.

A voice draws my attention back to the steps of my castle. "Ah, Rydel. There you are." Erathan's large frame descends the stairs, his bald head shining in the midday sun, his blond-red beard flaming down his chest, the two braids swaying with his steps. He holds out an arm, and I clasp his forearm, catching his thoughts. '*How soon can I get in his library?*' As he says, "Happy Solstice."

"To you as well, Erathan. I hope the journey wasn't too bad?"

He shakes his head. "No. The weather held us up for a day just beyond the border, but otherwise, for this time of year, it was fine."

The three of us turn, heading into the castle, the large wood doors open to the cold winter air. But even so, as soon as we're inside, the heat of the many blazing fires, torches, and candles warms my skin.

Erathan glances at Luc's arm, gesturing at the cut. "Did you have some trouble in the city?"

I shrug. "A few rebels denouncing my reign in South Leiren, claiming allegiance to Adastra."

Luc takes another swallow of his ale, and I do the same. Erathan frowns. "I still haven't heard word nor wild hair about this Adastra. It worries me, Rydel. This cousin of Ravaxina's shouldn't be able to hide this well."

Shrugging again, I finish my ale, refusing to let Erathan see the unease that's churning in my gut. Setting the empty mug on a small wood table pressed against the wall in the hall, I say, "He'll have to come out of the shadows, eventually. There's a rebel being brought to the dungeons as we speak. I'll know more soon."

I gesture to Luc and my pants. "We are going to get out these wet clothes." I look around, making eye contact with a servant. She tucks her cleaning rag into her apron as she crosses to us, bowing. "Take King Erathan to the library."

She nods, but before Erathan leaves to follow her, he smiles. "Caught my eagerness, did you?"

I smile. "I understand. And we did make a deal, after all." He nods with a grin, and I hold out a hand, directing him to follow the servant. "I've placed some books, texts, and scrolls on the desk I thought might be the most useful but help yourself to anything in the library."

He nods again before following the servant, throwing over this shoulder, "If I don't emerge in time, please have someone fetch me before dinner. I want time to change."

"Of course."

Luc and I head in the opposite direction, climbing the stairs to our wing, passing the guards who are keeping any of my guests from wandering into my private space.

I pause at Luc's door. "Meet you back here. Just give me enough time to change." I glance at his arm. "Do we need to call the healer?"

He pokes a finger at the cut, his other fingers still wrapped around his near-empty mug. "No. I'll wash it off and slap a bandage on it. It's not too deep. I'll be fine."

"Thanks for the assistance back there."

He smiles. "You could have dropped them all at once."

I grin back. "Yeah, but what fun would that have been?"

He laughs, and I can't help myself. I lean forward, catching his lips with mine. A second later, our tongues are swirling around each other. My hand grips his neck as his free arm wraps around my back. He is home for me, and kissing him is both calming and exhilarating.

The sensation makes me dizzy, and I pull back, noting his lips are red from the scratch of my beard. I lick my own lips, raw from his facial hair.

His eyes watch my mouth before he smiles. "I think you're right."

"About what?"

"The Heart Stone. Erathan seems ... fine, normal. I'd expect a wince or twinge or something." Luc rolls his shoulders before leaning back in so we're a mere breath apart. "Plus, he would have gone rock hard if he felt my desire for you. You're right. It's fake."

I smile, smacking my lips to his with a loud kiss before shoving him back into his door. "Stop distracting me."

He chuckles, fumbling with the handle before practically falling across the threshold. I walk down the hall, turning the corner and nodding at the guards before pushing into my rooms. Changing quickly into a forest-green pair of pants and a black tunic with green and gold embroidery along the collar and sleeves. I shrug into my chest harness, securing my thigh sheath, and sliding into a fur lined vest. I took my crown off to change, so I grip it, the gold points biting into the skin of my palms before I place it on my head, pulling half my dark-blond hair back into a knot.

Luc is closing his door behind him as I come back down the hall. My eyes travel down his body. His black hair is wet, combed back from his face, showcasing his brilliant blue eyes. I admire his black leather vest, the gold emblem of the broken crown shimmering slightly over his right breast. Under the vest, a black shirt hugs his muscular shoulders. My mouth waters as my gaze travels down his tan pants tucked into tall black boots as he asks, "You want to go question the man from the square now?"

I'd love nothing more. Using my power to hurt those who would hurt me or Luc is one of my favorite past times. And the temptation to delay putting on my show for the high families is almost too great to turn down. But I shake my head.

"As much as I want to ... for many reasons"—he chuckles, knowing me well—"he'll keep just fine down in the dungeons. I'll deal with him in a bit. I've neglected the guests too long. If I don't make an appearance, I'm afraid they'll start searching for me. Then I'll never get away."

"The burdens of being King."

We both smirk, but as we head toward the throne room, I stiffen my back, readying to deal with the circus I'm about to face—the high families of Leiren, South Leiren, and Adren. Luckily, not all the families come to the solstice celebrations, though this year is more well attended than any of those in the past, what with me claiming Trislen and the treaty with Adren. I'm sure everyone is eager to make a good impression on the King of the Mind Stone.

Luc whispers, "Here we go. Let the spectacle begin."

I chuckle, but my muscles tense up as we pass through the door behind my throne. Crossing the dais, I stand before my throne, and the crowded room goes quiet, but the noise in my head erupts. I clench my hands to keep from rubbing my temples.

Here we go indeed.

28

The sun set two hours ago, but there's still several hours until midnight. It's been a non-stop parade of brightly colored clothes, overdone faces, forced smiles, and a string of 'eligible daughters' curtsying and looking up at me with demure looks.

I rub my temple with one hand as my other clenches in a fist in my pocket. My crown digs into my skull, and I shrug out of my fur-lined vest, tossing it at a servant who fumbles to catch it before carrying it off, presumably to my rooms. I pinch the fabric of my shirt, fanning it away from my body, trying to find some relief from the stifling heat of the fires and the press of bodies milling about in my throne room.

The western wall of windows looks out to the gardens where torch-light flickers down gravel paths. A few people are strolling down the walkways cleared of snow. I glance to the left, where the long tables line the entire length. Food and drink cover every inch of the wooden surfaces. Roast boar, lamb, deer, and even ham weigh down the tables. Spiced vegetables, several stews, boiled potatoes, and roasted squash spills down the line, followed closely by baked goods of every sort. The scent of apple pies, scones, tarts, and sweet breads draws me to that end of the table. I snatch a tart, popping it in my mouth, almost moaning at the sweet and tart flavors. Grabbing another, I snag a crystal glass of sparkling wine, and as I lift the glass to my lips, I spy a man striding my way. His dark hair is slicked back and is graying at the temples. He runs a broad hand down the front of his wine-red velvet vest before tugging his dark jacket into place. He must be melting in those clothes.

With short little steps, a girl tries to keep up with him. Her red velvet dress matches the man's vest, and I assume she's his daughter. Great. Another one. Gods, this one can't be more than fifteen. Fuck no. Her eyes flit between her father's back and my face. She attempts a smile in my direction, but her eyes are too wide, and I don't miss how her hands clench the skirts of her dress. I barely stifle a groan as her father's thoughts weave through the noise.

'This girl better make a good impression. This is our chance. Finally, she can be of some use.'

The girl's quiet thoughts slip between her father's.

'Oh gods, there he is. The Crown Breaker. He's ... he's ... he's so big. He looks strong. I've never been with a man. Her fingers unclench, then clench again. Smile. I have to remember to smile. And father said to push my chest forward. Try to catch the king's eye. Say what he wants to hear. Oh gods, I can't do this.

No. Just no.

I snap my head to the right, acting like I heard my name called. I nod at my imaginary companion and quickly cross the room, leaving the annoyed man behind, but not before I catch the wave of relief from the girl.

I smirk as I pass through one of the glass doors. The cold air slaps me in the face, forcing a sharp exhale from my lungs. Her father seemed like a real ass but being saddled with me would not have been much better.

Moving down the path, I brush past a short pale woman wrapped in a cloak with a hint of green silk poking between the folds, the fabric swishing loudly as she bows. I have to angle to the side slightly, brushing against a tall hedge to pass a group of three, talking in hushed tones over plates clutched in their hands. I bump the back of one man, a little harder than necessary, bringing their attention to me.

"Oh! I'm so sorry, your Majesty. I didn't realize it was you." The woman of the group flushes, the pink of her cheeks matching her garish dress, her breasts practically spilling out the top of her bodice which is on display by her open fur-lined cloak. Her long blond hair slides over her shoulder and spills down her cleavage as she bows, glancing up at me with a smile, her breath steaming out in little clouds.

The other two men bow deeply, muttering their apologies, but I keep moving. Turning a corner, and another until I come to a deserted section of the gardens. The torchlight is farther spaced out, and pools of shadow dip between the flickering light. Stopping in a darkened pocket of space, I drop onto a stone bench, the cold immediately seeping through my pants. I rub my temples before running my hands down my face with a deep exhale.

Mumbling to myself, I scratch my freshly trimmed beard. "Why do I do this every year?"

"Because as antisocial as that Stone has made you, you still enjoy a party."

My arms come to rest on my thighs as Luc comes to stand next to me, taking a seat and crossing his outstretched legs at the ankles. Reaching for my crown, the small points dig into my hand as I lift it from my head, scratching my other hand across my scalp with a sigh. "Yes, well, this one has worn thin."

Luc chuckles. "There does seem to be more suitors than there have been in the past."

Closing my eyes, I groan. "Did you see that last one headed my way?"

"Shit." Luc turns, angling his face toward me. "He was going to present her to you?" I nod and Luc huffs. "She was what, fourteen?"

I shrug, opening my eyes, staring at the barren branches of a tree across the path. "Doesn't matter."

Luc is quiet for a long moment, and as the silence draws out, I turn to look at him with a question in my eyes. He averts his gaze, staring at his boots. "You'll need an heir eventually, Ry."

"Maybe, maybe not."

His eyes lift back to mine as he smirks. "What's that supposed to mean?"

"I don't want a queen consort." Luc opens his mouth, but I cut him off. "If I come across someone who I can stand to be around for more than one full minute, I may consider it. But—"

Luc clicks his tongue. "You only need a handful of minutes to 'plant your seed,' then you don't need to worry about being around her."

I chuckle. "True, but then there will be a child." Both our eyes go sad for a moment, and I nod. "I'm enough of a bastard to know I wouldn't be the best father. I'd never be as bad as mine, but still, how can I subject a child to"—I wave a hand at myself—"this." I smile. "Plus, having the unfiltered thoughts of a child in my head all the time might finally drive me mad."

Luc shakes his head with a quiet laugh. "So what then? We've done all this to just let your legacy die?"

"I'm thirty-four. I'm not headed to the underworld tomorrow. Besides, there's no actual law that says my successor has to be my heir. I can name whomever I want to carry on my legacy."

"I suppose. But an heir would be ... tidier."

"Tidy? So says the man who hasn't seen his floor through the piles of his clothes in years." We both laugh. "Maybe I'll plunge the kingdom into chaos and name Asha as my successor as the next Queen."

"The cook?" He throws his head back, laughing. "That would be entertaining for sure."

We rise, turning back the way we came. I spin my crown around my hand before placing it back on my head. We pass the cleared stage area where the fire dancers will perform after my toast at midnight. A few people are still braving the cold, milling about, and some thoughts flit through my mind revealing secret rendezvous happening in the shadowed corners of the gardens.

Now that's a great use of time. Glancing up, I notice the position of the large mother moon high in the sky. The edge of the child moon is just breaking the horizon, so there's still a little time before midnight.

I grab Luc's hand, pulling him to the left, snaking through an outer section of the hedge maze before emerging at the stone fountain. The large wolf howling to the sky is silent, the stream of water that normally flows from his jaws frozen in an icy stream. A curved stone wall partially encloses the fountain off from the rest of the gardens, and I press Luc's back against the wall.

His hands rise to frame my face, and I do the same, our affection and love for each other reflecting back at us through the other's eyes.

I lean in, my lips whispering against his. "Uh sahe'a iyai." *I love you.*

His lips curl up in a small smile as I kiss him slowly, savoring his warmth, his strength, his taste. My cock twitches as he runs his tongue over my bottom lip, but I keep the kiss gentle. My hands thread through his hair, nails scraping his scalp, and he wraps one hand around my neck, the other around my waist, holding me tight.

I moan as our straining cocks press together through our clothes, and Luc slides his tongue between my lips, licking me like I'm his favorite treat—he's certainly mine. I could stay here all night, in Luc's arms, safe in his embrace, tasting him, loving him, and letting him love me.

My skin is flushed, and I don't even register the cold as we pull apart slightly, eyes locked on each other. His hand leaves my neck, fingers trailing up my throat and over my jaw, cupping my face once again. I shiver at the look of possession and love in his eyes before tilting my head back, catching the glow of the small moon rising over the horizon, quickly making its way through the night sky to join its mother.

I sigh, my breath puffing into the air as I look back at Luc. "We should get back. Once I make this toast, the festivities should properly distract the guests, and maybe you and I can slip away ... have a little celebration of our own."

I raise an eyebrow, smiling, but Luc's returning smile doesn't quite reach his eyes. "Ry, I need to tell you something."

I press a quick kiss to his mouth, grabbing and squeezing his ass for good measure. "Later. I'll have your cock in my mouth, driving you to the edge before you're shouting my name as I take you from behind." His pupils dilate, and I grip my cock over my pants, now fully erect from my wandering thoughts of having Luc sweaty and panting under me. "I'm going to have my fill of you, then we can talk. But first, I need to make this damn toast."

He begins to object, but I'm already turning, his footsteps crunching on the gravel behind me as we break from the gardens. We step into the pool of light streaming from the throne room, climbing the steps to the doors. Striding through, the crowd parts as we advance toward the dais. I grab a mug of ale from a passing servant, Luc snatching one as well. He stays at the base of the steps as I climb them, turning to face the crowd.

The room is silent, but their thoughts are a rush of sound in my mind, like the rumble of stampeding horses. Luckily, I'm far enough away from the closest guests to keep out individual thoughts.

Without preamble, I raise my mug, everyone following suit. I pause, catching movement from the back of the room. Casin pushes through the open door, his eyes meeting Luc's with a sense of urgency on his face.

My voice rings out. "Here's to the sun's rebirth! Here's to the warming of Mother Earth! Here's to the light as it grows strong! Here's to the days as they grow long! Here's to Solstice and its feast! May fortunes be increased!"

Casin is making his way around the edge of the crowd as Luc's voice carries across the room. "Hail, King Rydel!"

The crowd answers. "Hail, King Rydel!"

Luc's voice gets louder. "Hail, Leiren!"

They all answer. "Hail, Leiren!"

"Hail, Solstice!"

"Hail, Solstice!"

And with that, we all drink. I turn toward the doors, gesturing at the gardens beyond. "Let the celebration begin!"

A lone figure dressed all in black appears in the garden, and fire erupts from her mouth as she spits flames into the sky. The crowd oohs and claps, quickly filing from the throne room, pushing into the frosty night to watch the fire dancers.

Casin climbs the steps quickly, saluting. "Your Majesty, dire news from Runic in South Leiren."

Luc joins us, taking the small slip of paper clutched in Casin's hands. Luc's eyes go wide as he reads the message, Casin saying, "The capital is under attack. A large force claiming allegiance to Adastra is fighting their way to the palace. Runic and our forces are holding them back, but he says if they don't receive reinforcements, we will lose South Leiren."

29

My heart is racing, rage trembling my fingers as I reach for the message. Luc passes it to me, and I skim through the words, my anger and bafflement growing.

"How the fuck? Have they actually sighted Adastra? There's no way he could have made landfall *and* gathered a force in such a short amount of time."

Casin just shakes his head. "That's all we know."

I snap my head to the right. "War room."

The three of us practically jog to the small room, leaving the celebrating crowd behind. Closing the door, we cross the room, each leaning over the table, hands pressed to the map. My eyes lift to Casin. "Go retrieve Erathan. He's more than likely in the library."

Casin rushes from the room, closing the door behind him.

Luc taps a finger to the map as I push off the table, palming my dagger, letting it dance between my fingers.

Luc's voice is thoughtful as he continues tapping. "I don't know how many of our forces we can safely spare to send south. We need to watch our backs here, in case Adastra attacks Farden as well, what with the trouble with rebels lately."

"I just don't understand how this is possible?"

Luc stops his tapping, pressing both hands flat, looking up at me. "Maybe he's been in Imoria all along."

My dagger stills for a moment before I pick up the soothing movement again. "Well, shit."

Casin comes back in, Erathan hot on his heels, his brow pinched, his fingers stained from running them over texts all day and into the night. "What's going on, Rydel?"

"Adastra has attacked South Leiren." His eyes go wide. "My forces are holding them back, but they need reinforcements."

Before I can ask, Erathan nods. "I'll send a bird to Adren immediately. I can have half of my forces deploy at once. Half of that number will head to the south, and I can have a quarter of my remaining forces head here. We will hold Imoria against this Adastra."

I frown, eyes traveling over the map. "I'm tempted to have you send all your available forces south."

I look at Luc, who nods. "We can hold the north. We need as many soldiers as we can spare in the south."

Erathan's frown deepens, but he nods. "If you're sure ..." When we both nod, he straightens. "Where's the bird house?"

Casin steps forward. "I'll take you."

I round the table, holding out my hand. Erathan clasps my forearm with a strong grip. "Thank you, Erathan. I was not expecting to call in the terms of our treaty so soon."

His teeth appear through his red beard with his smile. "I've been buried in your library all day. I'm ready to return the favor."

Our arms drop. "Any luck?"

He tilts his head. "Perhaps. There's several promising texts. At one point, I'm certain the stone got warmer. And there is one passage in particular that I have hope will point me in the right direction."

Doubt scrapes under my skin. Could his Stone be real after all? Has he found something that might unlock the little pink stone hanging around his neck?

Erathan shakes his head. "But for now, I need to send word to my army."

I nod, doing my best to shrug off the doubt, and Casin and Erathan quickly leave the room.

Luc comes to my side. "I should go south."

"*We* should go south. I probably shouldn't have left."

"Ry—"

"No, Luc. I need to go. My magic will bring this conflict to a quick end. I won't waste lives when I have the power to bring Adastra to his knees." I meet his eyes. "And I don't want to go without you. I want yo —no, I *need* you at my side."

He grins. "Well then, let's go mess with Adastra's plans of grandeur. Casin will take command here. We'll have to shuffle these guests out of the palace and *tactfully* send Erathan home."

"I can be tactful." Luc smirks. "And we'll let the guests enjoy the night. No reason to raise fear and panic. Not yet. Our soldiers will send everyone home in the morning."

I scratch my beard, looking at the map, but my eyes are unfocused, thinking through options. "Maybe we can travel south with Erathan. It'll be slower than I want, but we can use the time to discuss tactics and plans. We can drop him in Adren, and push on to South Leiren."

Luc nods with a knowing smile. "Gives you extra time to sort through Erathan's thoughts."

"He's tough to read. His mind is strong, but yes." My grin matches his, but it quickly falls as recollection hits me. "The rebel prisoner from the square."

Comprehension crosses Luc's face, and we leave the war room without another word. Our boots tap out a quick rhythm on the stone floor as we walk down hallways, briefly muted by a thick rug as we cut through an open room with a few plush chairs and couches comfortably spread out. Several guests, opting to stay within the warmth of the castle than brave the cold outside to watch the entertainment, eye us as we quickly pass through.

The sharp rap of stone underfoot picks back up as we turn down another hallway before Luc slides his key from his pocket, inserting it with a quiet snick into the lock of the door.

The cold in the dungeon is intense enough to draw an involuntary cough from my lungs. Luc nods at the guard standing at the end of the corridor, but my gaze focuses on the third cell down on the left.

The man, stripped of his cloak, leans against the stone of the back wall of his cell, one knee pulled up to his chest with his forearm resting on it. His other leg stretches out before him, like he's relaxing in a comfortable bed, not in a freezing cell under my castle with near catatonic prisoners keeping him company.

I keep my eyes on the man as I address the guard. "Any movement from the other prisoners?"

"No, your Majesty. Everyone is still deep within the magic."

The prisoner's voice floats from his cell, his tone casual, amused even. "Quite the collection you have down here. How long can you keep them like this?"

My eyes hold his dark brown ones, a smile on my face. "Until they die."

He tilts his head, looking at the woman in the cell behind me, his brown hair falling around his face before he tucks it behind an ear, revealing a scar that looks like a brand that puckers the skin on his neck below his ear.

He shifts to respond, but I cut him off. "Is Adastra in South Leiren?"

'Yes.' "Yes, he's in Trislen. He's been there for years."

My muscles tense at his admission, but I hold my body still, keeping my face neutral. I have no idea how I missed coming across even a whisper of a thought about Adastra when I was in the south. It doesn't make sense.

"How large are his forces?"

"I don't know, but enough to take back our country."

I push into his mind, sparking pain, and I grin at his wince. His fingers twitch, and I know he's resisting rubbing his temples. My voice thunders through his mind without me having to say a word. "*Adastra will be dead before he reaches the gates of my Southern palace.*"

My magic tears at his mind, and a trickle of blood escapes his ear, the red line snaking down the dark brown skin of his neck. Luc leans a shoulder against the cell behind us, arms crossed. I can feel his eyes on me, watching me wield the magic. I barely keep from licking my lips at the thought of running my hands over every inch of Luc's glorious skin. Later.

The prisoner groans in pain, dropping his head slightly. "Aye, your power may be able to hold what you stole, but then again"—he wipes the blood from his skin, smearing it over his fingers—"maybe not."

Luc smirks with a snorted chuckle. "This Adastra won't be the first bastard to think he can withstand or beat the magic of the Mind Stone. He'll just be another corpse to add to that number."

The prisoner's laugh echoes through my mind as he calmly smiles at Luc. *'This is perfect.'* I'm thrown by the prisoner's amusement, missing his first few spoken words. "... told if the opportunity presented itself, I was to deliver this message to the Captain." His eyes leave Luc's face, traveling down to rest on his chest before climbing back to his face. "Adastra knows your secrets, Captain Lucaryn."

Luc pushes off the bars of the cell at his back, his arms dropping to his sides as he steps forward. I can feel his tension ratcheting up as his fists clench.

Secrets?

The prisoner leans forward, a grin lifting his face in a crazed expression, his wide eyes landing on me. "And he knows you've somehow been able to keep your secrets from your king."

I smile, a small chuckle passing through my lips. "If you think a few lies will come between—"

"Keys." Luc's eyes stay fixed to the prisoner, but he thrusts out his right arm in the guard's direction at the end of the hall.

The metallic clink of keys being pulled from their hook is the only sound in the now silent dungeon. The ring flies through the air, and Luc uses his periphery to snatch it. As Luc quickly thumbs through the keys, sliding the necessary one into the cell door, a strange and unsettling feeling blooms in my chest.

Uncertainty.

Luc shoves open the door, the iron slamming against the bars with a loud clang. He strides into the small space like a storm cloud, grabbing the prisoner by the neck and pulling him to his feet. He has to rise on his toes to keep from choking as Luc pulls him to his face.

"Who is Adastra?"

The toes of prisoner's boots scrape on the stone floor as he fights for purchase, but a small smile crosses his face. "I don't know. I haven't had the pleasure of meeting him in person."

Luc looks over his shoulder at me, his jaw clenched, a question in his eyes. I rip into the prisoner's mind, and he groans, going slack in Luc's grip as I search for a face to go with the name. There's nothing. Only written notes or messages delivered by second or third parties. I shake my head at Luc, who turns back to the prisoner. I expect him to scoff, to throw the obvious lies back in the prisoner's face, but Luc squeezes his neck tighter, growling out one word.

"How?"

I take a single step into the cell, the space now cramped with all three of us in the tiny space. "Captain, don't fall prey to this man's schemes. Stand back and let me see what I can find."

Luc shakes his head, holding the prisoner's gaze, but the prisoner's smile widens, despite the stranglehold Luc has on him.

The prisoner looks past Luc at me. "Adastra, the true King of Trislen, the true King of Imoria"—he licks his lips, his hands finally grasping Luc's wrists in an attempt to gasp in more air—"has visions. He has natural born magic."

30

Luc drops the prisoner, backing away until he stands at my side. The man lands on his hands and knees, coughing and gasping with a chuckle.

I cross my arms, relaxing. "Well, now you've shown your hand. Lies. All lies. Magic died out centuries ago. The Stones are all that's left. So whatever game Adastra is playing, it won't work. Parlor tricks or drug-induced fever dreams will not be enough to win him the throne."

The prisoner lifts his head, staring at me through the strands of dirty brown hair hanging limp over his eyes.

"Our goddess, Circeon, has chosen lord Adastra to herald the rebirth of magic into our world, and you will fall before the goddess' will." He sits back, propping himself on his left hip and hand. "You have the means to see the truth in my mind." He waves his right hand at a still-tense Luc. "But you should ask your Captain to reveal his secrets. Then you will know the absolute truth of things."

I roll my eyes, palming my dagger, letting the familiar caress of the leather hilt calm my racing thoughts. The blade glints in the light of the torches as it twirls through my fingers. "Oh, rest assured, your mind is mine, and the pain will be unlike anything you have ever experienced. I will take you apart. I will see all of you, all those little hidden memories even you've forgotten. And when I'm through making you my plaything, you—"

One long stride carries Luc back to the prisoner. His strong hands grab his head, and before I can say anything, he wrenches the prisoner's head, snapping his neck and tossing him to the floor with a thud.

I toss up my hands. "Why'd you do that? You killed him before I could play with him."

Luc strides out of the cell, tossing the keys back to the guard. I follow, doubt and fear threatening to close my throat.

I pause as the guard calls out. "Your Majesty, do we burn the body, or would you like him sent somewhere as a message?"

I glance at the crumpled body of the prisoner, then carry my gaze down one side of the cells and the other. Sixteen prisoners, all slowly dying within their nightmares.

"Send him to South Leiren and drop his body outside one of Adastra's camps, where a patrol will be sure to find it. Make sure a message is staked to his corpse with these two words, 'Nice try'."

The guard smiles with a nod. "Of course, your Majesty. I will arrange it on shift change."

The door at the top of the stairs creeks open and slams shut as Luc leaves the dungeons.

Another glance around fills me with resolve. Enough playing. I wave my hand in an unnecessary gesture, my magic hitting each prisoner's mind, shutting them all down. Soft rustling and quiet thumps follow the falling bodies of the now dead prisoners.

"No need to wait. Handle it now."

The guard's wide eyes travel down the cells before he nods. "Yes, your Majesty."

I take the stairs two at a time, bursting through the door, ready to hunt Luc down, but the door stops shy of slamming into the wall as Luc grabs it. "We need to talk."

My heart sinks into my stomach, but I refuse to let the small seed of doubt grow. I step through the door, allowing Luc to close and lock it behind us. Before he turns back around, I squeeze his shoulder, feeling his tense muscles under my palm.

"Okay, Luc. War room?"

His head drops, his hands pressed to the wood door. "No."

I force my voice to remain calm even though all I want to do is draw Luc into my arms and feel his wrapped around me, sure and strong. "Okay. My rooms or yours?"

"Mine."

I let my hand slide from his shoulder as he pushes off the door, turning without meeting my gaze and striding toward the stairs that lead to our wing. Ours. We've built this together, and no matter what, I won't let the machinations of a mad pretender king pull Luc and me apart.

But dread worms its way into my chest, threatening to strangle the air from my lungs as I follow Luc. Neither of us notice the guests celebrating the solstice as we pass through the castle with unhurried but steady steps. Drunk laughter, the clink of glasses, the giggling of blushing suitors, the low rumble of advances being made, loud toasts being shouted over the heads of the revelers ... all of it washes over me.

His hand rubs at his chest, and I ache to slide the magic into his mind. My fingers tremble with the desire to know his thoughts, and the Stone burns in my back, reaching, straining for Luc. But I hold it back, barely, focusing the magic on the revelers, their happy, drunk thoughts spiraling through my mind.

I pause as Luc and I reach the base of the stairs, turning to the guard on the right. "No matter what, no one comes up here." I point a finger in his face. "No one."

He nods, swallowing at the look in my eyes. I jog up the stairs, catching up to Luc in the hall and following him into his rooms. The inward sweep of his door is slow, hindered by several books and what looks like a shirt that were piled behind the door. I step over a crumpled towel, hearing Luc close and lock the door behind us. Picking my way across the room, I stop in the center, his bedchamber to my left, his sitting area behind me, and a small office to my right. The fire is warm at my back; the crackle breaking up the silence.

Luc crosses the room, determination in his eyes, not bothering to avoid the mess, just stepping on or kicking aside whatever is in his path. His hands frame my face, fingers combing through my short beard, before he presses his mouth to mine.

My doubts melt away. Luc is mine. We are a team. It's always been us against the world, and I love him. I trust him. I press my hands to his chest, fisting the fabric of his shirt to hold him to me. He breaks the kiss, leaning his forehead against mine.

A single tear falls down Luc's face, his brilliant blue eyes shimmering with fear and pain. And just like that, panic, fear, and doubt spike through my heart as he whispers, "Surh iyai as iyais sis. Surh iyai as sahuhr nea." *Thank you for your trust. Thank you for loving me.*

He steps back, pulling his vest off, yanking his shirt over his head. The next moment, there's a dagger in his hand, and he's slicing across the scar from Kahar's strike all those weeks ago. "Luc! What the hell!"

I cross to him, ready to rip the blade from his hand, but I'm stopped in my tracks as he digs his fingers into the open wound before holding out his hand to me. My eyes dart between his bloody fingers to the cut on his chest where blood runs in thin ribbons down his torso. There, pinched between his fingers, is a small pink stone smeared in my best friend's blood.

My eyes snap to his. "Is that ...? How? What?" I let my poorly formed questions die off.

My brain refuses to function.

Arm still outstretched to me, Luc nods. "The Heart Stone."

31

M y head falls back as my laughter bellows around the small room. When I look back at Luc, his puzzled expression is just too much. Wrapping my hand around his bloody, outstretched fingers, I push his arm down to his side before kissing him with a loud smack of my lips. Our noses brush as I laugh against his mouth.

"Fuck, Luc. I'm so relieved."

And I am. A weight slides from my shoulders, and I feel like I might float away, so I grip his shoulders to keep myself grounded.

"You're not angry?"

I lean back, taking in the worry and ... fear in his eyes. "No, Luc. Why would I be? We have the Stones!"

He steps back, holding up his palm, presenting the bloody stone. His voice is flat, eyes averted, staring at his hand. "You have them now, Ry."

My brows furrow. Wrapping my hand around his, I close his fingers around the Stone, but I don't let him go. "Why didn't you tell me?"

He tries to pull free, but I hold tight, not willing to let him go, not willing to let him put physical distance between us because the emotional distance he's trying to create is breaking my heart. I almost rub my chest to keep the panic at bay.

He sighs. "All those texts, those passages, Ry. The magic of the Mind Stone already takes such a toll on you. What if the lore is right? What if the Heart Stone sends you over the edge into madness? What if I lose you?" *'What if you see?'*

His high emotions shove that small thought at me, and I wonder what he could mean, but I grip him tighter.

"Then you keep it."

His eyes snap to mine, wide and unbelieving. "But ... you, you've wanted the Stones since we were kids. They have always been the goal. They—"

"No. Lucaryn." My hand caresses his cheek, his beard scraping against my palm. "Getting us both to the top has been the goal. Keeping us safe has been the goal. Making sure no one can hold power over us, that has been the goal. The Stones are just a means to that end."

I lift his clenched hand, mine still wrapped around it, and press his bloody fingers to my lips. "Now we are untouchable. You and I will control Imoria through mind and will. Our enemies will fall like glowing embers before us."

The toe of my boots kicks up against his as I step closer. "It's you and me, Luc. Always." Our breath mingles, and his gaze dances between my eyes and my lips. My cock hardens with wanting him, but I hold still, waiting.

Painfully slowly, his face moves toward mine, and as his lips hover over mine, he swallows, whispering, "There's more." A quick press of his lips to mine is all I get to savor before he takes a step back. My palms sweat, and my heart is racing as he fists his hands at his sides. "You need to go into my memories. You need to see what happened *that* night." My brows furrow, and his arms tremble with how tight he's squeezing his fists. "You need to see what actually happened."

I stare at him with no idea what he could possibly mean, but his extreme tension is making me even more nervous, and a bead of sweat slides down my back. His entire body is stiff, and his knuckles are white from digging his fingers into his palms. His eyes dart around the room, avoiding me, and his voice cracks between us, pulling me from my rising panic.

"Just go into my mind, Rydel. Find the night ... that ... *that* night."

I take a step forward, holding out my hand, but he throws up an arm, stepping back and away from me. I feel like I'm losing everything in this moment, and I don't know why or how.

"Do it! You need to know, and if you don't see it for yourself, you won't believe me."

I hold his gaze for another long moment before nodding warily. I've never wanted to do something less than I do right now, but I push into Luc's mind as gently as possible. His small wince of pain almost has me drawing out before I've even seen anything, but he shakes his head. "Don't go soft on me now."

I grit my teeth against the pain I know I'm causing him, and my body aches uncomfortably from using the magic, like it knows I don't want to use the power against Luc, and now it's resisting me.

Rushing through his memories, I search for the one from that night. I'm tempted to stop and watch our first kiss from his perspective, but I push on until finally, a familiar shack of a house comes into view. I focus on the memory and sink into Luc's consciousness, experiencing that night from his point of view.

Lucaryn

My small hands clench tight as Ry's father's shouts reach me from where I stand outside. I was coming over to ask Rydel if he wanted to go bathe at the river together since I know he dislikes bathing at home, then maybe I could convince him to eat some food at my house. Ry hates handouts, but we're partners, friends, and he's usually quick to accept any excuse to get out of his house and away from his father.

But with his father in a rage, it's going to be harder to get Ry out tonight. I storm toward the door, the spaces between the planks of wood gaping more than they used to since his father refuses to do any repairs to the house, making Ry do everything like he's a slave, not his son.

Ry's father's words ring out along with the flat slapping sound of some-thing hard striking skin. "You are a weak," he strikes again, "useless," and another, "boy, and—"

I throw open the door, rage like a living thing in my chest. "Stop it!"

My voice freezes the room for a moment, and Ry whips his head around, seeing me in the open doorway. My fingernails dig into my palms, and I'd expect to see blood trickling down my hands if I bothered to look.

"Luc, no." I can tell Ry means for his words to come out as a command, but a whisper is all he can manage around his obvious agony.

His father chuckles. "Ah, your little friend is here to save you, boy."

What an asshole. I stand tall. I may only be ten, but I work hard and am already building muscle over my lean frame. I'm not completely helpless.

Rydel winces as his father tsks. "You're little boys. You know nothing of this world. You know nothing of true pain. But you will."

I catch the sound of Ry's fingernails splitting and cracking as he digs them into the table. His voice is a little stronger as he defends me. "Do your worst old ma—"

His father's fist connects with Ry's jaw, silencing him. My best friend's body goes slack for a moment, hanging over the table, and just as he shakes his head, his father reaches for him, knocking over a chair in his anger. His hand wraps around Ry's throat, hauling him off the floor, punching him over and over. There's a sickening crunch as Ry's nose breaks and his left cheek collapses. His left eye is already swollen shut, and blood drips down his face, but his grunts and groans have gone silent, and I know that's not a good sign.

Enough.

I rush his father, pounding my fists against his back, hoping to at least divert his attention away from Ry. "Stop it, you bastard! You're going to kill your son!"

Ry's one working eye is scouring the floor as his father's grip tightens around his throat. Pain erupts along the side of my face as his father back-hands me with his free hand. I stumble back, hitting the kitchen counter before crumpling to the ground.

Suddenly, Ry's arm snaps out, punching his father in the throat, hard. I almost whoop a cheer as choking gasps sputter from his father's lips. He's dropped Ry, who is patting the floor, blood covering most of his face. I attempt to push myself to stand, but something in my side cracked when I hit the counter, maybe a rib, and the pain steals my breath for a moment. I try to ignore it, to push through. Ry needs me.

Around his coughing, Ry's father stands over him, hand rubbing his throat. "Nice try, you ... little shit, but you are not strong enough to go against me. You'll never be strong enough." His father's laugh almost drowns out the metallic scrape of steel as Ry's hand wraps around the hilt of his father's sword. "You think you can use my sword against me, boy?"

Ry raises the sword, attempting to push up to a kneeling position to stand, and I grip the edge of the counter to join him. But the next moment, Ry's eyes roll back in his head, and he collapses unconscious in a pool of his own blood.

The rage within me explodes, and the world around me slows down as I shove to my feet and sprint across the room. The pain is gone. The adrenaline is carrying me through this moment, and I'm grateful because tonight, Ry will be freed of this man, of this place.

I drop to my knees, sliding easily on the blood slicked floor right past his smirking father. The sword is in my hand before I even register picking it up, and like I'd practiced the move a million times, by body twists, and I spin on my knees, using both hands to slice the heavy blade across his father's stomach.

The rush of blood past my ears mutes his bellow. His hands clutch his stomach, trying to hold himself together as he stumbles back, sending another chair clattering to the floor. I'm on my feet with my next breath, thrusting the blade into his chest, following him as he falls onto the table. There's a squelching sound as I rip the sword free to step clear as the table flips with his weight, landing half on his back before rolling over. I glance at him lying facedown, breaths shallow, but he's unmoving.

A high-pitched screaming reaches my ears.

"Help! Someone help! Guards, someone, please!" Ry's sister's eyes are wide, trained on me, but as soon as I make eye contact with her, she bolts.

"Fuck."

I leap over the fallen chair, taking another down on the way as I tackle Yareen, her screams piercing the night. "Guards!"

That's the last thing I need, some of Ry's father's soldier buddies to show *up. I lift the sword and plunge it into her back. The sword is heavy, but the blade is sharp, easily slicing through skin, muscle, and bone. Her screams immediately turn to gurgles as she struggles, kicking her boots—boots Ry worked for and bought for her—against the worn wood floor.*

As soon as she stills, I stand, dragging the sword behind me, the scrape of metal against wood loud in the now near-silent house. I pause over Ry's father's body, counting his shallow breaths.

Ry moans, shifting his head, revealing the swollen mess of the side of his face.

With two hands, I raise the sword overhead and plunge it into his father's back, once, twice, three times. My breaths are coming harder, but I stand as still as I can, waiting to see if his back will rise again.

It doesn't, so I turn to the last person in this miserable family. Ry deserved so much better than what he was born with, and today he'll be free. I stop in front of his mother, her eyes vacant, her stringy hair hanging limply around her flushed face.

"Useless woman."

Her throat opens under the blade, and she doesn't even flinch. The only sign that she's aware of her life draining away is a slight quickening of her breaths before they stop.

Turning, I look back at Rydel. He's coming around, and now panic is quickly replacing the adrenaline. I've just killed my best friend's entire family. Sure, they were shit, but will Ry understand? Will he be able to forgive me? I just wanted him to be safe, to be free, but what if I lose him?

The sword falls with a loud clatter as my strength leaves me with that thought. I can't. I can't lose him. I love him.

Shit, shit, shit. What have I done?

But maybe ...

I bend down, forcing my fingers to grip the sword, sliding the hilt into Ry's hands. He intended to use it. I saw it in his eyes before he passed out— he meant to try to kill his father. If he believes he did this, if he thinks he freed himself ...

I'll feed his strength. I'll feed the darkness I know he hides. He has to believe he saved himself, and with that belief, we'll escape this place.

He slowly pushes up to his knees, his gaze snapping between the blood coating the floor and the sword in his hand.

"Ry?" *My voice startles even me, like a clap of thunder.*

My best friend looks up at me. "What happened?"

I bite my lip, frowning, hoping this will work. "It had to be done."

Ry's gaze peels away from me and scans the room, landing on his father laying in a pool of darkening blood

His eyes find his mother next before snapping to Yareen laying dead in the doorway.

His eyes crawl back to me. "What happened?"

"You don't remember anything?"

He shakes his head, and I kneel, pressing my hand to his shoulder. "You screamed. It was a sound like I've never heard. It stopped us all in our tracks." *I pause, swallowing.* "You don't remember?"

He shakes his head, and I bite my lip. I have to do this. It will make Ry stronger. "You shoved the sword into your father's stomach before ripping it out and slashing at him over and over. When he fell, Yareen screamed. She yelled for help, Ry. She yelled for the guards. I tried to grab her, but she kept screaming. The next thing I knew, you slid the sword between her ribs. It was so quiet, so quick, and she just fell."

I take a deep breath, folding my legs under me, blood squishing as I sit next to Ry.

"Then you calmly walked across the room, stared at your mother for a few seconds and sliced the blade over her throat."

I wave a hand at his father's body. "You came back and stabbed him again and again until you collapsed here." *I pause a moment, tilting my head at him, waiting for him to call me on my lie. When he remains silent, I can't help but ask again,* "You really don't remember?"

He shakes his head, licking his lips, even though they're covered in blood.

"I'm sorry, Ry."

He shifts to face me. "Why?"

"I didn't stop you. I didn't want to stop you. Should I have stopped you?"

He glances at Yara, then at his useless mother, finally landing on his father again. A smile lifts his lips, growing into an outright grin, and then he's laughing.

"Ry?"

321

He throws back his head and laughs louder. "No, Luc. You should not have stopped me."

He laughs again as he plants his hands on the floor, blood oozing between his fingers. He stands, looking around. "I did this, Luc, and I'm not sorry." He stares at his father. "I'm strong. So are you. We're strong. I will never take abuse again. I will never be powerless again. I'm gonna to rise to tha top. I will be untouchable. We will be untouchable."

I take a deep breath. Thank the gods. This will define Ry—in a good way. He believes in his strength now. He'll build off this moment.

And he won't hate me. He won't leave me behind.

He waves a hand around the small house. "We're getting out of here." He locks eyes with me. "You'll come with me, right?"

I smile and sigh. The look in eyes, filled with fire and determination, tells me Rydel could conquer the world if he wanted.

And I want to see it.

"Of course. It's always been you and me, Ry. And it always will be."

32

I pull from the memory, hearing the small sigh from Luc as he tries to shake off the pain. I just stare at him, my body oddly cold as I watch a tear well in his eye before falling down his cheek.

I can't close off his mind anymore. The trust I held as an absolute has shattered, and I think it broke something in me as well. Rationally, I understand why Luc did what he did, but rational thought is not winning this moment. Rage is.

'His eyes. He's angry. He has a right to be angry. But there's too much between us. We have to find a way through this.' "Ry, talk to me."

I shake my head, fisting my hair as I back away from him, stumbling over piles of clothes, clattering over a dirty dish. "Lucaryn, all this time!"

"I'm sorry." *'There wasn't a good time to tell you, and then too much time had passed.'* "I only meant to—"

'No! I know what you meant! I saw it all. I felt it all. The fact is, you didn't have enough faith in my friendship with you to choose you over my shit family. No matter how noble your reasons, you didn't believe in me, Lucaryn."

More tears spill down his face, running under his chin and dripping down onto his shirt. *'Please, please, please, please ...'*

I drop my hands, and they hang loosely at my sides. The feeling of ice spreading through my veins sends a numbing pain throughout my body. With every beat of my heart, it feels as if frost coats more of my chest. This hurts. This, *this* is agony. I haven't known pain until this moment. I'm being torn apart. My throat is tight, my eyes burn, and my heart, my heart just wants to stop its beating and end this suffering—and that makes me angry.

Anger is good. It's much better than heartbreak, so I cling to my rage. I tense my shoulders and take a step toward him. "The only one I trusted." I kick a slipper to the side. "The only one I loved."

His face scrunches up in pain. *'Loved? Past tense?'* He drops to a knee, clutching his chest.

"I don't know how I feel anymore, Lucaryn." Another step brings me before him. "The magic. The Heart Stone ... do you feel that? In your chest? That ache? That hole? I have a matching one, but mine's filled with ice." I lean down, pinching his chin between my fingers, lifting his face so I can stare into his bright blue eyes. I want to see it, his pain. "You thought letting me believe I'd been strong enough to kill my useless family would feed my strength, my darkness? Well, you were right. Your lies built me into the man who did whatever it took to get to the top. Your lies propelled me to the throne. Your lies made me"—I sweep a hand at myself—"this."

He curls his other leg under him, fully kneeling before me. The tears have stopped, but I'm waiting to see what I want to see. "Don't get me wrong, Lucaryn. I love who I am, who I've become. I love the power, the pain. I love the fear I inspire in others. But you lied. To me!" I slap my chest. "I would have understood, Lucaryn. I would have thanked you, and maybe I would have found my strength on my own, just by being with you."

A soft sob escapes his lips, but I hold tight to his chin. "But I guess we'll never know. I've been the villain of many people's stories, and, yes, I'm the bad guy, so ..."

His eyes go wide, and I force a grin, my icy rage cracking within me in a mix of satisfaction and agony. I see his fear the second before his thoughts scramble in my mind. *'No. No, Ry. Don't. We can find our way through this. Please. Don't fucking do this! Don't you dare!'* "Rydel. No!"

I push my magic at him, all gentleness gone. He grunts, and I welcome the physical pain to distract from the emotional anguish that is threatening to crush me. "Of all the people in my life, Lucaryn, I never thought *your* betrayal would be the one to break me." I let a single tear slide down my cheek. "But here we are."

My free hand uncurls his fingers, tugging the Heart Stone from his grip, sliding it in my pocket. He struggles against my magic, gripping my forearm. His whispered plea rushes from his lips. "Rydel, no! You know what the magic will do to you. Don't! Rydel! Fuck! No! "

I shove a stronger wave of magic at him, and his hands fall away. "You don't get to worry about me any longer."

My entire world shatters as tears silently track down his face, his eyes burning with anger at what I'm about to do to him. But then his eyes turn unfocused, falling into the loop I've chosen for him.

'Iyai suhrh iyai use'a nea? Ze'ass, se'a e'ae'asuhr uhr nisius. *You think you hate me? Well, the feeling is mutual.* His whispered thought is the last thing I hear before I stride from his room, locking it behind me.

33

Lucaryn

There's nothing I can do as my vision tunnels, but I hold on to Ry's image as long as possible. I have plenty of horrible memories he can stick me in, but this one, right here, might be the worst. I'm losing everything in this moment, and the pain is unlike anything I've ever known. Seeing that look of rage and hurt on Ry's face is worse than a dagger to the heart.

I feel myself slump back on my heels, and my breath slows; my tears still wetting my cheeks as my room fades to black ...

The plain wood door that leads into the throne room stands before me. I rub my chest, trying to find some relief from the swell of feelings that crowd inside me—mostly fear, some amusement. I shake my arms out at my sides. I have to focus. If he sees this lie, he might see the other from *that* night.

Pressing the door open on silent hinges, I step into the vaulted room, stopping next to the throne with feet planted slightly wider than my hips, and cross my arms over my chest. I wince at the movement as the wound Kahar gave me—a perfect place to hide the stone—

stretches with a twinge of pain. My reaction is small, but Rydel catches it, frowning at me with a question in his eyes. His hope slams into me, and I have to grit my teeth as I shake my head almost imperceptibly.

His focus spins back to the man kneeling before him, leaning over until his face nearly brushes the black velvety-smooth skin of Sakara's cheek. He places his right hand on his shoulder, and I smirk when the kneeling man glances at Rydel's empty middle finger.

Ry sheathes his dagger and holds his left hand before Sakara, palm up. He stares at it for a second before tilting his head back at the king.

Rydel chuckles, and I see him shift slightly. He must be catching thoughts of the two of them engaged in, well ... my breath hisses between my clenched teeth as Ry's arousal almost overwhelms me. The sight of him gripping Sakara's long black locs in his hand almost draws a groan from my throat. As Ry presses his lips close to Sakara's ear, his voice is loud enough to be heard throughout the throne room.

"I did enjoy having you in my bed, but that is over now." Chuckles float around the room, and Sakara's chest and cheeks redden. Ry flexes his fingers, and I can't help stare at the gesture as he says, "Hand it over."

Sakara doesn't move, and Ry sighs, releasing him, and steps back. Sakara's fear makes me want to turn and run from the room, while Ry's amusement, quickly turning to annoyance, makes me want to laugh. Add in the varying emotions of the other soldiers in the room, and it's such an overwhelming sensation that I couldn't move right now if I needed to. There's just too much ... everything.

Ry waves a hand at the nearest soldier, who starts searching Sakara.

Ry's tsk brings Sakara's gaze back to him. "I did ask nicely. Now you either submit to this search, or I make you."

Sakara's nostrils flare, fisting his hands at his sides, and his anger boils through my blood. But then a second later, a tingle of pleasure shivers down my spine as Rydel basks in his power—the magic that might kill him if I give him the Heart Stone.

The soldier finds the ring, and Ry steps forward, holding out his hand, and the soldier drops it. Rydel slides it onto the middle finger of his right hand before leaning down. I feel his malice coating his words as if it's my own feelings. "Sakara, my sweet. Did your Queen really think sending me a spy wrapped in such a tempting package would be all it would take to get her hands on the Mind Stone?"

Sakara taunts Ry, and tension and anticipation floods me from every corner of the room until it feels like I'm going to snap in two.

Ry steps behind Sakara. "Just because I fucked your Queen once, does not mean she knows me." Sakara tenses, his shoulders pinching together, and his fists are so tightly clenched, his knuckles are white. I glance down, noticing I've mirrored him, his fear and a small amount of defiance becoming my own.

Ry's dagger is once again rolling through his fingers as his eyes travel down Sakara's body. I feel a whisper of regret wash over Rydel before he shrugs it off. He crosses his arms, tapping his dagger against his bicep.

"Did you really think you could get past the Mind Stone?" He waves a hand dismissively. "No, don't answer. You presented yourself to me with such ... faith in your lies. *Truth* be told." He smiles, and my shoulders tense. He can't find out. "I was pleased at the idea of adding another spymaster to my court. But alas, your loyalty is not to me, and I can't let that stand."

Sakara's emotions go into a panic, sending my own breaths into shallow, little intakes before I'm able to slow them again.

I press my lips together to keep from laughing at Rydel's amusement. Ry chuckles. "Quite the predicament."

Fear and anger take over the amusement I feel from Ry as Sakara grimaces. "Does your cruelty know no end?"

Ry shrugs, dagger dancing in his hand. "You came to me. You tried to steal what is mine. Is my cruelty not justified?"

Sakara's eyes narrow, his anger growing. "Only someone with a soul as black as yours would ever consider cruelty justified."

I shift, my back aching from the onslaught of emotions. My jaw aches from clenching my teeth, and I'm dizzy from bouncing between the amusement, fear, anticipation, pleasure, rage, and indifference hitting me from moment to moment. And most of these emotions aren't mine.

If Ry doesn't get on with it, I'll run Sakara through myself. A subtle shake of Rydel's head keeps me in place. Even without using his magic on me, he knows me so well.

I can't lose him.

Ry grins, stilling his dagger, using the blade to flick dirt from under his nail. He does like to play with his victims. "My soul may be as black as the deepest pits of hell, but I'm not beyond gratitude. So, thank you. At least you gave me something in return for trying to steal from me." Ry's gaze suggestively travels down Sakara's body, and jealousy all my own flares in my chest.

But the glare Sakara shoots at Rydel draws a laugh from my lips, and I get another tickle of Ry's amusement as well. Sakara's brown eyes narrow even farther. "I didn't enjoy being in your bed."

"We both know that's not true. I never take what is not willingly offered ... to my bed anyway."

As Rydel leans down again, his mouth a whisper from Sakara's, and I lick my lips, wishing I could trade places with the kneeling man, if but for a moment.

Anger flares from Sakara, but Ry is already stepping back as Sakara's head jerks forward, intending to headbutt the king. Idiot.

A smile curls my lips as Rydel chuckles. "It's hard to surprise the owner of the Mind Stone."

I shake my head, forcing my face into a passive expression. I can't let all these emotions show. I can't let Ry know. Not yet. Not until I have a proper argument for him to let me keep the Stone—for his sake, not mine.

Forcing myself out of my thoughts, I catch up with the conversation; Sakara's voice still defiant. "I could have killed you many times over."

Sakara jerks back as Ry laughs, the sharp sound bouncing around the room, and several soldiers chuckle along, myself included. "Killing me was the last thing on your mind, sweet Sakara. I was just surprised it took you so long to make your move." His dagger picks up its movement once again, flicking through his hands. I swallow around the flood of arousal that punches my gut as I watch his dexterous fingers.

Ry tilts his head, his grin widening, and I can't help but grin at his delight in playing with Sakara. "You enjoyed yourself, and for a moment, I thought you might actually defect."

"You think too highly of your cock." Sakara's flutter of arousal is there, and my dick twitches. I've seen him. Ry's cock is everything he boasts it is ... and more.

Ry's excitement kicks up, speeding the beat of my heart. He offers Sakara an option ... death or imprisonment. Sheer bliss hits me as Ry rides the wave of hope that crashes from Sakara. This is his favorite part—mine too, if I'm honest—the moment when hope is crushed, leaving only fear.

There's chaotic fear dancing from Sakara like yellow lightning. I feel Rydel fighting to keep from adjusting himself as Sakara's terror washes over me. Ry loves the fear, loves the power, and I ... love him.

Sakara's eyes stay on the king before him, his feelings roiling with indecision.

Ry sighs. "Time's up."

His dagger slices across Sakara's throat, and his pain almost shoves a gasp from my lips as blood spills down his front and sprays across Ry's chest. Sakara falls to the side, choking gasps escaping him until he falls silent, eyes staring at nothing.

Ry stands, sheathing his dagger and walks toward the dais. His indifference settles me from the intensity of the emotions from a moment ago. He climbs the three steps and claps me on the shoulder, drawing a wince from my face. We head through the door I came through earlier, closing off the bloody throne room behind us, some emotions dying off to a subtle buzz vibrating around my ribcage.

Ry grins, his green eyes bright, his happiness at having me home like a balm to my own battered emotions. "Welcome home, Luc. What's got your face pinched in pain?"

I shrug, my black hair falling over my forehead from where it refuses to stay brushed back. I take a breath. Should I just tell him? Give him the Stone? No, it'll kill him, or drive him mad. He can't resist the power, the magic. He's searched for the Heart Stone for decades.

What's a few more years? I can handle the magic. I can handle anything to keep Ry safe.

I glance at him, sending Ry the memory that will act as my cover story. "Kahar."

Ry shakes his head, and I almost collapse at his acceptance. He's not digging any deeper. There's no suspicion coming off him. "I don't know why you insist on keeping that hell horse. He's a menace. We have a stable full of horses."

I rub at the left side of my chest. "He's as fearsome as my reputation. I have to stick with him at this point. Though the bruising is going to take forever to heal, and I'm going to have a pretty big scar."

"Serves you right."

I snort a laugh as we pass a single guard with a nod and climb the winding staircase that leads to our private wing. We are silent as Ry pushes open the large wood door to his suite. Two guards stand on either side. They nod as we pass through, closing the door behind us.

Ry's fingers work down the buttons on his once white shirt, now turned a dark red with Sakara's blood. I feel his disappointment a moment before he asks, "So, no luck on finding the Heart Stone?"

I walk to a cabinet built into a nook in the stone wall, opening a glass door and retrieving a bottle of whiskey. I uncork the top with a pop and take a swig straight from the bottle, letting the alcohol burn away my tension, or some of it at least. "All the markings we read about were there, even the inlaid trap at the cave entrance."

A sigh slides from his lips before he crosses the room, entering his washroom. He returns, his face and chest clean, sliding a blue tunic over his head. As he tucks it into his pants, he turns, facing me. "We have to find it. Before anyone else."

His desperation almost breaks me, but I toss back another big swallow of whiskey before holding it out to him, telling him about Erathan's hunters I ran into at the caves.

I've spun the lie.

My eyes burn with the threat of tears. I know I'm taking advantage of Ry's trust in me and telling myself it's for his own good isn't helping.

I remain silent, swallowing the churning bile, monitoring Rydel's emotions as he pulls his anger under control until it bleeds into satisfaction.

That wasn't an emotion I was expecting. My shoulders slump as his emotions slam into me ... resolve, disappointment, amusement.

I take a deep breath. "I'm sorry, Ry."

He waves his hand; the whiskey sloshing with the movement. "I'm just glad you're okay." And he is. His relief at my safe return washes over me like the cool water of a stream on a hot day. He lifts the bottle but pauses before it reaches his lips.

We talk about Erathan and Ravaxina, laying out plans on how to move forward now that Ry thinks Erathan has the Heart Stone. Guilt fills my chest, making it hard to breathe, so I stretch, my spine popping. "Okay. I'm sore and tired. I'm going to wash and get some sleep, unless you need anything else?" *Please don't need anything else right now.*

Thankfully, he shakes his head, heading to his desk. "No. Go rest. While we're waiting to hear back from our spies in Adren, I'm going to plot a few other locations I was researching. We'll continue to send out search parties, just in case. Plus, that will keep Rava's and Erathan's spies guessing."

I nod, knowing my eyes are pinched in pain, hoping he assumes it's the pain from the wound in my chest, and not the agony of lying yet again to my best friend. His smile almost draws tears from my eyes. "See you tomorrow."

I nod and rush from the room. It's done. If he ever finds out ...

We're sparring with the Sagas, and I can tell Ry is wound up as he goes after Casin ...

We're late getting on the road, and as Ry approaches, I know he's been with Asha. I like Asha, and I like that Ry has someone he can release some tension with without it being complicated, but I can't help the jealousy ...

Ry's warning echoes through my mind, and I have a split second to move. The arrow thuds into my chest, and fire spreads. Poison ...

Ry's gone. He's gone after Rava, because of me ...

I can't handle Ry's emotions. It's too much. Everything is too much. The cave in at the mines gives me an escape ...

Ry wants me. Gods, he wants *me*. Is this real? I don't think I've ever been this happy ...

He knows Erathan's Heart Stone is a fake. Should I just tell him?

...

These damn rebels using solstice to get to Ry? I don't think so ...

Adastra has ... magic? He ... knows. How? Shit.

Rydel knows. He's so angry. I wish he would just drive his dagger through my heart. It would hurt less ...

The plain wood door that leads into the throne room stands before me ...

34

I flick the dirt from under my nails. My forearms rest on my thighs, the rock I'm sitting on digging into my ass. My chest feels hollow, and I squeeze my eyes shut as my soldiers' pain and exhaustion become my own through the Heart Stone. My fingers scratch at the still-healing cut along my left forearm where the new Stone sits under my flesh. I try to push the magic outward to calm the soldiers, to build their resolve, but their thoughts clatter through my brain like a herd of stampeding horses.

A groan passes my lips, and my head falls into my hands.

Gods, this hurts. It's too much.

I'm broken.

The bland scent of creamed oats hits my nose, and when I crack my eyes open, there's a tin plate in front of my face held with a hand missing two fingers. I push it away, lifting my head.

Carelle frowns. "When was the last time you ate, your Majesty?"

I shrug, not sure. We've been on the Adren / Trislen border for the past two weeks and haven't been able to get any closer to the capital. Runic and my soldiers held the palace as long as they could, but when most of my South Leiren army turned their allegiance to Adastra—not surprisingly—reports came that Runic and several of my soldiers were taken captive. That was over a week ago, and I can only hope they are still alive.

Every move I make, Adastra's army and supporters are there to cut me off. I sent small teams to circle around from the east, only to receive word they were all either killed or captured before they even made it into the city. Three days ago, I took the main contingent of my army and pressed straight toward the capital. Adastra's forces were there. Traps were set, archers were in position, hidden pits had been dug ... I lost a lot of good soldiers that day.

I wince as I shift, my bruised ribs screaming from the rock I landed on when Kahar fell that day, the oil-slicked ground sliding his hooves out from under him. The hell horse is fine, a small hitch in his rear leg, but it will take more than that to take the demon horse down. Me too, for that matter.

'*He looks awful.*' I smirk at Carelle, and she ducks her head. "Sorry, your Majesty."

I shake my head. She's tired and doubtful that we'll succeed in taking down Adastra, and I have to fight to keep her exhaustion and doubts from becoming my own.

"Any new word on Adastra?"

"No." '*That Shadow Lord fella is—*'

Carelle takes a step back as I grunt, pushing to my feet. "What about the Shadow Lord?"

"He's here."

"Bring him to me. Now!"

Carelle's fear hits me before she turns on her heel and jogs off.

I sway, catching myself on the rock I was just sitting on. Little white stars dance before my eyes. I know my body needs fuel, but I can't seem to feel the pain of hunger through the thoughts and feelings crashing through me.

The books were right. Luc was right. This is too much.

Gods, Luc. Eyes closed or open, I keep seeing his tear-stained face, kneeling in his room as I left him behind. My heart cracks open again, but I shove off the rock as I feel Carelle's anxiety and hear the Shadow Lord's thoughts, '*The Crown Breaker is struggling with the magic.*'

His black clad form stops before me, and Carelle stands to the side. "I'm handling my magic. What have you learned of Adastra's power?"

He rubs his neck, canting his weight to one leg. "Not much new, your Majesty. His claim of possessing natural magic seems real." He waves a hand at me. "How else has he been able to stop your every advance?"

"Really good spies?"

I laugh, and Carelle cracks a smile, but Mica frowns. "You know better, your Majesty. You won't be able to kill him unless you get close to him." He pauses, lifting a delicate eyebrow. "That is your aim, is it not? To kill him?"

"Yes."

Mica nods, I feel his acceptance.

"But he seems to know your every move before you even make it. Your army is tired, Erathan's troops have retreated, and Adastra is gaining new supporters every day. Maybe you should think about *surrender* yielding the south."

Last week, as assassination attempt nearly took out Erathan, the spider's poisonous bite driving him into unconsciousness. His healers were able to counter the poison, but Erathan failed to wake. His people brought him back to Adren, taking his army with them.

I cited the treaty we signed, demanding his army stay to help us get to Adastra, and when that didn't work, I plied them with the magic of the Heart Stone, making them want to stay against their will. It worked for a day, but the strain was too much, and I passed out, waking the next morning to agonizing pain and the knowledge that Erathan's army was gone.

I step into Mica's space, expecting him to move away, but he holds his ground. "Maybe I should wonder a little more"—I press the magic into his mind and heart—"if you've been feeding Adastra information on me."

His eyes stay on mine, and the only outward sign that the magic is affecting him is a light sheen of sweat on his face. I calm his heart, pressing the magic to make him feel relaxed, compliant, and at the same time, I search his mind.

341

I've done this before, certain the Shadow Lord is hiding things from me, but now, just as before, I find memories of him sending his network into the city, reviewing reports of movements from both my army and Adastra's. His spies throughout Imoria reporting to him, and Mica collecting each morsel of information to be used when necessary. The man is cunning, smart, and well connected, but he hasn't been passing information on me to Adastra.

I let the magic go, unable to keep from stumbling back a step as piercing pain slams into my chest and through my temples. Mica just stares at me, but Carelle moves to come to my aid. I hold up a hand, stopping her.

I spit the sour taste of bile from my mouth before turning back to Mica. "Keep me apprised on any new information—no matter how insignificant."

He bows. "Of course, your Majesty."

When I say nothing else, he turns and strides off.

Carelle watches me, her worry and pity hitting me like a physical blow. *'He can't go on like this for much longer. Then where will we be? Adastra will take everything.'*

I rub my temples. "I'm not ready to hand Adastra the keys to Imoria just yet." *I need Luc.*

Shit. I shake my head, trying to expel Luc from my thoughts.

Shouts ring through the air. Fear, pain and death nearly knock me over. Carelle turns as a soldier sprints over to us. His thoughts slam into my mind. *'We're under attack. So many dead already. We were caught unawares.'* "Your Majesty. Adastra's army is closing in, fast. We've lost almost half of our front lines. Should we reinforce the front, or retreat?"

"I will not be pushed back any farther. I won't let Adastra keep pushing us around." I turn to Carelle. "Send who you can to the front."

No. "Your Majest—"

"No?"

She swallows. "If we keep pushing, we're all going to die. Then all of Leiren will burn."

I grip my hair, a few strands pulling free. The soldier's eyes bounce between Carelle and me. His shock at her bold words nearly brings a chuckle from my lips.

"Fine. Fine. We will—"

I stumble back, tripping over the rock as fire explodes in the near distance. Screams rip through the air, both of fear and pain, and triumph. I prop myself up, ignoring the shaking in my arms as I watch swarms of people wearing the black and green colors Adastra has adopted stream over the dead bodies of my soldiers, slashing and stabbing at anyone who still stands.

They're driven by hope ... hope that if Adastra controls Imoria, the goddess Circeon will once again bless these lands with natural magic.

Fools. Zealots.

But how the fuck did they get so close without me knowing?

I'm yanked to my feet, Carelle's grip bruising my upper arm.

The answer is simple. I can't focus the magic. It's too much. And after weeks of battle and of having the power slowly tear me apart, it's taking every ounce of strength I have to just remain standing each day.

My boots scrape over the ground as Carelle drags me away from the battle. I try to pull free, but her determination slams into me, mixing with the overwhelming agony of those dying just a few yards away.

I register her anger and the jubilation of a rebel a moment before Carelle releases me, swinging her sword to block a strike from one of Adastra's soldiers. They dance, each strike of their blades driving their emotions through me. Carelle's blade sinks into the man's chest, and I drop to my knees, vomiting into the crushed grass as I experience his death.

The ground greets me as I fall to my side. The smell of wet earth from the rains last night draws forth images of Luc. I moan, curling into a fetal potion as I feel every stab, every slash, every punch, every death.

A shrill whistle sounds above me, and Carelle shouts in my ear. "Your Majesty! We need to move!"

The thundering of hooves shakes the earth under my cheek, and I see Kahar through my tear-stained vision. I tense, sure he's going to

343

stomp on my head, wishing he would, to put me out of my misery, but he stops, dancing in place.

Carelle shouts, "Help me." And two pairs of hands grab me. The world tilts as I'm thrust onto Kahar's back. I wrap one hand around the pommel, the other weaves through his thick mane, holding tight.

I grit my teeth, forcing strength into my spine, looking down at Carelle and the other female soldier standing at her side, holding the reins of two horses. I clear my throat. "Call the retreat. Fall back. We're moving into Adren. Adastra's army has yet to cross the border. Let's see if we can catch some kind of gods damned break." I lick my lips, catching my breath as I struggle to stay upright. "When's the last you heard anything from the north?"

Carelle's brow furrows. "There hasn't been a bird or runner in over a week, your Majesty."

"Shit!" That long? Did I know this already? Yes. Yes. I vaguely remember asking yesterday. Shit. I'm losing my grip on reality. "They're being intercepted. Casin wouldn't fail." I scratch my beard then rub my fingers through my hair, trying to press away some of the pain. It doesn't work. "Okay. We retreat fully to Leiren. We can refresh supplies and regroup with fresh soldiers."

The two nod, and the second woman mounts and rides off.

An arrow zips past my head, and Carelle spins, deflecting another arrow before deftly cutting the archer down with a well thrown knife. I groan at the pain of death, and Kahar tosses his head. Carelle calls out, running back to me, "Go, your Majesty."

I grit my teeth, drawing my sword. "I leave with my soldiers."

Carelle and I scream as a thrown dagger sinks into her back. She reaches around, but can't grip the hilt, her pain becoming mine, and my back muscles tremble.

She spins, screaming at a group of nearby soldiers. "Go with our King! Protect him!" They mount quickly, turning their horses north. Carelle's eyes meet mine, and she nods. "Kahar, se'ase'aus." *Kahar, retreat.*

I pull back on the reins, but Kahar yanks them back. He leaps forward, and I'm barely able to keep my seat as he races north. The four soldiers fan their mounts out slightly, keeping pace while one races ahead.

The sounds of battle grow dim, the pain lessening with each pound of Kahar's hooves. As the magic quiets, my body trembles. Kahar doesn't slow, and I'm not sure if we've traveled for minutes or hours, but my eyes keep closing of their own accord. Sweat has plastered my clothes to my skin despite the snow-covered ground, and every strike of Kahar's hooves drives pain through my cracked ribs and aching head. I recognize Adren land, and a moment later, a small village comes into view.

The sound of our galloping horses draws a few people out of their homes, and eyes go wide as we storm into the center of the small gathering of buildings, slowing Kahar's pace to a trot, then a walk.

Again, fear, confusion, and pity strike me as a few people dare to come close. *'I think that's King Wescaryn. He looks sick.'* ... *'Has the war finally come to us? We should have left weeks ago.'* ... *'Please let him keep going. He can't stop here. He'll bring death to us all.'*

The voices fade, as does my vision. Silence closes around me like a wave crashing over my ankles, up my legs, pressing down on my shoulders until my head sinks under. I feel myself falling, and the hell horse actually sidesteps to try to keep me on his back, but air brushes against me as the ground rises fast.

I wake to hands groping, trying to lift me from the ground. I shove them back, my weak attempt doing nothing to move them, but the growl in my throat has the soldiers stumbling back. I roll to my hands and knees, breathing deep before pressing to one foot, then the other. I grip Kahar's saddle, pulling myself to standing as a woman approaches. She's concerned and terrified, but her concern has won over. She holds out trembling hands, holding a tin of water and a small loaf of bread.

I take the water, my fingers accidentally brushing hers, the contact intensifying the magic until I almost believe I am this woman, completely losing myself for a moment. I instinctively shove the power back, and she screams, dropping the bread, collapsing on the ground. Her breathing is shallow, her mind quiet in a fog of unconsciousness.

The few people who had gathered back away, one bending to scoop the woman up, carrying her off and into the perceived safety of a nearby house. The emotions and thoughts of the entire village swim through my body. I swallow, licking my lips before drinking the water. But it comes right back up.

The last few weeks with the Stones have felt like my body only has room for the magic. There's no room for food or drink, or even myself. I am magic, power, pain, and longing.

I climb onto Kahar, my voice quiet in the silence of the village. "I'd leave here if I were you. I don't know if Adastra will cross the border today, but you're not safe."

I don't know if anyone heard me, but I kick Kahar into a fast walk, and my soldiers follow. One leans in as we pass into open country once again. "Your Majesty, shouldn't we wait for the rest of the army?"

I shake my head, and that small movement nearly tumbles me from Kahar's back. I grip the pommel until my fingers turn white. "No. We press on. The army will follow." I have faith in Carelle ... if she's still alive.

Mile by mile, town by town, we move north. There's no word on my army in the south, and I just have to believe they are retreating.

The moment we pass into Leiren, we're met with ruin. The first village we come to is nothing but charred foundations and blackened bones. Anger spikes through me, chasing away some of the pain. Adastra's reach has come to my kingdom, and I was somehow left in the dark about it.

I tilt my head back, screaming to the sky, "What the fuck good is this magic if I can't even protect what's mine!" My shout startles the soldiers around me, their eyes wide. Kahar prances in place, his giant hooves kicking up soot.

We find more of the same in the next village, and the next. We finally come to a town with some life, but the people stay hidden in their homes, windows busted, doors splintered, and a few bodies hanging by their necks in the square, their frozen corpses feeding the crows.

Emotions and thoughts leak from the homes. They're scared.

They're angry. They were used as a message—for me. Their lives have no value other than conveying to me that I'm losing. That I'm broken.

I'd send soldiers to protect what's left of this village, but I don't know that I have any to spare. I might be able to find a few ...

My eyes close, and I slump in the saddle. Kahar works hard to keep me on his back as I alternate between sweating through my clothes then shivering with chills.

Finally, Fadren comes into view, but as we draw close, smug intimidation slides into my chest, and a moment later, thoughts slam into my mind. '*The north will fall. Adastra will rule, and magic will come back to the land.*'

I've heard many versions of this ballad of hope over the weeks. I roll my neck. Hell, what do I know? Maybe Adastra is goddess blessed. Maybe he will usher in a new age of magic, but I won't let him take my kingdom to do so.

As more thoughts slip through, I realize the rebels are watching the main roads into the capital, so we skirt the city.

I sway, dizzy with a hunger I can't feel through the pain of the magic. We wait for night to fall to sneak into my own city, into my own castle. The magic searches for traitorous thoughts or feelings of excitement or subversion, but all seems fairly ... normal if a little tense. Every mind feels on guard.

I stumble up the stairs with the four soldiers at my flank as well as several concerned guards rushing after me.

"Your Majesty! Please, let us help." ... "Where's the rest of the army? Sir, have we lost?" ... "Our cities and towns are under attack. Rebels have nearly overrun the capital." ...

Casin rounds a corner at a run. "Your Majesty," he pauses as he takes in my thin and dirty appearance, his concern washing over me before it's replaced with anger. Anger that my pride and arrogance brought us here. "Did you get my messages? We need—"

"Out!" I stumble through the set of doors into the long hall. "Everyone out!" My hand travels down the wall to help guide me as my vision wavers. A servant comes around a corner, stopping short at the sight before her. I point at her with my dagger, which I didn't even realize I had in my hand. "Everyone out. All the servants, aids, guards, cooks, everyone. OUT!"

My scream echos off the walls and through their minds, and by the time I hit the first step leading up to my wing of the castle, the thoughts and emotions bombarding me fade as the sound of rushing footsteps takes everyone from the castle.

I make it halfway up the stairs before my knees give out. I fail to catch myself, and my head hits the marble tread with a crunch.

The world goes dark.

I gasp as awareness comes flooding back, but for once, the pain of the magic doesn't crash into me. The silence of the castle greets me, but for one mind. Luc's.

I crawl up the stairs, pulling myself to my feet, my boots dragging down the seemingly endless hallway until I'm standing before Luc's door. My fingers tremble, and I can't seem to get enough air as I reach for the handle.

It's said that evil will inevitably fall to the good deeds of men ...

Not yet.

King Rydel and Captain Lucaryn's story will continue in
THE BROKEN KING

ALSO BY T. B. WIESE

Scan the code below for links to my Amazon author page where you'll find the next book in this series as well as all my other books.

You'll also find a link to my website for signed books and swag.

ACKNOWLEDGMENTS

A huge thank you to my readers. Without you, this crazy dream of being an author would not be possible.

To all my beta & ARC readers, thank you! You had a big hand in making this novel what it is today.

Thank you to Jo at Waypoint Academy. Your encouragement and insightful editing took this story to a whole other level.

And lastly, I want to thank all my friends and family for cheering me on and being as excited about my characters as I am—I love my tribe.

ABOUT THE AUTHOR

T. B. Wiese is a military spouse, dog mom, photographer, Disney nerd, and lover of spicy fantasy. She loves animals (She grew up with dogs and working with horses, including working at the Tri-Circle D Ranch at Disney World), so don't be surprised when you find yourself reading lovable animal characters in her novels.

If you'd like to keep up to date with future releases as well as new swag and sales, sign up for her newsletter:
https://www.tbwiese.com/subscribe

SCAN THE CODE WITH YOUR CAMERA APP FOR HER SOCIAL LINKS

Made in the USA
Columbia, SC
01 July 2024

8679f676-2b53-47dd-9961-03c0d9c678ffR01